The Moss Gatherers

TIA JONES

Gomer

The author wishes to acknowledge the support of a
Literature Wales's Writers' Bursary.

Published in 2013 by
Gomer Press, Llandysul, Ceredigion, SA44 4JL

ISBN 978 1 84851 667 0

A CIP record for this title is available from the British Library.

This book is published with the financial support of the
Welsh Books Council.

Printed and bound in Wales at
Gomer Press, Llandysul, Ceredigion

To my Mum with love

Acknowledgements

In no particular order other than as I remember their valued help in the different stages of this novel, I am indebted to my late grandmother, Lucie, who first alerted me to the historical importance of moss, having organised local, regular moss collections for the British Red Cross to use in the Second World War. To Owain Jones and Rhiannon Evans, the first to read my manuscript and give their encouragement and suggest improvements. To Ros Mclean and all the staff at my local library for their help in my research and free use of the internet when I had no connection at home. To Stephen Gomes for his geniality and sense of humour. My thanks to Anthony Owen for the use of his maps, sea charts and all the nautical knowledge that helped me make sense of the journey. To Angharad Butler for her regular updates and suggestions, and Gwilym Jones for clearing the picture. Also to Eleri Lewis for her valuable contributions. To Ceri Wyn Jones and Gomer, and to the sterling work of my editor, Francesca Rhydderch: her clarity has been a great asset. Last but always, my husband John and my family.

AROS A MYNED

Aros mae'r mynyddau mawr,
    Rhuo trostynt mae y gwynt;
Clywir eto gyda'r wawr
    Gân bugeiliaid megis cynt.
Eto tyf y llygad dydd
    O gylch traed y graig a'r bryn,
Ond bugeiliaid newydd sydd
    Ar yr hen fynyddoedd hyn.

Ar arferion Cymru gynt
    Newid ddaeth o rod i rod;
Mae cenhedlaeth wedi mynd
    A chenhedlaeth wedi dod.
Wedi oes dymhestlog hir
    Alun Mabon mwy nid yw,
Ond mae'r heniaith yn y tir
    A'r alawon hen yn fyw.

John Ceiriog Hughes
(Ceiriog)

1

In the cold morning he dressed quickly, gulping down his breakfast and filling his thermos flask before putting it into his canvas bag. Tying up his boots, Tegwyn Jones threw on his coat and pulled his grey ex-army Russian hat over his ears before leaving the empty house.

It was the same day that Simon Davies, his childhood neighbour, would be flying home from America. Approximately thirty two thousand feet below his flight path, Tegwyn, accompanied by Frank and Dic Rhyd-y-meirch, walked up a side of a steep hill, east of the small rural town of Llanfeni. They made their steady climb rising to over thirteen hundred feet, and the oldest of the men, Dic, stopped to catch his breath. Tegwyn waited for him, looking up at the white vapour left by the diminishing dot of a plane as it soared over the mountains and out west across the sea. Briefly the younger man thought he'd like to fly off somewhere, anywhere other than the place he'd been born and bred. Not that he was bitter or hated his life, but he'd jump at the chance for a change. A sharp gust of wind made him wince. 'Come on Dic,' he shouted down. 'Get a move on; it's freezing standing here.' He caught a mumble of complaint followed by a scraping of hobnailed boots on the granite outcrop as Dic, still muttering, had started off again. Satisfied the old codger was following, Tegwyn turned back into the wind, and bending his neck down like a beast of burden he pulled himself up the last steep bit, only to catch sight of Frank as he dipped out of sight over the brow of the hill.

Once up the sudden mass of sea spread out below them to the west like a large white shine, too bright for their running eyes, making them squint as they looked. Never quite the same, it was a view they knew well and on that early morning the sea lay beautifully still in a silver fluid expanse stretching to the horizon. They stood momentarily dazzled by the sea's glaze and the sheer size of the water's glistening skin. There was no boat, no wave – only a rippling gentle breathing movement under her surface. Turning inland the two men followed after Frank, who'd gone on in a hurry to make a start. But on the top, for all his chat, he'd sneaked a pause, a glance to the sea and then back to his Bedford van parked on the verge at the base of the hill. Resting alongside he could make out Dic's Ariel motorbike. As usual they'd left everything by the side of the road unlocked as there was nothing worth stealing and they knew that apart from a local car and the post nothing would travel along the remote road. Then he was off, scampering over heather, ever the one to set the pace and chivvy. By the time they'd caught up he'd already thrown down his sacks and was bent to his task.

He'd not climbed any hill to marvel at a view. He'd seen enough of seas, calm and rough, of wild salted winds that wizened hawthorn, ash and scrub oak. Enough of Atlantic gales of rain that soaked to the skin making brooks into rivers, bursting banks in flood. Enough too of snow and driven drifts that could bury sheep and shepherds, whole houses covered by the filthy stuff. Or the East winds that made the land so blisteringly hard for months on end that even the hill sheep gave up the ghost, freezing to their hill. He'd even witnessed an unlikely summer drought that frizzled off all the grasses where gorse and heather burned out of control, kept alight by the underlying peat, leaving the Welsh uplands looking more like a scene out of Africa.

Unlike his dreamy companions, Frank was there on the hill for the money his work would bring and a day away from his Misses. He was not there for a day out and was irritated by their leisurely stroll as the two romantics finally joined him.

'That's cost you the first pint already,' he said to them.

'Hold your horses, Frank, we've got all day. I've got to pace myself.'

'Pace yourself! Left to you we wouldn't get a bag filled.'

'Yeah, yeah,' said Dic, refusing to be goaded into working at a faster pace than he wanted. 'Well, don't let me keep you. No one's stopping you. You leave me do my own patch in peace!'

Behind the closed lids and outward appearance of nonchalance the sudden shuddering forced Simon to open his eyes, his dilated pupils showing his fear as he searched along the aisle for the telltale signs of imminent disaster. He tried to seem unconcerned, taking a nervous look at the rows in front of him, concentrating on the backs of strangers' heads, before he turned to look down the gangway behind him. It all seemed normal enough, enough to let go of his held breath, and he smiled almost apologetically at his immediate neighbour. He tried to stretch, his tense body stiff in the confined space. Up to then he had thought he might talk to her, but hearing her sneeze, her guttural phlegm losing into her hanky that she hastily put to her nose, made Simon wince as he pulled involuntarily into himself and as much as the tight space would allow, he turned his head away to his small window. Simon Davies was already exhausted by his fear of flying, dreading the laboriously slow journey along the single-tracked railway that took almost as long as his flight from America, back to Llanfeni.

He already resented having to be where he was, feeling doubly trapped. Enforced on this trip he didn't want to make; had avoided at the best of times, let alone now.

Just when his life was really taking off, his mother's timing couldn't have been worse. He promised himself he'd make his obligatory visit short to negate any setback and planned to be literally straight in, see his mother and then out. A cold on top of everything else was the last thing he needed. Damn the woman snivelling, his mother's illness, but most of all his uncle for ringing him up to let him know, thereby forcing his hand.

Simon Davies was a big man; he filled every inch of his allotted seat, overspilling the arm rests. Thick, wavy brown hair framed his full face, curling over the collar of his jacket. From any angle he sat impressively wide against the window seat, looking swarthy, Mediterranean. Only close up there was something about his eyes, not just the fright in them but the actual tone, the light-blue colour speckled with amber that stopped him from being beautiful. He emitted a hue of anger, his face and upper body warming like a manure heap as he sat in his window seat quietly humming, cooped up there with no option other than tolerate being stuck; bumped and wobbled in what felt like the inside of a washing machine. Every movement from the craft suggested the calamity he was anticipating. Time dragged, and he tried to resist the urge to look at his watch every few minutes as his body ached in its cramped position. The flight felt like an eternity as he stared out into the blue sky, his face awkwardly angled away from the contagious woman. He tried to concentrate on the positive and on what sent him to the US in the first place. Anything to take his mind off his fear. Without being drugged senseless there was no way he could relax, confined and squeezed, his knees bent and his size thirteen feet forced askew under the seat of the passenger in front. He would never be a relaxed seasoned traveller, however successful he might become.

Finally the grizzling baby in the opposite aisle made his decision for him as it erupted, screaming from the arms that were trying to cradle it. Secretly he envied the little scrap its vent of frustration as he pushed his button, alerting the attention of a stewardess. He smoothed back his hair, accidentally nudging the woman next to him who turned her watery eyes onto him, her red nose breathing all over him as she excused him, her voice nasal. 'Don't worry. We're packed in like sardines aren't we!' He winced, half-standing to squeeze past her and the other passengers into the aisle. Like an emerging butterfly there was no way he was going to force himself back into such a tight cocoon, not caring that he had been exposed, compromised somehow. His only thought was of self-preservation.

He was glad to leave the other passengers behind, the mish-mash of humanity randomly concertinaed together; the bawling infant and red-faced arguing parents, as he followed the steward to the sanction of the curtained-off section at the front of the plane. Not only the curtains marking the divide, but also the comparative quietness and space were an immediate oasis, and he made a mental note never to travel anything but business class in the future. Once settled, he allowed himself a glance around catching a face he vaguely recognised as he nodded across to him.

'*Iechyd Da!*'[1] the man said, raising a glass at him. His face was flushed from wining and dining, and he smiled at Simon as if to welcome him into their privileged fold. Simon could not quite place where he had seen him before, but there was a conceit about him that comes from being in the public eye. The self-importance of a smug man, who had done very well for himself. Simon stretched out his feet, still trying to put a name to the face as he glanced across again. When the stewardess came with his meal he asked her, discreetly. Of course once told, he recognised him as a member of the newly-formed Welsh Assembly with a large chunk of the delegates with him. They repaid his compliment of not recognising him either, and he felt irked by the slight, feeling at least more important and worthy to be there than them, on their all expenses paid trip. But he had to be careful not to bite the hand that was indirectly feeding him, so he smiled and sipped his red wine, thinking about his performance.

---

[1] Good health, Cheers.

With their feet firmly on the ground the three men resembled a desultory posse of deserters roughly dressed and armed with their rakes and sticks. Not a group you'd want to meet alone on a moorland, men with hardened hands and unshaven faces. They'd moved apart, working back towards each other as they gathered. Bunched and bending down, often as not on their knees in the damp, each man stooped, the shape of their backs rounded like armadillos; solid and strong-armed, men of the soil. Younger and altogether more agile, wiry, loose-ended like a whip, Tegwyn flicked between them, his Russian hat bobbing up and down like a rabbit.

'Tego – you can't miss him; he wears a Russian hat,' to anyone who came looking for him. A hat that Dic had given him, although he had originally picked it for himself. He'd stumbled across it at a furniture auction, held occasionally in the cattle market where he worked. He'd always fancied himself as a bit of a Russian, a revolutionary, and after looking at himself in the mirror to get it just right he had proudly worn it to the Fenni Arms where they'd made fun of him, pulling the flaps down so he looked stupid. Taking offence, he never wore it in public again and some months later, he gave it to Tego, who didn't care what he looked like, as long as it kept his head warm. To save face Dic kept the red hammer and sickle badge and accepted the pint of mild as payment.

So on that cold clear morning, wearing bobble, Russian army and flat cap the three men looked a bizarre trio foraging on their perilous landscape like iguanas on rock, scraping up their bundles of the damp green mass. For over two hours they worked without talking, the exercise keeping them warm, and once they'd filled the outlying bags, they moved on, carrying the rest of the empty fertiliser bags with them to the wetter parts of the hill. They squelched into the peat-rich green mossy patches sunk between the coarse grasses in soggy ground, surrounded by knee-high thick heather that made it difficult to walk, careful to avoid large clumps of gorse, whose yellow flowers gave off the smell of coconut. Taking a bag each they dumped the rest in a pile, setting to work once more, each to their own patch as they raked the ground, gathering up bundles of the springy, wet velvet stuff. When enough of a bundle had been gathered they put it into the bags. Some mosses, close to the rock face, came away easily in swathes and these were rolled up like turf. Others were spread out to dry as the men continued working through the day, going around the outskirts of the hill before turning inwards again to the peat lakes in the middle. Regardless of how the weather turned, once up they'd stay for most of the daylight hours, sometimes talking, sometimes in companionable silence, three oddballs on the fringe in a time warp, collecting moss for a world where everything was wrapped in plastic. They gathered the moss for the dealer who made the money; arranging price, collection, selling on to the more lucrative markets.

They all had proper jobs, not just a bit of moss gathering; market drover, builder's mate and forestry worker. These wages were for the family, but it was the moss that provided them with their beer money so they were always keen to take an odd 'day off'. For all their strange looks they were polite if the land was privately owned, and Frank would ring first to ask permission before they gathered the moss and they were careful not to strip the place bare, so that the moss would re-grow, ensuring they'd never be short of beer.

They'd been at it bent double, raking for several hours without a break, and Dic was glad when Frank called a stop. He dropped down to where the filled bags had been stacked, using their bulk as a windbreak. He was glad to sit down and rest, the younger men joining him. They each had a flask of coffee or sweet tea, crisps, pork pie and a pickled egg. The only one who possessed a wife was Frank, who had a decent lunch box, and as usual he grudgingly shared his sandwiches with them.

'If you don't like it, you know what you can do,' he said as Dic turned up his nose at the pale pink of the fish paste. 'Cheeky bugger!'

'*Diolch*,' said Tego biting into his, grateful for any sandwich.

They sat, eating quickly, one hand holding onto the flask cup, careful not to spill any of the warming drink, slurping in between mouthfuls of bread.

'Have you heard how Elin Tŷ Coch is?' asked Frank, wiping his runny nose on the sleeve of his jacket. When he'd finished eating he pushed his bobble hat back, patting his pocket for the feel of his pouch.

'Still in hospital,' answered Dic, who lived nearest the village pub. 'Old Mervyn was on the hill when it happened. No one knows how long she'd been lying there but when he came home, he couldn't pick her up could he,' indicating one arm. 'He was in quite a state by the time the ambulance arrived.'

'Where was Richard, then?' asked Tegwyn. 'Chuck us it over, Frank,' he added seeing Frank with the tobacco. 'Ta,' he said catching the packet of ringers.

'Next time buy your own, scrounger.'

Teg bent lower against the sack to make a roll-up, pulling his jacket collar up as he tried to light his fag, missing what Frank had said.

'What'd you say?' he said, sucking the first pull of his cigarette into his lungs.

'He was away at market, deafo. Mervyn found her collapsed in the yard. Nesta thinks she disturbed an intruder. That, or else she fell and hit something. There was blood all over her face. He thought she was dead.'

'Poor sod. So Elin is really poorly then,' said Tego.

'*Duw, Duw*, awful and he was laughing his head off when it was happening.'

'Who, Mervyn?'

'Na, Richard of course. I saw him in the market, he was selling some calves. He was with Dafydd Esgair, and Ifan Foel, and old Miss Roberts was there.'

'She's a right sight!'

'Eighty plus.'

'In her seventies,' corrected Dic, always having to be right. 'She was there to buy a calf. You know, as she is.'

'Those old boots she wears, hessian sack over her coat tied with string, and her stick waving about?'

'All the rage, them Doc Martens!'

'What?'

'Never mind, Teg. Shut up or we'll be here all day.' They waited for Dic to tell his story.

'She got a bit of a crowd about her when the inspector came over—'

'RSPCA?'

'She'd be more than a match for him!'

'Hist, Teg.'

'Well, she stuck her finger up the poor animal's backside and smelt it,' said Dic.

'As one does!' added Frank, smiling broadly.

Dic acted out the scene for them, smelling his hand in disgust. 'And there he was striding over to her, his fish and chips in his greedy hands and before he could say anything, as bold as brass, she helped herself to one of his chips!' They all pulled a face, not needing Dic to fill them in but he did so, relishing the part. 'Yeah, her hand still yellow, you know like mustard. Well, you should have seen the inspector's face! But what could he say, ha! Not a thing, and he didn't know what to do with his dinner, holding it out like something dead the cat brought in.'

'So, what happened?'

'Took it! Cool as you like, chips in one hand, stick in the other and off she went to bid for the calf. All the boys cacking themselves!'

'Did she get her calf?'

'Yea, and a good dinner! Thomas knocked it down to her for virtually nothing and she got a cheer from the farmers. Didn't see the inspector after that!'

'Good old Roberts!'

The rest of the flight was uneventful and the periods of turbulence that had left him in a cold sweat had stopped. The dimming of the lights and bing bong voice instructing passengers to raise their seat backs and fasten belts announcing the preparation for landing, signifying the end to Simon's ordeal. He heard and felt a clanking somewhere underneath as the undercarriage opened and the plane banked, dropping, revving and dropping again in cloud. At least he was going down. He swallowed hard, chewing on imaginary gum to release the pressure in his ears as he tried to concentrate on his performance, thinking how lucky he'd been to get the break. Playing Musetto in *Don Giovanni*. He'd loved the challenge, performing every night to a full house, hoping James Barton's laryngitis would persist, at least long enough for him to make his mark. Clenching his eyes as she dropped again, *Annwyl Dduw*[2] he prayed to himself. Bounce, bounce again as rubber hit the tarmac, and the plane's engines were put into reverse thrust, sending out a powerful roar of arrival.

---

[2] Dear God

2

On the morning his mother had her fateful accident, Richard had indeed been away in the market, but what the men on the hill didn't know as they discussed his family was that he'd been detained on that morning.

For the first time since he could remember Richard had missed the afternoon milking, forgetting about his cows. He had been about to leave the car park with his unsold calves bunched in the back of his landrover, when a woman, a stranger hailed him.

'Thank goodness I caught you,' she said smiling at him, 'I've been waiting, hoping to spot you before you drove off.'

'Oh?' he said, taken aback at the direct approach and wondering if he'd done something wrong and was about to be penalized. More bloody red tape.

'Are you taking the calves home?'

'Yes.'

'Because if you were can I make you an offer for them?'

It was not what he had expected and any offer would have been better than the thought of taking them back, an unnecessary drain on space and foodstuff.

'You're not working for the ministry or a vet?'

'Why, do I look like one!'

'No, no.' He didn't add that never had someone come rushing up to him wanting to buy Friesian calves. She walked to the back of the landrover.

'I saw them in the ring. And this one's got such a cute face,' she'd said making a gooey baby noise as she stroked one on its forehead, its big ears stuck on to its head like a floppy appendage. 'You are so sweet, aren't you!'

'She'll make a good cross; Friesians are good growers and I'll give you a fiver for luck.' Richard was into his selling *spiel*, wishing he hadn't blurted it out as it made him feel cheap, but she didn't seem to mind. Money was obviously not her priority, or she wouldn't have been there in the first place.

'What would you have done with them, if I hadn't come along – had them slaughtered?'

'Probably given them to the hunt.'

'What?'

'I shouldn't be telling you this, but, here's no market for them. People don't want to know. And they're the wrong breed for the butchers, don't fatten easily. You don't have to have them I won't hold you to it.'

'No. I want them. They will cross out all right, make good mothers?'

'Yeah, they're very good milkers, and quiet, but the bull calves, well.' He shrugged.

'Would you be able to deliver them, drive them home for me?'

'Probably could. Depends how far? Where do you live?'

'It's only a few miles down the main road, Pen-y-coed Farm, you go straight over at the crossroads and then it's about six miles inland.'

'I think I could do that for you.'

'I keep Welsh Blacks; well, I've only just started. I've only got a few pedigree cows. Oh and two heifer calves and one bull calf now!'

He smiled at the thought of a few cows to make a living, and judging by her well-kept, attractive face, her body clothed in what he'd describe as 'posh county', he realised she had a bob or two to stuff into the gaping economic holes that he knew as modern-day farming.

'Got to start somewhere,' he said amiably, 'and the old Welsh Black is a dependable solid breed. Cross these out in eighteen months and they'll make good suckler cows.'

'It's what I've been told, so it's not all rubbish!'

'The blacks are docile and good doers, and if you cross them with a bigger continental breed you'll get some tidy beef cattle,' he said nodding at the two heifers. It made a nice change to chat to someone who seemed genuinely interested, and at the same time, Richard was glad to offload his unwanted calves. She'd saved him a depressing trip to the hunt kennels.

'I'm Penny Jordan.' She offered her hand. 'We've moved from London; well, Ralph, my husband still works in the city – he commutes, weekends and things – but I've moved down, permanently.'

'Richard,' he said, quickly wiping his hands on his trouser front before shaking hers. 'Richard Davies. I farm near Llanfeni. Tŷ Coch.'

'It's a beautiful part of the world.'

'Only a pity we can't get fat on the view!' Damn he'd done it again, moaning without thinking. What must she think?

'Yes,' she agreed. 'It's gorgeous, and great to get out of London. Will you follow me then?'

'Lead the way!'

He looked across to where she was pointing, not so much a car but a large, top of the range four-by-four and he felt chuffed, as he followed her out of the market in his muddy landrover, the waft from the young calves filling the cab. She was a bonus he hadn't been expecting.

It was like going back in time, driving into an unexpectedly old-fashioned and quaint farmyard, tucked away in a secluded valley, similar to how his own farm Tŷ Coch had once been. There were no new buildings and concrete, or heavy machinery. No silage, or plastic bales or old tyres. A variety of hens and a cockerel pecked around the restored stonework of the outbuildings and from the back door of the attractive square farmhouse a golden retriever lolled over to greet Penny as she got out of her car. Two fat, Thelwell-like ponies grazed in the field by the house; the smaller raised its head and whinnied at the sound of her voice as she came over to him.

'Those are my daughters' ponies,' she explained, 'but it's muggins here that does all the mucking out and exercising, when I've got time, while they're away at school.' She looked around the yard, 'If you can reverse back to one of these loose boxes, they should be all right in there.'

The sight of the ponies reminded him of his sister and he thought briefly how she'd judge them, as he backed the vehicle. He got out and smiling at Penny proceeded to lift each calf, one by one, and set them down into the deeply prepared bed of straw, where they stood a little wobbly and huddled together, unsure of their new surroundings.

'These calves, they'll be all right for my beef, won't they'? she asked, suddenly unsure of her rash purchase.

'Not as they are, but they'll make a good out cross, if you're not in any hurry for immediate profit.'

'I've set up my own company, producing a special meat brand under my own label. Primarily for the London market. I'm toying with the idea of going organic, I've been looking at conversion with the Soil Association and all that,' she added, not sure of his reaction.

'Oh.' Richard said noncommittally,

'That's what I thought, at first. But you know, some of the local restaurants said they'd be interested in buying free range, organic, so I'm starting small.' He couldn't remember when he'd last eaten out, not just burger and chips in the market but a proper sit-down job.

'I've got plans to go into pigs and perhaps poultry if it works out. People want to know where and how their meat is produced and the prices they're prepared to pay for locally sourced, traceable meat are very good.'

'London prices are a bit different from down here, though.'

'Sure, and it'll take time to build it all up, but I plan to make a name for myself, delivering to specialist outlets. They're paying good money for it in the South.'

'They can bring some down here if they've got too much. Your farm will eat money!' It came as a pleasant surprise that she laughed at his poor attempt at humour, her own demeanour friendly, relaxed and open. The opposite of sombre, weathered dourness facing disappointing prices. They stood by the door watching the calves sniff, still finding their feet after the journey.

'They'll soon settle. You've got a teat to start them off? Once they've learnt, they'll quickly move on to take it from a bucket.'

'Trust me not to think of that! Can you tell me what I need and then I can pop back to the agricultural merchant and pick them up. I need some more corn anyway.' She came back with a notepad and biro and Richard wrote down the essentials that she would need to feed and look after the calves.

'If you have any problems ring me. It's not far for me to pop over,' he said handing over the paper where he'd added his phone number and name of his farm.

'I hope you mean that, as I might just, being new to it all.'

By the time he left it was much later than he'd realised, and he felt slightly guilty realising he'd been away so long, leaving his wife home before him, no doubt wondering where he was and why hadn't got back in time for the milking instead of leaving it to his mam and uncle. 'What the hell,' he thought to himself, if for once he wasn't there – he was always so dependable. Driving home he felt good, happily thinking of Penny showing him round the farm, her questions and interest making him feel important as she asked him his opinion on her cattle. He smiled to himself as he remembered her smiling at him. In some ways she reminded him of his sister Bethan.

It was not only Richard who thought of Bethan that afternoon. The conversation on the hill about the Tŷ Coch family had also awaken a longing in Tegwyn as he lay against the moss thinking of her. Both happy memories were, however, marred by events. In Richard's case he came home to find out his mother had had some sort of accident and had been rushed to hospital, and his brief pleasurable interlude had been replaced by his guilt for not being home, and Tego, well, there were so many incidents where he shouldn't have and did and some where he hadn't and should have, that they'd all become jumbled, a Welsh *cawl*[3] on a constant slow cook.

Tegwyn didn't know better than anyone else who would and who might not die under any circumstances, but his thoughts were not of Elin's predicament but of her daughter, Bethan, her name bringing back bittersweet memories.

He thought of Tŷ Coch farm where Bethan grew up only a couple of fields from him, where he lived with his parents on their smallholding, Tan-y-bryn. Fair-haired, blue-eyed Beth, so much nicer than her taciturn brother, Richard. Beth who later used to serve him a pint at the Feni Arms where she worked part time. That was before she left the village and moved to Cardiff to train as a nurse. Suddenly impatient, Tegwyn was eager to be off the hill.

'Hurry up it's bloody freezing, come on, just these two to finish. Call it a day.' The sun had gone, leaving the hill bleak and the three men had had enough, packing up for the day as the chill crept back into the hill, and the sea steel grey and uninviting. Having stopped work Tegwyn felt the throb more strongly. He inspected the raw sore on his hand, unhealed, gooey like phlegm.

---

[3] Welsh stew

'You ought to have that looked at Teg. Your finger could fall off,' said Dic coming over to examine the old cut.

'You might as well talk to the wind – he won't listen,' said Frank.

'It's been like this for two weeks and hasn't fallen off yet.'

'Here, wrap some moss round it.'

'Gerr off,' said Tego, pulling his hand away, 'You'll get it septic.'

'Ah! It's already gone bad. Look, this stuff will clean it up.' Dic attempted to put a soggy bit of moss on the offending finger. 'It was what they used in the war on open wounds. Stopped them getting gangrene.'

'Where did you hear that rubbish?'

'Yeah, I can just see them dropping bombs and wrapping the bloodied bits in moss!'

'Not the last war, dumbo. The Crimea, and then the Great War. You know, like maggots, and leeches. In those days they used moss. No antibiotics then, and it worked. Saved a lot of lives.'

'Whatever. Since when do you know anything about the Crimea?'

'Jesus Christ, Tego. Don't get him started – we'll never get him off the hill.'

'You may mock me, but I know what I know. One of my ancestors went to the Crimea. I've got stuff at home to prove it.'

'Yeah, yeah, Dic, one of your I don't know how many great-uncles kept a diary. Or so you've told us all, a million times.'

'It's true. William Morgan was nursed by Florence Nightingale. I'm telling you.'

They all knew it was a load of poppycock, another beer-fuelled story of Dic's. Just like his notion that the footage of astronauts first landing on the moon was in fact an episode of *Thunderbirds* and no amount of persuasion would change Dic's opinion.

'And Dic Morgan's specialist subject is The Crimean War!'

'No, no his *Mastermind* subject is moss, Tegwyn!' laughed Frank.

'You've been watching too much telly – it's done your head in!' said Tegwyn, flinging the piece of moss to one side. 'Here's to a whole new market opening! This stuff will make our fortunes!' He crept over to Dic, a dirty finger on his lips. 'Sh, you never know who's listening. Better not let on or some bossy prick will put a stop to it, or steal it,' winking across to Frank, laughing at Dic and his fanciful ideas.

'You know Bethan's coming home as well?' Dic said, changing the subject and looking across at Tegwyn to see his reaction.

'And Simon,' Frank added.

'Who told you that?'

'In the pub. She's flying from Ireland.'

'Isn't he singing abroad?'

'I read about it in the paper, some tour.'

'With the WNO[4], isn't it? They must have rung him, told him to get back in case, you know.'

'She's hardly been back since she's been married. Odd that, seeing as it's only a short trip on the ferry or plane.'

There was a short pause, each thinking their own thoughts, before Tegwyn mentioned her name, attempting to sound unconcerned, as if in afterthought.

'Beth will be upset to see her Mam so poorly.'

'It's only a couple of hours for her to fly to Cardiff. Or Liverpool. That'll cost something, but he's not short of a bob, is he, Teg!'

'Remember their wedding? Him and that swanky car he had, and money about the place like confetti. Hell of a send-off she had that day, wasn't it!'

---

[4] Welsh National Opera

'He never found out who did that to his car.'

They hadn't seen Bethan since her marriage and now she was on her way home to see her sick mother.

3

Tegwyn Jones, or as everyone local is known by where they live, Tegwyn Tan-y-bryn, had known Bethan all of her early life.

When he heard of the accident he'd been one of the first to go out looking for Ianto, knowing time was of the essence and if the farmer had got himself in trouble he'd be needing immediate help. It was precarious landscape to raise livestock, and every day was potentially lethal. He hadn't waited for any organised search, and being a neighbour he knew Tŷ Coch land and where Ianto might be.

The family would have searched the yard, outbuildings and fields close to home and failing to find him or any telltale signs of an accident Tegwyn had gone searching the cliffs from Tŷ Coch, looking both north and south of Llanfeni. He remembered climbing down at the far side, onto the beach and walking back along the shoreline, finding nothing. In the event it had been Mervyn who'd stopped his van, noting the field gate open and swinging out onto the road. He was the first to walk into the field and see the skid marks, the brown slide like a gigantic snail's trail towards the sheer cliff. When the weather and sea were calm, Ianto's tractor was clearly visible in the deep water where it remained, rusting slowly over the ensuing years. Having lost their father and chief worker, neighbours rallied round the family for a short while, but they'd needed to get back to their own farms and it had been Tegwyn who had filled the gap, continuing to help with the milking when Elin and her children couldn't cope. Older than Richard but still not much more than a lad himself, the extent of their grief had shocked him. Tegwyn hadn't been prepared for such misery or to witness the desolation of the sad little girl, helpless in the face of what had happened. It had made a lasting impression on him and he'd set himself the task of trying to cheer her up and to put a smile back on her face. He hadn't cared less that Richard had wished to send him away, repeatedly causing him grief and resenting him being there. Beggars couldn't be choosers and they were lucky of another pair of hands, a farm lad used to dealing with cows. Richard had always been jealous of Tegwyn, ever since he'd ridden his father's cob and won the local race, reducing Richard to the sidelines as a spectator to watch with his mother from behind the ropes. Of course he knew it went deeper and he wasn't the complete fool he pretended to be, knowing his mother and Ianto had been close friends before he'd married Elin and he might only have been a teenager at the time, but the way his own mother Liz, had reacted to Ianto's death had been revealing. That Liz also was struggling to cope with Ianto's death was obvious and she'd set out on a bitter campaign of hate, which hadn't exactly endeared her son to the bereaved family.

Her railing against Mervyn had the opposite effect on Tegwyn, who'd sided with the Davies family. So his own father was weak and lazy and his mother a bit of a slut and Tegwyn spent most of his time across the fields helping them at Tŷ Coch in those raw early days following Ianto's death.

Those early months had been a challenge and he'd worked dog days, trying to do a man's job for no recompense other than to make Bethan smile. Why? He couldn't answer that, not then. Soon the little girl tagged after him and never having had anyone ever admire him, Tegwyn liked knowing she did. He hadn't cared that she was only six just so long as he got her to smile, to acknowledge his presence with those brilliant blue eyes. He'd never forgotten the day she'd giggled, laughing again and speaking, briefly forgetting her trauma and afterwards, he'd walked home across the fields feeling like he'd won first prize in a raffle. The first time he'd been made to feel important, even though she was a sad, lost little girl.

Mi gwrddais i â merch fach ddel, lawr ar lan y môr, he hummed. They could think what they liked – what did he care, Tego, the village clown with all his tomfoolery? Squirting her with milk if she dared come near enough to the cow, to his wheelies in the yard, or running her round in the wheelbarrow bumping her over the ruts until her giggling turned to pleas to stop. Anything that helped her to survive the initial shock of losing her father so that she was able to return to school after a month and resume the normal activities of a young girl, leaving the teenager Tegwyn suddenly bereft and lost without his young audience. He had made the difference to her life and when Mervyn moved in to live with them and he wasn't needed anymore, the bond between them had stayed. He continued to make her laugh, acting the clown in everything he did and he made sure they still bumped into each other. Only it wasn't the same as when he'd been on the farm, at her home almost as part of the family. He'd felt the tut-tutting and pointing, the upset it caused him of being accused openly in the pub as showing 'an unhealthy interest', a fight he'd subsequently lost in the car park and his fart of a father calling him a dirty dog, telling him to leave off. Worse that his mother encouraged him with a grotesque wink and nod making it out for something else. The power of innuendo, of women and chapel, of everybody knowing everybody else's business; who was related to who, tracing back generations.

He did the only job he knew, a labourer and forestry contractor and occasionally he got lucky, catching her as he stayed hidden by the high bank as she rode her pony. Passing him unshod and bareback, he'd watch the pony cantering on the beach with Bethan on her back, uninhibited and free, the moment special, private.

'Wakey, wakey, Tego.' Frank nudged him, waving a hand in front of his face. 'No guesses where you were.'

'What?' The two men waiting for his answer to the question he hadn't heard.

'Seven, then. Mind you bring those new flights, my last set of darts have had it. And you owe me a pint.'

'Like hell I do.' He was selfishly pleased that Elin's accident was bringing Bethan home and already planning a way to make sure he'd meet her, even if it meant going over to Tŷ Coch and call on her.

That evening, the Llanfeni Arms darts team was thrashed by the Red Lion side, not helped by the skinful of beer Dic, Frank and Tego had consumed, and by the end of the evening, after a poor rendition of 'Mae Hen Wlad Fy Nhadau', Tegwyn trundled home over the fields to the council smallholding Tan-y-bryn. He hadn't moved or progressed far in life and his short marriage to Dawn had ended the day she took off with the fruit and veg market trader and went to live with him in Liverpool, leaving Tegwyn no option but to go back to his parents.

As he stumbled back over the fields, staggering drunkenly, he commiserated with himself that he was well out of it. Always having a go at him, to do this, remember that. He forgot her birthday and their anniversary. 'Aah!' he said out loud, swaying from side to side. He could have fallen over the cliff he was so pissed, but instinct got him back to the yard where his clobber lay strewn. Machinery and clothes that had been another reason for her nagging. His menial job wasn't good enough, lowering the tone of her house with his 'junk'. Dawn used to complain of his smell, his reek of diesel and sweat. 'Good riddance to yer,' he slurred. At least now he could leave his greasy clothes on the floor and he had the use of the lean-to for his County tractor, winches and chainsaw and fuel. There was little danger of anyone coming uninvited up the rough track to Tan-y-bryn. From habit he didn't need to put any lights on as he felt for the two steps, the handle and stairs to his small back bedroom which he'd grown up in. Still fuzzy with alcohol, he sat on the bed in the darkness burping loudly as he undressed, leaving the pile of jeans, shirt and jumper on the floor. He kept his vest, pants and socks on, and without closing the curtains, he collapsed into a noisy sleep.

4

On the day that Elin had been found unconscious in the yard Mervyn had already been up onto the hill to check the late lambers. The morning had started as a promising day bathed in early sunshine. The first of the house-martins dipped in and out from under the eaves, checking last year's nest, and Mervyn, who'd been up before the sunrise, saw them, their safe return lifting him as he walked back to the cottage for breakfast and to tell Elin the harbingers of summer were back. Once the morning milking was over and Richard had gone to market, he had a bite to eat, and as it was such a bright spring morning, Mervyn decided to walk rather than take the quad bike to check the sheep on the common, leaving Elin some peace to potter about without having to make dinner.

He was old and took his time to climb, pulling slowly up onto the common land, to their bit of the hill where their sheep grazed. He was in no particular hurry, stopping often to look, leaning on his stick gazing down to the fields he'd spent a lifetime working; each contour and shape as familiar to him as his hand. He could see the black and white shapes of the cows back in the field and even from his high vantage point he reckoned he could pick out one or two of his favourite cows. Watching the scene acted out in miniature he could tell it was nearing nine. The milk tanker gone, the post van parked up, as Jonesy stopped for his usual cuppa at the stores, catching up on any news duly delivered with their post. All the familiarity filled him with a quiet pleasure, being part and parcel of the small community. He caught the sound of the train, the diesel engine pulling its two carriages on the single track, a steady clickety-clack, accentuated as it travelled away through the granite tunnels pulling steadily east from the coast, gaining speed through the hewn rock channels that echoed its departure, then he saw it again, passing through fields where sheep grazed unperturbed.

The school bus was en route, stopping to pick up farm children and from where he watched, he knew who they were. It was part of the privilege of living one's whole life in the same place. Every time he stopped, his dog also stopped a few yards ahead, coming back to push his muzzle against his master, asking to be stroked. Once he spotted sheep he became a different animal, pausing, standing stiff like a pointer, setting and watching intently. 'That'll do, Taff.' Mervyn called him to his side as ewe and lamb bounded off, the sheep snorting from a safe distance. As they covered the ground looking for any problems, Mervyn alerted by his dog's behaviour, he noticed a ewe lying close to the partially demolished slate wall. She had distanced herself from the main flock, using the wall for privacy and shelter. Her eyes were now fixed on the dog as it moved towards her, set low as if it was stalking her, waiting for his master's signal. 'Taff,' he called him quietly, clicking his tongue to make the dog back off so as not to disturb the ewe into getting up. Giving her enough space, but being near enough to hand in case she needed help, he watched as she struggled; her uppermost hind leg raised in a circular movement, straining then getting up to smell the ground, turn round and resettle and push again. Mervyn knew the ewe needed time and so, leaving her in peace, he took his dog off to check the rest of his flock before coming back to her. As he walked through the scattered flock, the young lambs remained lying with their mothers grazing near by. At the sight of the dog they bleated a warning, trotting back to their offspring, standing next to their lambs, protective. Most of the lambs had come, but near a patch of gorse he found a newly-born lamb with its uppermost eye gouged out by crows, and half its tongue bitten off. It had also been attacked, by the look of the umbilical cord where half its innards had been drawn. He touched it, still wet but cold, dead a few hours. Uncharacteristically, its mother was nowhere to be seen. He would remember the spot to go back to it, before he left the hill, in case she returned. He had a shepherd's eye – he'd recognise her again and with the bike and Richard's help they could catch her and bring her and her dead lamb down to the yard where he'd skin it and wrap its pelt around a twin lamb for the ewe to foster, fooling her into believing it was her own. He looked up at the ash for the culprit. Beady black crows watching him from their nest. He'd like to shoot them, not that it would make any difference. Like the gull to the sea, the crows had become numerous, kings of the hill. Mervyn turned to walk back to the ewe he'd left by the wall hoping she'd have delivered her lamb. When he returned there was still no lamb, a sign of complications. He knew he'd have to catch the sheep before she made a run for it, clicking his finger to bring his dog forward, not taking his eyes off the wary sheep. Too late she got up to run as shepherd and dog had anticipated her move, and Mervyn swung his crook to catch her round her neck. 'That'll do, Taff,' he said again as he struggled to hold the ewe. Holding a back leg he forced her over onto her side, using his weight to keep her down, while he put his fingers in to feel for feet or nose. Nothing but wool encased in membrane, as he had suspected. Between him and his dog they kept the sheep flat as Mervyn felt for a bit of baler twine in his pocket. This he inserted into the back end of the ewe using his fingers to feel for a hock before pushing deeper. The sheep moaned as he forced his fingers along the leg until he could reach a folded-up hoof. He had to push against her contractions knowing he caused her added distress, but he managed to loop the twine over the soft horn. He pulled gently on the string which pulled the back leg straight, allowing it to come through the birth canal. With one back leg out he re-used the string to draw the other one and with both presented he could afford to pull the breech lamb. Like all such births it was slow to live, its black-buttoned nose full of fluid. Still not breathing Mervyn got up, roughly swinging the lamb from its back legs to force a breath and clear its lungs. It then gasped, sputtering fluid. He squeezed excess mucus from its nose and mouth, hitting it on its chest to encourage the heart, before he lay it in front of its mother. Amber eyes stared solidly back at him, unblinking. When he put the tip of a reed into the lamb's ear it shook its slimy head and the ewe, seeing movement, showed a sudden interest, bending her face to smell and then to lick her lamb, newly defiant as she bleated protectively at the wet bundle. It shook its head again, and made a small phlegmy bleat.

Gently he got up, bending down and away from the ewe, and only after he'd moved several yards off did he bend down, wiping the slime from his hands on nearby grass. Calling his dog to him, they slipped away to leave the sheep in peace. As he walked homewards he felt uplifted by the experience and patted his dog, feeling less stiff and old as he made his way down to Tŷ Coch, the fields flattening in front of him.

With the men out, and Nesta and Rhian at school, Elin had the place to herself. The morning sun warmed the concrete, releasing the smell of cow and earth, of animals that grazed. To Elin it was a smell of life: dried warm cowpats, sweet grasses carried on a breeze of salt that lingered in the very masonry of her house and farm, giving everything a lived-in and homely feel.

As she pottered, picking up an odd bucket and brushing the area around her cottage, Y Bwthyn, she sighed at the state of her shrubs. Any that had grown higher than the protective wall had been rudely pruned by the cows in their twice daily trek to and from the milking parlour. It would have been easier not to have bothered, but she'd always loved plants and had a running battle with the cows as she scuttled out to shoo them on, as their tongues stretched out, curling round any stray shoot that came into reach. Barbed wire seemed no barrier to such determined, outstretched necks and like praying mantis in fast forward they would swipe mouthfuls of her flowering currants, forsythia, hydrangea or buddleia as they ambled past her door swishing a tail and side kicking as Taff barked at their heels. Elin had long since learnt to keep only the plants that could survive such fierce pruning, a fair price for farmhouse manure.

Life was funny, she thought to herself as she walked over to the farmhouse removing a stubborn ash seedling from a crack in the concrete. By the door her daughter-in-law's tidy formal pots sat looking strangely artificial.

Nesta hated the smell of the farm. She liked everything contained, tidily conforming and confined to its allotted place. Elin knew that she would prefer to receive artificial flowers rather than a bunch that would wilt, die and make a mess. Inside the farmhouse it was the same: the wall structure had remained, but little else that Elin could remember was left of her stamp. Time had moved on and Nesta had filled Tŷ Coch with bought fragrances, pot pourris and chemical products to disguise the smell of nature. This eradication of what had been part of Elin's life didn't bother her any more – after all hadn't she done exactly the same thing a generation earlier? But she had felt a sharp pull when Nesta had taken out the old Rayburn and replaced it with a hob and split-level oven and grill and extractor fan. It wasn't as if her daughter-in-law was a good cook or had any interest in food, as they tended to live off ready-made, microwave meals. None of this was important or mattered, and she'd got used to it over time, but what Elin minded and had to witness day in, day out was Nesta's indifference to her son. She could not forgive her for it and was glad she was out most days teaching and Richard shared his midday meal in the cottage with them. It was a chance to give him proper food. She allowed herself a smile, remembering how important the Rayburn had been for her at the time of installation, and how naïve she had been then, looking back at the event in her seventies. It was a sure sign of getting old, she thought, admonishing herself for being sentimental, and pulled herself up from the sun-warmed pebble-dashed wall.

On her way back to her cottage she thought she had heard a noise. She heard it again, an odd sound, and she went towards the cowshed to identify the source, curious but half-expecting to see Mervyn or an animal somewhere it shouldn't be. She called 'Hello,' but there was no reply or movement. Tentatively she followed where she thought it had originated, by the side of the milking parlour. She put her hand up as a visor against the sun's glare, trying to see down the narrow, shaded track. There was a door ajar at the far end but apart from this nothing was visible. Perhaps it was only the fact her eye had caught the sight of the door left open that had attracted her attention. She went up to close it, disappointed that her hearing was becoming less acute, yet still with the belief that she had been right and there was something odd and it was too early for anyone to have come home.

By the time Mervyn got home, following his dog, he was tired, ready for a cup of tea and sit down and about to open the garden gate into their cottage, when Taff, always obedient and to his side, suddenly ran off, making a beeline to the far side of the milking parlour. '*Tydyma Taff*,' he called, and when the border collie didn't come back, Mervyn followed him to see what had sent him running. Half-hidden by the corner of the cowshed wall he saw her sprawled, unmoving body lying on the gravel, her pinny still tied around her middle. He rushed over to his wife; the dried blood across her face was still dark and damp around her ear. He knew not to move her as he went down on his knees, putting his face next to hers to feel for any signs of breathing as he gently touched her pale cheek. Her scrawny legs lay awkwardly under her and one of her shoes had come off. So typical of her, and untypical of most the older farmers' wives not to have bothered with tights or stockings, nothing to disguise her varicose veins running vividly like a map of railway lines up her legs. Elin never could sit still, she always had to be busy, on her feet, helping. He could not bear to see her like this, that he had not been with her when whatever happened had happened to her alone.

'Elin, what's happened? Did you fall? Has someone done this to you?' Without leaving her side he stood, searching frantically for something that would help explain why she was there in such a condition. There was no loose horse or cow, no animal that could have hurt her, no person or any sign she'd been using some machinery and had an accident. Nothing dangerous was to hand or anything he could see that seemed extraordinary. It all looked tidy and the same as when he had left in the early morning. 'Oh, Elin fach! Speak to me. Please Elin!' Reluctant to leave her in case she came round needing to see a familiar face, he had to take the risk leaving her again on her own as he ran as fast as he was able to the house.

'I don't know how long – it could be an hour, or more. There was no one else at home.' He listened to the question, pulling the telephone cord tight so that he could see part of her from the kitchen window. 'Yes, I think she is breathing.' He listened intently for the next question, answering in a hurry, 'No, I haven't moved her.' Again the composed voice enquiring and his answer,

'Yes, Tŷ Coch.' A pause. 'Yes, the farmhouse. It's on the outskirts of Llanfeni.' He listened again to more instructions, all the while agitated and needing to be back by her side, wasting valuable minutes on the phone. 'Please hurry.' Clumsily he replaced the receiver and rushed back out to her, grabbing some overalls from the hook on the door, something to put over her to keep her warm, waiting for the ambulance. They had been attached each end of a yoke, having spent their time working together on the farm, each job done jointly, sharing. They were separated only in sleep and then each old body folded close in years of habit. Until now, when suddenly with no warning he found her lying in front of him in the yard, bleeding and motionless. His beloved wife.

5

Relieved to be down and on firm ground, Simon didn't mind the jostle of the Underground. He'd come with little luggage and was happy to stand, swaying from side to side as he leaned on the upright pole as the tube rattled along. He changed twice, and once above ground he walked briskly for his train connection, knowing he still had several hours of travel ahead of him and that before the journey's end he'd be utterly exhausted.

There was little time between connections and he walked hurriedly to the waiting train, tripping over a suitcase that two women had dumped, stopping in the middle of the platform to embrace.

'Watch where you're going,' said one of them as Simon half-fell over the obstacle.

'Sorry,' he muttered, cross that it was their fault and not his but on seeing their faces full of the happiness at being reunited, he couldn't help but smile apologetically back. One of them reminded him of Bethan and the thought of seeing her again raised his spirits.

One last change on what had been a long slog added to his sense of dread as Simon neared his home. He recognised familiar landmarks blurring by as the train slowed slightly through the small rural stations where only their long names and empty platforms flashed a reminder of a different age. The station houses had long since been sold off and converted into B&Bs or private homes. The horn sounded as the train passed unmanned gates through remote farms or over a bridge running close to the estuary and sea. The place was empty out of season; bleak and beautiful. He was going home, back to his roots; steep mountains of shaley soils and trees permanently slanted. At least the long journey had given him some time to adjust, to come down from the heady heights of an American platform to a humble farm and a very different way of life. He didn't want to be reminded of it all. He hoped his sister Beth would meet him at Llanfeni station. She'd want to hear all his news, and she had that knack of making one feel good, a welcome tonic in what he knew would be a depressing reunion. As the train pulled through familiar landmarks, he thought of how it had been Beth who'd always been upbeat when he'd first started on his musical career. She was the one who came to meet him off a train or bus and even his first flight from Cardiff, and he realised how much he'd missed her support. She was one of life's rare optimists.

Simon hadn't wanted to come home, not now, not any more. He knew Richard would resent Uncle Mervyn's phone call, begging him to fly home, and it was only because of his uncle's insistence that he had caved in.

6

The Atlantic sea was in benevolent mood, gently marking another high tide. Bethan turned from the river's mouth away from the few boats moored in it and walked along the narrow band of sand above the high water following a line of hoof prints still defined in the wet sand. It was a habit that had been instilled in her as a little girl, when she had followed the hoof prints of her father's cobs, using a bit of seaweed as a tail, trotting along the beach.

Although renowned for their mountain ponies and cobs, it was the Irish who were the horse riders. Thinking of home, Bethan didn't notice that the man rowing among the moored boats was watching her. Unbeknown to her, he often did keep an eye out for the girl who walked alone, half-hoping she'd spot him and come over and pass the time. Intent on her walk, she hadn't noticed him today and Peter O'Donoghue did not call or try to wave across at her. Only the seagulls acknowledged her presence, taking off just for a few yards to keep ahead of her as they moved along the beach. When they realised she had no food, they took to the air properly to plop down onto deeper water, several bobbing up and down on the unbroken waves.

It could have been the same water, the Irish Sea part of the same vast ocean, and for a moment the thought both consoled and troubled her. She had walked so often with the sea as company, alone or with her brothers on empty clifftops in out-of-season months which she preferred to the busier summer. Today at least, she was still facing in the same direction, even if the coastline did not have the gentle curve of Cardigan Bay, only open sea stretching to America.

Bethan sat down on a damp rock, sharing the space with limpet and barnacle, looking into a flooded rockpool where red anemones opened their sticky fingers in the high tide. Putting her hand into the water she lifted the skirts of the bladderwrack, looking for crab. The tide was on the turn, exposing other lumps of rock shining with clusters of mussels clamped tight at their sides. She traipsed her regular solitary route, her head down. She noticed a shell rolling gently in the water and bent down to pick it out, putting it to her ear to hear the perpetual rushing sound. It was a silly childish act that brought sudden tears, as she stood there desolate, the shell limp in her hands, thinking of her home and her mother. Enough. She had to pull herself together, she thought, taking a deep breath into the salt air as she continued walking, the sea befriending her as it always did, lifting her mood.

She must have walked for about an hour before she heard a regular chugging sound of a small engine and looking out she caught sight of a boat making its way around the far point and out of sight. She should turn for home but instead she took off her wellingtons, stuffing her socks inside, leaving them on the sand, and walked barefoot in the water, initially a sharp cold turning tepid as her feet adjusted to the temperature and she splashed, sending spray upwards in subtle colours of green, blue and silver. Before she knew it, she was late and would have to hurry to get back in time.

As usual her husband Malcolm was out with his horses and her mother-in-law was there to give her a look of admonishment accompanied by 'Where have you been? Malcolm's been looking all over for you!'

'Liar,' she thought. 'You knew I was down by the sea.' But she stood mute, saying nothing to the woman whose mean thin lips tightened in accusation. 'He couldn't wait any longer. He's too busy a man to chase round after you on one of your whims! He's left you a message.'

She shrugged, uninterested, and was glad Malcolm had already left. She knew that her mother-in-law's reference to him being away on business was a euphemism for a good time off with the lads, down south for the racing at Tralee: horses, boozing, business, always a bit of skirt, with an occasional bit of fervent Catholicism thrown in for good measure. From there who knew what or where, left on a free-rein with money he never seemed to have worked for. It could be days before he returned home and then he wouldn't tell how, where or what he'd been doing, always a phone ringing in his pocket or by his ear as he'd turn his back to her. There were other things besides.

'Your brother rang. Said it was urgent.'

7

It had not been how she had envisaged it would be and they hadn't been married more than a few months when he had taken her to her first meeting, introducing her as if she were one of his horses, 'a strong mare', as he'd put it, 'with plenty of bone, that would do a grand out cross', as he'd patted her on her bottom to general laughter. What could she do but laugh with them, taking it as a compliment, joining in with the joke?

She caught the thrill of his racing, that made her blood rise as the crowd cheered at the sight of the thoroughbreds and their jockeys galloped past. Standing so close to the rails it sent a tingle down her spine as they sped by the single-railed fence that separated the course from the spectators. She had been so pleased with herself, choosing the horse that won, a bit of beginner's luck. It was all new to her, having to look at the horses in the paddock and then walk along the rows of bookies amidst the regulars who knew the game, looking for the best odds. She remembered feeling self-conscious, a novice, uncertain of what was written up in chalk on the boards, not understanding the jargon being shouted out. The hand waving tick-tack. The place was packed with people consumed by racing – it was a national obsession and Bethan had been staggered to see the amount of money exchanged by the most unlikely of hands. Overcoats, leather jackets, outdated blouson noir, and some with just shirts on, all unanimously fixed on the sport of horse racing and of gambling.

They weren't just men, but women and nuns and she'd even spotted more than one dog collar, and witnessed a horse's blessing, for God's sake! People who seemed on the surface hardly able to keep themselves warm in ill-chosen clothes still handing over fivers, tenners and twenties like they were nothing more than a packet of cigarettes. She had felt almost a cheat asking for two pounds each way, naming her horse, and panicking when asked what number it was. She didn't know, and couldn't remember any details; or who was riding it, the jockey's colours or the trainer. She'd retained only the useless information that had attracted her, it being dark chestnut with a white stripe. Someone laughed, calling out its number, nudging her from behind, pointing out the details in his race card, held firmly in a hand used to working outside.

'Whatever he said,' she'd told the bookie who'd already known which horse and issued her with a ticket. She threaded her way around from them, more comfortable in the quieter throng that had already bet and like her had taken a place against the rails.

With her blue eyes and fair complexion she could have been one of them but there was something, more than just the feeling of being new to racing, that set her apart in her woollen, rich, aubergine-coloured coat and lichen green beret that she wore jauntily over her unruly fair hair. She'd laughed as much as the rest of them, and was ready with her warm friendly smile and open face. 'Big boned' was what he'd called her, with hands and feet that could never be described as petite. She waited in anticipation for the cry, 'They're off.'

On the rails between the last jump and the finishing post, she leaned over to catch them passing, enthralled by the spectacle of movement and colour as pounding hooves thundered on. All at full stretch using the rail as steerage up to the winning post. Impulsively she jumped and yelled with the other spectators, cheering them past the post, except Malcolm, an old hand, who showed little emotion, only a slight movement at the corner of his mouth, enough to know it was a result for him as well. He raised an eyebrow at her, acknowledging her win, waving her to follow the rest of the lucky punters already making their way to the winners' enclosure. The first, second and third horses came into the small squared-off space, flanks heaving with their nostrils distended in rapid breathing. They waited before the announcement of 'weighed in' before they could collect their winnings. Onlookers gathered round, and clapped the jockey as he dismounted – 'Well done Liam,' and he raised his stick to his cap in acknowledgement, lightly jumping off his steaming mount, talking to the connections as the small pancake-thin saddle with ludicrous short stirrups was taken off the hot, panting horse. Only so close up to them did Beth see through the silk shirt tucked into a lean middle. The jockey was as fit and lithe as his mount, a body wasted for the weights. Standing next to the sweating, spent animal Bethan realised how brave they were. She was no expert rider but knew the perils of riding short. How did they manage, perching themselves on horses they'd never sat before, high onto the withers of half-wild, running machines with nothing but balance to keep them there?

All three jockeys were keen to cut short any post mortem of the race, anxious to be away from owners, trainers and onlookers, wanting to get on with the weighing, before changing, and out again for the next race. As Beth started to turn away she was surprised to see someone throw a bucket of water over the still heaving body of one of the horses; steam rising in the cold. As she walked back towards the main part of the course she scanned the milling faces for her husband, expecting to find him waiting for her. She wanted to share her thrill of winning and ask him about the practice of throwing cold water on a hot horse. She had always been taught to rug up after work or a horse was likely to catch pneumonia.

There was something about looking into a crowd that is unnerving, Beth felt, scanning for him in the mob of people. Then she caught a sudden snake-eyed, unblinking look from a stranger who in that split second knew she was lost, making her feel vulnerable, of being caught out somehow. It was similar to the feeling of travelling on a train or bus knowing someone was staring, assessing. The thing she'd learnt was not to look back, to give no eye contact, it was always a trap and Beth turned away from the unwanted eye, wishing she could see the familiar slim form, dark hair and hatless head that was Malcolm. She tried to follow the next two races, preoccupied in her search and becoming increasingly edgy by his absence, with a sense of someone else behind her shoulder. Just as she started to the steward's office, he came up from behind, making her jump as he placed a hand on her shoulder. She turned almost gasping as he smiled his one-sided smile. Then he'd laughed at her silly fright and indignation, saying he'd been there all the time, only his wife couldn't recognise her own husband! His phone rang; immediately he pulled it from his pocket, his bitten nails squeezing the button as he put it to his ear distracted and already moving away from her.

Early on, at the beginning of it all, he had been proud to take her with him, an asset on his arm to charm and grace his contacts and after the racing there were always parties that rolled on into the small hours. There was also a time when he was inexplicably absent. He never explained his absences despite her questions and pleas, and the public solicitousness he showered onto his new wife were tinged with a falseness, always holding something back. He seemed to enjoy seeing her at odds, to watch her being less able at something than he was. Just like he enjoyed keeping her in the dark so that she would say something that exposed her ignorance.

As soon as they were man and wife and she had moved across to Ireland, he became a different person. That first autumn when she had made the mistake of saying she could ride, he set her up. Like most of his neighbours, Malcolm rode to hounds most weeks. Not here any talk of banning or a phoney drag hunt substitute – the local hunt ran unrehearsed, straight line over any terrain type, with bogs, banks, gaping ditches an added bit of 'crack' to be taken in the horses' stride, all flat out after an elusive and very canny fox.

He'd put her on a beautiful but highly-strung thoroughbred and she felt as brittle as the falling autumn leaves as hunt members and spectators stood round laughing, drinking and smoking while the hounds milled round, whining to be off. The liquor stuck in her dry throat before giving her a warm jolt of dutch courage. A gutsy girl, she tried to stick it even though her arms were being pulled out of their sockets as the mare careered after the leading group, a horn calling them on, the forward group already a field in front, galloping after the huntsman and speckles of racing hounds. Malcolm hadn't waited – he had a reputation to keep, the first and most fearless across country. Inevitably she came off as the mare jumped too boldly, and stumbled on landing before finding a leg to right herself and bolt off riderless. Sore, wet and winded, Beth groggily got up onto all fours and pulled herself out of the ditch. 'Bastard,' she'd thought. Not the mare but her husband to have put her on a firecracker. A couple of onlookers walked across from the lane to help her. 'You

all right Miss? You took a bit of a tumble. The mare's taken off.'
She tried to acquit herself of the guilt she felt. The trainer's wife
falling off.

'She came down on her knees—'

'You're lucky she threw you clear. Here take a swig of this,
it'll help.' The man handed her his flask. Its thankfully eye-
wateringly strong contents prevented any gush of emotion.

He came cantering back, leading the muddied riderless
mare, jumped off and ran over to her. 'They told me you'd come
a cropper! You poor darling. Are you all right?'

'No, I'm not. What have you put me on? She was so busy
fighting for her head I couldn't get her to slow down, to even look
at the ditch. She's got no brakes and a mouth like lead.'

'Well, I've brought her back. Here, let me give you a leg up.'
Was that all the concern he felt? Did he really think she was
going to remount an animal that, like a train with a full head of
steam, was ready to bolt.

'Malcolm! I could have been killed! And all you can think
about is remounting. Do you think I'm mad?' she'd remonstrated.
'I haven't got a death wish.'

He laughed at her.

'I think that's a bit of an exaggeration. Look, she's had a blow,
she's settled down now. Your mistake was trying to slow her. You
should have let her go, and given her her head. She'd have looked
after you. Come on darling, I'll give you a leg up.' She had felt like
telling him to piss off but in front of strangers she couldn't say
much and being stuck out in the country some miles from their
starting point her options were very limited. Also, her pride was
at stake. She didn't want the whole county to know he'd married
a woman with no backbone. Reluctantly she remounted on his
promise to stay by her and go gently, quietly resolved never to
ride the mare he'd so 'carefully chosen' for her again.

In hindsight it had been her error to tell him she could ride.

Hunting in Ireland was a world away from hacking around the lanes of Llanfeni, and she now wished she'd never have shown him their Welsh cobs at Tŷ Coch, as if horses were an important part of her life when they had been her late father, Ianto's passion.

On the morning of their marriage, she'd arrived at the chapel in a gig driven by Uncle Mervyn, pulled by a favourite old pony, and perhaps this had given Malcolm the wrong idea. Or perhaps not, as in hindsight she suspected he'd already known she was no expert with horses and was easily unnerved. She was capable of sitting on a sensible cob who had no aspirations to jump round Aintree and after her first experience with hounds, she didn't go again, preferring her own company. Occasionally she'd follow on foot, but usually she kept away from the hunting field, keeping her riding to the broad-backed short coupled Freddie, who was happy to tramp her around the lanes, with perhaps a rare, very steady canter on the grass verge.

8

Anxious that she was late, Bethan hastened back to the square Georgian house, walking briskly by the yard surrounded on three sides by the rows of boxes that overlooked the well and beyond to what had once been a garden. The comings and goings all focused on the boxes, which had been designed so that they faced seaward. 'Fresh salt air,' as she had been told ever since her arrival, was an important factor in keeping the horses healthy.

Never quiet, there was always work with the horses, stable lads and girls exercising them, grooming, feeding and mucking out, Malcolm keeping them on a tight rein, and it was only when he wasn't around that the atmosphere relaxed enough for the boys to give her a friendly wave.

Coming in from outside, the house felt unused and damp as Bethan ran to pick up the ringing telephone. Her mother-in-law followed her in, wanting to hear what the news was. She replaced the receiver, Richard's words still ringing in her ears, standing in her boots that had made a small puddle on the flagstones. Avoiding Moira's quizzical gaze, Beth walked back to the scullery to remove her boots with a jackboot. Her socks were still damp from her walk in the sea as she left her boots lined up with an array of others, giving her time to collect her thoughts before facing the barrage of questions from her mother-in-law. She was waiting in the kitchen, which was only marginally warmer than the rest of the house, with the ancient range sluggishly reluctant with any heat.

'Bad news?' she asked, looking eagerly at Bethan's face, hoping for tears. A catastrophe?

Bethan didn't want to tell her anything, especially not about home.

'What's happened?'

'My mother's ill.'

'Oh?' Slightly disappointed.

'She's had an accident.'

'An accident? On the farm?'

'I don't know, Moira. Richard wasn't sure. She was on her own at the time. I have to go home.' She took a moment to register.

'Of course you do. I'll look after Clare, she'll be no trouble with me.'

'Over my dead body,' she thought, but said. 'I wouldn't dream of leaving her. I'll take her with me, make it a sort of holiday, seeing as we still haven't been. It might help Mam, to see her granddaughter.' Thinking of her mother, Beth longed to be there, back at the farm and the house that had been her home.

She turned to get a cup from the cupboard and, not bothering to use the antique hotplate that was barely warm to the touch, she walked back to the pantry for cold water and an electric kettle. Everything in the house was a hike, drinking water in the pantry then to the scullery with its low sink and cold stone floor where the vegetables were kept cool next to a large fridge for the milk. Saucepans lined the open shelves, the upper ones taken up by jars of stewed fruit, jams and marmalade, enough to feed the neighbourhood, and judging by the rust on the lids, they'd had been made pre-war and had not been in great demand.

During her first winter she'd seen a rat jump down from the sack of potatoes and scuttle quite casually, along the line of the skirting board, under the door, out along the passage and under the back door. At the time it had upset her and Malcolm's answer had been to put his dog, 'Big,' a cross bred, rough-coated sort of greyhound on it and have a rat hunt which revealed a mound of the animal's droppings hidden behind the softening sack of carrots. No rat.

It wasn't that the O'Connor family couldn't afford to upgrade the rambling old home, to make it into a more comfortable mansion with mod cons, a central heating system that wasn't operated by an archaic boiler that billowed fumes and swallowed coal only to produce tepid water that gurgled along yards of lead piping giving any unsuspecting visitor a stomach upset. No wonder they were all mad, rapidly driving Beth the same way. Mother and son didn't see the need, or wish, to change.

Arriving the very first time as Malcolm's wife had left her speechless. The whole place had come as an appalling shock, not at all as he'd described it to her. Far from greeting her as she'd expected, at least initially, her mother-in-law had made her dislike of her daughter-in-law horribly plain. She'd hardly acknowledged her, proffering a cold slim hand just as Bethan was about to embrace her in a friendly hug. She might have looked like her son, but she'd obviously not agreed with his choice of wife, making it her business to let Bethan know she did not approve of her.

In those first frosty months, Moira had taken a perverse pleasure in watching Bethan struggle to find her feet; the house was inhospitable, cold and damp. It was very different from her Welsh home with its cosy, lived-in kitchen and Welsh lilt emitting from the radio, *bara brith* or Welsh cakes in a tin handy in case of any visitors. At the Conna Stud a bottle of liquor was the only liquid, and there was no food. Mother and son seemed to live on air and gin, and the most simple tasks were made complicated as kitchen implements and appliances, when there were any, were either broken or so archaic as to be useless so that making a simple cup of tea was a challenge. By the time Bethan had conquered some quirk in the ramshackle old mansion, another small irritation would pop up to thwart her; to produce a hot cup of tea was something approaching a miracle. Yet when she suggested to Malcolm that they could upgrade some of the appliances he'd laughed, pulling her to him kissing her, teasing her for not liking his home or the place's quaintness, side-tracking the issue as he swung her up in his arms and towards the stairs and their bedroom.

It was all so different from her old home. Nowhere near so big or grand, Elin had always made sure Tŷ Coch was warm and welcoming. Beth had a pang for home, for being wrapped up and cosy with her Mam.

She was not going to let Moira defeat her, and so she persevered for several months before resigning herself to cold or smoky rooms giving up lighting, yet alone keeping any fire going long enough to produce any penetrating heat. It was bad enough that Malcolm's mother was still in situ, when he'd promised her she wouldn't be living with them. Beth knew that while Moira remained in the family home, she wasn't going to get her own way. As a temporary measure she resorted to wearing layers of thick clothing. Not surprisingly there were rarely any guests and none who stayed over; most of their gatherings took place after a day's racing where interested parties had already fuelled up with liquor, mother and son keeping themselves warm by topping anything wet up with a slug of whisky.

The local racing syndicates were obviously well used to the house, almost relishing its bizarreness as they praised their hosts. What a character his late father the legendary Pat O'Connor had been, and how his son was a chip off the old block, didn't she think? Having never met him, what could she do but nod and smile, keeping off the drink, pretending with lemon and soda but no gin. Boring little puritan, he called her.

She'd had her phase of drinking in Cardiff and once too often been so drunk she'd been unable to walk, needing police assistance and ending up in a cell for the night for being drunk and disorderly. The fright and shame had been enough for her never to allow herself to get in such a state again. Now, she hated smelling it on Malcolm's breath and although he tried to tease her into having a small one, to join in with the party, she wasn't tempted, preferring tea or coffee. In concession, she'd given up the traipse for milk, taking her drink black and in the summer, as there was always a fresh lemon in the house for Moira's gin and tonic, Bethan developed the continental taste of having a slice in her tea.

Grudgingly she had to hand it to Moira for having managed to raise a family without help in such an inconvenient house. What she couldn't understand was why, when they seemed to have plenty of money for anything equine, why nothing had been done to improve what could have been a beautiful home. Why had the family let it run to wrack and ruin when with some renovation and refurbishment it could sit comfortably in the pages of *Country Life* or *The Field*, and be worth a small fortune to the hunting, racing, shooting and fishing fraternity. Did they enjoy living in such an uncomfortable pickle? Surely travelling around with his horses Malcolm must notice the huge discrepancy? Or was it, as she grew to suspect of him, a kind of inverted snobbery that because they could afford not to, they preferred to live uncomfortably? Done up, it would serve as a watering hole for English supporters of field sports who were in the process of being banned from wearing red coats and tally ho-ing after foxes. Set in spectacular scenery, Conna House could be stunning but instead they'd let it go, a mausoleum of what it had been. Carpets, where there were any, were threadbare on stone floors and any guests braving the stairs would find the rail perilously unsound. The wood had been painted over, the various shades of light blue revealing the patching up of earlier hues applied to the deal timber. The fawn-coloured, loose stair carpet was lethal to a careless tread or bearer of a tray, as she'd learnt to her cost.

The drawing room looked out onto a small lawn. The room was permanently chilly and the inefficient fire with damp logs hissed more than burned. Sea air penetrated the surfaces: wood, stone and fabric all ceding to seeping saltwater. At least there were beautiful views, the light across the bay constantly changing, and Bethan often caught herself idling in front of one of two sets of full-length windows that looked out onto the sea.

Faded, once smart lined curtains were hooked back to take full advantage of the view, and after enough alcohol, the room could be beautiful, its shabbiness part of its charm. Hard-backed books propped up the broken leg of a piece of furniture, the easy chairs easier to sit down on than get up from. Rugs covered the need for repair so that those that knew the household chose to stand. Need for a lavatory could take one on a trek down a cellar-like passage to steps with no light. The running water was cold unless one was prepared to wait, letting the tap run until eventually the trickle would turn tepid. Coming back into the hall an elegant George III mahogany table was pushed up against the wall for support. It wobbled unsteadily to the touch and the heavily-shaded lamp helped conceal the damp patches on the wall. There were several portrait paintings in heavy frames depicting serious faces of men and women who, Bethan later discovered, had nothing to do with the O'Connor family but at least hid some of the peeling paint. The three forty-watt bulbs in the candelabra in the hall gave out a shadowy light, enough just to see print on paper but not strong enough to allow a reader to decipher it without going over to the light of a window. For all its dilapidation, it was still a hauntingly attractive place, breathtaking and isolated by the sea, and at least Beth reminded herself she was lucky to have found someone she loved and who loved her.

Moira was the thorn and there was no way Beth could see the sweet old lady in her mother-in-law. Far from being frail as Malcolm had described her, Moria was in the rudest of health and had never been ill. She was furious with her son's choice of bride and never had any intention of attending their wedding whatever cock-and-bull story her son might have told her. Knowing her better now, Bethan could see for herself Mrs O'Connor had never been too anything to travel over for their wedding, whether in mourning for the death of her husband or not. Weak was not a word to use in conjunction with her mother-in-law. Her small frame was erect like a waiting heron, and her steely eyes steadfast.

Discovering how it really was, Bethan was very angry with Malcolm for lying. Why hadn't he told her his mother didn't approve? It wouldn't have changed how she had felt about him and it would have prepared her for the encounter. Bethan felt duped, particularly disappointed to understand that it was her husband who had lied and not his mother, as he'd led her to believe.

It wasn't surprising, then, that Bethan tried to give Moira a wide berth and spent as much time as possible out of doors when Malcolm was away on business. She tried to make the best of it, giving the stud a go, and ignoring Moira. When the lads realised she was no threat, that she was not a superior riding woman with her own plans for the yard, they relaxed, happy enough to have the boss's wife mucking in and making them laugh. One of the girls, Eileen, wore the typical horsey uniform of breeches and boots, pink tee shirt, collar always up under a royal blue jumper and jerkin, a healthily tanned face, mascara, and pink lipstick and after initial scrutiny, gave Beth a wide berth. She looked the epitome of the ya ya brigade who did the circuit at Badminton and Burghley, and Beth was sure she had an excellent seat as well. Liam, the head lad, even though he must have been near forty, oversaw the day-to-day feeeding and exercising when Malcolm was away.

There was no question of the boss's wife 'working' on a daily basis in the yard and after her experience on the hunting field, Bethan was relieved not to have to handle fizzy young thoroughbreds. Anyhow he'd made it plain he wanted a family. 'No wife of mine is going to be carrying other people's bedpans; I married you to have you all to myself. Exclusive rights!' He'd laughed at her, and seeing her unsure, came towards her with one of his melting smiles. 'There's plenty to keep you occupied,' he said, gently pulling her hair from her face. 'I've more than enough money for the both of us and, anyway,' he said as he started to kiss her, first on her eyebrows, 'how could we practise making babies if you're away working in some hospital ward?' His kisses continued down her face, tracing the shape of her neck, and deftly he started to undo her shirt button, tickling her collar bone with his tongue. It didn't always happen in the bedroom but inevitably led to sex somewhere in the rambling house, where she giggled at the thought of being caught doing something she shouldn't. Always in the back of her mind was the ticking clock, her nubile age running out, and she'd seen enough heartbreak of couples in the fertility clinics. Convenient yet insensitively situated next to the maternity ward and crying babies, women failing to conceive in their late thirties. So love-making and sex were always a good idea. She was petrified she'd left it too late to conceive and to distract her from counting cycles, she tried to busy herself by spending her time a bit like his dog, tracking her husband while trying to be useful without getting in the way.

When he wasn't there she'd explore the coastline, anything rather than being cooped up with Moira. He promised her that as soon as she was pregnant he'd make his mother move. The bungalow he'd started was still at the foundation stage and there was no sign of recent work.

It was different on the days the owners came, where she was expected to dress more appropriately, not looking like a farm hand, standing next to her husband, smiling and making the right noises although she knew very little about the horse's potential, form or breeding. She left Moira take centre stage.

After his father died Malcolm had had a clean out of the stud. He got rid of the horses nearing the end of their racing careers. He sold what he could to the hunting or eventing field, keeping a couple of the best mares for breeding. But he'd bought in so that his yard was full of unraced stock, youngsters that had some way to go before they could be expected to win any serious money at the bigger racecourses. Bethan did wonder where the money came from to pay for everything, especially as her husband was careful not to overexpose his young horses. She had to hand it to him, he had a knack of seeing things she couldn't spot, instinctively choosing a race the horse was capable of winning; bumpers, hurdles and steeplechasing. One drawback was that a small field would result in small prize money. Occasionally he'd open up to her saying how he felt the pressure, how much was expected of him being the son of the famous Pat O'Connor, who'd trained a winner at Cheltenham and Aintree. Ambitious, he wanted to better his father's record, and he was going to do it his way.

In contrast to Beth's jeans and jumper, Moira would come down every morning immaculately turned-out considering the upstairs ensuite facilities, in smart clothes more in keeping with the twenties; shapely stockinged legs beneath a pencil tweed skirt, silk shirt, woollen cardigan and pearls. She did not approve of Beth's casual clothes, complaining she was letting the side down, giving out the wrong impression. 'To who?' Beth asked, getting up sulkily from the table to make the trek for a cup of coffee, her footsteps echoing the emptiness, not bothering to wait for the reply.

'What will they think of you going out like that. You're not one of the stable lads!' Moira had waited until she returned and Bethan had to sit through the same spiel about how fantastic the late Mr Patrick O'Connor was, 'If Patrick was alive he'd never let any daughter-in-law of his go about like that.' Beth opted for a simple breakfast in the kitchen, leaving her bloody-minded mother-in-law alone in her hall.

However he was portrayed by his grieving widow, though, the saintly holiness of the late Patrick O'Connor was not reflected in the array of photographs proudly displayed on mantelpieces and walls. Studying a close-up she noticed her husband's sliver crucifix around the man's neck and staring out at her was a tough, hard-looking man, the dark suit and the whiteness of his shirt only emphasizing the contrast. He had a mass of curly grey hair around his full, ruddy face.

The background, usually a public occasion where he was being bestowed with a silver plate or cup which he held aloft in big, country hands, was surrounded by people clapping and cheering the man responsible for making them money.

9

Mervyn had worked at it for months beforehand, keeping it under a roof to protect it from the weather. Once the date was fixed he'd set himself the task, his way of giving her a good send off. Working late with the night pitch-black outside, it had echoes of the old days when he'd often laboured into the small hours; forging and hammering metals to mend farm machinery, or working horse shoes for the different farm horses on his books. Occasionally he'd get a request for an elaborate fire grate, weather vane, or door knocker.

That was a different time and being considerably older with only one arm he was slower, tiring easily. It had been hot work and he chose to sit away from the hearth. Elin hadn't the heart to tell him not to bother, that Beth wasn't that fussed. His pride was at stake so she helped him where she could, scrubbing and later painting, using spit and saddle soap to supple up the unused straps. In the kitchen she brought in what work she could so that by the day of the wedding all the leather was polished and the brass fittings shone.

The harness had been lovingly overhauled, the pad newly wool-flocked and fully lined. Mervyn made sure the breast collar fitted over the bearing surfaces. He had even gone to the trouble of using double weight hide for the traces, not that there would be any great weight to bear. He'd bought new cupped blinkers in case some fool drove past too close. He wanted nothing to upset her day.

He'd brought the pony in from the fields months before, first long reining her down the lanes before putting her back between the shafts as a reminder of what she'd originally been broken in to do. Nursing away in Cardiff, Beth had no idea what her uncle and mother had planned or that they had secretly cancelled the chauffeur-driven car. In the longer evenings once the lambing was over, Mervyn would drive the little mare around the lanes, and closer to the big day in the newly-restored, light gig.

They had made the ferry's bar their own, and in a fog of tobacco smoke amid the sweetness of stout they were out to enjoy themselves: shaggy dog stories lubricated by drink that drooled out in a silly end for any still listening. An odd half-hearted attempt to sing, nothing like the Welsh, who would sing their hearts out. There can't have been more than thirty in the party but it felt as if half of the county had come over with him to give him a good time. Untroubled by the ship's roll, they duly arrived at Fishguard leaden with duty free, transferring onto the coach that had been pre-arranged to collect them. Malcolm had travelled over on an earlier ferry, needing a clear head in order to drive his car along the coastal road to Llanfeni.

Again that night they were in full swing, their fun infectious, swamping the quiet, slightly dour Welsh village, and laughter from the Feni Arms was heard well into the night, the Irish making the Welsh merry.

Having failed to make Malcolm's stag night, because he couldn't get a relief milker for the weekend, nor expect his mother and uncle to run the farm for three days while he was in Ireland, Richard made sure he wasn't going to miss another party. He, Nesta and Simon had turned up promptly at the pub. Drinking quickly but being less capable than his Irish companions, Richard was already well on his way before last orders. With his arm around Malcolm's shoulders he attempted to impart a secret he'd already told him sober.

'I checked it, it. It'll be safe there away from...' he nodded his head in obvious exaggeration at the locals, at Frank, Dic and Tegwyn. Dei and Jean and Iwan were immersed in Irish hospitality, never having been known to refuse a drink, their glasses no sooner empty than refilled. 'They won't find it there, doesn't matter what pranks they might—,' Richard added with a slur in his voice, nodding his head in an unnecessary way, pointing towards his Welsh neighbours, his eyes blurring in a watery alcoholic haze. With a bed at the pub it wouldn't matter what lengths the local lads went to in order to block the bridegroom's way to the chapel as was the tradition, as Malcolm would be able to walk over the fields if necessary to the chapel.

Above the Celtic babble, Dermot's voice shouted out for another refill to cheers. Johnny Moynahan, Malcolm's brother-in-law, attempted the river dance, an arm over Tim and Liam as he spilled his beer over the latter's shirt as he tried to keep his upper body erect as he kicked his legs. He got the laughs and clapping that encouraged him to quicken the tempo. He slipped, nearly falling onto Liam and Rory, who held him up, taking his glass from him and ordering another pint as he lurched over towards the bar, laughing to Richard and Malcolm with Jerome and Rory. Affectionately he put his arm over Richard's shoulder

'He's a grand lad, though I say it myself,' cuffing Malcolm who smiled back at him.

'Ah you're drunk, Johnny! Go on with you!' laughed Cormac. 'Drink up.'

Together and from the back, the Welsh voices started. Led by Simon, Nesta joining in wavy soprano; Gwynfor, Dei, Iorri, Gwen, Mair and even Dic and Frank and Tego, not known for their voices, joined in singing. The visitors looked across to the group of locals that had formed by the wall. Freely they sang, first 'Land of my Fathers', then 'Sosban Fach' and 'Bread of Heaven', all familiar from the rugby internationals, all heart-stirring passionate stuff. Outside in the car park, Richard had succumbed and was throwing up what he'd earlier happily swallowed. Just for Malcolm's benefit, Nesta started the chorus of 'Lawr ar Lan y Môr'[5] taken up by them, all winking and

---

[5] Down by the Sea

nudging the groom, the meaning of the simple folk song soon explained by an obliging bystander. Then the signature tune, 'Delilah', everyone thinking themselves a Tom Jones, joining in 'I felt the knife in my hand and she laughed no more! My, My, My, Delilah, Da da da da da,' at which point Tegwyn who had been sitting staring more and more sullenly at his half-empty glass got up, gave Malcolm a shove and pushed roughly past the rowdy group. He stomped out into the cold fresh air and strode angrily away.

Rosaleen lay on the bed watching the late night film, but her telephone conversation with her mother where perhaps she'd over-egged her story left her with a metallic taste in her mouth. She'd got the reaction she'd sought; Moira scathing in her replies to the picture her daughter had painted, sarcastic and vitriolic.

'Chapel, common, and no money! If your father were alive he'd be putting a stop to his antics.'

'I've told them you're too ill to attend.'

'Why? I've never had a day's illness in my life! You tell them what you like, but I'll not cross the sea to witness my son making a clown of himself. And you can tell the little trollop there'll be no welcome for her on these shores.'

Richard didn't remember how he'd got home but seemed to recall his brother and wife manhandling him on the stairs. He had no recollection of taking his clothes off or getting under the sheets but in the dawn amid the smell of cow and milk, he felt wretched, his stomach churning queasily. That particular morning the normally mild, quiet man hated his farm and his cows, cross with himself for getting so paralytic. He wanted to lie down, not have to face the practice at the chapel. Luckily it was Friday and he had another day to recover.

Beth missed the evening, having the sense to take herself off to spend her last couple of nights at home with her Mam. Even though she knew it would be a good do, she was a superstitious bride, believing it to be unlucky to see the groom beforehand. She had no wish to tempt fate,.

'What's wrong with Dad?' Rhian asked the following morning as her father rushed out of the bedroom without a word of how she looked.

'Nothing, *cariad*,' her mother answered still half-dressed and trying to apply make-up. 'Nerves.'

She got up from the dressing table and took her daughter by the hand. 'Don't you look beautiful, Rhian! Give me a twirl!' The girl spun round in her bridesmaid dress.

'You look lovely. Beautiful. Has Nain seen you? See if she's in the kitchen. She'll help you with your headdress and your posy. Tell her I'll be down in a minute. Don't go across the yard.' She called in afterthought as Rhian had already left.

Had they forgotten that Beth was back in her old room and could clearly hear them through the walls? Perhaps she should have slept in the cottage with her Mam and Uncle Merv, only Simon was staying there and she had wanted to have her last night as a spinster in her old home. As the voices rose in the next bedroom, Bethan caught the tail-end of their conversation, her brother's quiet, monosyllabic answers to Nesta's edgier, defensive voice. She could tell they were having a disagreement by the intonation as Nesta's voice edged louder and upwards, and her brother's became quieter, colder, his sister knowing it a sign of his anger. She wanted to make a noise to let them know she was there, and could hear them. Not today on her wedding day. She got up, opening her door loudly and clattered downstairs, bumping into her mother who'd already come across from her cottage. The facial expressions of both women were uncomfortable, both aware of the row. Elin raised her eyebrows to the ceiling asking her daughter silently, who responded with a shrug. The voices ceased and too brightly Elin asked, 'Did you sleep well?'

'Surprisingly.'

'I thought you'd like some help to get ready.'

'Thanks Mam. We've plenty of time.'

'Rhian's already dressed. I've just seen her go across the yard.'

'Don't let her mother know. She'll throw a fit.'

'It's been swept clean. She wanted a word with Mervyn.'

'Oh?'

'Something about the time to leave. Never you mind. Come on or you'll be late.'

'I can, today Mam!'

'Remember Rosaleen and Jimmy will be waiting outside the chapel. Do you think he'll behave?'

'He's a little tearaway. Rhian can keep an eye on him.'

'Richard said his father is a real case. Well, he was on Thursday night.'

'From what I've heard Richard wasn't in any fit state to comment about anybody.'

No one mentioned Johnny's wife Rosaleen, Malcolm's sister, who had looked on the whole evening in the Feni with disapproval, refusing to join in the rowdy party

As Elin followed Beth upstairs, she paused on the landing. 'I do need a quick word with Rich.'

'Oh?'

'Nothing to worry about. You make a start, I'll be there now.'

She knocked tentatively on their bedroom door and Nesta opened the door.

Is everything all right?'

'Yes, of course.'

'I wanted a quick word with Rich before he goes out.'

Nesta slipped past, 'He's in the bathroom,' and she continued down to the kitchen and out of the family's way.

When Elin returned to Beth, she was sitting in front of the mirror deciding what to do about her hair.

'Richard's all right isn't he Mam?'

'Fine. Having too much to drink on Thursday hasn't helped. He's worried about his speech. You know in front of all those people. You know how shy he is.'

'If it worries him that much, I could ask Simon to do it instead? Have you seen him this morning?'

'He's taken that piece of music down to the chapel. No. Beth, you mustn't ask him to do it instead of Richard. He'll be offended. He's your eldest brother and he's been working on it for weeks. He'll do it beautifully when the time comes.'

Ianto would have been proud of his daughter, if he could have seen her on that morning, sitting by her uncle as he drove the gig, clicking on the smart cob. Siani carried her small ears alert and her head high, her black coat shining from her grooming. She spanked out her trot along the high-banked road towards the chapel. It was a picture that any father would have been rightly pleased to see, but especially in Bethan's case. His only daughter was getting married, in style to a rich, landed, husband with horses.

Llanfeni locals had turned out, lining the verge and spilling out around the entrance of the chapel, cameras snapping the pony and trap. Elin had made her daughter posies of wildflowers which she'd tied along the back of the gig; fragrant evergreen myrtle leaf, to assist fertility, blue flowers of borage, wild thyme, meadow rue and feverfew using what she remembered from one of the herbal recipes passed down from Mair, Mervyn's mother. She combined the herbs with the more usual pinks, and dog roses. The bride's white satin dress showed Beth to her best advantage, and she looked happy and expectant as she left in the trap.

Uncle and niece were met at the chapel's door by Elin, who was waiting with her grand-daughter Rhian. From the inside Nesta's organ playing drifted out to greet them. Elin held onto Jimmy, who was tugging impatiently, much more interested in the pony and trap than a bride.

A lucky sunny day, azure blue with a gentle breeze on the clifftop. The collection of cars that had parked tight to the verge along the road gleamed like multi-coloured ladybirds in the sun and the small white nonconformist chapel with its uninterrupted expansive view over Cardigan Bay looked more like a setting from a Greek holiday brochure than the wild Welsh coast.

After the vows and whilst the newly married couple were signing the register, Mervyn, flanked by Richard and Simon, stood in front of the pulpit to the opening bars of 'Bara Angylion Duw'. The three voices rose together, the old man's powerful still melodic base underpinning Richard's light baritone and Simon who had the biggest, richest voice that pulled apart in virtuoso only to come back, joining together in union to finish in a deep sonorous wave that resonated out through the chapel walls to the bystanders and local well-wishers who listened on the cliff top. Gulls soared above the still sea in a day of promises.

The Davies family had booked the only suitable hotel, situated two miles north of the village standing up on the hill, separated from the sea by sand dunes, a golf course, and railway line. There were the inevitable photographs as the guests hung around trying not to look bored or hungry. At least the smokers had something to do, lighting up to pass the time – 'nice service, didn't the bride look stunning, make a lovely couple' – while quietly longing to slip away to the bar for something stronger than the sparkling wine.

Eventually, laden with drinks, guests drifted to find their allotted places on the tables that filled the large function room. Everything was crisp white, with each place setting adorned with a small packet of sugared almonds for the men and a wooden love spoon for the women. Silver and gold stars had been sprinkled around the base of each glass vase of the fresh flowers on every table.

Eventually the top table came to sit and everybody clapped

as they entered. 'Must have cost a fortune,' muttered Edwina looking appreciatively around the room, making a quick calculated guess at numbers and the cost of a three-course meal for them all.

'Fair play,' said her husband Alun, 'They've done her proud.'

'Hell of a send-off,' agreed Elwyn. 'And I thought the dairy farmers were having a bad time of it!'

'*Tew fel hwch y felin*!'[6] laughed Dafydd.

In the same vein Gwynfor, who ran the local bakery and cafe, added, 'Have you ever seen a farmer on a bike? And I'm sure his family helped. Beth's done very well for herself, Ianto would have been proud of her.' He rubbed his thumb and forefingers together with a chuckle and nod to the rest of the table. The farmers got stuck in as soon as their soup arrived, dunking their rolls of bread into the hot potato and leek broth. They were country men with healthy appetites who treated eating as a serious business, and chatter was kept on hold until stomachs had been filled.

Although it was still early in the season Malcolm had insisted the guests be spoilt with Wales's best, and so roast Welsh lamb was served with all the trimmings as well as new potatoes from Pembrokeshire; gravy, mint sauce and redcurrant jelly to top it off. He'd also had a word with the management to bring more wine and make sure there was plenty behind the bar. The Welsh might like their food, but the Irish couldn't survive a wedding without alcohol.

As waitresses cleared plates from the main course, Dermot got up, tapped on his glass, relaxed and easy, and when he'd got everybody's attention he started reading out a few cards, sending himself up with his poor Welsh pronunciation, and even poorer attempt at the accent. After enough for a joke, he gave up, giving

---

[6] Fat as a miller's sow, i.e. fat on other people's corn

the rest of the cards to the brothers, Richard and Simon, to read out. It helped break the ice for Richard who was about to stand up and make his speech. There was much banging of spoons by way of encouragement. He cleared his throat, then, speaking in his native tongue, he thanked and praised his sister, mother, and uncle, wife, daughter and late father Ianto. Then switching to English, he welcomed his brother-in-law to his home, village, and country of Wales, even trying his hand at a joke, thanking him for taking his sister off his hands. He raised his glass as everybody got to their feet to toast the bride and groom. Tegwyn held his glass up with the rest of his table but did not take a sip of his sparkling wine, his face fixed in a false smile, his eyes screwed up, pained.

The best man Dermot got to his feet, relishing his part, commanding the floor with his anecdotes which the Welsh had never heard and the groom only wished he hadn't.

'The last wedding I went to, it was explained to me the difference between guts and balls and as the lovely Bethan is about to spend the rest of her life with Malcolm, who, as we who know him, is full of both, I think I'd better define the two definitions, as there is a medical distinction.' A nudge from Liam knowing what to expect as Malcolm raised his eyebrows in mock horror to the heavens. 'We'll take the guts first,' said the Irishman. 'Guts is arriving home after a night out with the boys and being met by your wife with a broom in her hand and having the guts to ask her, "Are you still cleaning or are you off out somewhere?"' Sniggers and appreciative guffaws came from the married men and the Irish. Dermot was well practised at producing punch lines; he waited for the right amount of laughter and then proceeded. 'Balls on the other hand,' he said, smiling round the room and then back at the bride and groom. 'Balls is coming home late after a night out with the lads, smelling of perfume and beer with lipstick on your collar and slapping your

wife on the arse and having the balls to say, "You're next fatty!"'
The room exploded into raucous laughter as Dermot beamed
across, 'So you've been warned, Beth!' He raised his glass, calling
for a toast as the laughter subsided.

There was a pause for trifle and pyramids of richly chocolate-
covered profiteroles, fresh cream and more drink to the
detriment of the speeches. Coffee helped to sober everyone up,
with trays laden with cheeses, lava biscuits and cream crackers.
Guests got up to stretch their legs and chat at other tables, the
men gravitating to the bar. Then came more photographs of the
cake and further toasts. Some of the older generation of Welsh
were wanting a cup of tea.

It was nearing dusk by the time Beth and Malcolm had
changed and were ready to leave, surrounded by the wedding
guests who slapped their backs and slurred good wishes of
advice. Tegwyn mingled among them, waiting for the car that
would take them away. Dermot had brought Malcolm's vintage
MG sports car round to the front of the hotel. Its chrome bumper
and fittings, as well as the spoked wheels, had all been spotlessly
cleaned and polished for the occasion. Freshly scored marks on
the side spoiled the highly polished car in an ugly scarring along
the pristine body. They had been made with a sharp instrument,
the end of a key or knife blade. Malcolm could not hide his shock
at seeing his car mutilated, rubbing a finger along the line. He felt
it as keenly as if someone had slapped his face; a gauntlet thrown
down, and he looked around for the culprit, then to Dermot
and his brother-in-law for an explanation. A feeble attempt of
a joke from someone in the crowd came as Richard started to
apologise.

'I can't understand it Malcolm. It's been locked up and out
of sight since you came.' Things could have got ugly, but with
everyone watching and his bride already in the leather passenger
seat smiling at her well-wishers, Malcolm shrugged it off and got

in, revved the engine up and to the sound of tin cans trailing behind them, they drove off. Two miles away he stopped the car, and got out to detach the cans and take a closer look at the damage. She would recall that face of his, but for the first time it shocked her to see him so angry, his fist clenched closed, waving it back at the village.

Beth's last glimpse of her home had been of her mother in the car's mirror. Standing in the road, her arm up in a final wave of goodbye, watching the car drive away with her daughter, being driven off with the man of her dreams. Seeing her mother there, Beth had a sudden fleeting ache for the figure left behind and everything that had been her home.

10

After the couple had gone, Elin did not go back to join the party, leaving it to the young to dance and drink the night away. At home where hours earlier the house had been full of her children's voices, only discarded items were left. Months of preparation and build-up were over in a flash, the family coming together briefly before fragmenting again. Marooned in moments of memory, Elin wandered around the empty house, touching a cushion here, a bit of furniture there, as if by doing so she would recapture some part of them, their growing up and leaving. Upstairs she came across Beth's wash bag left in the bathroom, her flannel still damp on the sink. She picked it up and smelt her daughter, letting the tears she'd held back all day fall.

He'd come into her life, charming first her and then her family. Effusive and laden with gifts, he praised them and their enterprise, making all the right noises as Richard showed him round: the new milking parlour, fields under plough, quality silage, sheep and Welsh cob, keeping his best to last, his Friesians.

What excited Malcolm had been their horses. He showed his equine knowledge as he viewed the two stallions, a colt, eight mares and foals. Standing in the yard, he'd watched as Richard trotted the Welsh section D stallion along the dirt track and Elin, who was preparing their supper watched through the kitchen window She'd felt a shiver, an irrational unease; his stance, leaning nonchalantly against the farm shed wall with the sun's rays sinking behind him. It was reminiscent of that time when Ianto had showed off his cob so many years before. The same trick to catch her daughter. The minor incident caused a surge of protectiveness for her daughter and Elin had wanted to grab her to warn her. Instead she watched her loving, generous Beth laugh happily with the Irishman she'd brought home.

She'd encouraged Beth to leave home in the first place, glad that she'd had chosen a nursing career, putting distance between her and the unsuitable Tegwyn Jones. The older, almost gypsy boy with connections to her past life. Tegwyn, reminding her of Liz and her husband's infidelity. Like all mothers she'd fretted, watching her daughter growing up. Dates that came to nothing. Or worse, Beth had come home elated, only to be crestfallen as she'd fallen in love, been promised the world, and slept with him only for him to leave her. It chipped away at her confidence and Elin thought Malcolm had done the same. Only he came back to claim her. She had not been convinced of his story, but wished to believe it for the sake of her daughter. She hadn't liked the word he used when he returned: 'Claim,' he'd said. Not a nice word; its connotation predatory.

In late summer, he'd driven her north passing through the permanent grey bleakness of Blaenau Ffestiniog to Betws-y-coed with its the alpine features. Steep sides covered in Douglas Fir.

The fast running waters of the Conwy cutting through the rock like a silver knife, streaming over boulders into swirling pools of brown. He hadn't allowed her to linger with other tourists but continued on up to Llyn Ogwen. The still soft ephemeral greens of summer belied a harsher hidden terrain and dark rocks towered over a thousand feet high, a truer representation of the long, ice-hewn winters. Majestic mountains that made one gasp; awe-inspiring, impregnable and immovable, guarding golden sands that distended west to Llŷn and north to Anglesey.

It was Beth who'd gawked like a tourist at her country's splendour. Malcolm was less moved, as if it was commonplace, a panorama he'd seen before. He'd laughed at her easy pleasure and calls of, 'Look, look, slow down,' and 'Pull over, we must stop here – I've just got to take a photo!' as she touched him on the arm, pointing across to another vista. As ever, he'd meticulously planned the trip, refusing to be distracted. A schedule to keep as he sped through the last leg of their journey, driving too fast for the mountainous roads, frightening his passenger, so she'd been relieved when they reached the bridge. Above the fierce Menai he finally slowed down, driving carefully along the island roads to a pine forest, coming to stop at Newborough beach on Anglesey.

They came to Llanddwyn, a wide curve away from the estuary and big tides, its shallow still water shimmering under the sun's light. She followed him to the far end of the beach where the rocks offered some seclusion from the last of the daytrippers, leaving them virtually alone. The subdued water was refreshing, still silky warm after a day's sun and his girl was altogether more natural and better in water than him. She'd dived like a porpoise, coming up in front of him to kiss him, wanting to make love there, but he was nervous and he'd swum back to the shore in short sharp strokes. Later she would realise he hated water, especially the sea.

Returning from their walk she had stopped to look into Dwynwen's well, superstitiously searching for movement in its depths for eels.[7] Before she could see if there were any, he'd dropped a stone in, shattering the mirrored surface. A raven perched on a fir branch, called out and looking up into the trees. Beth was surprised to see so many of them. Shiny, black-coated and inquisitive they'd come in to roost in the firs that bordered the sand. At Tŷ Coch she had only ever seen the odd nesting couple, but here by the beach they seemed more like a gang, a menace of Hell's Angels. Congregating en masse, looking for some action in youthful agitation as they stretched their leathered fringed wings, croaking to each other. A whole helmeted black army of them on their outposts, up to no good; gimlet-eyed scanning Malcolm and Beth below, beaks like flick knives. She'd felt they were being observed, searching for a chink of weakness and that she was doing something wrong. Or she'd misread their intention and they were her guardians. Rook and magpie would follow, and the starling would single her out in unwritten time to understand.

'Marry me,' he had said, slipping a beautiful emerald green ring onto her finger, where in that silvered moonlit night the light trailed a path over the navy-blue silent water in invitation to Ireland.

---

[7] Folklore states that if eels were seen in the well, the husband would remain faithful.

11

Bethan had fallen in love with the romance of it all, of being swept off her feet by him to live in Ireland among galloping racehorses. She'd expected to fit in. In Ireland horses are always close by but how elusive to breed. Dominant horse colours passed down from the ponies of Connemara, the arab or the Carmague and Welsh Mountain: iron, dappled, roan, and blue, dun, and on through the coloured skewbald and piebald tinker ponies. Separated by the garden, lanky-legged, glossy-coated thoroughbreds grazed the new Conna stud grass. Mares were turned out to spring pastures where their foals squealed and bucked, their short tails erect like toothbrushes as they pranced back to their mothers. What the house lacked in comfort the horses had in abundance. Everything was geared to them, and the yard was run like clockwork and the all-weather gallop complemented the sandy beach less than a mile down the quiet road.

Unlike doctors, the local vets were on twenty-four hour, seven-day stand by in case of any equine emergency. No stone was left unturned if it meant saving a valuable animal. Bethan had learnt early in their marriage that humans could hurt, or drink themselves to death if they wanted, being more dispensable than a well-bred thoroughbred. When she witnessed her first accident it had shocked her to find the injured jockey left to his own fate, whilst Malcolm ordered the other stable lads to pursue the careering horse. When it was finally caught it was painstakingly checked for any injury and treated. Stupidly she'd expected her husband to offer some sympathy to the unfortunate jockey, but he'd been furious with the rider, blaming him for a lack of horsemanship that could have cost thousands. She remembered him reprimanding her, that she knew nothing about horses. Having been humiliated Beth had gone back to the house, wishing that she'd never met him.

Upstairs on the landing on top of a chest of drawers was another array of photos of Patrick and his family. These were different from those of him suited and holding a cup, or other trophy for the camera. These photos were of the family man. Bethan picked up a faded frame of the family group, examining the small boy in it to see if she could recognise any of Malcolm's features beside his parents. Presumably the little girl was Rosaleen. Behind the shot was a row of brightly-painted guest houses. Both children were in shorts holding ice creams and smiling at the camera. At the photo's edge the rusty framework of a small pier in an almost empty beach on an out-of-season day. Although they smiled bravely, the young faces couldn't disguise the fact that it was cold. Still cross with him, she studied the boy's face in particular, noting his mother's look, seated beside her. His mousey brown curly hair, and slim frame nothing like the ruddy-faced, big, flint-eyed man sitting staring out.

Holding the photo up to the window, Bethan wondered who had taken it and where. Somewhere in Ireland probably and as she put it back, she noted Moira's hand holding the boy's. She thought it an odd thing for a mother to choose the son's rather than the daughter's hand and wondered if Malcolm had ever been seriously ill, and not the robust man she knew?

Moira blamed her late husband for the union. If he hadn't insisted in going over to Chepstow, Malcolm and Bethan would never have met. They arrived over with one of Patrick's up-and-coming steeplechasers, the five-year-old grey gelding, Fergus Blue. He was well bred and just beginning to come into his own. By Precious Gem, a stallion with a huge turn of speed out of a Dunrunner staying mare, he expected big things from his horse. He'd won well at home, and had shown a good jump with finishing speed and could become a possibility for Cheltenham.

He'd travelled over on the ferry sensibly enough and Malcolm watched as his father took control, full of noise in front of the camera, pulling him into the shot and slapping him on the back as his successor, but in reality he might as well have been one of the punters for all the difference he made to the running of the stud. Patrick knew many of the faces, calling his son over for an introduction, pleased to have him by his side, then, like some kid he'd send him on a schoolboy errand so that he could talk in private, 'doing the deal' as he called it.

The horse had come in second without pulling out all the stops and Patrick, nodding at his jockey was quietly delighted, confirming the bigger fixture in March. Moira was given a different version of what happened at the late-night party that had ensued that ended with Malcolm in hospital in the Heath, needing several stitches in his head.

The father wouldn't take no for an answer, pushing his son to drink himself silly in 'The Prince of Wales'. The sight of his blood had sobered Patrick enough to throw his money about, smiles and threats in equal measure, demanding consultants at three in the morning. In the event a registrar came to face him and assess the damage. Malcolm's head had bled like a pig, putting the fear of God into Patrick and it was no wonder he hadn't given his wife the true story, blaming the Welsh for his own stupidity. In the middle of his son's impromptu striptease on top of a pub table, Malcolm had managed to get his foot stuck in his trousers, lost his balance and fallen, bare-bottomed to the clapping crowd to the chant of 'Get 'em off, get 'em off!' He was lucky it had been the edge of the table and not glass that had cut him. In the event he'd been rushed to hospital and kept in overnight for observation. During the small hours Bethan Davies, the night nurse on duty had taken his temperature, blood pressure and pulse and made him a cup of tea as he recovered from concussion to a savage hangover.

12

Richard came into the kitchen, the smell of warm cows and milk lingering on his overalls. The table had been cleared except for a single bowl and packet of corn flakes. There was no sign of anyone, although the kettle was still hot to touch and the cups and saucers warm on the draining board. They can't have been gone long, so he called. There was no reply. He set about making his own simple breakfast washed down with a mug of strong tea, and switched on the telly for the news and weather forecast.

He felt irritable, having obviously been left out of the recent family discussion whilst he was busy milking. Last night hadn't gone very well, ending with a row. He shooed the cat off his chair as he stretched his legs, trying to relax, flinging his coat onto the settee. He needed to know if anyone had rung the hospital that morning to find out how Elin was, and had Simon, or Bethan contacted home to confirm their arrival. He was frustrated there was no one to ask, and typically no one had thought to leave him a message on the table. Apart from his Uncle Mervyn, it was he who should be making the decisions, not left in limbo while Nesta discussed his mother's fate. What was really niggling him, if he were honest, was his sister's attitude. A couple of years ago he'd have thought her behaviour totally out of character. She'd changed so much that Richard felt he didn't know her anymore.

When she had finally returned his call she had seemed distracted. Of course she'd made all the right noises and perhaps, he reasoned, going over their conversation in his head, that by not being there, she didn't realise how serious Elin's condition was, but in his heart, he knew it was a flimsy excuse. As a nurse she would understand the implications. Their mother could die before Beth seemed bothered enough to sort out a flight or ferry and on the phone she had seemed more concerned with who'd look after Clare if she came. 'Selfish pig,' he said aloud. The last thing he wanted was for his brother Simon to get there before her.

On the news a black and white cow on the screen caught his attention as it staggered on its feet, and he grabbed the remote to turn up the volume. It was a repeat of the same footing the media played over and over whenever there was some new development of anything about mad cow disease. They seemed to relish the picture of the poor cow stumbling, incapable of walking. A man in a white coat was on record saying it was a minimal risk to humans. Then the camera switched to a man from the ministry who confirmed that a further outbreak of BSE had been found, and MAFF was taking the preventative measures of prohibiting all bovine material from entering food that was fed to cattle. Richard watched the rehash of the old news waiting for the new twist, each repercussion another nail in the farming coffin. The by now familiar shot of John Gummer's child spitting the hot mouthful of beef burger out and the voiceover announcing over three hundred new cases had occurred in a week. Then the usual spiel about how much money in compensation the farmers with infected cattle were getting and how it was costing the nation, as Professor Lacey demanded the slaughter of all herds where there was an infection.

Richard sighed at the depressing news, watching for where the footage was leading to. It didn't bode well. Mr Dorrell, the minister for Health, and Mr Hogg, the minister for Agriculture, Fisheries and Food appeared on the screen. They admitted that ten people with the new form of CJD2 had been diagnosed, eight of whom had died. The excuse and knee-jerk reaction from Europe was to ban the export of all cattle from the UK immediately. Typical bloody French, he thought, knowing only too well that the problem would be wider than just British-based, but that the UK farming industry would take the brunt of any fall-out. Richard shook his head in dismay, thankful he'd sold his last batch of calves. Making a profit was hard enough and this was a crisis British agriculture could do without. He'd been farming long enough to know the implications would be life-changing. He thought of Penny and how she'd react to the breaking news and he hoped that it might prompt her to ring him.

Angry with the mess and total incompetence that the politicians were making of the crisis, he picked up his cap, gulped down the last of his lukewarm tea, and went back out across the yard to check on the last batch of animal food. Smelling a handful of cake from the hopper, he wondered how was he to tell what was in the sweet brown, slightly waxy cake pieces. He broke one between his fingers, feeling and looking for something other than crushed cereal and molasses. No odour, or texture that indicated anything remotely animal derived as he went down the list of ingredients of protein, fibre, minerals sugar beet and vitamins. He'd turned the cows out only a short while ago, but nevertheless the news had unsettled him enough to go over to their field to check them in order to reassure himself. No sign of staggering, cold or sore feet. Standing over the gate, he watched them graze, chewing gently. His docile, homebred, boney-hipped, piebald Friesian cows. After years of breeding and milking them, he was attached to them and they'd always been more important to him than the Welsh cobs.

After his father's death and Mervyn's accident, he'd sold off much of the equine stock, keeping just the core breed that his Dad had been so proud of. He'd all but given up showing and only kept a stallion, two colts that he planned to sell and five mares. His daughter Rhian turned her nose up at anything he suggested and without Bethan there, and Mervyn too old, he would have liked to get rid of all the horses altogether. Looking around his farm he could have felt pleased with his achievement; nothing obvious to an untrained eye, but under his hand, the land had improved over the years. It had taken him to middle age before he could stand in a field satisfied with what he saw, and just as he'd thought he could relax a little, this new crisis threatened to overwhelm him. He was helpless to prevent it and the unit wouldn't survive without the regular dairy cheque that kept them afloat. He walked back down the lane parallel with the cliffs, feeling fate conspiring against him. He looked out at the sea, its immenseness emphasizing the smallness of man. Despite it all his family had survived, farming the marginal land, and the Davies family still owned the land and hadn't sold out like so many milk farmers.

Conveniently he forgot his wife's contribution towards the farm's upkeep, refusing to admit even to himself, it was her teacher's pay-packet that helped the family farm from going under. His mother, who had managed to keep them all together, was languishing in the cottage, unable to give him any advice and with his brother and sister's imminent arrival in what threatened to become another agricultural crisis, Richard wondered if he would be able to cope. He realised how much he still relied on his mother's knowledge and good sense. He only hoped she would improve and regain some of her functions. He so needed her still to keep the farm and family in balance.

By the time he'd got back, Mervyn was in the yard. He had one boot on the hose as he tried to switch off the tap with his only hand. Richard called, coming over to help him. He felt an unusual wave of sympathy for the old man unable to manage the simple task of turning off a tap. 'Here, I've got it,' he said taking the hose off him. 'Have you heard from the hospital Merv?'

He nodded 'No change, but she's had a better night.'

'Well, that's something. We'll go in again this evening.' Mervyn seemed lost, not knowing what to do to fill his time, unable to settle to anything. Richard touched him on the shoulder.

'Have you had your dinner? Bacon and eggs do?'

They walked together towards the back door of the farmhouse.

'Simon should be home by then. He's landed and on the train up.'

Richard's moment of sympathy drained away. He wished his stepfather had said nothing. He didn't want to see Simon. He screwed up his eyes as if walking into the sun.

13

'Bring her with you, I'm sure we can find a camp bed and if you're worried we can put it in your room. That's no problem.'

'Is Simon home yet?'

Always bloody Simon, he thought trying to hide the irritation from his voice. 'He's spoken to Mervyn, he's landed. And he was in the middle of an important tour,' he added pointedly.

'Rich, don't give me such a hard time. I said I was coming didn't I? I'm trying to find a flight. It's just Malcolm's... Mam would understand.'

'What?' he cut across impatiently. 'You don't need to ask him do you! He can surely spare you for a few days.'

'It's not that.'

'Well, what? Mam really needs to see you Beth! I can't believe it's money. If you're that short, I can lend you the fare.'

'Oh Rich, of course I don't need your money. Look, I'm coming even if it's via Fishguard. I'll ring you then. It'll be so good to see you, to have some time at home.'

'Yes, you haven't been home for so long.'

He put the phone back on its hook, pleased that she was coming home, something positive he could tell his mother when he went to see her that evening.

Simon's homecoming might be like rain after drought for Mervyn but for his elder brother, it brought all sorts of dormant thoughts to the surface. Richard looked around the familiar kitchen remembering their childhood. Waiting for the prodigal son, the anticipation of having to greet him and pretend, like the rest of the family, to be delighted to see him was not something Richard was looking forward to. It brought back unpleasant memories soured in adolescence. The endless rows he'd had with his mother. He hadn't been such a dutiful son then, doing his utmost to force her to take sides. He'd accused her of collusion, even of her plotting to kill his father. After the accident, when baby Simon had arrived he'd charged her of cheating on Ianto.

Buoyed up by Simon coming home, Mervyn went back to the cottage to change out of his work clothes, ready to greet Simon when he finally came through the farm gates. The old man's obvious pleasure and expectation had further needled Richard, who didn't want to be part of any joyous reunion. The farm had managed without his help, run like it had always been, by Richard and his mother, Mam making the dairy efficient, paying attention to detail day in day out, up each morning at four and the milk cheque at the end of each month.

Elin and Mervyn had indulged Simon, the *cyw melyn olaf*[8], allowing him to be spoilt, and he'd got away with doing very few farm chores. Instead, he'd entertained them, making them smile indulgently at any misdemeanour. When they realised he could sing, really sing, well that was it. After the discovery he was excused virtually anything. In Richard's eyes, he was cheeky as well as being bone idle. It had been Richard who'd saved the spoilt brat's life and look how he'd repaid him! He didn't like to see the jealousy in his face, trying to smile, to hide his feelings, surprised at seeing his resemblance to his father. His hair had

---

[8] youngest chick in the brood

thinned, revealing an ugly white line of forehead, which he kept under his flat cap, pulling it up and down on his head just like Ianto used to, when agitated or in thought. His close-set, brown eyes seemed to accentuate his rather long nose and when capless, his bare forehead dominated his pale face. He did not have the usual ruddy colour that reflected a lifetime spent in the open air. Had he grown into his father, short-tempered, always seeing other people's grass greener? He wished his mother was there to greet her returning children. Married and in his forties he still instinctively turned to her and not his wife for support. She had always been there for him, stepping into the breach, sorting out the worries: illness, money, animals and humans. Long before Nesta. 'Nesta,' he brooded over her name. His wife, who couldn't wait to leave every morning. Her keenness had been especially acute this morning, almost palpable as she crossed the yard, in dainty heeled shoes, her music bag over her arm, stepping gingerly over the concrete. He thought she resembled a cat avoiding water, careful not to put her feet in anything unsavoury. Following her, Rhian slouching and sulky in customary black, slumped into the passenger seat. Safe behind the wheel with the ignition on, Nesta could afford to look back at the house and smile, raising a hand to no one as they drove off, not caring if he saw her off or not.

She had been only too happy to volunteer to pick up Simon, and for once Rhian would have to tolerate the school bus and walk the half mile of lane. Neither were interested in the news of a farming crisis, or Richard or his cows. Perhaps it would have been different if he'd grabbed the opportunity when it had been there for the taking. When they were both young and thought themselves in love. A *twmpath* dance when youth's optimism had burst out and he'd felt like Fred Astaire as he had swept Nesta along to the music. Instead, he'd waited, prevaricating, sitting on the proverbial barbed wire fence while she went off to study music in college and he stayed on the farm, his way of life making him introverted. They kept together, drifting like flotsam, until finally by their mid-thirties, they decided to settle. Not for the right reasons, and as he'd suspected she'd only said yes because she wasn't going to make it as a musician and there had been no better offer.

He'd known at the time only he didn't want to admit it, preferring to pretend everything was fine. His trips down to Cardiff were fun and not a charade where he'd watch her perform. Later they'd go on for a meal and chat, Nesta full of the capital while he quietly fretted about his farm and the cows. If he was honest he didn't even like the harp; he preferred watching an international, and in his efforts to look tidy he alienated himself from the sloppy, lax, jean-hanging scruffy uniform of her student friends.

By the time Richard had finished the afternoon milking and sent the cows back out to the fields, he heard a car pull into the yard. For a moment he'd hoped it was Beth, but from the lane he saw his brother's head through the hedge. All the unease he'd felt ever since he knew his brother was coming home resurfaced and he remained concealed, watching Simon pull his cases from the boot, sharing a joke with Nesta. Unseen he watched them walk across the yard together, Nesta laughing unnecessarily loudly at something he said. His height was accentuated by her shortness, and he looked tanned, debonair. Richard didn't want to meet him as he was, unshaved in working clothes, smelling of cow and manure.

14

After she put the receiver down she felt his disapproval, his admonishment still reverberating through the flex. She didn't need him to tell her she'd let her mother down, her feeble excuses insulting.

The door banging open made her jump and she quickly turned round.

'I thought you'd gone to town?' she said defensively, moving away from the phone.

She felt his lopsided smile.

'I had, but I forgot something. Moira said your mother's had an accident?' Standing in the sunlight Bethan could not see his expression, leaving her at a disadvantage, as he plainly saw her fright. His dog waited quietly at the door.

'I'm sorry if I frightened you, darling. Of course you've had unsettling news. Your poor mother. Is she going to be OK?'

Bethan shrugged. 'Richard says Mam's still not come round. Simon's on his way back from America. I must go—'

'Of course. You must go Beth. Sort out a flight and I'll drive you to the airport. I am sorry about Elin. It's only right you must be there for her. You are her daughter—'

His ringing mobile interrupted them as he pulled it from his pocket.

'Joe,' he said into the handset, then there was a pause as he half turned his back to her. 'You know I don't, not like that. Wait, and I'll sort it.' He slipped the phone back into his pocket.

'Shall I put it on your card?' she asked.

Still thinking about the call, he didn't seem to register her query.

'Sure.'

'Hopefully we shouldn't be more than a few days.'

'We? I can't come with you Beth—'

'No, I knew you wouldn't be able. I meant me and Clare.'

'Oh you'll take Clare with you? Of course. Put it all on my card.'

They both knew she had no other means.

Hearing her father's voice, Clare came trotting down the hallway to where they were. In her hand she carried a few drooping wild flowers, holding them out for her Dad.

'Daddy, Daddy!'

'Who's my little cherub,' he said, sweeping her up into his arms. 'Come on, I've got a little treat for you while Mam's packing,' and he carried her off.

'Is Mam going away?' her voice trailed.

After they'd left Beth felt suspicious of his simple acceptance of her going, when he normally made a fuss of her most simple excursions, wanting to know her exact whereabouts.

Much later that afternoon, long after she'd booked the flight and packed and he hadn't answered his mobile, she began to wonder where they were, but before she resorted to going over to ask her mother-in-law, she heard his car drive up. Clare was obviously overtired.

'I expected you home hours ago,' she said over her daughter's head. 'Where have you been?'

'Daddy says we're going on a plane, in the sky, Mum?' she said pointing to the ceiling.

'Why where you so long?' she asked him, 'I thought you might have had an accident…'

'A bit of business in Killarney. It took longer than I thought.' Clare was jumping up and down demanding her attention.

'Are we going now? Are we?'

'If you're a good girl. We're going tomorrow. To Wales. To see Nain, your other granny and Mervyn. And Uncle Richard and Uncle Simon.'

'In the air?'

'Yes, flying over in an airplane. Now it's way past your supper. Then you'll need a bath so you're all clean for the trip. Come on, Clare.'

She fell asleep immediately but later in the evening, she came downstairs. Looking flushed and beginning to cry, without warning she was sick all over the carpet. The action of vomiting frightening her. Beth leapt up from the sofa, holding her as she continued to throw up, trying to reassure her, keeping her head down as she pulled her hair away from her face as Clare cried between the bouts. Coming in to see what the commotion was about, Malcolm seeing the scene rushed off to get a towel and bowl of water.

Once the bout of being sick had subsided, and she had quietened down, he carried his daughter back upstairs with Beth following. Sitting on her father's lap, Beth changed the soiled sheets and together they washed and changed her, putting her into a clean nightie. Beth took her temperature before tucking her into bed.

'Sh, there my love, you'll feel better now.'

'I won't be sick again?'

'I don't think so. You go to sleep now.'

'You won't leave me, Mam?'

She shook her head. 'I'll sit here till you're asleep. And I'll leave the light on and the door open. Mummy and Daddy will only be next door.'

She left her daughter asleep and crept downstairs to clean up the mess. Trying not to become nauseous herself, she needed to examine the contents on the carpet to better understand what had caused her daughter's sudden bout of sickness.

'She's never been car sick before,' she said to Malcolm. 'Did you give her lots of sweets or fizzy drinks?'

'No, and they wouldn't have given her a temperature. She

only had an ice-cream on the way home. Perhaps she's caught a bug.'

'I hope not. Do you think she has? We're off first thing in the morning.'

'Well, there's nothing you can do tonight. We'll just have to see how she is, and if need be you'll have to cancel going—'

'Malcolm, you know I can't do that.'

'OK, then leave Clare at home. Mother and I can look after her. You won't be gone for long? Not more than a few days, will you?'

Then he took off the cross he always wore around his neck, got up and put it over her head, kissing her. 'I insist you wear it; do it for me will you? It'll keep you safe until you come home.'

15

Unable to face their inevitable joy at seeing the prodigal son returning, Richard cut back over his fields, needing to put space between him and Simon. He followed the small stream up into the wood, away from them and the house, to a parcel of land not joined to the farm. There was a roofless walled ruin of a barn that housed a family of owls; as he walked through the trees, his tension dissipated.

In echo, the sound of the cuckoo rang through the trees and he paused his walking, searching for the elusive bird of spring. It remained hidden in the leaf of young oak and fragile filigree leaf of ash. The afternoon sun filtered through onto grey lichen, making it almost phosphorus bright. Around trunks there were patches of wood sorrel and underfoot it was slippery. Richard smelt their scent before reaching the swathe of bluebells growing under the trees.

He was glad he'd come to this place. For a change, dependable old Richard would not be there for them. Let the rest of the family get on with it and perhaps his younger brother could dirty his hands, just for once. He knew he'd be unable to leave them to do the jobs badly, but he wouldn't go back until he'd climbed to the top to see the crag of mountainside, purple moor of heather and peat. He was a dyed-in-the-wool farmer's son tied to the land, where his path had been worn by his father's footsteps. Secure and safe yet precarious and untenable, weighed down with the history of family, generations working the same land. Much easier to have been Simon, who'd cut and run, free to do what he wanted. Perhaps that's what Richard envied the most: Simon's success only adding to his own sense of failure. He'd lost out somehow and somewhere in all the hours of manual labour, failing to achieve. Pushing no boundary other than his own small plot of land where he worked tirelessly, going to bed each night physically spent.

His brother returning prompted self-doubt like bothersome horseflies. Richard eventually made his way back to the farm to greet Simon, but he dreaded the threat that would expose him, forcing him out, a hermit crab from its shell. He'd experienced this gnawing feeling before when his father died and it was like going back in time: he was waiting for something to explode that would change everything. Sitting heavily like cloud building to impending storm, the row that would surely ensue would be like the rumble of thunder, sending the leaves twitching in the sudden burst of wind. As he reached his home fields, the first heavy drops of rain started to fall.

He came into the kitchen and was greeted by bits of bright wrapping paper left strewn on the table, and a bunch of flowers in pride of place on the sideboard. Fancy packets of American cookies and boxes of chocolates had been piled neatly on the table. There were some parcels still left wrapped but before he had time to nose, Rhian came bursting in on him.

'Hiya Dad, have you seen what Uncle Si's bought me?' She gave him a twirl, showing off her new top, pointing to it when she realised he wasn't sure what was new. 'Designer label, look,' she said, drawing his attention to a rip in the faded material.

'Fantastic.' Rhian was too busy looking at herself in the mirror to pick up her father's sarcasm. 'Did all this come from your uncle?' He raised his eyebrows at the table.

'Flowers for Mum and another bunch for Nain as well as those biscuits. But don't worry Dad, he hasn't forgotten you. I think this is for you,' she said picking up a package.' She called out. 'Mam, Uncle Si, Dad's back, can he open his present?'

Simon came through the door, filling the kitchen with his size, and on seeing his brother, he smiled, coming across to shake hands and give his brother a hug in greeting. His hand was smooth in his brother's rough grasp, and his aftershave smelt strong after the fresh air. At least Richard wouldn't have to put up with him in the farmhouse as he would be staying across the yard, keeping his uncle company. The spare room was for Bethan. He sniffed, turning to put the kettle on as he wiped his nose on his sleeve.

'So how are things?' Simon asked tentatively.

'You mean Mam? You didn't stop by to see her on your way home?'

'Give him a chance Richard! He's been travelling for nearly twenty-four hours!' said Nesta.

'I thought I'd wait until I'd seen you first. And I'd prefer it if we could go together? It might be less of a shock to her, if she saw me with you. Less confusing. How is she Rich?'

'She was a bit better yesterday, wasn't she?' said Mervyn.

Richard hadn't thought she'd improved even though the doctor had tried to reassure him, saying his mother needed time to recover. It had been a shock to see her lying there so unalive, with one side of her face drooped, and Richard doubted if she would ever remember him. But perhaps hearing and seeing Bethan and Simon would in some way jolt her clogged brain.

Standing next to his youngest nephew, Mervyn looked diminished in his clean shirt, the one empty sleeve pinned up against his chest. He'd somehow shrunk and Simon noted to himself how much he'd aged in the time he hadn't been home.

'I didn't see much change from yesterday, Merv.' Richard turned to his brother. 'You know she's had a stroke? She won't recognise you.'

'Just because she doesn't show any signs, you don't know what's going on inside her head. Perhaps she knows and understands, only she can't talk to us,' reasoned the old man.

'It could be weeks before we know the extent of the damage and whether it's permanent. How long are you planning to stay over for?'

'They've been very good about it and said as long as I like, but I can't leave them in the lurch for too long.' He didn't add that his mother's illness couldn't have come at a worse time and if his uncle hadn't insisted, he'd have kept in touch over the phone, until the tour had finished. 'Beth not here?' he asked. Nesta made a grimace.

'She's on her way.' Richard did not elaborate.

'I thought she'd have been the first home.'

'We've been ringing her but she hasn't been able to get away,' said Mervyn.

'There's Malcolm's business and the little girl,' defended Richard.

'Not like me you mean!'

'Elin will be so glad to see you, son,' Mervyn said patting him on his sleeve. 'Seeing and hearing you could be just what she needs to pull her round.'

'Fair play to you. A big effort to come all this way,' added Nesta unnecessarily.

Richard wished his wife would shut up about his brother's effort. 'The flight. How many hours? Then that awful slow train. And no sleep. I'd be exhausted!'

Nesta continued to prattle on, 'Such a pity Elin had to fall ill just now, with the tour and everything. Mozart's Musetto with the WNO, that's really a big break. It's quite something!'

'It doesn't matter about that, I'd never have not come.'

Richard felt the lie. It may have been a career-defining opportunity, potentially lost.

'What time are we going over?' Simon looked around at his brother for confirmation.

'I've got the cattle to finish, they don't do themselves. And I'll need to wash and change out of my work clothes.'

'Do you want a hand?' Simon hoped his offer would be declined.

'Don't you think of it. I'll help Richard, you need to relax, have a shower. I've put the immersion on so there's plenty of hot water in the cottage and Nesta's made the bed's up if you want a rest,' said Mervyn. 'Visiting hours are from seven till nine.'

It hadn't been so bad, Richard thought, patting a rump of a cow as they herded out along the track, their empty udders swinging loosely as they walked back to the field. The heavy shower over, cows back grazing, and preoccupied with chores, Richard felt better now that the initial meeting had been and Simon had said he wouldn't be staying long.

After Nesta's tea of cold ham, cheese, and egg salad, bread and butter, and bought apple tart, they piled into the Daihatsu, hastily brushed out by Richard in order to remove the worst of the farming debris. It still smelt strongly bucolic.

Simon sat in the front not just because he was considered a guest, but because of his bulk. Richard had to admit he looked good in his camel-coloured chinos, and blue open-necked shirt. His manicured fingernails and long brown fingers rested on the large bunch of flowers and box of chocolates across his lap and even his aftershave seemed sophisticated. Richard opened his window.

'Richard! It's blowing a gale in the back. Do you have to have your window open?'

'Yea Dad, we're freezing.'

Reluctantly he wound it up, feeling his brother's bulk too close, not helped by being cooped up as they were, the twisting roads forcing their bodies to sway like kelp in tide, rubbing against each other on the twenty miles to the hospital.

They walked through automatic doors along a wide sloping corridor past wards with poetic-sounding Welsh names until they reached the Llannerch-y-môr ward, passing bays of convalescing patients until they reached Elin's by the window. Quietly and tentatively, as if afraid of waking her, they came to sit beside her. Mervyn noticed she had had her nightdress changed although she was still supported by pillows and remained unmoving in her bed. Automatically the family group lowered their voices in the public environment and Richard felt self-conscious at having to see his mother's disability so publicly exposed. Nesta was the first to pull up a chair and motioned to Rhain, who made a complaining face but went to get one for Mervyn. Awkwardly Simon leaned over her with his gifts still in his hands, as he vaguely tried to give them to her. Seeing no response, he put them down on her table and took one of her limp hands in his. Richard felt a twinge of gratitude that his mother offered no acknowledgement. At least she showed no preference. It was awkward being there, trying to fit round her bed, not knowing what to say or do. Nesta smiled sympathetically at the other visitors sitting with patients in various post-operative stages; still happily drugged up, groggy, sore but getting better, slowly walking with drip in tow, to and from the toilets. They shared a common face of relief of having survived the anaesthetic and only Elin was not like them, lying inert, her sheet that moved to her breathing the only indication of life. When her eyes flickered, Simon momentarily experienced the same hope Richard had a few days before as she lay there, a little dribble escaping from the corner of her mouth.

Rhian, who up to then had seemed more interested in her cherry-coloured, fingernails, without thinking suggested something that had come up in class.

'Perhaps Nain's caught mad cow disease.' Her father looked at her sharply, his mouth puckering in disapproval.

'What? Are you completely stupid. Rhian! Of course Mam hasn't got that.' Underneath her pale make-up, Rhian blushed at her father's insult scraping back her chair, her posture stubborn, defensive.

'Well, it could be. You don't know, Dad. People have caught it from eating meat. It's in the news enough.'

'What's got into you Rhian, your head's full of rubbish.' She'd obviously touched a nerve.

'Mr Warburton says it's been proved—'

'Who?'

'My science teacher. He was saying in class that there is a direct correlation between BSE and CJD.'

'You can tell Mr War from me, he's wrong and he's no right saying it in a classroom.'

'Your Dad's right, Rhi. I don't think for a minute Elin has anything like that. She's always been very careful in what she eats and even growing up, long before any BSE, everything she put in front of us was always homemade.'

Mervyn patted Rhian on her arm, thinking she was about to cry. 'Your Nain's had a stroke, cariad, part of getting old, that's all.' A trolley pushed by two auxiliaries came along asking patients if they wanted tea or a hot chocolate and seeing the lovely bunch of flowers, picked them up from Elin's table.

'What beautiful flowers, shall I put them in a vase for her?' She took an appreciative sniff, 'Smell these, Jean, aren't they gorgeous?'

Simon looked at his watch, wanting to leave. He found the scene stifling and he was dropping with tiredness. It wasn't difficult to catch the friction between Richard, Nesta and Rhian between his mother lying still, assiduously tended to by his heartbroken uncle. It was all too depressing and he wished he hadn't been summoned home to witness it. At least if Richard and Nesta were happy it would be easier. Thank goodness Beth was coming home to lighten the load. He'd have preferred it if his mother had had an accident or something that could improve and mend. Sitting there looking at her he remembered how fit and jolly she'd been the last time he'd seen her. He could feel Richard watching him. He sensed his hostility towards him, and it didn't help that Nesta was buoyant; all busy and matter-of-fact, fussing over his flowers and the get well cards. It was a relief when Richard indicated that they should leave. Collectively they got up and Nesta busied herself returning the chairs, not wishing to see her husband or brother-in-law kiss their mother. Rhian had already stomped off.

Richard said nothing as he drove them back, dipping his headlights to spasmodic flurries of traffic coming against him in the blackness of the country road.

'How did you see your Mam?' Mervyn asked Simon hopefully.

'In some ways, better than I'd anticipated, Uncle Merv. You know, she's not wasting away like some old people do.'

'No, you're right. Your mother's always been a strong person. The doctors said it'll take time.'

In the privacy of their bedroom Richard was still seething.

'I don't know what's come over Rhian. I mean where did she get that crazy idea from? How could she think our cows or our farm for that matter could have that disease?' Nesta, her face covered in night cream, shrugged her shoulders.

'She didn't mean any harm. She's only repeating what she's heard in school.'

'Ever since she moved to Secondary, she's got her head filled with rubbish. We don't even know who she's mixing with! Vegetarian hippies full of drugs. I've a good mind to go over and have a word with the headmaster—'

'Mistress,' she corrected him.

'Headmistress, then. I'm not having my daughter brainwashed.' He got into bed, pulling up the duvet, waiting for his wife to get in beside him and switch off her bedside light. They didn't kiss and she turned to her side.

'I don't know why she's become so different. She used to love being part of the Young Farmers and the Urdd. She was great, remember, in the Eisteddfod?'

'Yes but that was two years ago. Things change and she's growing up fast. She still does drama.'

'Yeah, but its a different sort now. Not mixing with the locals, is she?'

'They're still youth groups, Richard.'

'They're a different type to us. Who knows who she's with.'

'She's just hanging out. A kid who's growing up, Richard. Going through a stage, and the more you fuss the more she'll react against you. Pretend you don't notice and it'll pass.'

'Like you do?'

It hung between them until he changed tack. 'Simon looked well, don't you think?'

A noncommittal 'Hmm' came from his wife.

'Get anything nice from him? I didn't think much of the shirt he bought Rhian. Torn and faded.'

'That's the fashion. She loved it. Thinks it's really cool.'

'Did he give you anything nice?'

'Flowers, for the house.'

'Oh? Nothing special?' he added spitefully.

'Nothing, Rich. You know exactly what he came with. A tee shirt for Rhian, and the rest for Merv. The bottle of perfume you've obviously seen is for your sister Bethan.'

'Never mind, he's here in person; that is the best present!'

'You've always been jealous of him.' There, she'd said it, out in the open like a bad fart lingering in the bedclothes.

'We both know that's not true.'

So he wanted a full-blown row.

'Do me a favour. It's plain for anyone to see. You can barely stand to be next to him.'

'Is that what turned you on, him being my brother?' Careful, the ground suddenly precipitous and the use of words needing extreme delicacy in the order with which they would come from her mouth. She lowered and softened her voice, not wanting the row to escalate.

'Look Rich, I know you're upset tonight. What with your Mam ill, and Rhian speaking stupidly, and Simon here and Bethan not turning up. But don't hurt yourself with something that isn't or never was.' Her hand moved across to touch his pyjamas. 'Please Rich, I like him as your brother, as part of our family, that's all.'

He was sitting up in the darkness, tense like a rod. She heard him release a deep sigh and silently hoped he'd let the matter drop as she gently squeezed his arm.

'Please Rich, let it go. *Nos da*.'[9]

In the dark he continued to think, unsleeping. Of course his wife was right, it was plain to see he was jealous of Simon.

---

[9] Good night

Unlike her younger brother, when Bethan did arrive she had only a backpack and no presents. 'I'm sorry I haven't brought anything for anyone,' she said flinging her rucksack down. 'In the end it was all a bit of a rush what with Clare and everything.' She already felt guilty being the last home.

'Nothing serious, sis?'

'No, she was sick in the night with a bit of a temp., and I didn't want to risk her flying.' She hugged each of them in turn, Richard's tinge of farmyard a sweet remembered smell from childhood and she felt a sharp pang of regret of everything she'd left behind, coming back to them now whilst the matriarch weakened, a pack member returned to help them all pull together.

They sat in the kitchen; everything was like it used to be, only it wasn't. Nothing stands still and each family member had moved on. It was difficult to look at Simon and see him as her little brother. He'd become so sophisticated and grown-up: of course, he was still affectionate as he tried to tease her but things weren't quite as easy or relaxed as they had been when they were children. Ever serious, even Richard seemed to have aged and shrunk as if the burden of being the eldest, carrying the weight of the farm on his shoulders, was physically weighing him down. After Simon had turned in for the night, going over with Mervyn to the cottage, and Nesta had left them to catch up, did they relax in each other's company. Both had changed in the few years making it impossible to go back; no longer children of a single unit. Tŷ Coch was still important but it was no longer core, whatever the wish. The error lay on both sides. She knew it had been especially difficult for Richard, the member of the family who hadn't left home, expecting it all to stay the same, and both brother and sister had been naïve to expect such a thing. Even her solid older brother, who like the landscape he worked seemed unchanged to a casual glance, was a different person.

'I know it's been hardest for you, Rich. I should have come home more.'

'Fair play, you're busy with your own family and daughter. I understand that.'

'I feel I've let you down.'

'Well, it's good to have you home now, Beth.' He put his hand on her shoulder and she hugged him again, feeling some of his disappointment, his hopes and aspirations diminished.

The friction between the two brothers was palpable, and whenever they shared the same space Richard retreated into himself as he always did under pressure, hardly speaking when in the house, spending all his time out of doors working. How different Bethan felt about her old home without her mother there. The meals were awkward, the food was shop-bought. Nothing was homemade and like the artificial taste, conversation was stilted, petering out to the sound of cutlery. Uncle Mervyn was the only person who was genuinely grateful the children had come home to offer their support.

The tables had turned and it seemed it was no longer Bethan who needed comforting. Now Richard looked lost, fighting to hold his footing where in the past he'd been her brick, her big brother who'd hug her tight and let her share his room and hold his hand to go down the lane. She wondered if there had been a family row already, and not for the first time Bethan felt she'd let the side down, culpable for being late, for not going home regularly to see them all. In the old days she would have asked her brothers straight, but life's baggage had made it complicated and she didn't feel she knew them or had the right to pry. She wouldn't have thanked them if they did it to her. She immediately became defensive whenever Richard started to ask about her life in Ireland.

16

Now she was back, she wanted a chance to be alone to revisit the place where she'd lost her father, a place that still haunted her dreams. From the farm's lane she caught the smell of cow, their soft pats warming in the sun, a smell that always reminded her of her home. Barely reaching his thigh, she used to trot by her father's side to his quick impatient stride, as he walked down the high-banked farm lane to call the cows in. Now as she wondered down the same lane, through the same fields between uncompromising mountain and sea, where rocks had succumbed to tides, and the huge hole near the cliff still hissed and boomed with every wave, she missed him not being there.

Bethan climbed over the stile and continued to walk, keeping away from the cliff's edge. What was it about the sea that always uplifted her but at the same time made her think of mortality? Deserted and isolated, she walked on the narrow winding route out of sight or sound except of bird and water. Gull called on upward airs above sheer cliff face. Malevolently below, black bludgeons of rock lurked under the water. A dangerous place as she recalled a news flash; the finding of two bodies, a middle-aged man and wife found dead at the bottom of the drop, their dog left whining on the path. Not just her father, but in her childhood there had been another body, this time a woman's found washed up on incoming tide. Precipitous rocks less incriminating yet precise, lethal as any weapon leaving the sea and tide to wash away any evidence. Possessively the sea wasn't always obliging, keeping a corpse for weeks before finally letting what was left to surface. Bethan had promised herself that she wouldn't become morbid and the point of her walk to the place had been for love and memory of her father.

She passed the point of the accident, and in the shelter of the cove she caught the pungent smell of gorse, its yellow brilliance tracing away from the cliff's path. On the rock outcrops patches of lichen interspersed with soft mounds of pink thrift. Away from the cliff's edge in the shelter of the bank, scented bladder campion was in flower and where the spring ran down from the farm's field, the water collected in a humid, boggy patch and cluster of flowers; hoary cress and yellow marsh marigolds whose dark green leaves seemed to attract all the insects blown from the salt wind. A slow trickle seeped down over the cliff path in a damp slide. She looked out onto the familiar landmarks that had been etched in her memory. Although the coastal cliff was being continuously eaten by the sea, the standing outcrops remained, stranded in their watery outposts. Here, where the sea in its own time had spewed up the bloated body of her Dad, semi-submerged as it floated on a calm day in the gentle ripples off the Llanfeni shoreline.

Of course there'd be no sign of any metal, which would have been eroded by the salt, but she needed to look into the green unbroken water rolling inwards, over the place where the tractor had fallen. To her adult eyes it now seemed smaller, the reality less of a nightmare. The two stacks of granite rock had remained loyal. Like giant tomb stones they stood sentry duty over his grave. It felt better, now that she could see the place again, and looking out across the sea, she was glad she couldn't see Ireland; the thought somehow would tarnish her father's watery shrine.

She was glad to be back, in the company of her brothers to smile at a shared reminiscence, until the phone rang. Too eagerly she answered it. 'In case it's from the hospital,' she said. Knowing that her mother would now never see where she lived and the time had been lost to share the connection of place, so they could not share her daughter, or her life in Ireland, made her regret she'd hadn't insisted on bringing Clare with her.

'It's a shame Clare-Marie couldn't come with you, so at least you wouldn't be in such a hurry to get back. I can't believe you're thinking of going this Friday, you've only just arrived,' Richard said preempting her thoughts.

'I know Rich, but Malcolm won't drop everything for long. You know what it's like with the farm.'

'You've only been home once since you married, Beth. Be fair to Mam. He can afford to let you stay a couple of weeks.'

'I know it sounds really selfish, but it's not like that, Rich. Mam's illness isn't going to get resolved quickly. She could be like this for some time. I promise I'll pop back much more regularly, and next time I'll make sure Clare comes with me, even if Malcolm can't.'

The truth of her sister's prognosis of their mother's condition was something he'd been dreading, a nurse's blunt statement, but probably accurate. They sat not needing to speak, the two of them alone in the farmhouse kitchen, its shape unchanged, the clock still ticking on the same place on the wall even though the furniture and paint had changed several times since its original buttermilk, waiting, trying to work out what would be best for their mother, but both aware that it would be Richard who'd have to take the brunt of caring for her.

'Have you asked Simon what he thinks?'

'I don't see what it's got to do with him. He's so rarely home, flying all over the place.'

'I feel I've let you down, Rich. I know I haven't been over as much as I thought I would, but you can't blame it all on Simon. His career demands everything and if he doesn't take the opportunity there mightn't be another chance.'

'You don't have to make excuses for him.'

I'm not but she is his mother as well, Rich, and he'll want to help. Fair play – look how he's dropped everything and come. Shows me up! Where is he?'

'In the cottage with Mervyn.'

'He's offered cash. You know, if Mam needs special care.'

'Will it come to that?'

'I don't know but I wouldn't be surprised. If she doesn't recover, a stroke is very debilitating.'

'We'll have to make the cottage suitable for her and get a bed downstairs.'

'Won't be easy for Mervyn either,' Richard flippantly waved one hand up. 'He's very limited in what he can do.'

She sighed, thinking of all the problems ahead of them. Until now Elin and Mervyn had been fit and fiercely independent, looking after each other and doing their bit on the farm to help. Suddenly it had all changed and they'd slipped down the steeper slope of old age and a greater dependence on others.

'It could be worse Rich. She could have Alzheimer's.'

'Does she know who we are?'

'I think so, she just can't find the mechanism to tell us. That might come back with a bit of time.'

'It's all right for you. You'll be nice and cosy back in Ireland by then. But what am I to do, Beth? Who's going to look after Mam? I've got the farm, all the animals.'

'It's not going to be easy. There's Nesta and Rhian, and Mervyn will do his utmost, and there are the social services. If she's out before the end of the week, I can help you establish a routine so it won't be so difficult.'

'Can't you stay a bit longer? Please Beth. Ring Malcolm up.'

'Please don't make it harder for me. I've got to get back on Friday. I'm sorry, but I can't change it. Not this time.'

She already felt guilty, but Malcolm had done little to reassure her on the phone, something she couldn't explain to her brother. How could she tell him she'd made a big mistake, and she rarely left her daughter on her own, and never more than a day? She didn't trust either her husband or her mother-in-law to look after Clare.

How could she put any of this into words, to tell her soft,

old-fashioned, stick-in-the-mud, kind brother, and worry him further with her fears or worries about her future? He had enough on his plate and things didn't feel good between him and Nesta. Bethan's anxieties were undercurrents, a murkiness in her marriage which she would have to sort, and when Malcolm had bothered to contact her he'd said Clare was getting better but still in bed and not quite right. He played her, and when she'd quizzed him, he had to admit he'd not had a doctor to her as he didn't think she was ill enough, but she was missing her mother.

The next day, borrowing her brother's pick-up, she drove off to the hospital to try and find out what her mother's prognosis was. She hadn't gone a few miles before roadworks brought her to a halt. A short distance in front of the red triangle sign a man held up his hand at her telling her to wait. She could hear a chainsaw but couldn't see round the corner of the bend where the work was obviously being carried out. She hoped they weren't going to make her wait for long, looking at her watch and knowing the doctors wouldn't be on the wards for long. Within a few minutes another man, wearing a bright yellow hard hat, came round the corner carrying a chainsaw. Seeing the vehicle he walked over.

'Sorry about the wait, we're nearly finished,' he said, barely looking at the driver. 'Just got to saw the branches so we can move them—'

'Tegwyn?' Surprised, he turned to look at her, recognising her immediately with a huge grin. He pulled back his helmet.

'Bethan Tŷ Coch!' It never occurred to her to say O'Connor. 'Well, I'll be blowed. I thought I recognised the pick-up. If I'd known it was you, I wouldn't have cleared the road so quickly! Well, well, if it isn't our lovely Beth come home!' He couldn't get his thoughts together, the things he'd said so often to her in his head. 'I heard you were coming. I was sorry to hear about your Mam. How is she?'

'Not so good, I'm afraid.'

He didn't want to waste their time talking about Elin, knowing the lights would change and he wouldn't be able to stall her. 'I'd recognise you anywhere.'

What to say, that he still had longings for her? That he always had and would always love her? His brain was numbed by the surprise of seeing her so unexpectedly.

'You haven't changed!' he said, unable not to smile at her, delighted to see her in the flesh.

'You have.' She didn't add that he seemed to have gone up in the world, no longer the gypsy boy she remembered, still with his 'come to bed' eyes.

'For the better, I hope?'

She didn't answer, smiling back at him

'I didn't know it was you under that hat. Since when have you been doing this?' She pointed vaguely up towards a tree on the side of the road.

'Quite a few years. Pays much better than forestry work, tree surgery, and there's plenty of jobs from the council needing to cut trees by roads and things.'

'Have you given up your moss gathering ?'

'No. I still go up with them. To keep Dic and Frank out of trouble. You know, the odd Saturday. Why?'

'No reason, really. I just remembered you doing it.'

'Oh.' He was desperately thinking of ways to delay her, anything to prevent her from going so that he could tell her how he still felt.

'Do you like it over there, living in Ireland? Can't be as good as Wales!'

She shook her head at him, 'No, there's nowhere's as good as home, is there Tego! You know that! But I do live in a lovely spot and did you know, I'm a mum? I have a lovely little girl.'

'She'd have to be gorgeous, only got to look at her mother!'

'Still the same old Tego. You've lost none of your old charm!'
Back to schoolgirl flirting. A horn behind her made her notice
the green light. 'Look, I've got to go Teg, or I'll miss the doctor.'

'What? Oh. Sorry, of course. They can wait,' he nodded at the
impatient driver behind her,

'Let me just move the branches or your brother will give me
grief scratching his bloody van.'

'What's new!' He laughed, trying to keep it light, and not
show how keen he was, how he'd never forgotten her. He waved
the traffic behind her to pull out to pass Beth's car. 'Will you
be home long?' He cleared his throat, to hide the need from his
voice, wishing he'd shaved and he looked better for her, so she
could see him in his best light.

'Sadly not. I've got to fly back on Friday. Clare, my daughter's
been poorly, so I need to get back.'

'Oh.' He was disappointed. What could he say? Under the
circumstances he could hardly ask her out for a drink, and
because he could not think of anything else quick enough, said
rather lamely, 'But I might see you then, before you go back?'

Poor deluded fool, was he expecting her to suggest meeting
up, or pop over to Tan-y-bryn for a cup of tea and chat? Her
face, her eyes, still beautiful blue, smiled at him. He had to
take his hand off the car window and move away from her. He
yanked the last few small branches that obstructed the side of
the road, letting her and another two other cars pass so that she
couldn't stop longer even if she wanted to. 'Thanks, Tegs, good
to see you again,' she said leaning out of her window, as she
drove past.

He stood looking along the empty tarmac where she'd just
driven, feeling elated and flat at the same time, that she'd been
and gone. He knew he would have to see her before she went
back on Friday.

Belatedly, whilst his mother was still in hospital, Richard worked on her wall, raising the height to help protect her shrubs from the cows. It had always been a bone of contention and now that she was ill he felt guilty that he'd left the job so long. He hoped she'd notice the change when she came home. It was his way of letting her know how much he wanted her to get better.

While Bethan was out, the hospital rang to let them know that Elin's condition was no longer acute and they would be discharging her. Despite Richard's pleas of not being ready or able to cope, the administrative staff were sympathetic but firm. They were always short of beds and they needed Elin's for emergencies. So on the morning Elin was to come home, Richard was up as usual, rising before five, sharing the first light with his animals. He called his cows, as he'd done for the past thirty years, most of whom had already collected near the field gate. As they filed past down the lane and into the collecting yard, he patted an odd, shining black rump affectionately, cross that his daughter could ever think of them as disease-ridden. The first dozen went into their allocated places, wet-wide noses down as Richard wiped their udders before putting on the milking claws, the air sucking them onto the teats, stimulating the flow of the morning's milk into stainless steel; pulsating, rhythmic reassuring, milky white bone-building nourishment, gallon upon gallon.

Having been discharged, Elin Davies came home from hospital with her three children waiting to help settle her in. Two days later, both Bethan and Simon would be gone, leaving Richard to pick it all up. Only Mervyn meant what he said about being there to help, while Nesta suggested putting her on the list for a nursing home. Rhian, who had convinced herself her grandmother was suffering the effects of CJD, was unwilling to do anything in case she got contaminated, making her father even more angry with her. The media had infected his own daughter's brain against farming, farmers, and against him. As he turned the cows out he knew that it had been an opportune reason for Rhian to react the way she had. She was rebelling and her father wasn't cool, being a man of the soil. She would have preferred him to be arty, a pop musician, not a farmer producing milk and meat. Bottled spring water or crops of flax, or a soya derivative would have been fine. When she'd been a little girl, she hadn't disliked the smell, the dirty ordinariness of the farm, and she'd liked the animals then. He blamed the school and the company she kept, and her mother's influence. And as she'd grown up, living so far out of it when you needed transport to do anything was a real pain, as it meant she was dependent on her parents for any ferrying around. Unlike many of the other kids, they didn't go abroad for holidays, the farm and animals preventing them. Closing the gate as the last cow trundled through, he knew she couldn't wait to grow up so she could leave.

Y Bwthyn had been adapted for Elin's return, and the small parlour turned into a makeshift bedroom for her. There was no hope of getting her up and down stairs and they'd thought she'd appreciate being near the window where she'd be able to watch the comings and goings of the farm. They'd been told how important it was for her recovery to keep her stimulated so Mervyn had made a posy using some of her precious herbs; echoes of the horse doctor in a bygone age which he'd put on her windowsill. At least it was spring and there was the summer to look forward to; hawthorn and may followed by honeysuckle and dog rose. It was too late now to acquire her herbal knowledge and Richard regretted he'd never taken her garden seriously, utilising every bit of green for his cattle, sheep and horses. He didn't know the medicinal properties of the herbs she'd used as his father had scorned her, pooh-poohing it as fanciful rubbish, even though on more than one occasion he'd seen him sneakily resorting to Mair's and Mervyn's herbal remedy to treat a sick animal. If his mother recovered he promised himself he'd retrieve some of her knowledge and write her remedies down, and he couldn't bear to think of the yard with all its necessary concrete without his mother's lifelong fringes of flora that had brought medicine as well as perfume and colour to the farm's functional surroundings. It was so much a part of her.

17

Simon left the next day and Beth witnessed the uneasy handshake of the brothers, the hollow platitudes in the yard. She hugged him fondly in her turn, making him promise to visit her in Ireland. Nesta was already in her car waiting to drive him to the station.

'I thought you were teaching?' Richard had questioned her at supper the night before.

'It's very sweet of you Nesta, but I can get a taxi.' Simon had offered.

'I haven't got a lesson until twelve and it's not far to go round.'

'It's in the opposite direction-'

'Look, let me get a taxi, or Beth could – would you mind? Save any fuss.'

'Sure, if I can use the pick-up? I'm not insured to drive any other car.'

'As Nesta's obviously sorted it out you might as well go with her. I need the pick-up,' said Richard settling the point.

Simon smiled nervously as he picked up his suitcase. The journey was awkward as Nesta talked needlessly, until she mentioned the Cardiff Singer of the World competition. It was not a memory he wanted to be reminded of, the culmination of what had been up to then a fantastic week. Richard had been at home to milk and a bout of flu prevented Elin and Mervyn from attending, so that only Nesta and Bethan went. No longer just eisteddfodau, and primarily Welsh, but St David's Hall in Cardiff where he received the wider exposure and a bigger television audience. He had been praised as 'a promising young baritone with a big future'. He'd sailed through his heat to the final which he didn't win, but he had been heard and seen; a face to put to the voice.

The sudden placing of her hand on his thigh caused him a knee-jerk reaction. The spotlight, success and booze were no excuse for what followed that night. He had allowed it to happen and as he sat frozen, he recoiled from the recollection of his brother's long-term girlfriend, his sister-in-law to be, lying under him naked in a double bed at The Hilton. She'd shared his passion for music and had helped him, accompanying him on the piano when he practised but he hadn't seen it as anything other than sisterly affection. A bit of teasing, cajoling, fluttering of eyelashes – silly insignificant flirting that suited both their egos. After the competition, he'd been on a high and before he fully realised where it was leading, his pants were down. The act could not be retracted, however he had later tried to eradicate it from his memory. Worse still it worried him that having been rejected by him, Nesta had gone back to his brother to marry him. Since then he'd kept his distance so as never to be alone with her, until now. In her car, her hand on his leg making him want to retch. He removed it roughly, hoping she'd get the hint, his thought only the end of the journey where he could escape onto a train. He had a flash of an image of Helena and then the tortured look on his brother's face as they'd departed. How long had he known?

She'd pulled over and stopped the car in some empty lane.

'There's no one to see us and I've waited all week to be alone with you.'

111

'For heaven's sake, Nesta. I'm not interested. You're my sister-in-law—'

'So? It didn't stop you before.'

'What? That was years ago and I was drunk.' He needed to get to the station without a scene. 'I was young and the concert went to my head. A silly schoolboy incident. That's all it ever was.'

'I still fancy you.'

'I think Richard knows.'

'So what if he does? We weren't married then, so where's the problem?'

'You were his girl, Nesta. Look, we're family. Can't you forget it ever happened, like I have?' His brother knowing made it all the worse, adding an unwanted validity to what had been a drunken incident he'd liked to have eradicated. At the time he'd wanted to confess everything to Richard but never did. How could he tell him it was Nesta who'd come on to him and that he was too drunk to prevent what happened? So much luckier and easier to escape from the close, tight-knit, narrow community, singing his way out to liberation, admiration and beautiful women all over the world. It was easy to be an expat, where he could be proud to be known as a Welshman, from the land of song, singing in Italian, French or German and occasionally Welsh.

Whilst she dumped Simon sulkily at the station, Richard spent the whole day brooding about them. Did she think he couldn't see what was going on, as she'd got into her car all smiles, stinking of her cheap scent and readily applied lipstick? Bethan also witnessed the departure, having heard husband and wife arguing in their bedroom the night before. When it was her turn to leave she knew that he didn't have the cosy support of his family that she'd assumed. Things at Tŷ Coch weren't right and she felt bad about abandoning him. After the early milking Richard insisted on driving her down to Cardiff airport. She said her goodbyes feeling suitably guilty: her bedridden mother gave no reaction to her kiss, and a forlorn hug from Mervyn, even though he tried to put a brave face on it. Elin would need twenty-four hour care. In the car Richard didn't bring up the row and Bethan, whilst wanting to show her support, was reluctant to say anything. She knew that once said it could not be unsaid and there could no longer be any pretence and that what she needed, before she left, was the image of her home being secure. Her brother and mother always there to give it permanence. She hugged him close outside the departure doors.

'At least you've always been loyal, little sis,' he said making her feel more guilty.

Flying home she regretted they hadn't been able to speak freely, sharing their problems like they had as children. Hesitant and cautious, her brother had needed more time than she'd allowed, so that neither was quite ready for divulgences. Their misgivings, missed opportunities and wrong choices had added up to a failure, so they'd kept things close, only their tight embrace at separation showing the extent of how they really felt, already too late as each let go.

Her wobbly feelings were forgotten as soon as she saw Clare racing excitedly towards her, calling out 'Mum,' in genuine joy. She swept her up into her arms, kissing her and then put her down again to see Malcolm following his daughter at a nonchalant pace. He kissed her lightly as Clare pulled at her sleeve, wanting all the attention.

'I thought you'd be glad to see her and I promised her a trip to the airport if she was good.'

'But is she well enough? Are you better, darling? Mam's been so worried about you.' The little girl looked puzzled.

'You were sick, remember when I left.' She made a face, a half-hearted nod, unsure.

'Is that why you went away?'

113

'No. Of course not.'

'Mam's not going away again and leaving us are you?'

'No, darling. And next time, I'll take you with me. I promise. I thought about you every day when I was with Nain and Uncle Richard. Here, I've got a present for you,' and she pulled a soft, curly-coated toy out of her carrier bag. 'There, it's a woolly sheep from Wales!'

18

He never thought he would see the day when he would be pleased, in fact delighted to find one of his calves sick and fate on his side. He'd been in the house when the phone rang.

'Are you sure you wouldn't mind popping over?' she'd asked him. 'It could be nothing.' He hoped ideally it would be a small illness. Nothing too complicated so he'd be able to solve the problem while getting to know her better. He wouldn't have been so quick to offer assistance if it had been another buyer, but he'd insisted it was no bother to pop over to see what was wrong with one of the calves he'd sold to her.

They looked well settled down in their new home but Richard was more excited to be in her company than look at any calves who'd inquisitively grouped around them. Penny wasn't about to fall into his arms as he'd daydreamed she might. She was more concerned about her sick animal. Watching her as well as the stock Richard thought she seemed a little more heavily made up than the day in the market and with it a little less ebullient than before. Having conjured up a flight of fancy in the intervening weeks, the truth was that Richard was just a farmer she happened to have bought stock off, and one of the calves was obviously bothered, with froth coming from its mouth, as it coughed, lowering its head, and throwing a front hoof forward as if to paw the ground.

'He's been fine until yesterday. Is it serious, do you think?' she asked him. 'Does he need a vet?' He had an impulse to kiss her, to take her in his arms and make love to her. Instead he had to study the calf as it moved, agitated and uncomfortable, shaking its head.

'It doesn't look too serious. I need to catch it. I wonder could we drive them into a box? Easier if we keep them all together.'

'They've only got to see the bucket and they'll follow me. They're very tame.'

'Oh, OK then. If you get them a bucket of their milk, I'll try and grab him from behind when he's got his head in it.'

She came back out with a half-bucket of reconstituted warm milk and the calves all jostled to get their heads in first. Once the sick calf was distracted, Richard made his grab, wrapping both arms around its neck before it could pull its head out of the bucket. The other calves shot off, startled by the stranded calf's unceremonious bellowing. Using his weight Richard floored it, and before it could escape, skillfully brought its four fetlocks together, tying them tightly with rope. With the calf immobilised and Penny on her knees stroking its head, Richard proceeded to eliminate all the obvious calf ailments he'd had a lifetime of diagnosing. It looked well with no temperature, no scour, no runny nose or dull eyes. It was too young for any mineral deficiency, nor did the stomach seem distended to indicate a sign of blockage. He didn't want to get it wrong, to miss his chance to impress her, but he couldn't see for the life of him anything wrong with the calf. He was about to admit defeat when the calf started to chew, to rotate its jaws, frothing as it twisted its tongue out of its mouth. Squatting on his heels, Richard pulled the tongue out. 'Here, can you hold this?' She held the calf's tongue, which immediately slipped from her grasp. 'Sorry.'

'Try again.' This time she pulled it, keeping a firm grip and allowing Richard to put his hand into the protesting animal's mouth. Quickly he felt along the jaw to the back of the mouth, where, he felt a solid object wedged.

'Ah, I think I've found something – can you hold the tongue up, a little bit more?' He felt around with his thumb and forefinger as the calf struggled. Penny squeaked as the wriggling tongue slipped from her grasp again.

'Damn,' she said. 'He pulled and I couldn't hold. Sorry, I'm not very good at this.'

'Not to worry, one more time,' said Richard as he pulled the calf's tongue again. Before the calf could retrieve its tongue from Penny's grip, Richard pulled the offending object out of the calf's mouth. He held a small, stout twig between his fingers. 'This is the problem. He must have been chewing on a bit of branch and got it stuck in his mouth. He should be all right now, just a bit bruised.' He wiped his slimy hands on the grass, 'You'd better stand back when I let him go.'

Penny got to her feet, patting her calf. 'I hope you know how lucky you are to have Mr— I've forgotten your name, how awful of me—'

'Richard, Richard Davies. Everyone one calls me Rich Tŷ Coch.'

'—Richard Davies come over just to help you, you silly old thing,' she said to the calf. He smiled at her saying his name, the name she'd forgotten, as he bent his head to undo the rope, not wanting her to see how pleased he felt. Then he stood up and back to protect her as he released the calf who veered up and careered across the field to the other calves.

'Thank you, Richard, I didn't know what to do.' He attempted to wipe his hands on his trousers. 'Any time. It's nice to see them doing so well. You've obviously got a knack for stock.'

The compliment pleased her and he saw her lighten up now

that the calf was fine. 'You need to wash the slime off, why don't you come inside for a coffee?' She lead the way back to the house and into the kitchen with Richard in tow, still pleased with himself that he'd been able to solve the problem in front of her, secretly knowing it to be down to luck rather than good judgement that he'd found the solution to the calf's illness.

The kitchen wasn't as tidy as he remembered; there were no flowers or homemade smell of baking. When she had her back to him he looked across the room to the oak dresser with it rows of blue and white china plates. In the middle was a framed photograph of a smiling man between two girls. She turned and saw him looking. Her mouth trembled. He swallowed the question he was about to ask, instead filling the space with small talk.

'You've done a fine job on them; they've grown well in a short time.'

She brought two mugs of coffee over to the table and as he smiled his thanks to her she burst into tears, turning away from him, looking for a hanky. She got up, putting her hands to her face, apologising, still shaking. 'I'm sorry,' she said in a muffled voice. 'I've had a really bad day.'

Richard went to her, taking her in his arms, and held her sobbing frame. 'Shoo, there, there you let it out, it'll be all right. You cry on my shoulders,' cradling her, wishing their intimacy was due to happier circumstances but still glad of an excuse to hold her in his arms.

She made an effort, pulling herself away. 'God, what must you think of me, I'm sorry. I saw you look at the photo and it set me off. No, it's not that, they're all fine,' she said in case he jumped to the wrong conclusion. 'Ralph, my husband came over last week. I stupidly thought it was in celebration of all this,' she said looking round. 'Our venture into the country idyll and the birth of our new joint company. How stupid can I have been!' Richard said nothing, looking at her intently longing to take her back in his arms. 'How wrong I was! I threw the champagne at him. I wish I'd hit him. Do you know why he came? Dragging himself all the way down from London? To tell me he was leaving. He's been having an affair. A "colleague" was his word for it. Some savvy little lady based in New York. And there was I thinking he was busy making money, feeling sorry for him coming home jet-lagged and exhausted, working all hours to put money into this, when all the time he was screwing her, glad to keep me away and occupied, out of his hair.'

What could Richard say, thinking how lovely she looked and how crazy the man must be to cheat on her. 'Oh don't worry,' she went on. 'He can easily afford all this – the farm's small fry compared to what he earns. To think he did it just to get me out of the way, that's what hurts.' Tears started anew as she realised how blind she'd been. 'He's probably using our house in Hampstead to entertain her, the bastard.'

'I should have called earlier. I've just been so busy and my Mam had a stroke and it's all been a mess at home.'

'The last thing you need is me and my problems.'

'That's not true. Your husband must be mad, with someone as beautiful as you for his wife.' He shouldn't have said it, but it was what he felt and her blotched, sad face smiled briefly at the compliment. It became suddenly awkward between them. It was not the time to flirt, to tell her he'd fantasised about her, ever since their meeting in Llanfeni market. That her marital problems could prevent him calling on her and she'd be so mixed up, she might move away before she'd had the chance to settle in the country. Nor would she be in the frame of mind to consider a romance once this meeting was over. Richard wondered on what grounds he could see her. How to make up a plausible excuse to call on her again? She didn't wait to see him off; instead she pulled the door. It was an embarrassing closure to her sorry outburst. He drove home in an ambivalent mood; elated and despondent and regardless of there being any attraction on her part, he knew she'd be preoccupied and he quietly cursed the timing of the husband's confession.

He kept himself out of the house, only coming in for meals and spending more time with his mother. He longed to tell her about Penny, knowing she'd like her, her enthusiasm for farming and her can-do attitude, similar to Elin's own. 'I wish you could talk to me, Mam,' he said, sitting next to her bed. 'There's so much I want to tell you and get your advice on. I think you can hear me, can't you, Mam?' He touched her hand, hoping for a response, her hand warm against the blanket. How could he tell her he had fallen in love and wanted her to meet his new woman whilst his wife and daughter were a stone's throw away in the farmhouse, where they sat down at the end of the day, Nesta and Richard barely making conversation whilst Rhian flitted in and out again like a bat at dusk, avoiding their questions as she deftly slipped out of the back door and down the road to some waiting car. They didn't even row about her anymore, her clothes, her gaunt complexion or about where she was going or with whom. Richard lost the will to communicate, choosing to keep his mother company, unspeaking, thinking about Penny. On one such evening as he was going through her post, he opened an envelope with an invitation inside. A trip to Castell Gwyn with the Royal Forestry Society group. He'd heard it was situated in a beautiful garden and, looking across to his mother slouched opposite, he knew she'd not be able to go.

He rang when the house was empty, rehearsing what to say as he listened to the ring tone, only to be disappointed as the answer phone kicked in. He didn't leave a message, but came in again, just before the afternoon milking and tried again and as the phone clicked into the message, he heard her voice talking. 'Hello, hello?— hang on,' as she switched off the answer phone. 'There that's better. Who is it?' she said

'Me, Rich, Richard Davies. Tŷ Coch.'

'Of course. Sorry I've literally rushed in to pick up the phone, door's wide open, shopping on the floor and my brain still in the car. Yes, of course I know who you are. The calf's much better. Thriving.'

'And you? I was really ringing up to see how you were, the calf was just an excuse.' He tried to laugh to keep it light. 'I wanted to know if you like a trip to the gardens at Castell Gwyn? I've got an invitation for two and no one to go with.'

'What a surprise, but isn't there someone in your family you'd prefer to take?'

'Nope. My wife hates flowers and my mother's not well enough, so rather than waste the tickets I thought you might like to come. Have you seen the gardens? It's just the right time for them with the rhododendrons and azaleas out. We could have a pub lunch or take a picnic. I'd love the excuse to go.' He could hear her weigh it up, hesitating. 'I would have to be back for the afternoon milking so it wouldn't be a long day, just a few hours. It would make my day if you'd say yes?' He wanted to say something that would force her, but said nothing, hoping she'd agree.

'What day did you say it was?' she asked, 'I suppose I could, if you're sure no one else—'

'Great, I'll pick you up at ten.' He put the phone down before she could change her mind knowing he'd caught her on the hop, unable to think of a reason to say no. He was happier than he had been for months. He felt no guilt, just a sense of tingling anticipation whenever he thought of the trip. The two-week gap seemed to move in slow motion and he made sure he wasn't in the house so he couldn't pick up the phone in case she rang to say she'd changed her mind.

The beauty of the gardens eased any early awkwardness between them as they walked along the gravel path;

rhododendrons and azaleas were in full flower. They followed the group under the branches of impressive redwoods and giant firs, down various paths ending in amazing views framed by majestic mountains. Still chilly out of the sun, the group collected under new, lettuce-textured leaves, smiling conspiratorially at each other as the megaphone was passed around to different society members who wished to ask a question from the tour or raise a query about a species of tree, disease or general woodland policy.

Richard thought the questions would never end, leaving no time for the picnic, but at last society officials finally switched off, leaving them to wander as they wished.

Sitting on Penny's rug against a wall where the sun had warmed the stone, Richard enjoyed the intimacy of sharing a picnic with her. The mixing of what they'd brought: her rug, his coat, her plates, his flask of coffee, parcels of food, carefully wrapped in greaseproof paper or tinfoil. Freshly baked bread with bits of dried tomato and olive, that he'd never tried before. Homemade pâté she'd made, and slices of rare beef, lettuce and wholegrain mustard. Stilton and Welsh goat's cheese and an individual egg custard tart dusted with nutmeg for dessert. Well fed, they relaxed in the fickle spring sunshine, Richard not wanting to ask about her family and by association spoil his special day with her.

'Thank you so much,' she said beginning to tidy up the picnic bits.

'It's me who should be doing the thanking. Lovely food and company.'

'I meant for the other day,' she said. He reached over and took her hand. 'For letting me cry on you. I'm sorry for making a scene. It came as a shock, and you caught me just at the wrong time. And then you were so kind.'

'I'm glad it was me, Penny.' If his words surprised her she didn't reveal her emotions other than to smile at him. 'Life is full of ups and downs. We all have our share of them. Sometimes when it all seems bleak, things can turn round.'

'Do you believe that?'

'It could end up for the better in the long run.'

'I don't see how.'

'It's because it's still fresh. When I first met you, I remember thinking how bubbly and full of life you were compared to us dull farmers.'

'He wants a divorce. He's moving to America and, like civilised people, we're sharing the girls. School here where they're settled and holidays between us. I can't believe how stupid I've been for not seeing it! All those trips abroad, never home for more than a day, itching to be off.'

'It wasn't you being stupid if you ask me.'

'I'm a clever, successful woman, Richard. I should have read the signs staring me in the face, only I didn't see them. I didn't suspect anything.'

'Why should you have? Trust is what a marriage is based on isn't it? And you trusted him.' She caught his eye, then quickly looked away again as she screwed up the flask.

'Here, let me take that,' he said, and she handed the flask across and got up from the rug. 'Damn', he thought, not wanting the picnic to end on a bitter note. He picked up their shared rug, shaking out their shapes and residue of crumbs before folding it up for her. 'Have you decided what you'll do?' he inquired, fearful that her answer was about to shatter his pipe dream.

'I'm not going, if that's what you're asking. I came down here to run a business and I intend to try, with or without him. He never was any good with the countryside or animals.'

'Well done you!' He almost whooped for joy. 'You'll do just great – I know you will!'

She laughed at his misplaced optimism.

'I'll show him he's not going to wreck the rest of my life.'

'Atta girl, that's the spirit. Just keep out of milk production and you'll do fine.'

'And dairy farmers?' He didn't know how to answer her.

'I'm teasing you, Rich.'

'Whew! For a minute I thought I'd put my foot in it.'

'Only your toe.'

'I wouldn't advise you to go into milk. So many are giving up.

'But not you?'

'I must be mad! I'm even having to sell an old barn off, just to keep going.'

'Are you?'

'What, mad?' He laughed, glad her mood had lightened.

'No, selling a barn.'

'Yes, on the outskirts of the village I've a bit of land and barn. I'd prefer not to sell but it'll help the cash flow. It's not the answer but it'll help keep the bank off my back.'

'In a nice spot?'

'It's got potential. He didn't mention it had been something his mother bought when she'd married Ianto and how she would hate for him to sell it. 'It's got a small wood and stream but the land's too steep for anything other than rough grazing. Nantygaseg.' She looked quizzically at him. 'Means the mare's stream. I've got someone coming to look at it next week.'

'Has it got planning?'

'Outline. I could take you there, if you'd like. There's a fantastic view from the hill.'

'Perhaps.' Seeing he'd been pushing too eagerly, he changed tack.

'And now I know you'll be staying permanently, when and if you need anything, you promise to ask?'

'You bet.'

'Good, that's settled. You'll see I'm quite handy with a tractor and a spade.'

'And calves.'

Following the alloted lunch break, people had started to re-group, forcing Richard to make a move reluctantly to join them and as they walked back she asked him, 'If milk production is so dire, and there's no other option, why don't you produce under your own label?'

'I'm not sure going alone is the right thing for me.'

'Better than being ripped off by the supermarkets, isn't it? Or go into cheese, and yoghurts are much more popular. Everybody's health conscious. Or go the opposite way and make luxury ice cream.'

'We used to. My grandmother made cheese, and Mam too for a short time. Then everything went mechanised and people didn't want homemade. Today the consumer wants everything wrapped up in plastic, as far removed from the animal that produced it as possible.'

'It's all changing again, Rich. There's a growing demand in the city for local, home-produced products. Less plastic and packaging, more brown paper and cheesecloth. That's what I'm counting on, selling my meat, outdoor-reared, traceable and local.'

'Local?'

'What I mean is not from Argentina or New Zealand. More green. Perhaps I'm being naïve, I hardly know the first thing about real farming. I'm on my own, out of my depth and to top it all my financial backer's found himself a new market, the pig!'

'I've no money but I can help with the graft.'

'And you know about animal husbandry.'

'And I'm local, easily traceable, only down the road!'

'Thank you Richard. We might just have the beginnings of a successful partnership. And I might have a friend to help me out.'

'Anytime.' He beamed at her, pleased to be called a friend.

That was her brave face. What he didn't see were her nights of anguish, breaking down after she replaced the receiver, having told her girls she was fine and coping, but actually ranting in the small hours in her empty house.

However painful, Richard thought, at least Penny's situation was better than his. Given time Penny would move on, whereas without the financial means he was stuck. The farm and animals and lack of money were the only reason he remained with Nesta.

19

After Clare had gone to bed and they'd finished supper and opened another bottle, Malcolm pulled her into his arms, kissing her like an old romantic. He removed his cross from her neck and put it back around his own, kissing her. He led the way to bed, and made love to her the way he used to when he had first courted her. After he'd fallen asleep she lay awake wondering whether the problems in their marriage were significant or like everybody's marriages, full of ebb and flow. Deep down she knew she was kidding herself, that from the beginning their courtship had been singular, out of the modern step. 'Spooning' was how he'd phrased it, and part of his appeal had been his old-fashioned ways. He'd send her long letters written by hand often containing poetry, a rarity in the computer age.

'Did you write this?' she'd asked him once and he'd shrugged.

'What do you think?' He never answered a question he didn't want to, leaving Bethan open in any argument.

'So, you've come back,' had been her mother-in-law's comment.

'Clare seems totally recovered so you don't need to come over. I let her go to the playgroup.'

'All the thanks I get! Don't you think I can look after a child?'

'You know that's not what I meant. She seems fully recovered that's all.'

'She's been as right as rain. As soon as she'd sicked up all that sugar and fizz you gave her. Call yourself a good mother.'

Bethan wasn't going to give her the satisfaction of knowing her son had lied to her, but as soon as Moira left, Bethan went in search of him. It seemed he'd deliberately made Clare sick, fibbing about her recuperation, so she'd have to come straight back.

She found him in the stables office, one hand on the phone and the other too close to Eileen's bottom to hide where it had just been. He raised it casually, away from the groom's leg. 'You make sure it's delivered and let me worry about the rest. Ring me later, yeah about four.' Eileen sidled towards the door. 'Take the afternoon exercising, I won't be back with Liam in time.' He switched his attention. 'Darling, what a nice surprise. What can I do you for?' He slipped his mobile into his jacket pocket

'Why did you lie about Clare?' she blurted out, furious at him for everything she saw. 'What sort of father would fill his own daughter with sweets and fizzy drinks to make her ill, just to stop her coming with me to see her Granny? How could you Malcolm?'

'Hey, hey, angel, what's brought all this on?' He got up from the desk, all concerned as he attempted to put an arm around her. She pulled away from him.

'No, Malcolm. You're not going to get out of things that way. In her usual polite and succinct way, your dear mother launched at me, accusing me of stuffing Clare full of rubbish and that there has been nothing wrong with her – 'right as rain' were her exact words, and accused me of gallivanting! Rich, isn't it! And as well you know, I'd never have left her here if I thought she was fit to travel.'

'Wouldn't you? And this, your home.'

'Fuck you, Malcolm. You're capable of almost anything – All those things you told me about your Dad dying and your mother not coping, stricken with grief. All lies. Do you know when you're telling the truth?'

'You should never believe everything my mother tells you.'

'Why not? She seems to speak more truth than you.'

'What's the woman been filling your head with now, and you believe my mother rather than me? Beth, Beth. It's her way of getting back at me. Don't you see?'

He lowered his voice. 'She's never forgiven me for Kieran's death. She blames me for what happened,' he started to explain.

'Who's Kieran?' Bethan asked, sidetracked by the sudden revelation.

'My little brother.'

'Now you've got a brother? It's the first I've heard. Why didn't you tell me?'

'Had. It's painful, in the past and I didn't want to frighten you off.'

'And you don't think you are now?'

'You remember the picture you asked me about? The one of us by the seaside, upstairs on the landing?'

She nodded, waiting for him to continue.

'You thought it was of me with Rosaleen and my parents. It was of Kieran. I wasn't in the shot. It was me taking the photo.'

'So why didn't you tell me before? I never knew of his existence.' She was visibly shocked that he'd kept such information from her. 'Why on earth didn't you tell me, Malcolm?'

'Because what happened was tragic, and I didn't want you involved in that bad part of my life. I didn't want you to become contaminated by it.'

'But I'm your wife, Malcolm. I thought we shared everything. Shouldn't we?'

'You're right, of course darling, and it was very wrong of me,

I know. But once I'd started to conceal it, I couldn't find the right time to tell you. Do you see? When? After six months, or a year and then you got pregnant with Clare. Not the time to give you a shock. Oh, by the way I had a brother who died.'

'But surely your mother or sister or someone could have told me rather keeping me in the dark?'

'We never discuss it. We never openly mention it, but I'm sure we all still think of him. I know I do, every day of my life.'

'Oh Malcolm. I'm so sorry. You should have told me, used me as a support. Isn't that what marriage is all about?'

'Would you feel the same, if I told you I killed him?'

She gasped at his revelation, her hand involuntarily covering her mouth.

'You killed him?' she almost whispered. 'How?'

'I did as far as my parents are concerned.'

She reeled from the news, unable to fully comprehend him, seeing his face contort as if in pain, waiting for him to go on. 'There was only a couple of years between us and like most kids we hung out together. He was everything I'm not. Clever at school, a good sportsman, a natural on horseback. He could do no wrong; he was the apple of his mother's eye.' She looked at him to see if he was envious. 'No, don't get me wrong, I wasn't jealous of him, you can't be jealous of someone who idolises you, can you? I didn't mind he was good at everything. In fact it took the pressure off me, as all their energies went into Kieran, leaving me to do what I liked.'

'When did it happen?' she knew that by asking when, he'd also tell her how it happened, having gone this far.

'I was nineteen and it was just around his sixteenth birthday. There was a group of us gone down to the sands, larking about with a few cars, you know, racing some souped-up banger along the beach. We often did it. We made a fire, got some booze and a bit of dope, nothing wow, you know. Anyhow I was driving, sort of racing Michael Flynn home when I hit some loose gravel on the road. I don't remember the rest, but I must have overreacted and, well, we ended up with the car on its roof in a field. I remember thinking, I like this song, the radio was still on 'Jail Break', Thin Lizzy. Funny how you can remember exactly some bits of something and the rest is just a blur, you know. I knew I was stuck, something was pinning me down and I hadn't realised we were upside-down and Kieran wasn't talking. Strange you know, I didn't twig that blood was dripping up my face and into my hair and I couldn't turn to see him, so I asked him if he was OK'

'God, Malcolm, I'm sorry.'

'Lucky really, otherwise I would have lost it. Freaked me out, wouldn't it, if you had to see your brother lying next to you, all smashed up, eyes staring, full of blood. And his pretty boy face, all wrong, mangled. By the time help arrived I must have blacked out.'

'How appalling.'

'I remember coming round, in a quiet room on my own, a bit like a convent you know, with the dim lights and a candle and a picture of the Virgin Mary above the holy water. A nurse or someone in white leaning over checking me and I asking if he was all right. She said I was to rest and he was doing fine,

'Doing fine, the hell he was. I don't know when or how long after that, but I heard my father's voice booming outside in the corridor and another voice, my mother trying to get him to be quieter. Outside my door I heard him ask if Kieran was going to be OK and the nurse, nun or doctor, a woman anyhow say he was conscious, with a broken collarbone, broken ribs, collapsed lung and broken leg, but that God willing, he should recover. Then I heard my mother ask about me and the doctor say he was very sorry they'd tried everything to save me. 'Thank God Kieran is safe,' were the last words I heard before they crept into my room.'

'But I thought—'

'Yes, so did they. Someone must have muddled our two names and it was Kieran who died, not me. In that deceptive light my mother didn't immediately recognise the doctor's mistake. I suppose I was covered in tubes and bandages. I heard her whispering to my father, 'Thank Blessed Jesus it's not Kieran. At least he's been saved, Pat.'

'Then they realised it was me, my eyes and face looking through the bandages. Well! I shall never forget their look of abhorrence. I don't care how drugged up I was, it was plain for me to see.'

'What did they say, when they realised?'

'Of course my Pa denied it, saying I was only semi-conscious, and drugged up and I'd dreamt it. Said it was all part of my guilt. My mother's never denied it.'

'How awful, Malcolm. I don't know what to say.'

'It left me speechless too.'

She was stunned; what could she say?

'So you see Beth, we're not very close, my mother and me. Not what you might think it is. We're not the close-knit typical Irish Catholic family.'

At last she was privy to what had happened to him as a teenager: the bombshell he'd just dropped explained his sometimes odd behaviour, and why he had a problem with trust. All those poignant sad poems that he'd sent her were part of his confession and she had been the anonymous priest, the sea acting as the veiled curtain. No wonder his love was tinged with an irredeemable grief, a place she could not touch. She had thought it had been about her, but now she realised he'd written about the loss of his brother.

He used to take off suddenly, leaving her with an absence that he never explained, leaving her to try and puzzle him out. She'd read and reread his words, trying to understand the meaning to the beautiful tortured words, kissing his 'x' before she put them under her pillow to dream of him. They were of an unconditional love, yet as she saw it now, not love for her but his love for Kieran. His feelings of grief for Kieran were mixed up with falling in love with her. His erratic behaviour and unexpected outbursts were passionate and wild, yet always scheming so she never knew where she stood. Now they finally made sense. Always caught, his wife hanging like a fly by some thread over a ravine, half-expecting a knife to cut through the strand of silk that bound her to him. A knife that he liked to wield in some grotesque game that reduced her to begging. She'd draw back from his threats of violence, learning resilience, learning to survive, and to love less. He'd lived with it for over ten years, the razor-raw sharpness of his guilt. Beth resisted the urge to put her arms around him. To give him the love he'd been deprived of, as if it would make up for it. It would be another mistake and only make him hate her for the pity.

'Ah! I see you're suitably shocked. Not close! I despise her! Can you imagine that, Beth? To hate your own mother, hoping something nasty, something slow and malingering will get her. You always ask for the truth so now you have it. See, I'm a long way from being the dutiful loving son.'

'So why do you stay here? Wouldn't it be easier to move away?'

'And let her off seeing me every day and reminding her of Kieran! Let her suffer as well, it's the least she deserves.'

She recalled how he'd suddenly clammed up at the beach in Anglesey, hating the water and the dunes, and her teasing him. She'd had enough years to reconsider why she'd ever chosen to marry him. Why she'd naively jumped into it without finding out more about him. Had she been that desperate that she'd closed her eyes and leapt, knowing that she was jumping over a cliff? They had needed to have more in common than their

131

chance meeting, more to survive a life together. Learning about Kieran brought them closer, having both lost a special member of family to the sea and whereas she still loved the vast, ever rolling green swell of ocean, Malcolm hated it.

Alone in the house, she looked at the photo again. Taking it from its place, its removal left a stained lined margin like a sin. As she peered into the faces, she thought it strange that no one had ever mentioned anything to her. Family and community keeping it quiet, hermetically sealed like some potentially lethal disease, contained. With her new knowledge she now could see that the little boy in the photo wasn't Malcolm. She tried to scrutinize Moira's face as she leaned protectively towards Kieran, her hand over his, to see if she could read such favouritism. Had she been part of Malcolm's plan to get back at his parents? After his discharge from the Heath, there'd been no reason for him to contact her again and he'd turned up, out of the blue, persistent in his courtship. He was good at secrets, never letting her know where he'd arranged to take her, and when they were together, he made her feel exceptional, and she fell in love with him. He gave her something she was not used to, spoiling her with treats. On the farm, work and making ends meet were all-consuming. Any time off was connected with it; selling animals, seeing machinery, going to an auction, calling with the vet, and if they were lucky a quick stop for fish and chips on the way home. With Malcolm the day was for her alone and after he took her racing at Chepstow and after she'd backed an outsider that won, he'd insisted on champagne.

Not with him a greasy kebab and can of lager in some lay-by. It was a world away from her usual Saturday night out, tottering on alcohol that tasted like pop in a low-ceilinged night-club basement, dancing to electronic mixes, spilling out onto the streets in the small hours, drunk and disorderly, where middle-aged men ogled girls, hoping to take advantage.

Shirts that failed to conceal their paunches protruded over trouser waistbands. These men were old enough to be their fathers, predatory and certain. Like a lot of young girls, Beth had stumbled out in her youth, the bright neon the only light she could focus on.

Thinking about that time Beth was reminded of having just seen Tegwyn again. How she and he'd changed and yet he was still the Tegwyn she'd known since childhood. She'd been lucky he'd been there on one of those nights, he'd picked her up when she was drunk and helped her back to his car. Lost to alcohol and pill, the music still pounded in her ears. In a quiet lane where he could have done anything, he pulled over, helping her out so she could throw up in the ditch and afterwards he drove her home in the pouring rain in his clapped-out old car, the radio dodgy, playing country intermittently. It had been her last night at home before leaving for Cardiff but he hadn't said any of the things he'd planned to, and now she was too gone to hear. He should have walked into the night club and pulled her out instead of loitering outside until it was too late. Only he didn't want her gang of friends to see him, think he was another dirty middle-aged creep on the pull. So what did he do? Give her a sprig of white heather, which she promptly dropped in the mud. He picked it up and shoved it into her coat pocket as she lurched from his car, as he tried to kiss her, swaying with her. He'd half carried her to Tŷ Coch's back door, whispering his undying love to deaf ears, begging her not to go.

'*Nos da*, Tego,'[10] were her parting words as she stumbled into the back kitchen.

Later, he'd found one of her earrings on the car floor of the passenger seat and he'd wrapped it up carefully and hidden it away in an old tobacco tin as a memento.

---

[10] Good night

Beth had been glad to be out of it, distanced from the small coastal town, enjoying city life where everyone was up for making money and living fast, each for himself, with no petty small-town restraint. Cardiff was still part of Wales for all its makeover, the promise of devolution, new Welsh Assembly and proposed bay developments and gaps left by coal and steel, rugby and male voice choirs, glossed over with pedestriansed precincts and its high fashion and smart new hotels that still catered for the rugby crowds and Valleys visitors. She'd been caught up in the hype, feeling empowered at being part of the excitement as Cardiff expanded and by the time Simon moved down to study music, she had made a home for herself in the city. She enjoyed taking him round, sharing her favourite cafes and trendy bars and Welsh-speaking pubs; Italian restaurants, clubs and cinema complex.

When she was based in Cardiff, her family gravitated towards her, coming down more regularly than the once a year for an international, and whenever Richard came down to see Nesta, they would all meet up, joskins striding out along the city pavements, walking like farmers to cover the ground as if on a hill.

It had been fun then, especially at the beginning when it was all new, but at some point things changed. Like milk on the turn, the singing competition was the catalyst for the souring. Richard's visits stopped, and when he did come down there was none of the fun and when she asked if things were all right he just shrugged it off, blaming work. Simon would no longer join them, always finding an excuse and Bethan felt like a gooseberry in the threesome, between Richard and Nesta. She had been there, but never knew what exactly had happened that night, sitting in the audience with Nesta, proudly applauding her little brother's performance. Afterwards she'd shared a celebratory drink before going back to bed, ready for an early morning hospital shift, so that when they heard that Nesta was moving back to Llanfeni, it came as a surprise, and far from splitting up with Richard as Beth had expected to hear, she and Rich had finally decided to marry. It was a quiet family affair and the reception as stiff as a Sunday service, their vows echoing in the cold chapel, and only good singing lifted the ceremony. Beth felt it was more like a funeral.

She was glad to go back to Cardiff. She was a natural nurse, caring and astute, working and gaining experience to become a staff nurse. The same could not be said about her personal life. Perhaps her fair hair, bubbly personality and her father's glad, blue eyes attracted the wrong sort of man. She had short-lived affairs, living for the moment, everything that home was not and at that time in her life Beth hadn't wanted a ponderous, safe, cautious man like her brother Richard. She'd encouraged the frisson with Tegwyn and although her mother and brother blamed him, she knew she'd lead him on, deliberately hanging around after school, loitering in their lane hoping to meet him. The smell of him, a man's body, his sweat mixed with pine resin, earthy peat and tobacco, untamed, capricious. Old enough to know better, he'd chatted her up, fourteen going on twenty.

By the time she'd reached her late twenties she had good reason to regret the choices she'd made. There were men who'd left her feeling used and flat. She'd had the same roller coaster ride with different partners, and like some euphoric junkie, the lows of the inevitable break-up had taken longer to get over as time went by. Insidiously her youthfulness was giving way to the older, knowing woman who looked back at her in the mirror. She was done with her bit of partying, of drinking and sleeping around and now it was her turn to see her options narrow, understanding her sister-in-law's panic and her decision to move back to Llanfeni and settle for Richard. Full of people and noise and work, city life was becoming lonely, making Beth think more of the her home. Of her mother, her brothers, the farm and Tegwyn, and she was ready to pack her bags and go back, content to work in the cottage hospital. That was before she met Malcolm and it had all changed again and suddenly city life was exhilarating as she walked on the air that was full of him. From the start he'd been different from her other lovers. He was like a pre-set missile with her as his target, determined. Always attentive, almost overwhelming, he'd lavish her with surprises. Doing things she was not used to, with a lifestyle to match. Extravagant and on the move, he popped in and out of her life, turning up at odd times unannounced, calling in on his way to or from somewhere. Always with a business deal in hand, in-between somewhere, calling in to see his Beth. A sucker for it all, listening to his accent, his soft lilt that could charm the hind leg off a donkey, amiable in tailored suit as he winked at her, making her believe that she was part of him. She loved his lopsided smile that revealed an imperfect set of front teeth, making him look more boyish, more appealing. Hidden by well-made clothes he had another imperfection, a slight limp that only showed when he ran, like asking a horse to be trotted up, a tiny unsoundness, the result of an old injury he quickly dismissed.

In those early months she thought that she had begun to know him – there were little things that made him unique to her, his quirky habits that endeared him, irascible and unpredictable, constantly surprising her. Arriving back tired from a difficult time on the ward, Beth hadn't noticed his first letter lying carelessly on the floor with the usual junk mail, and it had been one of her flatmates who'd brought it into the kitchen for her. Not recognising the writing, she opened it in the kitchen, looking to the end to see who'd written it.

'Go on, Beth – who's it from?' Carys had asked, looking over her shoulder as Bethan blushed, hiding it as she realised it was from Malcolm, wanting to read it in private. His small slanted scrawl was difficult to decipher initially, until she realised he was left-handed. What he wrote had astonished her. How many hours had Bethan sat in her nurse's room, looking across the tarmac car park to the hospital, reading and rereading his letters, dreaming of them together, as she worked through her shifts. There was the luxury of holding paper instead of the more usual text or email, and his first letter was typical of the way he did things, eccentric, old-fashioned, and she treasured the envelope and the pages. Not pages of sentimental love, but a window, an insight on how he looked at life. He'd often finish with a line or two of poetry and she was never sure if he'd composed them or borrowed them. In her nurse's digs she would imagine him huddled over his composition, seemingly uncomfortable and at odds with paper and pen, looking out over the water and thinking of her.

She didn't always understand his poetry and was shy of asking him, not wishing to show her ignorance, but she did pick up on its melancholy, wishing he didn't have to leave her on those Sunday evenings, feeling flat without him.

Then he would turn up again and take her out to dine. Absent-minded rubbing his thumb over the tips of his first two fingers as he spoke, as if he were winnowing, pondering the choices on the extensive menu. He'd whisper sweet nothings as he took her off to bed, telling her she was everything he'd ever wanted and he was going to whisk her off to his homeland to make babies who'd all be brilliant horsemen. With her at his side, the Conna stud would be the best. Bethan was only too willing to ride his dream, galloping beside him on the sandy beaches on fiery, fine-skinned thoroughbreds as they splashed along the edge of the water, flying in the wind and roar of the surf.

He enjoyed telling her about his home, and his plans. The special lay of the land, the grasses that made horses thrive so, and his ideas for breeding the next generation of winners. He couldn't wait to take her there.

'Sure,' he said. 'There's was nothing better for keeping them sound than the sea. You wait till you get there!'

'I can't wait!' she'd teased him, her heart on her sleeve. 'And to meet your father and mother and the rest of your family.'

She'd unwittingly said the wrong thing. His crooked smile halted, turning suddenly, and his urgent rush of enthusiasm was brought up short pulled like a horse's gag, checked. His eyes, half-closed, were suddenly louche as he looked away from her.

'Perhaps,' he'd muttered, meaning a definite no. 'He's often away.' He didn't want to talk about him and rather forcibly he pulled her into his arms, kissing her, saying over her shoulder so she couldn't see his face, 'They'll all love you to death, so, but I'm not for sharing you!'

'Perhaps you've a gorgeous cousin or brother!' she'd laughed.

He stopped kissing her, squeezing her arm forcibly. 'What?'

Again she'd inadvertently touched a nerve, 'No rivalry! So you don't have to share me.'

'Oh, I see.'

'Malcolm, you're squeezing my arm.'

'Sorry,' he said letting go of his grip, his face easing. She didn't know why she'd said what she said, harmless words that seemed to set him off. Perhaps she'd subconsciously been thinking of her own brothers.

She had plenty of time to reflect, to play over and over their last meeting, trying to understand what had prompted his abrupt and complete disappearance. What had she missed? What was it about her raising his family that had so obviously upset him? Whatever it was, the implications had caused him to flee. Words she'd said in love, that had made him edgy, restless suddenly and wanting to be away, away from her and Wales. Her innocuous comments that triggered something, leaving her standing there watching him drive off, the red rear eyes of the car like a fox. A sly stealth, a silent violence.

Nothing followed: no note, no message, no contact. He'd severed all communication, leaving her wretched and bewildered, wondering what she'd done to cause such drastic flight. Had she been such a naïve country girl to have totally misunderstood anything he'd said to her in the four months they'd been dating? Dating, an out-of-date word. She persistently asked herself why the complete shutdown to any of her phone calls or letters. Of course she'd tried to get hold of him but had never managed to make personal contact so she didn't know whether her messages or her letters were ever delivered. When she asked who was she speaking to on the other end of the line, the question was never answered. The female voice always said, 'I'm sorry Mr Malcolm is not available,' and the phone was put down. No explanation or answer of any kind. She was tempted to do a missing persons but she ducked out, knowing he was alive and had run away to avoid her.

Her nursing friends rallied round, Carys saying she always thought him a bit wired, full of sympathy yet intrigued, loving the drama and mystery of her friend's let-down. Some nurses were more vitriolic, blaming men for all the world's woes. For all their support and words of encouragement, Beth couldn't come to terms with her sudden abandonment. Had she pushed the agenda, seemingly desperate to have him. Was marriage the issue? Yet it had been Malcolm who had talked openly of marriage and babies and their life together and it had been his suggestion she would soon become Mrs O'Connor, he who had bought her a fine Irish stone for her pretty finger.

For weeks she worked in a daze of having lost like a bereavement, and in the instant she woke each morning she was still full of him, momentarily ecstatic before the reality of her situation hit, leaving her to sink into despondency.

She didn't know just how long he'd been watching her before he presented himself, reappearing. During her shift she'd felt something at her back, a stickiness in her uniform that made her pull at the fastening of her bra strap. Several times she'd turned, half-expecting to see someone she knew, only every time she turned there was nothing, no one other than the usual shuffle of patients along hospital corridors. Then she saw him walk into her ward, coming into the green grey like some prophet from the wilderness.

He was so apologetic, effusive in his missing of her, of his tortured enforced separation. She led him hurriedly away, away from the peering faces, away from the gaping windows, dropped jaws of a nosey building, pacing down the corridor whilst he continued to remonstrate, pleading with her to stop. She didn't want the scene, not in front of the nurses and bedridden. Once inside his parked car she spat questions at him, losing all the control and dignity she'd promised herself to keep in the event he ever turned up again.

'Why? Why, Malcolm, did you do it?' she'd shouted at him, not caring that another couple sitting in their car next to them watched them arguing. Bethan was past caring about what other people thought, having already been humiliated for three months, and kept on, raising her pitch in uncontrolled fury as she shrieked at his pathetic answers, pummelling his chest in fury.

'You didn't even have the guts to speak to me, to tell me yourself for goodness sake! All I got was some woman, your wife for all I know?

'No, no wife, Beth. My mother.'

'Well, your mother. I don't know which is worse, telling me or saying you were not available. Not available, Malcolm! You piece of shit! You can go to hell.'

'You've every right to be angry—'

'Angry! You've no idea! What the hell is wrong with you? One minute you want to share everything, possessive, and the next thing you vanish.'

'I'm so sorry, and I understand why you're so cross. I would feel the same in your shoes. I know I let you down—'

'Let me down!' She repeated everything he said in utter bewilderment. 'Three thousand feet up, and you let me plummet, no rip cord, nothing! I hate you, fuck you. I never want to see you again, Malcolm.' She made a move to open the door and he tried to restrain her, begging her to at least let him try to explain. She sat stonily, looking ahead at the plain building, trying not to break down as she thought of all the misery he'd caused her. She heard the emotional tremor in his voice as he searched for the words that might stop her from opening the car door. They both sat looking ahead and from the corner of her eye she could see his knuckles, gripping onto the steering wheel, clutching for some sort of support.

'You have every right to hate me, to never want to see me again, but I couldn't help it. I so wanted to ring you, to run away from everything at home and to be back in your arms.'

'Rubbish, Malcolm! I was here, waiting. What about me, how do you think I felt? It wasn't me who vanished off the face of the earth.' Empathizing the 'me' pointedly. 'I rang and rang, like a demented loony. I even wrote to you – oh don't pretend you didn't get any of my letters! I wrote in case you needed some space, to give you some time and distance so that you could choose how to contact me. And what did I get? Absolutely nothing. Being dead would have been easier! What is it with you? Do you get off on it, hearing me pleading, like some sort of sicko? Go and drop dead you bastard! I never ever want to see your face again.'

'My father died. He collapsed, dead before he hit the floor. Out of the blue, totally unexpected.'

He felt her body language shift fractionally, absorbing his words. He needed to choose his next words with the utmost care so as not to lose the little gain of sympathy he'd managed to retrieve. How could he explain it to her so that she would forgive him?

'Anyone normal would have rung. I would have understood if only you'd told me and explained things. You could have leaned on me, Mal. I thought you had died, got sick, had an appalling accident, or you'd been killed.'

She'd used her nickname for him, a softening he'd recognised. Instantly he took one hand off the steering wheel, his long fingers tentatively touching the hem of her dress, a spider feeling the tension in its web as a fly touches. She sat with her lips pressing together as she felt him touch her, her blotched face still full of hurt. Her grimace tempered, as his eyes met hers, before she looked away unseeing to the rows of parked cars and the impersonal window reflections of the hospital building.

'Part of me did die,' he said melodramatically. 'Not being able to speak or to see you. Each day I could feel you slipping away my beautiful Welsh princess, and I couldn't do anything about it.'

Just his luck to stumble on the name her father had called her, that helped weaken her resolve. It had started, that trickle, and continued as his voice choked and he quickly wiped his hand across his hazel eyes. She was less decided.

'Darling, you have to believe how I wanted to contact you. Every minute of every day I thought of you. It was, it became impossible. I can't explain, only you were in a different world—'

She wouldn't let him finish talking such gibberish, again angry with such feeble excuses. 'Hardly, Malcolm! A couple of hours over the sea. Don't make me out to be some sort of unfeeling monster. I would have understood that you couldn't come over, but just to leave me in a void, imagining the worst. How could you? And now you come back to say you love me?'

'I know my behaviour was bizarre, but I was in shock,' he said defensively, 'and there was my mother,' – a pause – 'and my sister.' Still she didn't see the need for her absolute exclusion, waiting for him to expand. 'We had no warning you see, nothing. He'd always been the life and soul of the whole place, the business, any party, he was the boss. And when he dropped down dead on the gallops – well. My mother has taken it very hard. I thought she was in danger of taking her own life. I couldn't leave her alone. Not for a minute; she was unhinged by it.' He lowered his head against the wheel so she wasn't sure if he was crying. Everything she'd determined to do if he ever turned up, crumbled away when he looked up at her, unashamed tears running down his face. She couldn't bear to see him crying so pitifully, and soft-hearted Beth put her arms around his forlorn form, cradling his head in her arms as he wept. Any residue of anger was punctured by his sadness.

'I was very close to him,' he said quietly into her lap, and like a priest she stroked his hair in absolution acquitting him of blame, and in that moment when he seemed in so much need of her forgiveness, she loved him all the more. She should have said no, sent him packing, the completely callous shit.

20

Tegwyn didn't see the walker covering the ground, as the lie of the hill and high heather camouflaged him from view. Not until he'd reached the top of the ridge did the trekker break from his steady uphill pull, standing to enjoy the views that surrounded him. He turned to look back along the way he'd come, satisfied with the progress he'd made, having walked several miles from the farmhouse in the distance. Rare hiding grouse cackled their presence as a small covey took flight, flying fast and tight to the hill, instinctively dropping below the rise to avoid a bird of prey or gun. He noted the dark green regimented lines of fir inland.

Any brook hooded by conifer would have killed off life, now too acid for fish.

To his south, six white giants on stout unmoving trunks waved their colossal arms as another elemental source was being tapped. Dear Wales with its men of soil, slate, coal, and steel, to forests and dammed water, and now wind farms in a bid to help keep the population fuelled. In his position and field of expertise, he had reason to approve of the harnessing of nature for a sustainable energy in the world that he considered was on the brink of an abyss. Being up on the wind-blown, peopleless hill, he felt a oneness with the place, of childhood holidays, and he was glad that he'd made the effort to find the time for his trek, wanting to locate a possible green source for himself.

Tegwyn was stooped in his task, wet bundles of *mwswg coch* or blood moss piling up around him. The appearance of the stranger from nowhere made him jump, as he still did every time low-flying jets caught him unawares and his reaction was one of anger. The emptiness of the moor was made suddenly too full by the presence of this tall, gaunt man. Gripping his rake, Tegwyn Jones stood up, shaking slightly, and scowled at the man bearing down at him from above.

'Oi, you. You're trampling my work,' he said testily. The man stepped to one side.

'Sphagnum, the most common form,' he said, adding some Latin so that Tegwyn had no idea what he was on about. 'A much underrated, valuable little plant. May I enquire to where does it go? Where does it end up?'

'Why? I've got permission.'

'Yes, yes, quite,' the stranger agreed, not wishing to antagonize, realising he'd startled the worker.

'Did you want something?' Defence was the best form of attack in case he was to be accused of trespassing. The man could be a petty little official about to put a stop to his beer money with some new rule or regulation. The thin, tall man seemed unperturbed by Tegwyn's somewhat hostile attitude, nor did he answer his question, but instead carried on with his own story.

'I only ask because I can recollect stories of an old great-aunt gathering moss for the Red Cross for the Great War. She came from the South West, my great aunt, near Widecombe-in-the-Moor, not so unlike here. And,' he said bending to pick up a small quantity of the moss, 'there's plenty of this stuff, red, yellow and green.' He became absorbed with the bundle in his hand, ignoring Tegwyn. Minutes passed and Tegwyn, bored and getting cold, coughed loudly, making a show of needing to get on. 'It reminds me of her, this stuff, and my childhood days up on Dartmoor. Quite similar in many ways.'

'So? What did she do with it?' asked Tegwyn, vaguely interested and realising the man was not going to move on in a hurry. 'What was it good for? Packaging, plants or what?'

'Of sorts, I suppose. They used it as a disinfectant. To help treat the wounded. Not in this state, of course. Initially it had to be pulled out of the bogs, just like you're doing there, then it was dried by constant turning.'

'So that's where bog roll comes from!' The man stalled, momentarily taken aback by Tegwyn's comment. He smiled, seeing the joke. 'Quite so.' Surprised at Tegwyn's accurate historical fact, he paused unsure as to continue.

'Then what? Like Dic said, you put it on cuts? He tried to put it on mine here,' proffering his dirty wet hand at the man.

'Well, there's a bit more to it than that, but fundamentally, yes.'

So old Dic wasn't talking *rwtsh*[11] and the running sore on his finger really had healed better because he'd insisted on wrapping it in moss. 'Well, who would have believed it, and I thought he was off with the fairies. You ought to meet him, get on well with

---

[11] rubbish

145

him. He can talk about any subject under the sun. Normally he'd be with me, but he's got bronchitis and didn't fancy the walk.'

'It's quite a pull up.'

'When they first landed men on the moon, Dic wouldn't believe the pictures on the telly. He reckoned it was a set-up, you know like those *Thunderbird* puppets, and yet you've proved him right about this stuff.'

'Life never ceases to amaze. Did your friend – Dic was it? – Did he explain the process to you?'

'Nah, we tried to gag him before he got properly started or we'd still be up there and no moss gathered. He probably doesn't know, not that that would stop him.'

'It hasn't changed; people are still gathering it in much the same way as you're doing by hand. By volunteers, which is where my family come into it. Once the moss had had a chance to dry off, it was transported and put indoors, ideally in a house with many floors where it could be laid out with a furnace on the ground floor so that the hot air circulated up to dry it out further.'

'Sounds a hell of a lot of work to get a bit of dried grass.'

'Let me explain.' He was a bit like old Dic, knowing everything, but as he was a stranger Tegwyn felt obliged to listen. Anyhow he didn't mind having a bit of company, as long as he didn't go on for hours. 'After it got to resemble the dryness of hay, it was spread out again, this time over a metal grille over a series of hot pipes. It was left until it was really dry, but importantly it retained its soft springy form. Only then could it be used for dressings. It took a worker several hours to make a finished dressing, two ounces of moss into each muslin bag, I can't remember the exact measurements, but not quite a foot square.' Tegwyn had realised he was listening to a perfectionist where no detail was going to be left untold, so he just nodded, letting his mind drift. 'Then it would have been sublimated, no doubt highly corrosive, so rubber gloves would have been worn to prevent skin burns, before it was squeezed through a mangle to get rid of the excess fluid, and then it was dried again to return it to its original two ounce weight. Clever, isn't it!' It was not a question and Tego remained silent, quite sure he hadn't understood everything nor was he really listening. In fact he was beginning to regret that he'd showed any interest in the first place. 'They packed them into packets of twelve, meticulously wrapping them in two layers of paper to prevent any infection from the outside. These were used for the domestic market, for the injured soldiers lucky enough to be sent home. But the bulk of the dressings went abroad, baled up in their thousands. They covered them in a waterproof coating to stop them getting wet by sea spray on the crossing over the Channel and then they were transported to the front to the troops.'

He waited for Tegwyn's response.

'Did they work?'

'I'll say they did. Saved thousands of soldiers from dying from infected wounds.'

'*Duw, Duw* – this soggy mass?'

'You wouldn't think moss is four times more absorbent than cotton wool, would you?'

'No.'

'The dressings were so successful that, even though volunteers made them in their thousands, they could never keep up with the demand. It doesn't say a lot for our leaders at the time, eh? All that futile waste of life for those poor buggers, brought down like flies, with only dried moss to stop the bleeding of such heinous wounds. Days of the Empire, eh?'

'So where does the disinfectant bit come in, was it in that stuff they covered it in?'

'Partially, but the moss has natural iodine in it which acts as an antiseptic. It was this that helped cleanse and begin the process of knitting back the broken tissue after the bleeding stopped. It was very effective, layered between the lint bandages.

In fact it worked so well the practice was brought back and moss from the hills of the UK was gathered again by groups of volunteers in the last world war.'

'They used this stuff? Instead of antibiotics?' Tegwyn said, somewhat surprised and not sure if he entirely believed the man.

'No, no. It replaced cotton wool, saving thousands of pounds. The operation and effort made by the various depots were recognised by the king and queen who made a visit to one. It was in the papers. Oh, what was it called? It'll come in a minute.'

'Somewhere in London?'

'London?' No it was his turn to look incredulous. 'Good heavens, no! No, up in Scotland, where they had most of the depots. Mull and Carrbridge, I remember now. 1941 if my memory serves me correctly. So you see just how important this humble little plant had been. The Red Cross worked in conjunction with the Department of Health and they didn't just use it for dressings, but stretcher pillows, splint pads and the like. And County York hospital reported that the moss dressings were very successful when used for "iron lung" patients.'[12]

'Cor! Bit of a let-down today. All I do is flog it on to a wholesaler, who sells it to garden centres for hanging baskets and the like.'

'Rather a waste.'

'It grows again, and we always get enough rain.' He'd suddenly had enough of the history lesson, wanting to get on. The man had begun to irritate, yet he seemed slow to take the hint as Tegwyn picked up his rake, bending to his work. Wasting time that was his dwindling beer money.

'You must be from around here. I'm staying in Llanfeni, I've been to look over a barn for sale; 'Nantygaseg', I think it's called, some man called Davies. Do you know him?'

---

[12] British Red Cross Museum and Archives

'Davies, Tŷ Coch.' At the mention of the family he thought of Bethan.

'My name's Arthur, Dr Arthur Trelawny,' the man said proffering a firm hand.

'Oh, a doc. We could do with another, we've more vets than doctors and there's always a queue in the surgery.'

He laughed, 'Not that sort of doctor. More of a research scientist. Look, I know we have only just met, but actually I came up here to look for you. I was told you'd be here.'

'Oh?' Tegwyn was put on his guard, wondering what he'd done that was about to catch up with him.

'It might seem a bit unusual, but also rather appropriate. I've got this proposition.'

Tegwyn never trusted propositions. In the past he'd come off worse.

'What?' was all he muttered.

Undaunted by the muted reply, Doctor Trelawny continued.

'If it works it could make you money.'

'Oh, yeah? What would I have to do?'

'What you're doing now but for a lot more money. I think you could be exactly the right person for the job. Would you be interested?'

'Depends?'

'A moss gatherer,' the doctor said simply. 'It's all about moss.'

To celebrate his new job, Tegwyn called in the pub, staggering home several hours later where he collapsed fully clothed on his unmade bed and fell asleep. His body twitched in dream.

His ears pounded with the roar of the cannons and his clothes stuck to him, clammy-cold. He could no longer feel the horse that he'd ridden, butcher-boy style through the volley of cannons, his sabre flashing as he hollered a bloodcurdling cry to the Cossacks, and with Turks, their *yataghans*[13] drawn; he galloped with them through the smoke-filled valley. He heard the neigh of terror from his horse as it fell instantly, catapulting him clear. He saw it crabbing desperately at the air with its hooves. In hanging time he sensed other movement around him. He did not move his head or try to comprehend, only to lie still at last, under the blackness of a sky. The ground was hard, thin soil with rough rock, no bed to lie on when she came to him. Her voice was urgent yet gentle, and in the darkness he thought he could make out a cross or was it a brooch she wore? Then she smiled like she used to and he caught her sweet smell as she leaned over him to wipe his brow, undoing his brass buttons, eager as a lover. He took her in his arms as he had done so often in his dreams, trying to slow time to savour her fragrance. That scent that transported him back, away from the Caucasus across the Black Sea, westwards to an equally ancient place where water runs pure off slate under the rarified air. Mountains of peat and moss and the smell of Welsh rain where the ancestors of the Welsh black cattle *Bos Longifrons* and *Brachyceros*[14] used to roam. There where the untainted, peat-nourished mosses thrived; all colours of green, dark to fade and patches of yellow, brown to rich crimson-wet, in iodine. In such a place he looked into her deep-blue eyes, stroking her corn-coloured hair, whispering his love. A place he was no longer a tongue-tied youth but an adroit lover. He bent down, tracing his lips along her neck, nibbling at her ear lobe.

'Sh,' she intimated her pleasure, leaning into him, her body shielding him from the cannons' clamour and with her soft laughter, bubbling like a stream over the boulders of his body. He loved her.

She cleaved to him, her hands deft as silkworm, searched out

---

[13] Turkish sword
[14] ancient long-haired cattle

his wounds, covering them with a gossamer cloth that stopped his teeth from their violent chattering. His body ceased its fearful shaking as she buried him in her moss. Lint strips warmed him in reddish hue. He remembered thinking clearly that he'd have been content to die like this, wrapped in her arms.

For her part she was also willing to give him everything, not giving it a second thought to go back into the black cold wet, waist-deep in mire, in order to lug armfuls of moss out of the peat water. On the bank she had carefully and meticulously separated out any trace of grass, twig, bilberry or heather. No heath, only the most pure spaghnum, the Welsh *mwswg coch*[15].

'*F'annwyl, fy nghariad,*[16]' she whispered, caressing him softly, away from his putrid stinking bed, away from his misery and pain to a lucid, love-bright light. No longer a bed of suppuration, or rotting flesh but one of sweet mountain air. The cost to himself irrelevant as he lay at last, sated in her arms.

What brutish force that wrenched him from his haven? What sudden jolt pulled him up, with a voice so poisonous? Mercury-quick in soft Irish lilt calling her name, his Beth, his own Florence Nightingale. The butcher's courageous noble steed standing above them panting hard as it snatched at its bit with flanks covered in blood and sweat as it heaved laboriously from its strenuous effort. In that demon night Tegwyn watched the horse's blanket of warm steam rising to envelope them, muffling the battle's sound. The horse had been maimed and sways of his once glorious chestnut skin had been ripped off, the huge gashes from wither, girth, hindquarter to tail shining bloody in the dark. Not by Tegwyn's hands to cause such savagery, 'Brave, poor horse,' he thought as he watched it flinching and shaking, mortally wounded like he was. Like the fallen soldier, the horse had galloped his heart out for love.

---

[15] red moss
[16] My dearest, my darling

The humble beast serving the false master. A dressed-up piece of muck in leather boots and flashing sword and swank of colour like a bird of paradise. The Sergeant Malcolm O'Connor, renegade, bent over him, all solicitous in mock concern. Casual as you like, then shouted at him to address a commanding officer in the proper manner, bloody mercenary kicking him with his spurred boot as with free hands he touched up his girl. Lying there gaping, he couldn't even give voice to his threat, to tell him to get off her. To leave his girl alone or he'd break his sodding neck. He had a nerve, taunting him in front of her. Pathetic, he watched; it was all he could do from where he lay unable to express any counter; fumbling to co-ordinate his soggy brain to his legs and arms, to get up and hit the spurious thief.

'Cannon to the right of them, cannon to the left of them, cannon behind them!'' The bastard stealing his girl and as he tried to stir, to get up and cut him down, his wounds retched a hideous viscous yellow, breaking out of their moss skins, rendering him weak and helpless. The phoney officer then ran his steel blade along Tegwyn's skin, scoring it like a razor. 'No sweetmeat here for you, sonny Jim!' and as he walked away with the lovely, fair-haired Bethan on his arm, his spurs clinked with his laughter.

21

Richard sat looking at the literature, listening to the man as he read out facts and figures. He hadn't realised how much change it would mean if he decided to go ahead. The financial incentives were tempting, and in the first year he would make money even if it meant reducing his stock number and corresponding milk yield.

'We recommend you reduce your stock level for the first year, as you'll be pushed for early spring grass without artificial fertiliser.' The grassland was used to its regular fix of nitrogen and he was concerned about the quantity and quality of a silage crop without the chemical boost.

'How will the grass compare?' Richard asked.

'Better in the long run, once the soil stabilises. We'd suggest you plant with red clover which will help promote natural nitrogen, and by going organic you'll very quickly appreciate your farmyard manure as a real asset.'

'How long will it take before I can sell my milk as organic?'

'Two years to convert, but we do allow a little bit of flexibility. Take your first year Friesian heifers for instance – you'd be able to graze them on a nonorganic land and still rate them as organic as long as they come back to Tŷ Coch before the winter. It'll help give you a bit of space whilst you transfer to the organic system and your farm has time to adjust. It's why the payments are made annually on a sliding scale,' said the man from the Welsh Office's agricultural department. Richard had done his sums: the demand for organic milk would push the price up to twenty-seven pence instead of the eighteen he was getting. It would also give him a good excuse to contact Penny, as she'd given him the idea in the first place. She might be interested in taking on more heifers.

'I've decided were going to switch to organic,' he announced some weeks later when the three of them – Nesta, Richard and Rhian – were in the room.

'Sh, Dad I'm watching *Eastenders*.' said Rhian, switching up the volume. Nesta shrugged her shoulders.

'Will it cost more?' was all she said as she turned to clear away a mug left on the table. He didn't know why he bothered. Their total lack of interest made him cross; it was his hard, daily slog that kept them fed. He got up and switched the television off.

'Oi, I was watching that!' Rhian said angrily.

'It's about time you listened to me. I thought you'd be pleased. You know, veggie, no chemicals and all that.'

'Eh? What planet are you on Dad? I don't know what you're talking about.'

'Because you can't be bothered to listen. And I'll have less of your cheek, girl.' She was about to go off in a huff, when uncharacteristically, he pulled her arm and stopped her leaving. He wanted her to hear him out for a change, instead of always walking off in mid-sentence, but he was shocked to feel how thin her arm was under her layers of clothes.

'I thought you'd be pro what I'm doing, changing the farm to organic. I've had the Soil Association here and everything. They've been round all the stock and fields and in principle they've approved us for the scheme.'

'Cool,' she said pulling a face at him. 'Have you told the cows?'

'What the hell's gone wrong with you, Rhian, eh?' He let her arm go, where it drooped limply by her side. Her heavily made-up eyes stared, blanking at a point behind him.

'I don't know what you're about. I've had enough of all this,' he said pulling her black jumper 'Your silly clothes and there's nothing of you, under all that black. You don't eat properly.'

'Whatever.'

'No, it's not whatever. Look at her, Nesta.' He looked to his wife for support.

'Tell him, Mam; I do eat, just not what he wants me to. Liver and bacon to make me grow strong on the steroids you farmers give your animals,' she said sarcastically.

'Cheeky little madam! Get your facts rights. They've been banned for years and meat's much better for you than those beans and veggie burgers, judging by how you look. If we were meant to live on leaves and fruit we'd still be swinging from the trees!'

'It's like talking to a caveman! I'm not going to end up like Nain.'

'Huh! No danger of that! The rate you're going you'll be lucky to get anywhere near her age. And for your information, even monkeys eat meat when they can catch some! I saw it on the telly with that animal bloke.'

She pushed past him, mouth turned down, slammed the door then stomped up stairs. Another door banged shut and then he heard some heavy metal blasting.

'You might have said something.' He directed this at his wife, but she had her back to him, drying her hands on the tea towel.

'You said enough for the both of us. You're always so heavy-handed with her.'

'I'm not. Just because I don't indulge her. You just give in to her, let her do whatever she wants and look at the mess she's in.'

'I see. So it's all my fault now? Do you ever talk to her to find out who she is? You've no idea what makes her tick.'

'Rubbing me up the wrong way is one. And those ridiculous clothes she wears. We're into summer and she's in black, heavy make-up and heavy boots. She looks a bloody fright.'

'See! It's a phase. You used to rebel against your parents, didn't you. That's if you can remember back that far.'

'All we ever did was play some pop music and wear our hair over the collar. What's happening to Rhian is different; she's really alienating herself from me and the farm. It's come to the point when she needs to see a doctor. What she's got is anorexia.'

'Don't be so melodramatic, of course she hasn't.'

'I don't mind her disagreeing with me if only she'd eat properly. Her loopy ideas are wrecking her health.'

'It's just how the young are these days; conscious of how they look. Rhian likes to be like her friends, that's all.'

'And you obviously approve? You've always hated being here in the middle of nowhere.'

'Blame me as usual.'

'Well, it's true isn't it? Admit it. You'd never have married me if your lover hadn't done a runner would you? Come on Nesta, it's not like you to be shy. Cat got your tongue?'

'If I'd known it was going to be like this, no, I wouldn't have married you.'

'What do you mean, if you'd known? Of course you bloody knew. You grew up round here. You knew exactly what it would be like! No, what threw you was the other bloke, wasn't it? The one you set your heart on, only he didn't want to know, so you came crawling back to the stupid older brother, a consolation prize, keeping it in the family.'

'I don't know what you're talking about.'.

'Come on Nesta, we both know. When he went down to Cardiff, you looked after him, didn't you? Including all the services.'

'Of course I looked after him – he was your little brother. Anything else would have been odd. I kept an eye out for him, made sure he was OK. So? Where's the big deal?'

'Sleeping with him is the big deal.'

'We never did.'

'He told me you did. After the Cardiff concert. He got blind drunk and before he realised you'd got him in bed in The Hilton, where you came onto him like a pro.At least he had the decency to scarper, not like you, a second-rate music teacher, crawling back to your old sucker of a fiancé.'

'It wasn't like that. Not in the way you mean.'

'Perhaps you thought I'd remind you of him. Hmm?'

'You! You might be his brother but you're not a patch on him!' She spat the words at him, hurt and full of scorn. Why let him know that Simon had been appalled at what he'd done, fleeing the next morning and ever since had done his best to avoid her, ducking her phone calls, always too busy to catch up, until she finally got the message. When the family was expected back at Tŷ Coch, he used work commitments as a reason not to come home and only turned up at their wedding because Richard had especially asked him to sing in the chapel. It would have been too difficult to make up a plausible excuse.

'I remember confiding in you before you ever went away. You knew how mixed up I was about Dad's death and Mam expecting and then Mervyn coming to live with us. You fucking well knew I thought the baby was Mervyn's and not Dad's. I buried it, accepting him when he came. After what we'd been through, it was the only way to survive.'

She said nothing. What was there to say? 'Do you know the worst thing about it all,' he said, 'is I loved him as a true brother. Much more than I ever loved you.'

He left her there, mouth turned down, sour and miserable, the thin veneer of them together as a couple stripped clean off. Richard moved into the cottage with his stepfather and mother. Rather than go through with a divorce, he left his wife and daughter in the farmhouse. He didn't tell Mervyn what the final row had been about, not wishing to cover old ground and reopen healed wounds. After all, the old boy had been good to him, in many ways better than his real father Ianto ever was, and Mervyn had stood by him when he needed him. He'd given years of his life to put the farm back on a secure footing in his quiet unassuming way, and without Mervyn, the family and their farm would never have survived. Devoted to Elin as he was, he'd tolerated Richard's adolescent taunts with his characteristic quiet restraint, risking his life for him and losing an arm in the process, and there was no way now Richard was going to revisit an old pain. However much he blamed Simon for what happened between him and Nesta, he was not about to share it with Mervyn on the mantelpiece, who thought the world of his operatic son, even proudly keeping Simon's postcards from the different destinations where he performed.

For a short while it seemed to work, living in the cottage away from Nesta: she kept her car and comings and goings to one side of the yard and Richard his truck and tractor to the other. They rarely met and barely acknowledged the other's existence. There was only Rhian between them, awkward after the row with her dad, but he would not abandon her to that bitch of a woman. He'd fight to get her back, to have her as she had been, his little girl.

In his hurry to see Penny, he had to slam on his brakes to avoid a van coming up the lane. Cursing and already late, he pulled in to make space so that the other vehicle could pass. He was surprised to see Tegwyn unwind the window.

'I wasn't expecting to meet anyone on the lane.'

'No, I could tell that!'

'I'm in a hurry.' He didn't want to be delayed by Tegwyn but he noticed some flowers on the passenger seat. 'You come to see Mam? That'll cheer her up.' Richard noticed Tegwyn had also spruced himself up, both men having changed out of their usual working clothes.

'I haven't called before now, so I thought—'

'She'll love the flowers.'

'Oh, yes. How is she doing?'

He seemed a bit embarrassed, neither of them wanting the unavoidable exchange.

'I've got an appointment, but go in, Mam's in the cottage. There's no one else around, but don't expect her to speak. Mervyn shouldn't be long.'

Only afterwards as he neared Penny's place did he realise that like himself, Tegwyn had been on a different mission to the one he'd assumed. It was not his mother but Beth he'd hoped to see, unaware that she'd already gone back to Ireland. For the first time Richard felt vaguely sorry for Tego.

22

Malcolm's recent revelations helped Bethan understand the O'Connor situation better, forgiving him some of his idiosyncrasies. The same could not be said for his mother, Moira. If their relationship had been frosty up to then, it was now ice.

'I see your wife's full of her usual charm,' she'd say sarcastically to her son when they'd been forced to share a post-syndicate do in the big house, adding, 'She's like snow off a ditch,' not caring who heard her comment as Bethan blanked her, indicating a loose screw, winding her finger against her temple. Whenever they had to be in the same room Beth remained deadpan, her eyes flat in her blame for her. For everything she had done to Malcolm. His unhappiness was down to her. His arrogance, rudeness, and underhand manner were all because of his mother. No wonder he'd resorted to secrecy, needing to protect himself from his parents by damage limitation. Little wonder Malcolm concealed things as a safety mechanism, and if now his wife saw him act rudely, at least she understood. Now that she finally understood some of his past Bethan felt she was more in control of their life together, and with their daughter Clare she felt hopeful they'd be able to bridge the gaps in their marriage.

Armed with better insight, she tackled the yard more confidently, belatedly keeping Eileen in her place and becoming more her old self, teasing and joking around. She even started to ride again, cantering along the beach on the low tide, loving the feel of salt air and water and the rhythm of her Irish cob as it cantered through the surf's edge.

Excluded and ostracised by her daughter-in-law, Moira viewed the comings and goings of the stud from her bungalow. She discerned the brighter step and sometimes when Clare was with her mother, dressed in the pink paraphernalia of a little girl, they'd stop, pointing to her window, Clare hoping to see her Granny appear so that she could wave in that capacity of simple happiness. Like a spring lamb feeling of rip and skip, an exclusive facility of young. Watching, Moira softened as she saw her granddaughter pointing to her house, her small face screwing up in laughter as she splashed into a puddle. Her resentment reserved for the mother; smiling, calling, holding her daughter's hand then letting her run to the demand of 'Look at me', as Clare 'raced off' for a few feet.

'You're lucky he still speaks to you, after what you did to him. I don't want you to have anything to do with looking after Clare or any of my children! You're not fit to be a mother,' had smarted, causing her to look back, to retrace. Behind the glass, Moira's memory was of a different mother, where there had been no spontaneous whoops for joy. Any sound of happiness had been uttered by her sister and not her. No, her domain had been a place of dislike and rejection so intense that it left a lasting scar. Worse than being just poor and inept, it had been the arrant, constant show of disfavour that had eroded any feeling that might have been considered jolly. A blight that her own mother had given birth to twins, girls at that. Her father had only ever been a hint in her memory, as he came back briefly between long absences; loud and rough, smelling of tobacco, and whisky, itching to get back to the sea. He left the rearing of his twins, Moira and Maeve, to their mother. To charity when the money ran out and the protective soutane of the Catholic faith. God, help us all for the religions we have dressed you up in, where an empty room or open field would have been a better place than where they sent young Moira. Her life blighted so early, destroying that little pocket in any human existence that should hold gaiety. Her mother had chosen to keep only one daughter, and Maeve had been her favourite. So at five Moira had been cast off in a peopled sea of the unwanted; to swim or drown in institutionalized homes, run by the fervent for the dammed.

Eventually and reluctantly two spinster aunts came to reclaim her; like a piece of battered luggage they removed her to the west of Ireland, to the middle of a blank empty nothingness where it rained for weeks on end, steel sheets of water over the desolate landscape. Day after day until the very bogs bled black in saturation. Although the two aunts had no love, no affection for her, they clothed and fed her after a fashion, and more importantly she learned to read and write, to do her sums at the cold school. It was a consolation that she had a good brain despite Miss Gubby, a lay teacher whose mission was to thwart any sparkle of advancement shown by the disadvantaged children under her care. Being entrusted by the clergy, she had a *carte blanche* to inflict her own cruelty and prejudices. She took particular offence to Moira who showed some spark, some promise and aptitude for learning. Miss Gubby inflicted her own injuries, pulling her up in front of every class for ridicule: her clothing, her ignorance, her lack of piety, any excuse to punish the small child. To hit, pinch, isolate and trip up, to exclude the already excluded. But despite her attempts, Moira learned her books, by some ancient gene that although not favoured by her parents, came through. She was clever, petite and pert, with bright eyes.

In country ways, just as a ewe once hefted[17] to a place needs no fence to keep her there, there is also an odd, errant sheep who will actively search for any gap in wall or fence. Once through, no amount of fortification will keep her contained. So it was with Moira. She'd seen a gap in the fence, that day when he had walked into the place, accidentally mistaking her for a guest in the only hotel in the depressing town. They both happened by chance to meet in a place where passing trade was rare, and they saw the funny side as they waited interminably for the drink

[17] To be bound to a place by a natural restraint, like a flock of sheep hefted to an open hillside

he'd offered her. Once through that initial gap, Moira did not care that all might be lost; words of 'ruin, loose and disgrace', meant little to her, for as she'd been told ad infinitum, she was already beyond reproach. Regardless of any consequence she had been prepared to take the gamble rather than return to her miserable life in the clutches of those pernicious and mean aunts. As it turned out, Patrick had never shown any interest in her background; he didn't ask for any history, nor gave her any of his, other than being a country boy with a wild streak himself, and so they jumped through the fence together, headed for the better pastures.

They ran away to Dublin where they married in a whirlwind of pleasure. There was live music in the bars they ate and drank at. They went to a cinema or a dance and then to a day out at the races. He could lay a brick and had an eye for a bargain, but most important, he was the first person who had made her feel loved, wanted and despite what came after, all his infidelities, she would not forget his gift of love for her. Uncouth, rough and ready, it was nothing compared to what she had been used to, and better a rough hand than no hand at all. She didn't mind his lack of books or learning. Only Patrick knew how to make her feel desired, how to make her want him so she would cry out in those early, hungry days. And he was clever, taking risks with little to lose, grabbing his chance while others deliberated. Behind him she kept the tabs, well practised by those austere, tight women. Steadily he made money, buying run-down shacks to rebuild them and sell them off in profit. Three children later and a rich hardened husband used to getting his own way, Moira had learned not to interfere in his affairs. To let him and not plead. Later in their marriage she had her card parties, her bridge days that occupied her, intense through booze and smoke playing for the important pennies, while he was away gambling his shirt on the horses, bricks and mortar.

She had the best of thirty years to be well-rehearsed, astute in the ways of men, and she did not need some slip of a girl moving in. Worse, to accuse her of lying, of not loving her own son! What had she ever seen? How little she knew about life compared to Moira. Had she been there when Malcolm was a baby? No, but as his mother Moira had watched him as he developed and grew, witnessing deeds that fed a mother's doubt. Incidents that added up to something not quite right, a propensity in her son that worried. A leaning toward bad. If Bethan could have seen him then, encouraging his little brother to danger. Like the time he pushed his brother into a wasps' nest. For the spite? Jealousy? She couldn't say for sure. In all the commotion that ensued in the mass of angry insects and stings, she'd raced him back into the house, shouting for Patrick who later took a rage, beating him with a stirrup leather. She remembered she did nothing to prevent him, soothing the crying Kieran all swollen and bumpy faced, covered in ugly bitten blotches with the centre marked by the sting. Was it her fault as their mother that Kieran had been so much easier to love, placid and wanting to please? Malcolm seemed intent on causing trouble, doing things deliberately that promoted her prejudice, so that by the time he had reached double figures, his mother had committed him to the very same pattern of rejection that had been hers to bear as family history repeated itself.

Now, the cheek of it; she had to suffer his jumped-up Welsh nothing. How dare she judge her! If only she'd known the lengths she'd gone to to try and make Malcolm feel cherished. How often had he refused his mother's arms, her cuddles, preferring his own, solitary company. She'd catch him sitting on the stairs, eavesdropping, wanting them to fight, to see her humiliated by her husband so she'd cry, rushing from the room to catch him with a satisfied smile in his face. Where did Rosaleen fit in to this jigsaw of family life? As a bossy elder sister who told tales. Yet for all of it, Kieran looked up to him as some sort of God, following him naïvely, unaware of his corruption, his face giving him away at the time of questioning. He could not lie like his elder brother. Malcolm was mercurial-tongued, fibbing more effortlessly than he told any truth.

No mother could ever forgive the casual behaviour behind the wheel that had killed her best son. It didn't matter afterwards that he said he never meant to. Playing his usual silly buggers, a game of Russian roulette topped off with a joint. What did he expect? Immortality? And now his wife wanted, no demanded she rewrite their history. A family of whom she knew nothing, that had nothing to do with her. The only thing she was right about was that Moira had wished he'd never married her, this woman from Wales. She had not been privy to any of the thirty formative years she'd had as his mother to see and experience at first hand her son's deceptive, manipulative ways. Only she knew that underneath his charm lurked an altogether more sinister person used to getting his own way.

23

In the attic Richard found the old wooden cheese press, which, apart from needing a good clean, seemed to be intact. For the last few weeks, he'd already been experimenting in the kitchen, keeping a small amount of the milk back in order to attempt to make a soft, cream cheese. If only his mother could help him, show him how she used to do her cheeses as a young wife. She had been showing signs of improving, and perhaps if he took the press to her he'd provoke a reaction. She had made cheese in a time when there was less choice for consumers and all milk was precious. There was no skimmed, semi, rich, Jersey – just milk with its half-inch of cream in the neck of the bottle. Since the demise of the Milk Marketing Board, life for the dairy farmer was more precarious, if less restrictive and Richard knew he needed to change, he had to become innovative if he was to survive the downturn in the price he was being paid for his milk.

'Do you remember Mam, how you used to make the cheese? Well, I'm going to start it up again. Could you help me? Show me how it's done? Just nod if I'm doing it right.'

He attempted to assemble the press as Elin watched, trying to talk, her speech slurred but responsive and between them, Richard thought he had understood her and was thrilled with, taking it as a positive sign she approved. Clumsily he tried to hug her.

'Perhaps Penny's right, Mam, and shoppers' attitudes are changing and now is a good time to diversify, to make a new niche for ourselves in the health-conscious consumer market. You think so, don't you, Mam?' He could have sworn his mother nodded. 'Why,' he reasoned 'should we let the French be the only producers of specialist cheeses?' "Caws Tŷ Coch Cheese", Mam, eh?' It had an easy ring to it and once he had the brand name established in his head, the idea of becoming a specialist cheese producer started to appeal. It fitted in with the conversion away from intensive to extensive, organic farming. It might even meet with his daughter's approval. 'At least vegetarians aren't averse to eating cheese,' he thought, although it was in his view ironic that they conveniently forgot that calves had to be produced in order to get the milk. Who was he to quibble if it meant more customers, and his unwanted young bull calves would still be sent to slaughter just as they'd always been. At least the French ate and enjoyed veal, creating a demand for the otherwise wasted young meat.

He didn't consider his wife in any of his new plans, but at least in this new way he hoped he would be able to re-engage with Rhian. He was eager to start and be in regular contact with his new business partner, Penny. They'd need new equipment, stainless steel machinery, and he needed advice on the best market. Whether he was best setting up in the traditional way, using unpasteurised milk, natural preservatives, flavouring and colour. His life was suddenly looking more promising than it had done for a long time and at last Richard went about his farm with a renewed sense of purpose. He also needed a way out of his unhappy marriage, a resolution that didn't involve going over a cliff. Unlike in his mother's day there was no stigma to divorce, only the huge problem of settling their finances. He had no doubt Nesta would want her fair dues for the fifteen years they'd been married, and when she had her money she would move away.

Like most of his neighbours, the farm was already mortgaged and the only way of realising the money needed would be to sell up. He tried to put it to the back of his mind, to blank it so as not to hate her as she threatened to take the farm that had been in his family for generations. He did not want it to be him who lost the farm, consoling himself with the thought that the money was tied up and she would have to approach the bank, and as a partnership there was also his mother and stepfather to consider. Separating had been easy but the business side of it would be far more complicated. He had considered asking Malcolm via his sister for a loan, and even his brother Simon, who was earning a good whack. Unable to find a solution he switched his mind to Penny, thinking of her as he did his day's work, imagining her with him on his farm, sharing the milking, each cow letting down her milk while in his mind he uttered soft endearments absorbed by the cows, their languid eyes all knowing as they burped contentment. Chewing the cud, with an odd flicker of a black ear as if they approved of what he said. He'd always talked to his cows; descendants of the *Bos Longifrons* that had been man's lifeline, his companion since antiquity, the very air of them venerable. Richard felt stupidly happy, like one of his heifers let out after a winter confined indoors, he wanted to throw his cap in the air, to unclog his middle-aged, soil-bound feet and leap up, over some gate or hedge, knowing she loved her cows, that she might grow to love him.

Someone else had signed for the letter in his absence and over a cup of coffee during the first rehearsal break of the day, Simon opened it in the cafe, not recognising the writing on the envelope. He read it quickly, his expression changing as he came to her news and the implications of their splitting up. Simon knew he would have to contact his brother, however unpalatable the thought.

He tried to choose his moment, a time on the farm when darkness had fallen so his brother would be in, and hopefully alone so that no one could hear their conversation. Richard's almost cheery voice took him by surprise.

'I'm so sorry, Richard.' He wished he could put the clock back and his drunken union never have taken place. 'You were my childhood hero, saving my life and look how I repaid you! What can I do now, Rich, to make amends? Is there no hope of a reconciliation?'

'Between you and me?'

'I meant you and her. I know what I did was unforgivable.'

Richard had a sudden impulse to tell his younger brother it didn't matter any more, that he'd forgiven him because it had let him off the hook. He had fallen in love and Simon had actually helped him escape and he felt a bit mean, concealing the truth from him. Instead he turned the subject to money.

'She's looking for another post, and once she's found something she'll move away. I don't know what Rhian wants to do, but there'll always be a home for her here, with me and her Nain and Taid.'

There was a pause.

'Once Nesta's sorted, and she's made this very clear, she wants paying out. You know the farm business is tied up to the bank.'

'Bit quick of her isn't it?'

'She's been wanting to go for years. She only waited until Rhian was old enough to make her own decision, apparently.'

'Do you know how much she will settle for?' asked Simon, thinking how much his brother was going to ask him for.

'No, but she'd be a fool to ask for anything less than her rights. Probably a few hundred thousand.'

Where the hell would a dairy farmer on the pittance paid to him, the seventeen pence a litre of milk from the supermarket, be able to find that sort of money! Both brothers knew the impossibility of raising it without selling off capital assets.

'Could you sell off any outbuildings? That old barn?'

'I've already put Nantygaseg on the market.'

'On the plus side the housing market is on the up, so it should fetch a fair price. Have you had planning?'

'Outline, but it's not so easy these days. The council's making us jump through so many hoops and they all cost. It should go for a bit but nothing like the prices down in Cardiff. Barely scratch the surface of what she wants.'

'No, I suppose not.'

'So that just leaves a couple of hundred thousand short.'

'And Yr Efail. Could you do something there?'

'Perhaps, but not immediately. It's let. Next you'll be suggesting I chuck Mam and Merv out onto the street. Don't you think I haven't been through every possibility already.'

'Can't she have it in instalments?'

'She won't.'

'Not even for you to have some time to raise the cash?'

'The minimum legal requirement I think is how she put it. She always was a bitch.'

'Of course I'll help, Rich. I'll see what I can come up with.'

'Selling the farm is not an option Simon, just in case you thought it was. I won't sell the farm ever.'

'I understand. No, nor should you, Rich.'

After he put the phone down he thought to ring Bethan, to find out if Richard had approached her and Malcolm for a loan. Thinking about it between rehearsals he decided to switch his flight home, and go via Shannon or Cork or better still get a ferry over and if his news was good, he could call on them at Tŷ Coch on his way back to Cardiff.

24

It was a warm, still day and she'd prepared a picnic. Clare was excited, running down the sand to Kenny, who was already waiting by the water's edge. He sat as Liam rowed them out to his father's boat. Once on board he steadied the dingy, helping to lift Clare onto the bigger vessel. Kenny passed up the picnic, and with a bit of banter offered to lift Beth across. Wearing shorts and trainers, she was quite capable of scrambling onto the fishing boat using the rope to help pull her up. She was glad to be there, as Malcolm had been reluctant to agree to the trip. Clare had gone to bed overexcited after her father had eventually given in and allowed her to go. It had to be calm, totally flat, and Beth had promised to go only a short distance from the shore. Malcolm insisted Clare wear a life jacket before leaving and on no account was she to take it off.

The weather couldn't have been kinder, sunny and still, and they would only be out for a few hours. Hugging the shoreline so that they'd be able to swim back to the shore in the event of some catastrophe. 'God, he fussed,' Beth thought to herself, glad to be aboard and away from the land in case he came running down having changed his mind. She had deliberately left her new mobile phone at home so he couldn't contact them. Hadn't she often been out with old Pete, and Malcolm knew he was a local man who knew the coast and sea well. Much less risky than riding a horse, and Liam, his son, and Kenny were aboard to help.

They set off, much to Clare's delight who sat between her mother and the boys, near the front, holding Bethan's hand, watching the bow break the glass surface of the water.

Bethan felt invigorated by the expanse of water, glad to be away from the stud and Malcolm's family home. Clare excitedly jumped up and down, pointing back to the shore, to the village, to her nursery classroom by the school. There was their house and Granny's bungalow and the horses grazing in the paddocks. She'd forgotten any nerves, laughing and shouting over the engine to the lads to see the gulls that followed the boat, waving back to Pete who sat keeping one hand on the rudder and the other holding his pipe, when it wasn't between his teeth. He took them round the point, before pulling clear of the coastline and out towards a small island of rock sitting less than a mile out.

'There's normally a good chance we'll run into a mackerel shoal on the top of the tide,' Pete called across to her. 'Look, look Clare, did you see the seal?'

He pointed his pipe at the seal sitting in the water just to the bow of the boat. With its head out of the water looking like a wet labrador, it lolled for them, big black eyes inspecting them.

'Where? I can't see it, Mam.'

'Look. There,' said Liam, holding her up above the seat so that she had a better view over the boat's side. 'Where Dad's pointing to, watch the water. It'll probably come up again,'

'There!' The seal obligingly reappeared, as curious to watch as to be watched and Clare squealed her delight. 'Look, he's got whiskers, Mam!'

'And he's spotty! Did you see?' Pete steered the boat closer cutting the engine to allow Clare to see the seal close up. It squeezed its nostrils, blinking its eyes, before slipping back down under the surface leaving no ripple, vanishing.

On the lee side of the island, Pete slowed the engine, letting the boat idle, drifting with the tide. He came over to give them each a line. With a piece of lead at the bottom each trace had four or five spinning hooks interspersed along it. Liam stood close to Beth, the gentle movement of the boat causing their arms to nudge together as they held their lines. Kenny sat out towards the stern, pretending not to see.

'When you put it in the water, the fish think it's bait so they come up and grab it,' Pete explained to Clare. 'Here, I'll throw it over, then you hold on to it.' Pete threw the weight and line that plopped and sped downwards, then gave the line to Clare to hold. There was nothing at first as the boat moved forward in low gear. All of a sudden there was a rush of them, silvery glistening flashes as the lines were pulled up with dangling dappled silver green, mackerel. They flapped, slithering on the floor of the boat as Pete helped knock them off their hooks. Liam picked Beth's up, kissing it before putting it into the plastic box. Clare made a face, not sure of all the fish flapping against her legs writhing to get back into water. Her mother was exhilarated but also a little sad to see them marooned. Part of her wanted to tip the bucket back into the sea.

'Ah, I'm good myself, Johnny. How's Jimmy? And that lovely sister of mine, Rosaleen?'

Malcolm hardly waited for the answer, as he fiddled with the cord of his open binoculars, looking out to sea, nodding his head, not listening but wanting to get to the point of the phonecall. 'You got any of that stuff left over from last summer?'

Johnny O'Moynahan couldn't think what stuff he was

referring to. He supplied his brother-in-law with an awful lot of veterinary products in any given month.

'Not sure what that'll be, Malcolm,' he hedged.

'You know, for that mare we couldn't sort? The one that broke the railings.'

That narrowed it down marginally as many racehorses were apt to jump out. Johnny took a minute to register, trying to remember just what his brother-in-law was looking for. Malcolm jogged his memory. 'The one we couldn't foal. She brought that big brute of a colt, nearly killed her remember? We had to put ropes and a pulley on her. Pulled it like a flippin' cow!'

'She in foal again?' He asked surprised. 'You want something to quieten her?'

'Yeah, you got any about? You know, something you could pop over with?'

'I think I can find some for you. I've got a TB testing to do this afternoon. Is it urgent?'

'It can wait, she's not due yet. Tonight will be fine.' He expected him to put the phone down but Malcolm asked casually, 'It won't show up in any blood test?'

'No, but nothing's absolute. I'd give it a couple of days after, just to be safe.'

'And no ill effects, nothing long lasting? If I want to sell her?' he added.

'Depends on the mare and how she presents at foaling, but there shouldn't be. Put it in the neck and it'll make her dopey for a bit, as she starts to foal. To be safe I'd give it at the first sign so she doesn't get herself too worked up.'

'I don't want her to get into trouble. I'll sell her with the foal if it lives, as soon as I can.'

What he didn't add, but his brother-in-law understood, was he wouldn't want anything to show, nothing going through the book. It had been handy Rosaleen married a vet and Johnny was an affable easy-going bloke, who didn't nose. When he arrived, Malcolm conducted the business in person, storing the drug away, and paying him cash before he brought him into the house for a whisky.

Having come straight from the TB testing, he was on his own. He gave Beth his customary bear hug, and his huge voice boomed across the room, laughing and teasing his niece, making his usual fuss of any small children.

'A fishing trip no less! And you caught a whale? A shark? A conger eel? I know, a lobster. Or was it an old shoe? Neptune himself?'

'No,' she squealed at him. 'I caught seven fish, Uncle Johnny!'

'Go and show him, Clare, they're on the draining board,' said her mother. The little girl ran off to get her catch.

'I never had you as a fishing man, Malcolm.'

'And you'd be right! Wouldn't catch me in a boat! They went out with old Pete, you know, Liam's father.'

Clare came back carrying the plate of shinning gutted mackerel.

'You caught all those!' her uncle acclaimed, raising his voice in mock astonishment. 'Haven't you got a clever girl here! Enough fish for everyone to have two each for supper.'

'Mummy caught that one, and I caught this one, and Liam him, and Kenny that one and I caught—' and as she tried to single out another of hers, tilting the dish so that the whole catch of fish slid off onto the floor.

'Look they're so fresh they've got away. So you had yourselves quite a party on the boat!' her uncle said as he bent to help pick the fish back onto the dish, which Beth hurriedly took from Clare.

'Here. Let me take them. We'll put them under the grill. Now, I'm sure you can stay for a fresh mackerel or two can't you, Johnny?'

'No, I must away or I'll be in trouble with Boyle,' he said, running his hands under the sink and wiping them on the pantry towel. 'Trouble with a bull that's ripped himself in a delicate place. Trying to get where he shouldn't. He's caught himself on barbed wire, and no good for anything unless I mend his tackle. Another time.' They saw him to the door, standing arm in arm as he drove off.

'We had such a lovely time, you should come out with us,' Beth said to him over supper.

'Yes, Daddy, will you come next time?' asked Clare. 'And it's safe with Liam isn't it Mam? He says he can swim like a seal, Dad, and he'd save us.'

'Oh, did he just!'

'So, will you, Dad, please, and we can all go swimming again.'

'So, you went swimming, did you?'

She nodded, pleased with herself.

'Where did you swim? Out in the sea?' he asked

His daughter nodded her head, proud of her achievement.

'It was the sea, Clare, but right in the cove, next to the beach, Mal. You could stand in the sand.'

'No I didn't. I swam out of my depth, Dad.'

'I'm sure you did.' He turned to his wife, 'I didn't see you take your towels or swim things.'

'I swam in my pants. Like Mummy.'

'Really. Like your Mammy. Well, well, my little mermaid, it's way past your bedtime.

'So will you come, Daddy?'

'We'll see. You've had more than enough excitement for one day. Time for bed.'

When it was just the two of them he asked her, 'So, you went skinnydipping with the workmen, the stable lads! Must have been a sight for them.'

'Hardly. A quick dip that's all.'

'I'm sure they'll be talking about it in the yard and all over the county.'

'What? Not at all, Malcolm. Why do you have to make it sound smutty. Where's the harm? It was really hot and the water flat. It was good for Clare to swim in the sea. I didn't go naked Malcolm if that's what you're thinking.'

'If you think you're going to go off flaunting yourself in front of the men using Clare as an excuse, you can think again.'

'It's your business to stop me, is it? I don't tell you what to do, day in day out, off as free as a bird. Why the hell should you prevent me? Just because you don't want to, why should that stop me from having a tiny bit of fun! I didn't go without telling you. I don't stop you every time you go off without me, and let's face it, that's every bloody day of the week. And I don't know what the hell you're doing, do I? Or how often you take Eileen? You've no right, Malcolm, to tell me what I can and can't do. I have a right to a life.'

'Seems you had a right good time of it,'

'You should be proud of your daughter swimming. At least she hasn't got your fear. She loved the day and the fishing. Did she tell you she saw a seal?'

'And I wonder what else.'

She looked at him nodding his head as his mouth flattened in temper, staring at her.

'I can't see any harm. If you'd come out with us you'd see how innocent it all was.'

'I don't see me in a boat somehow, do you? And you had more than enough hands on deck.'

'You're deliberately trying to twist it so that you can spoil it. We never do anything as a family.'

He was impossible to reason with and so she left him to sulk, not wanting him to spoil her memory of their day in the boat, and he was right, she had enjoyed the men's company. He followed her.

'I won't have you going out with them again. Do you hear?' Before she refused his ultimatum, he turned to go out.

'That's right,' she called to his retreating back. 'Tell me what to do. Why is it you always have to have the last word. You have to be in charge!'

He didn't stop, opening the back door. 'Don't you want to hear my good news?'

He heard her but didn't turn. 'Don't wait up.'

She wanted to pick up her glass and chuck it his retreating footsteps, his shoes crunching on the gravel.

He'd obviously regretted his decision to let Clare go on the boat trip and the lads being there hadn't helped. But it had been Clare's innocent remark that had tipped the balance. He'd been all right until he realised they'd been swimming and yes, his wife had been virtually naked, in pants and tee shirt. Her devil-may-care attitude, her face when they returned still flushed from the sea air and excitement of being out in the boat for the day: goose and gander she'd justified, a one back for all his times up a skirt.

If he'd waited to hear what she was going to say instead of storming off, he'd have seen his silly folly. He could get on with it and she'd let him wait until he was in better form, before she'd bother to tell him the news.

Still peeved by his selfish attitude, Bethan decided to make a treat of it and do a bit of shopping while she was in the city. She rang to make a morning appointment so she'd have time for some shopping and a chance to use his credit card. She had booked a hotel. The only downside was having to leave Clare behind with Moira.

25

Richard had changed and as she'd suggested he had put on his new shirt, leaving the top two buttons open. However he felt uncomfortable and resorted to a tie that went with his jacket and trousers. When he was dressed up, his workman hands seemed larger and he felt odd without his cap, so he went back into the kitchen to get his best one out of a drawer, folding it like a Cornish pasty and slipping it in the pocket of his jacket. In the yard he met the post van, and rather than carry the post around in the car, he took the day's brown envelopes, bundled together with an elastic band, back to the cottage. He quickly scanned them to see if there were any cheques that he'd take with him to the bank, then he came across a postcard. He knew it was one from his sister, the picture of the city centre and river with Greetings from Dublin written across the bottom. Hurriedly he flicked it over to read her wide scrawl 'A shopping spree and having a ball. Lots to do and see. Dublin's a great city. Off to see a show tonight before home tomorrow. Hope you're all well and Mam you're feeling better. Lots of love, Beth xxx.'

He left the letters on the table for Mervyn, the postcard on top, and then rushed out to his van and away down the road.

He met Penny at the showground where she was setting out her stand, a red and green banner bearing the words Wild Mountain Range across it, and underneath the Welsh Development Agency's logo of financial support of the venture. At least in Wales, they did try to help their farmers compete, to get new brands of good, locally-produced food out into the wider markets, more in keeping with the successful French branding.

He felt awkwardly self-conscious with his produce, his two baskets of Tŷ Coch cheese and a few dozen, plain single-sheeted leaflets explaining his new business. Unlike Penny he hadn't thought of displaying colour photos of his herd, his farm or dairy. No iconic pictures of contented cattle grazing. Nor had he thought to use the scenic views of land next to the coast. She on the other hand had prepared a beautiful laminated photograph of her farm and cattle, enlarged to make the backdrop of her stand.

The food hall was a very different selling place from the cattle market he was used to, where it was full of farmers only interested in selling to the few buyers, buying for a few big companies. No thrills, no panache, just dealers. Richard had never had to sell himself before, to stand in front of the general public with his wares. He was understandably nervous, not wanting to come up short in front of her. Penny worked with a professionalism that impressed him; from the layout of her stall, the detailed colour brochure with tear-off bit for further orders by post, the advertising on an internet web page, the vacuum packed burgers and other joints of meat, all neatly labelled with company logo and address in the chill compartment. On the counter top where everybody could see, she started to cook on the grill provided by the WDA. His pamphlet was dull beside hers, and his few cheeses looked paltry next to her vivid display. Nor had Richard any idea on how even to present his food to entice customers.

Typical British weather aided them as waves of showgoers came in to seek shelter from the heavy showers. Once under cover, it was up to the food exhibitors to tempt their captive audience into parting with their money. He needn't have worried, as he stood in her shadow watching, and learning. In the uniform white coat and obligatory white hat with her hair netted back, Penny visibly wooed the showgoers with her natural sales flair. She offered free samples off the grill, chatting to customers as she flipped more beefburgers onto the heat, the smell of sizzling warm meat seasoned with herbs enough to tempt the mackintoshed, wet country carnivores, coaxing them guilelessly into buying a vacuum pack of four, six or eight, all handy for supper, or freezer.

Good quality local convenience food. She smiled at the men but it was to the women, the decision makers of food buying that she gave her real attention. She'd had the foresight to bring some of her homemade chutneys and relishes; samples doled out on biscuits, sweet and savoury, hot and spicy, in saucers to go with her beefburgers. No sooner had she cooked a plateful, than they were eagerly taken by a queue of people so that she was continuously cooking more as she chatted, relaxed and easy, talking about food, recipes, enjoying the buzz of selling.

She didn't fuss when Richard got things wrong, as long as they were selling that was all that mattered and throughout the day, she managed to keep up a light banter, working each gathering that passed their stall; a jar of homemade chutney that would keep, and go beautifully with a slice of Richard's Tŷ Coch Welsh cheddar. Although the show was sixty miles from home, Richard knew several of the faces who called in at the food tent to have a look. A smile at him with Penny Jordan as they picked up a leaflet, no doubt holding back gossip. He would have done the same himself, but what caught him off guard was the appearance of Tegwyn Tan-y-bryn, dressed up as if he was off to a funeral, talking with someone he recognised but couldn't place. Then it registered, it was the man who'd come and looked over his barn. So what had Tegwyn do to with him and the other men who were talking animatedly? Apart from Tegwyn, they were obviously non-agricultural, civil servants from Cardiff. Their own brand, of soft-handed, brief-cased officials with polished shoes, who stood out from the farmers as they traipsed around the showground, trying to look important and interested in all things rural. Tegwyn spotted him and with his schoolboy smirk that had got him into so much trouble in the past, he came up to Richard and Penny.

'I'd heard you'd gone into something new,' he said, not unfriendly, winking at Richard. 'So are you going to introduce me? How'ya, *cariad*,' he said not waiting for Richard, as he offered a hand to Penny, who raised her blue plastic gloved ones.

'Hello, I'm Penny. Here, try a burger. I recommend the aubergine pickle.' She pointed at one of the saucers.

'Ta. Don't mind if I do. I'm a neighbour of his.'

'Are you?' She sounded interested.

'Yep. I live the other side, we border each other, don't we Rich? Tegwyn Jones, Tan-y-bryn. But everyone knows me as Tego.'

'So you farm?'

'Smallholding, just a few animals to keep my old folks happy. I was in forestry, until my employment with Doctor Trelawny here.'

The entourage gathered round, tasting the burgers offered but resisting any temptation to dig into their own pockets.

'So how's Bethan?' he asked Richard, as the others listened to Penny's spiel.

'Fine. Mam had a postcard from her this morning. From Dublin. She was up there shopping.'

'Next time you talk to her tell her I was asking after her. I'm sure she'll be impressed to hear that I've gone into business.'

'Oh? What line is that?' He asked waiting for a cock-and-bull story.

'Tell her medicine.'

'You a doctor! Now I've heard everything!'

'Not a doctor – medical science to be exact. With the doctor here.'

'Hello again. I didn't know you made your own cheese?' the doctor said.

'I'm just starting. We had to do something, with milk prices as they are.'

'How's it going? You seem very busy.' He looked round at the public interest.

'OK.' He didn't want to share Penny with them and didn't introduce them. 'Tegwyn's just told me he's in business with you?' He tried to keep the incredulity from his voice.

'That's right. We're in the process of developing a new market for an old problem. To do with healing, or the lack of it.'

'Really?' Thinking how the hell had Tegwyn got himself involved with something he knew nothing about. Richard watched his neighbour smiling broadly.

'You know we have an increasing problem in this country, well in the Western world generally with the overuse of antibiotics. Don't get me wrong, I applaud the huge advances made in medicine over the last fifty years. But there is a drawback, a price to pay for our over-reliance on modern medicines. Antibiotics are becoming less effective because they've been misused, for coughs and colds and simple ailments that don't need any treatment.'

Richard wondered if he was about to receive a lecture, similar to that of the Soil Association expert who'd spent hours condemning modern farming practices, the use of artificial fertiliser, crop-spraying and modern veterinary medicines that were administered willy nilly to animals to maximise profit. None of the farmers he knew went about in Bentleys! The reality was the consumer demanded cheap food. He was tempted to say something but the doctor continued. 'Our modern sores, you know the open running ones that won't heal because they've become resilient to antibiotics. I'm sure you've read about it in the press, doctors reverting back to using leeches, maggots and the like. Well, we're in the process, working with the development board here, as well as, and in conjunction with the findings from Glasgow and Nottingham Universities, who are doing several pilot schemes with a selection of patients—'

'And a famous Elastoplast manufacturer. With Royal approval,' Tegwyn couldn't resist adding, attempting a bow.

'Mr Tegwyn Jones here is an integral part of the business. If it succeeds, he'll be very busy. However it's in its infancy and we've only got the green light to go into very limited production. It's early days, but promising.'

'Yeah, but we're in production aren't we?'

'Well,' Dr Trelawny laughed modestly. 'We've made a start but we mustn't count our chickens just yet.'

'Good as,' said Tegwyn.

'It's not public knowledge, not for another month, so I'd prefer it to remain that way.' Irritated that Tegwyn talked too freely, he swiftly changed the topic of conversation. The funding would depend on the medical bandage company and the clinical results of further trials before more money was committed. As for the Prince of Wales, he had shown an interest, being an advocate of the alternative medicine movement but at this delicate stage, apart from showing a polite wish to be kept informed of the universities' trials, there was nothing more concrete. He'd have to reel in his new business partner, his moss gatherer who'd relished crowing to a neighbour.

'Oh,' was all Richard could say and Tegwyn was happy not to expand on his role as it sounded so much grander than it was.

'I'll buy a couple of packets, *cariad*, very tasty,' Tego smiled, handing over a crisp twenty-pound note. 'Remember, Rich, to give Beth my news next time you speak,' he added to Richard before walking off to catch up with his group that had moved on.

By the end of the day Penny had sold out and between them they tidied up their stall, leaving the showground and still running on adrenaline, she talked about her plans for them; beef, lamb, and pig as well as cheese, yoghurts, and ice cream. All he could do was smile admiringly.

She reminded him slightly of Beth, jolly and not someone to sit around moping. Meeting Tegwyn unexpectedly made him think of her and he thought that she would like Penny. Beth would have been good at the show and she'd have been better than her brother at selling. He regretted that she lived so far away in Ireland, but he thanked his lucky stars he'd gone to market that day and met Penny. Having seen her perform all day, he really believed that she would make her business a success and he was happy to follow in her wake.

For a change from the beach, Bethan took the small single-track road that led out and away from the village. Stone walls on either side snaked grey through the patchwork of fields. That morning Clare had gone to school wearing the new dress she'd brought home from Dublin, her white socks with embroidered, furry bumble bees an immediate favourite that had to be worn. Malcolm had greeted her off the train, and there was no taint of any row as he cuddled her in his arms after they'd made love.

Today, work had taken him away to Cork, so Bethan had the day, at least the morning to herself. What little early morning local traffic there was had gone, leaving a lull, and from the top of the small rise, she looked back at the stud. The old house looked impressive, its signs of wear and tear invisible from where she stood. 'This is where it looks at its best,' she thought to herself, and the next time she would remember to bring her camera to take a photo to send back home, so they could all continue to believe that she lived a life of grandeur! She'd have to be careful to avoid the shabby garden and eyesore of the hideous bungalow. In contrast the long view down to the yard surrounded by wooden fenced paddocks with horses grazing looked the business and she wanted her family to think she was doing well and was blissfully happy. Her life with Malcolm had improved and at least she felt she'd been able to paper over some of the cracks. And Clare was her great joy.

Looking away from the buildings towards the sheltered bay, she eyed the familiar array of small boats to see if she could spot Pete's 'Little Marie'. The tide was out and from where she stood, she couldn't see his boat. It painted a quaint, picturesque picture, somehow timeless, and she half-expected to see a donkey and smiling peasant come along the beach's edge to complete the preconceived idyll. She was in no hurry and sat on a wall, looking down on the tranquil scene below her, the sea's edge framed by the row of cottages that could have been old Fishguard, Aberaeron or Newport only different, no granite houses or imposing chapel on the land that ran flatter and more unruly to its sea.

From the distance a sound, carried by the water, buzzed, rising and falling getting louder until a black blob appeared from one of the bends, speeding along the winding road. Only the rounded shape of a helmet remained visible as it zigzagged its trail, coming towards her at amazing speed, revving annoyingly like an angry bluebottle. It sped past without a hint of slowing down, making her jump, coming up so close, the whoosh of wind on her bare legs making her pull them up hurriedly onto the wall. The motorbike receded quickly down towards the beach out of sight in the road's bends, only to come into view again, its noise following, a belated rev to signal the passing of the narrow humped bridge and out away to the other side. Lucky she hadn't been riding or worse, with Clare on her trike. Angry at the biker, she got down from the wall and continued on her walk, but the tranquillity and pleasure had gone. She felt irked by the biker's intrusion and decided to curtail her walk, dropping down to the pebbly end of the beach before turning for home. Malcolm would be due back by two. A car appeared and passed her before stopping in a lay-by made into the stone wall. The driver had got out and was leaning on the bonnet. At her approach he looked up, smiled as he shrugged at the map laid in front of him. His reflective sunglasses looked anonymously at her.

'Hi, there. You've guessed it, we seem to be lost,' he said in his easy American drawl. At this point a woman, perhaps his wife, got out of the car to take a look at the map.

'Dick said we should have taken a fork right back in that last town, for Killarney, but I've promised the folks back home we'll take some snaps of Bantry Bay.'

'Well, this road will take you along the coast to there,' Bethan said, emphasising the word 'will', 'but it's a slow road following the coast.' She leaned down to look at the map, and wiggled her hand to indicate the winding road. The woman moved closer to look at the map.

'It depends how much time you have and where you need to get to,' Beth said.

26

Hastily the man, helped by his accomplice, tied Bethan's hands and feet as she lay dazed, slumped on the ground. There was a noise in a distance, an insect flying in her haze. She remembered nothing more.

Using the open door as a shield they gagged her loose, silent, drooling mouth, and the third person, not a child but a small man got out from the back. He checked her eyes and pulse before sliding a needle into her arm. Between them they bundled her into the boot of the car. It didn't take more than a minute until her body was drugged and trussed up; it was all proficient and professionally executed. They'd taken care beforehand to choose the spot. The dip in the road that was conveniently hidden from view, with the lay-by and high wall helping to conceal it. Before they drove off the driver looked all around him, then briefly over the wall, sharp and quick, just to make sure no one was watching from any open field or from any boat that might have sailed onto that particular stretch of water. Quickly but quietly the car moved off.

When she came to, Bethan panicked, trying to move, to shout and scream under the gagging cloth; anything to attract attention. Her efforts nearly asphyxiated her, as she choked with barely enough oxygen to keep herself alive. Did she pass out? She didn't know, as it came in waves, in and out battling to keep from panicking again.

Bethan felt hot to the point of stifling, like a dog unable to pant; she couldn't breathe properly, and breathing only through her nose she had to resist the urge to gasp. She could hardly move her jaw or try to call for help and she had no idea how long she had lain there, bound, stiff and thirsty. Her head throbbed in the stale petrol-fumed air. She knew she was confined in a car's boot. She could move neither her arms nor legs and her body ached from the hours of being cramped and numb. She could blink but not much else, and when she tried to shift, she was only able to move her shoulders, inching like a caterpillar held by its thread as she struggled to touch the side of the metal, to bang it with her body. She'd struggled and given up trying to undo, or loosen any of the ropes, managing only to bruise her cheek in the attempt. Her jaw ached and the feeling of claustrophobia was smothering her like a heavy blanket.

Bound and gagged, she felt she was slowly being squeezed to death, as if a boa constrictor was squeezing her with each gasp, making it increasingly difficult to breathe. There was no movement, no distraction to help her fight her fear. She had no idea of time, of how long she had been cooped up. How long she'd been totally out before drifting back, in and out of consciousness. She had bouts of being really awake, lucid, petrified, fighting her confinement. It was to no avail, and she quickly succumbed to exhaustion, to the point of passing out. They were going to kill her or let her do it to herself in the boot of a stationary car in some place in the middle of nowhere.

She had no idea of how to gauge time, how to move seconds, minutes or hours forward with nothing to go on. No light, no sign of movement within her aluminum box. Was it so searingly hot? 'Dogs die in hot cars,' she kept repeating to herself, trying to keep calm and sane, fighting waves of hysteria. She had no way of knowing anything, as she drifted, light-headed, thankfully foggy until the agony of coming round, of being acutely alert to her plight, her throat razor dry. She was convinced she'd been abandoned to die slowly from lack of air and water. The realisation started a new wave of new panic, not as she'd thought when they had first grabbed her, to be murdered by some strangers, but just left to rot. She would prefer to face her torturers, at least to plead with them to know her fate.

She had no idea of time or place, or day or night. No giveaway, not even a sound coming from the outside, other than what she heard in her head. She strained every nerve to listen for something less than nothing. There was no fruition to her imaginings, no result other than to turn her mind, rapidly losing any sense, any reasoning. How quick to turn from sound to madness, going berserk in the space of what? A car boot of a few minutes, hours or was it days? It felt an eternity. Still no response, all her energy taken up for a single, muted, muffled thud that failed to signify anything as she lay wasted, her energy and mind sapped. She went from extremes, from being dozy, a half-wakening sleep in a twilight zone to one of severe agitation where her heart raced, and blood pounded in her ears. Had it turned cooler? Cold enough to make her shiver in shock. How long could she survive without going completely insane?

She tried to take control, to pull herself together, concentrating on one thing, the most important thing of her life, her daughter, Clare. To hold her face in her mind and not lose it, not to give in to the invisible dark foe. She forced herself to think of minutiae, Clare's each finger and toe at the time of her birth, tiny, pink and perfect. Bethan had a mother's instinct to fight like a tigress to protect its young, and she had to win this battle or die fighting it. Not to give in, but to keep breathing, to focus on staying calm. There was hope, and she knew Malcolm would be looking for her. Meticulously organising, and searching the whole of Ireland if necessary. She knew he'd be fastidious, pulling out all the stops to unravel her whereabouts. He had the capability of using whatever means to retrieve her. It would have made her cry for joy if she'd been able to see him combing the countryside for her, methodically forcing his way towards where she had been left abandoned. Waiting for him to find her.

27

Martha had crept from the house in the small hours carrying only what she'd carefully prepared and packed in the days preceding her planned departure. Only her elder sister Myfanwy knew her plans and had promised secrecy, at least until it was too late for her to be brought back.

With her were the precious sachets that her father used; herb derivative powders and pastes and liniments to keep the farm horses in work. After rumours of William Rhyd-y-meirch's injury in the field, Martha had waited, hoping for news, for some confirmation or for him to come home, until she could no longer bear the wait, packing only essentials and answering a call.

She was what the educated tough Derbyshire lady had been looking for; a young woman from the working classes who was used to hard work and would cope with the impossible conditions that lay ahead. But Martha had further criteria: she was a horse-doctor's daughter, with valuable medicinal knowledge as well as the need to find her betrothed, her William Morgan, and bring him back to Llanfeni. It was too late to wish he'd stayed, digging for a miserable existence in the lead mines of Dylife. Martha was set on a course to travel halfway round the world following a zealot. She was a ruthless, domineering woman on a mission. One of the few non-Catholics, Martha joined other nurses and nuns at Scutari just in time to witness the mass transport of the wounded following the disastrous battle of Balaklava. Irish Catholics made up over one third of the British army's rank and file, filtered with a scattering of any poor, able-bodied men.

She'd never imagined such chaos; nothing in her hard but sheltered life in remote Wales had prepared her for the atrocities she now faced. It was dreadfully overcrowded, and the dead and wounded lay together, sickness and disease intermingling on dirty mattresses that were crammed with injured men. The filthy floors compounded the problems, and outbreaks of cholera and diarrhoea hampered basic hygiene principles. The farm animals housed in Llanfeni lay in luxury compared to these soldiers. Martha worked until she dropped trying to help them in atrocious conditions where open wooden tubs served as hospital lavatories and disease spread like wildfire in the stifling heat.

Autumn brought further problems. With virtually no fresh running water, as most of the pipes had broken, there was no heating system in the makeshift hospital, but at least they had a roof over their heads, unlike many of the poor soldiers who'd been left to fend for themselves with woefully inadequate provisions. Their thin clothing left them drenched to the skin within minutes in the unremitting rain. In a belligerent, bloody-minded military cock-up run by rank and privilege, the foot soldiers had not been provided with any overcoats, blankets or even basic tents as they sat huddled like rats. Wet and freezing cold, they had nothing to protect themselves from the extreme weather that buffeted them across the Black Sea. They died in their thousands as their kit, tents, clothing and blankets were lost to the storms at sea as their boats were smashed by autumn storms. Hundreds died without firing a shot.

The ridiculously long hours were better than a stagnant waiting, and at least here, Martha was able to do something whilst she waited for news of her William. Her days were arduous, following instructions from the severe lady with the lamp, and the nurses did their best to comfort the wounded and dying that kept coming by ship from the Crimea. In reality there was little they could do: a sip of water, a kind ear and attempt to keep the hospital from becoming any filthier. Survivors of surgery, when available, were virtually nil and many of the nurses themselves became ill as they tended the men.

After several months of slog, Martha's piddlingly ineffectual reserve of potions and herbs had been used up and her spirit flagged as she realised the impossibility of ever finding her William Morgan. Debilitated by a bout of diarrhoea she was unable to rise from her bed for a week. A nun would come and check on her, to see that she had clean water to drink and to offer a prayer for her soul. Thanks in the main to her age and tough upbringing, Martha recovered sufficiently to return to the hospital and against advice she insisted on staying, still hoping of some news as she continued to question all who were able to speak as to whether they had come across or knew anything of William. It was always the same, nothing, but nothing was better. But at least it was easier to live with than the hope she'd had at the beginning.

It seemed years ago and not a few months since she'd got herself into a spiral of euphoria and misery, believing the snatches of information to be a genuine lead in her search for him. Only as months passed had the hopelessness of her task seeped in, slowly removing any sense of expectancy. Yet from habit she still asked. When one said he thought he knew someone with that name Martha just smiled in sympathetic disbelief. There was no leg and he would not see another day but he had a gentle lilting voice and soft blue eyes and he was some poor mother's son. He told her that he'd fought next to a Welshman, big and black-haired who sang in Welsh. He'd been felled, left calling out in a foreign language that only the Breton French understood, coming to him to carry him off. That was all he could say other than he himself came from Cork and wished for a priest to give him the last rites. Martha promised to fetch a nun. Before she could get back to him she was called to a desperate scene outside the hospital where a dishevelled man was heaped up against the wall. He was obviously in a bad way, weak and still losing blood from a wound in his side, and the two men who'd carried him were remonstrating with an orderly who refused their admittance. Nationalists were fighting under the Turkish army against the Russian infidels, but Martha was not interested in any religious priorities and would not leave him to die in such squalor. She led the way for the men to carry him onto a mattress in an outhouse that served as her bed. She did not understand a word they said but did her best to staunch the flow of blood with strips of cloth she tore from her bed, wrapping the last of her moss-filled liniment bandages that she'd saved for William. She gave him some water and left him, expecting him to die. The two men who'd brought him were Zouaves, men from the mountains renowned for their bravery, who waited outside, not willing to leave one of theirs on his own. For two days he wavered in no-man's-land, with Martha doing what she could after her long day in the hospital, before collapsing to sleep on the floor of her hut, listening to his laboured breathing, hoping her William was dead rather than going through this suffering.

They said little when they took him away, brandishing their *yataghans* and saluting. Perhaps he would be a lucky survivor.

How was she to know they'd witnessed the fight between an Irish volunteer, induced with a bounty, and a Welshman, over a silver cross taken from the neck of a dying Russian. The Welshman had challenged the thief who'd been about to snatch the trophy even before the Cossack had died, pretending to offer compassion, holding out an empty water bottle in order to steal. What spoils to take home! Silver treasures and precious stones plucked from the sick men of Europe. Using the superior mini-rifle taken from a dead Frenchman, the Irish soldier had picked off the Russians, helping himself to what he could find on their person. He got greedy and carelessly walked into musket range; luckily he was picked up by the French and transported to hospital, leaving the Welshman to the bayonet.

Martha would die without finding out what had happened to William. She would never get back to the hills of Wales, but she managed to trick them and get to Balaklava, dressing up as a *cantiniere*.[18] She'd trudged in the mud and pouring rain towards Sebastopol where she'd heard of his last whereabouts. Mud-filled trenches were littered with desperation, men praying for closure yet clinging to life on a futile final trip. From biting wind and rain to snow she trundled forward until her legs would no longer function, refusing to take the step her brain instructed. Her body, weak and nearly frozen to death failed, and exhausted, unable to move another step she stood in this desolate land, gently swaying like a sheaf of corn before she folded herself down to lie in the sludge, her face against the mud, dreaming of being united with him in their hills of home.

Would she die before he found her? Longing to be found she held on tenaciously for that moment of discovery. She knew Malcolm would not give up, but there was no sound, no indication that she'd even been missed. Bethan tried to rally, but in the absence

---

[18] female sutler

of any tangible hold, she slid back into despair, inching closer to death, letting herself believe she wouldn't survive, he wasn't coming and she'd never be found. She drifted again, giving in and letting go. Someone opened the boot in a rush of fresh air. Enough to catch the white of her eye before closing it to her silent scream. She felt movement, a car door being opened, a slight weight on the suspension, a door being clicked shut. The engine started up and the car was in motion, off again along an uneven surface as her body rolled against the sides of the car as it twisted its way, always in darkness.

28

'Malcolm it's me. Bethan's gone missing. Clare's come home on her own. No.' A pause. 'No one came to collect her from school. She walked. It was lucky I was in.'

'Or she would have just come home, Mother, and watched telly and had to wait for her her tea, that's all.'

'You seem to be taking it very coolly. How often does your wife go off without you knowing?'

'We don't live in the Gaza strip. She's probably just out and running late. Got held up somewhere. Is the car there?'

'Yes. And she left the house wide open. Anyone could have walked in. If you ask me, you need a word with your wife. It's very irresponsible, and to forget to pick up her own daughter.' But as she said the words she knew it sounded hollow and untrue to suggest Bethan was anything but a very good mother, and whatever else her daughter-in-law might be, she wasn't careless where Clare was concerned.

'Sorry, I can't hear you,' she said, raising her voice, calling 'Hello' into the empty receiver.

After a few minutes the phone rang again.

'I've stopped. There's a better signal here. Any sign of her yet?'

'No. She's vanished, disappeared!' Moira said whispering loudly so that Clare, who was watching children's telly, wouldn't hear.

'Don't be so alarmist! Have you checked with the lads to see if she's gone out riding or fishing with Pete? She's probably out walking.'

'It's the first thing I did. Of course I've checked. I might be old but I'm not losing my marbles, Malcolm.' Always quick to be defensive. Keep your hair on woman.

'Where's Clare now?'

'In front of the box. How long will you be? Where are you?'

'On the way home, about another twenty minutes. I called in with Dermot as I was passing his place, to see that two-year filly he was going on about.'

'Should I ring the Garda?'

'For heaven's sake mother, she's gone a couple of hours and you want the alert the whole of Ireland. You're over-reacting.'

'It may be much more than a couple of hours, Malcolm. We don't know do we? For all I know she may have been gone all day – I haven't seen her – but if you're not worried then why should I be? She's your wife!'

'Of course I'm concerned; I'm just not jumping to any conclusions. Wait until I get home. I'll come as fast as I can.'

He put the phone down before she could tell him to drive carefully, a phrase she often used. He felt it as a deliberate reminder.

She heard the sound of gravel being churned as he sped up. His slamming of a car door and brisk footsteps to the house. Before she could get there Clare had already run out to greet him and hug Big.

'Hello Daddy. Mummy's not here. I've had tea with Granny.'

'And you've been a good girl and very grown up and sensible to walk home from school on your own?'

She nodded. 'Where's Mam gone?'

'Oh, she's probably shopping, or gone for a long walk and forgotten the time. Don't you fret my little angel, she'll be home soon. I want a word with Granny. Can you give Big his supper? Don't give him too much, though.'

Having successfully prevented Clare from hearing their conversation, he quickly turned to his mother for information.

'Any news?' he asked quickly, more urgently, lowering his voice just in case Clare came skipping back down the corridor.

'Nothing. None of the stable lads have seen her since this morning when she went out along on the coast road.'

'On foot? Alone?'

'Of course she was alone, Malcolm. Who does she ever walk with?'

'And you've checked the boats?'

'Liam said his Da was out early morning but his boat was back on its mooring when I looked for it.'

'When was that?'

'Teatime. When Clare turned up on her own. You don't think something's happened to her?'

'I don't know what to think.' His face was no longer relaxed as he moved across towards the door.

'Where are you going now? You've only just come home. Shouldn't you alert the authorities?'

'As soon as I've checked upstairs.'

'She wasn't planning to leave you?'

'No. I'm sure she wasn't.'

'She'd never leave Clare behind. It doesn't make sense.' Malcolm leapt up the stairs, two at a time, up onto the landing, striding into their bedroom. From below, his mother could hear him rummaging. She listened to the opening and shutting of drawers, of his banging things down before coming down.

'Bag, mobile everything's here. Nothing's gone but herself and the clothes she was wearing.'

He tried to weigh it all up to decide the right course of action. 'If something has happened, and I can't think what, someone must know, Mother. I don't want the police involved. Because if something nasty's happened, it could put Beth's safety in jeopardy. You understand what I'm saying? Let me make a few more phone calls, first, and then if nothing we'll have to get the police involved.'

'Do you think something bad's happened to her, Malcolm?'

'Well she's not here, and you said yourself it isn't like her. Look how many times she rang home when she was in Dublin for one night. If you want to know, I'm worried sick.'

The scrape of the scullery door notified them of Clare's return, the child and dog pattering back along the flagstones. 'Keep Clare with you, I'll be in the car to make a few phone calls. If the house phone rings, don't pick it up. Come and get me.'

How to tell a four year old her mother's disappeared, leaving no trace, no clue of where she might be? Involuntary or voluntary, with no body, no scene of tragedy or accident. Nothing that would explain it and help them come to terms with the fact, if she was indeed dead, as Moira now feared. How would she be able to fill a mother's gap or tell the family in Wales she'd vanished?

But she was jumping the gun, letting her thoughts run wild, typical Celt, imagining the worst. She just didn't want her daughter-in-law to become one of the haunted faces portrayed briefly on television in and out in a surge of public pity following the aftermath of a personal atrocity, clutching a cherished worn photo of a face, already grown old, still fresh in their useless hope and sad eyes. Moira had already lost her beloved son.

They came to a sudden stop and for a moment Bethan thought she was going to be left in some sick game without even having the boot opened. Silence, then to her relief she felt movement within the car and a click that pre-empted that rush of fresh air, releasing the rankness of her prison: urine, sweat, her fear. She blinked, her eyes refusing to focus on the shadowed forms that loomed above her, their shapes muffled in with the darkness. She heard a rustle of outdoor clothing as one of the figures bent, his boot catching a bit of the car's bumper. 'Sh.' Another voice in the dark. Of course they'd have been stupid not to have chosen to open the boot at night to do their sort of work. Before she died, somehow Bethan had to let her family know how much she loved them To leave something behind, a clue or token that would comfort. Better to die under the rapist's or torturer's hands, leaving her body disregarded, decomposing to be found, rather than suffocate slowly in her metal grave, in a silence never to be discovered.

No innocent would be out in such a place with no movement; no light or shape other than dark. Think, think, catch a clue as to where she was or who they were. Wake up dull, slow brain for any scrap, any small thing that might aid the police later.

The open boot helped her breathe regularly, and the space she could not see smelt open. She sensed they were out in the country. No buildings, only a wall perhaps or just a darker deep running away in charcoal cloud. Was it water, a river or the sea she could hear? A dream wafting on the *bwlch* with her great-uncle, holding his cob's reins as he threw the brick-like shapes of the dried peat into the back of the tumbrel. A treat in September, a day off school to help him, the pitiful cry of a young buzzard calling above them. She suddenly realised what the smell was. They were about to bury her in a peat bog.

'Say anything, and I'll kill you.' A man's voice broke from the darkness as arms roughly held her torso against the rim of the open boot. He hauled her into an upright position. The other man, and yes she was sure they were two men, held onto her head, pulling the tape, twine and cloth from her mouth. She mouthed pathetically, unable to voice any word. Clumsily he poured liquid into her parched mouth which caused her to cough, unable to swallow.

'Shut up. Don't gulp. You'll get no more.' Then he tipped a little, more gently so she was able to swallow, a mouthful at a time. 'That's enough for now. Be quiet or he'll give you another needle.' Did she catch a hint of smile, a flash of gold in a tooth, as he jerked her head back, holding her firmly with his leather gloves as he sealed her mouth over? They pushed her stiff body, lifting her legs up and across so she lay on the other side. He pulled the boot lid down, that fatal small sound, a click engaging in metal, solid and secure that entombed her. Then the vibration as the engine started up and the feel of tyre on soil. A transition to road, of speeding up and driving straight. Somewhere the car stopped, doors opening closing, automatic lock then nothing. She'd been left, and as the car cooled she started to shiver.

'For the mother of God, Malcolm, will you ring the Garda? It's after two in the morning. We've heard nothing! If you won't, I will.'

'No, Mam, you could put her life in danger. Don't you see, if she's in some sort of trouble, it won't help. They'll only force things. It could end up killing Beth. I'll do it my way. I've got the boys onto it and they've only been gone a few hours. We still can't be sure she hasn't just gone off.'

'We both know that's a load of rubbish. I owe it to Clare, and I can't just sit here and do nothing. You've rung her family?'

'No.'

'Why not? You have to let them know!'

'What do I tell them? The Garda's bad enough without

involving the British police. I'm hoping one of my contacts will ring with news any time now. Even if I have to sit up all night. So why don't you go back to bed? I promise I'll come and get you the moment I hear anything. If I don't hear anything by then I'll ring the authorities.'

'You give me your word, Malcolm, to come and get me just as soon—'

'I promise.'

Reluctantly she left him standing looking out into the darkness, the curtains undrawn as if expecting a light from the beach or sea or perhaps a car's beam. His face was taut, his eyebrows drawn in, his whole body held in tense anticipation as if about to spark. Moira felt an unexpected tenderness for him, wanting to pull him into her arms, to tell him everything would be all right, that it wasn't his fault. She'd forgiven him.

He didn't go to bed but stayed up all night, sitting in his father's armchair, the leather arms crudely patched where they'd been worn through from constant rubbing of hands. He didn't sleep but sat waiting, watching as the dawn broke. He hadn't eaten anything, whisky and coffee and constant cigarettes his night-time companions. He felt the vibration before the tone that he'd been waiting for. Grabbing the mobile from his pocket he pressed the key as he stood up, going to the window for the best signal. He listened intently.

'How much?' He raised his eyebrows as he listened to the amount of money that was being demanded.

'Where? I need time to raise that. I must speak to her. You have to guarantee she is unharmed.' There was a pause then her voice, very quiet, just audible but unmistakably hers. He mustn't break down, or threaten her abductors. He had to stay in the present, think only for the moment to secure her safe release, whatever it would take. Then there would be time to sort the bastards out. 'Do whatever they say, Beth,' he said to her, trying to sound resolute and positive down the tentative phone link. 'I'll sort it all out—'

He caught her question.

'Yes, Clare's fine. Don't you worry, we'll have you home, I promise you my darling. I love you, my princess.' The phone was cut dead and he knew dialling a callback would be futile, they would have fixed the number: withheld or unknown. He checked for any texts or any other messages before slipping it back into his pocket and climbing the stairs to the spare bedroom to wake his mother. At least he had something concrete to tell her, that she hadn't done a runner. He had a ransom to find, crazy money, but she was alive, distant, distressed but alive, he'd spoken to her.

She held onto his voice. Her powers of reasoning like an electric short circuit, misfiring so she couldn't reason. Soosh. A sound, a movement, human, animal or was it the rustle of a tree? A gust of wind and the beginning of rain, a patter of mice on the bonnet. What comfort until it persisted, heavy and unrelenting on the top of her tin roof? Was this worse than her nothing? The hammering unrelenting rain, making her think she'd drown. She hardly noticed the car's movement anymore, that this time it was a different pattern, and when it stopped the two men were less careful, more predatory with her. They plucked her out like a leftover carcass, slamming the car door as she was lifted into the light. Wearing balaclavas and a stocking over their faces, one undid her mouth gag, offered her some water which she couldn't take, before the other untied her ropes, releasing her limbs that flopped loosely, unhinged. How far they carried her she didn't know, barely conscious as she was. No word was spoken, nothing exchanged. They put her down and quickly walked away. A car started up, the sound quickly fading.

She lay where she'd been dumped, incapable of standing, hardly capable of thinking, of drawing such fresh, sharp air that made her lungs hurt raw like breathing in an icy wind. Light-headed and giddy she tried to focus, to feel and touch solid ground, a floor of a building. Then she drifted away again, not realising she'd been dumped in a shack. It had wooden slatted walls and a corrugated roof with a small window and two wooden doors that closed in the middle with a chain and padlock.

It took time to adjust and what she saw and felt was real and not an hallucination. Like a pit pony, she'd come into the light, stumbling, as her eyes slowly recovered and were able to absorb daylight. She still had no idea of time or place, still lying where they'd propped her, slumped against the wall, blinking like some cold lizard, unable to gather the data until the sun warmed its body to make it function, or have a sense of anything. She did think she was alive, that where she was, was real, but she couldn't be sure. Her hands and eyes and brain had lied before. She lay resting, letting nature take over, tenaciously and persistently breathing in and out.

They found her at last, peering through a crack between the locked doors. Wrenching the flimsy frame, the rotting wood came away easily with a little force so that he almost fell onto her body, which was still curled where it had been left. Then there was a stretcher, blankets, and a lifting, a sense of being carried, carted off on another journey. No sirens or blue lights and this time the face that leaned over her was masked in white. But it wasn't dark and someone had wrapped her up in an aluminum foil blanket. A paramedic put another needle into her arm, staying next to her as they travelled, a hand touching hers to reassure and watch her pulse, to make sure she stayed with them.

29

It had taken him much longer than he'd anticipated, finally arranging a suitable time, having dithered and prevaricated before choosing a Saturday. Nesta and Rhian had taken an early train for a day's shopping in the city, so he had the place virtually to himself. He wanted his farm to make a good impression on Penny and hadn't made up his mind whether to introduce her to his mother and Uncle Mervyn.

Richard was excited by the thought of her coming, and kept looking at his watch, unable to settle to any job even though she wouldn't come before eleven. He listened for the sound of the traffic on the main road, waiting to hear a vehicle gearing down and turn into his lane.

Now that the day was here, he worried his farm would not live up to expectations. He looked around with a critical eye, trying to envisage it as Penny would see it. Hastily he'd tried to remove anything that was obviously his wife's, removing her photograph and knick-knacks in the kitchen. It was difficult when he chose to spend his nights in the cottage.

He searched for some nicer cups than the everyday mugs that Nesta put in front of him. The kitchen was drab, with no warmth. Would she judge him by his wife's poor taste? She already knew he and Nesta weren't happy, not pulling as one, in the ill-fitting yoke that was their union. He fidgeted, pulling the kettle off the stove, then changed again, taking off his shoes and jacket and back into his workman clothes. He'd feel better if he met her outside, in the yard where he felt more at home.

As so often in farming, in the event it was an animal who came to his aid, dictating the terms of his tryst, by falling sick an hour before she was due to arrive. So when she did come, she found him bent down attending to the calf. Taff came up to her, smelling her leg, putting his nose to her crotch and wagging his tail.

'Hello.' Her greeting made him start; he was unable to get up with his hands full of calf, smelling of milk and scour. He couldn't kiss her as he had planned to, not like this, but Penny didn't seem troubled, bending down to the sick calf.

'Can I do something to help?'

'I'm sorry, I hadn't planned to meet you smelling of calf crap!' he smiled apologetically. 'I need to get this solution down her. You couldn't keep her head up while I just try to get this tube in?' She helped the calf's head up as Richard forced the plastic tube into its mouth, pushing the length down into the animal's stomach.

'Why the lump on the tube?' she asked, watching him insert what seemed an awful lot of pipe down such a small animal, which the calf did its utmost to resist.

'The lump stops me pushing the tube accidentally into her lungs. This way as long as I'm careful, it can only go down into the stomach.' Attached to the other end of the tube was a sealed bag full of a warm pink fluid which Richard held above the calf. With his free hand he slid the clip, releasing the fluid down the tube.

'This is not how I'd envisaged it. You on your hand and knees and me smelling of—' he said sniffing his hands.

'And I thought you'd stage-managed it all for my benefit. Knowing I'm a soft touch for baby animals.'

'That's all right then, *cariad*.' His endearment slipped out, like a cab driver or brickie saying 'darling'. Only he meant it.

The pear-shaped face and big oval ears drooping made the calf look pathetically appealing. 'Is it serious? She seems very miserable, poor thing.'

'Scour. It dehydrates them very quickly. At this age they can go down very rapidly. One minute they're fine, you turn your back for a second and, well, you can see she's feeling very sorry for herself, and without fluid she could easily die. She might anyhow.' A typical pessimistic farmer.

'Like kids with diarrhoea. Gastroenteritis?'

'Exactly. Keep her off the milk and in here where it's out of the sun and hopefully she should feel better by this evening. I'll need to keep an eye on her, so I hope you don't mind being stuck on the farm for the day? Unless I ask my uncle.'

'No, I've been looking forward to it.'

'Good. We'd better check that none of the others are showing signs. It's a bugger once it's in the herd. It's very contagious.'

He needn't have worried. Later, having had a wash and coffee, they went together through his fields hand in hand, close and comfortable in each other's company. He showed her his herd of Friesians, the young stock and the few cobs he kept. Rather than sit indoors on such a sunny day, he should have thought of a picnic instead of bringing her back to the gloomy kitchen, where he had some cold ham ready. As he got the prepared food out, he was very conscious it wasn't good enough for her and wished he'd taken her out for a meal instead. Looking at the food she teased him about his lack of culinary skills, and from the bag she'd brought she produced a bottle of wine to go with his cheese, instead of the tea he would have made. It was very unWelsh, wine and at lunch time too. Not used to it, he found the drink loosened him. They had a couple of hours before he'd have to get the cows in. He'd have liked to take her to bed but before he put words to his thoughts, Penny suggested a stroll around his farm.

There were no walkers on the cliff path as they sauntered along, stopping to look across Cardigan Bay. The sea winked in refracted light, as roll on roll of wave gurgled around rocks. In the sweep of coast near to the point, she stopped again to take in the three stacks of granite in water, where swarms of white, querulous sea birds had collected. Some in flight, to monitor or feed, calling out obstreperously.

'It's so beautiful, Rich. I had no idea you lived quite so close to the sea.'

'Careful, it's sheer there,' he said, anxious that she should stand further back from the edge.

'No wonder you don't go on holiday, when you've got your own private cove! Can you get down there to the beach?' She asked him pointing. 'Do you swim?'

'Not here, but round the point there's a steepish path; it's OK so long as you're careful, and at low tide you can walk over the rocks to the beach. We used to swim here as kids. But I haven't for years. My wife thinks the water's polluted and prefers the safe chlorine of the local swimming pool, and as for my daughter, well, Rhian isn't into sports.'

'It looks so inviting.'

'I bet it's cold though.'

'It does look deep from here.' She peered down.

'Please don't go so close, you're making me jumpy.'

'You've no head for heights?'

'I lost my father here.'

'Oh, I'm sorry, Richard. Did he drown?'

The conversation's light mood changed and he had to answer her.

'We think he died before he hit the water. He lost control of the tractor; he was taking a silly risk, spreading a load of slag in the rain. He was in a hurry to be home for Beth's birthday party.'

'How awful!' Penny exclaimed, resisting her urge to quiz him.

'I shall never forget the day. Beth was six and Dad had bought her a Welsh Mountain pony. She was over the moon but he made her promise to wait until he got home for tea so that he could take her and her school friends out on it for the first time,' he explained. 'Mam's always been hopeless with horses. No one knows exactly what happened, only I remember the skid marks running down across that field over there.' He pointed across to a wide sloping field where cattle were grazing. 'Where the cattle are. I know it doesn't look that steep from here, but with a heavy load and rain it's a dangerous business.' She nodded, not really understanding the tractor mechanics. 'In Dad's day it was easier to tip them up, tractors weren't so safe. But you can still kill yourself on one today.'

'It must have been appalling for you all. How old were you Richard?'

'Sixteen. My dad was a very stubborn person. He'd take a risk rather than admit defeat. For years later you could see where he slid, like a scar down the field. He took the risk and lost everything. All for what? For his pride.'

'I'm sorry, Richard. I shouldn't have asked you to bring me here.'

'Well, now you know my murky past.'

'None of it was your fault.'

'I suppose not. But his death changed all our lives.'

'I couldn't see you not farming.'

'What! I'm afraid I'm very predictable, dull and boring.'

'I didn't mean it like that, Rich. And there's nothing wrong in being solid, dependable.

'I'll take that as a compliment.'

'It is a beautiful place, though,' she said, looking out across the stretch of water and cliff.

'I'm glad you like it. Despite everything, it's always been one of our favourite places and one of the first things Beth did when she was last over from Ireland was to come straight down here. It helps, you know.'

'I'd like to have met your sister.'

'If she had stayed for longer I would have tried to arrange it, but her visit was a mad dash and anyhow it might have been a bit awkward, you know, the timing and everything.'

'Is she like you?'

'The opposite. Very bubbly, pretty and easy-going. Everyone likes her. She reminds me of you. She's very, oh, what's the word I'm looking for, confident. Outward-going.'

'Well, I'm flattered. So why did she have to rush back?'

'Her little girl was sick – nothing serious but she couldn't stay on. I was bitterly disappointed. We rowed and we never do. But I felt she let Mam down.'

'She'll come again; it's no big deal from Ireland. You were young to have all that responsibility on your shoulders.'

'There was Mam and Beth as well. But it was a bad time in my life and looking back I don't know how we managed, really. I remember being angry and difficult, especially with my mam.'

'You were still a child, it's understandable,' she said, thinking of her eldest daughter who was being difficult since the split.

'Do you have any siblings?' he asked, wanting to change the topic.

'Only a sister, who lives in Australia.'

He gave her a shy 'silly old me' sort of smile, which made her want to hug him. She felt awkward as she took his hand, squeezing it, leaning into him to be held before they kissed. They'd have to start for home.

'It's good to be close,' she said, thinking of her family.

'I hardly see them any more. Beth's in Ireland and Simon's travelling around the world.'

'I didn't know you had another brother. Is he in agriculture?'

'Farming? No, never! He's the youngest and an opera singer. He has a busy lifestyle jet-setting all over the place.'

'Lucky him.'

'He's not like me. He has a huge booming voice; he's much taller, and broader and he's got masses of curly hair!' Richard pulled his farmer's cap up and down on his head, and for no reason, he burst into song:

'Os hoffech wybod sut
Mae dyn fel fi yn byw,
Mi ddysgais gan fy nhad
Grefft gyntaf dynol ryw ...
Rwy'n gorwedd efo'r hwyr
Ac yn codi efo'r wawr,
I ddilyn yr og ar ochr y glog
A chanlyn yr arad goch
Ar ben y mynydd mawr.'

'You're full of surprises, Rich. I never knew you could sing! I don't know what it was about but I've never been serenaded so beautifully before, and in Welsh!'

'A simple life, working the land, ploughing.'

'It sounded very romantic, thank you, Richard. I'll treasure the memory.' He was chuffed that she'd praised his singing and was inexpressively happy as they made their way back along the cliff path. As they passed the cottage Yr Efail, he commented that it was were Mervyn had been raised, and from the path he pointed over to what had been Mair's herb garden, explaining to Penny that it was where they made up the horse medicines in the old days, that Mair's father, Mervyn's grandfather, had been a renowned horse doctor and local farrier. Old traits passed down lived for longer in small rural communities where families moved less. He realised he'd talked a lot, perhaps too much. He undoubtedly wanted to share his whole life with her. By sharing his past it was easier to share his future.

'Like that man we met at the show?' she said after a pause.

He looked blank.

'You know, he said he was your neighbour. He came up to our stall with that professor?'

'Oh, him. Tegwyn. He's not like Mervyn. He's very different. He used to be pretty wild.'

'You don't like him?'

Richard shrugged. 'I think you're missing my point,' said Penny. 'What I meant was, the doctor he was with. Alternative medicine, like your blacksmith family.'

'Oh, I see. Yes, then more like him.'

'It has its followers and it's a growing market. Look at your prince. Royal approval. We could use that to our benefit. Perhaps we should include fresh herbs with the business. The obvious ones like rosemary for lamb, sage for sage and onion stuffing. Parsley and thyme are easy enough and you could add things like chives and garlic to your cheeses. I bet it would be popular. Then there's mustard, tarragon, marjoram. The list is endless, and lots of them have beneficial properties as well.'

'Would it be profitable?'

'It's something to think about. Now, where are all these cows you're so proud of? Remember, I only said I'd come today on condition you'd let me help with the afternoon milking!'

He called them home as he always had from force of habit rather than necessity as they had already collected and stood by the gate, avoiding the live strand of wire. They plodded down the lane after him, with Penny left to wait for the last few stragglers and close the gate, enjoying the sight of a herd of his cows swinging boney-hipped down the lane. She hadn't realised their feet were so sensitive as they carefully picked their way over the uneven stone, their piebald hides shining as they swished at flies. They waited their turn, with an odd toss of a head, tongue stretching out to clean each nostril as they took measure of her; a burp, ear flick, teeth slowly chewing round in a semi-circle under a nose glistening with moisture.

Richard watched out for her, hoping she was enjoying being in the middle of them, seeming to want to help. She washed their udders before he helped her put the claws on, all to the quiet rhythmic sound of milking. Man's sustenance in that ancient pish-pish of milking, not so far removed from the nomads with their camel, cow, goat and sheep; hefted like Richard was to an age-old song of land and toil.

She was unlike his wife, helping him milk with her hair tied back, calf and grass stains on her jeans, relaxed and laughing, immersed in the hum of it all, the smell of sweet cow and warm milk, her face wreathed in smiles. With a sense of achievement, she successfully managed to take off the claws as the cow raised a back leg, eager to leave now that her udder was empty, and make way for the next cow. The warm milk went through the cooler, to fill the stainless steel tank.

Now that they had mentioned their respective families, Richard knew he would have to introduce her to his at some stage, though he didn't want to. Their relationship, which had up to now been private was bound to change, but if their business venture was to work, which he desperately wanted it to, they would have to face the point when partners and children would have to meet.

He could handle the ex-partner, who wasn't interested anyway since he'd left her; it was Penny's daughters as well as his own that caused him concern. At least her daughters were away at a private school, and if the photos he'd seen were anything to go by they seemed happy, well-adjusted youngsters. How could he explain his own offspring? Rude when not monosyllabic, covered in body piercing and tattoos, dressed in black or, on a good day, in camouflage. Only home to change before heading out to no idea where. 'Out,' was the only answer he'd get as she slammed a door. She didn't just smoke; he was pretty sure she experimented with drugs with the yobs, as he referred to the set she chose to hang out with. His attempt to talk, to engage belatedly, inevitably ended in a row, topped off with an obscenity as she stomped out, banging a door as she went. Richard was ashamed not only of her, but how she'd got to the state she had.

Some, if not all the blame had to fall on him as her father, for not preventing it, or at least when he saw her slipping, putting a stop to her decline. But he'd failed, fighting with his wife instead, blaming Nesta for encouraging her. He'd taken refuge on his farm, been weak and he had let her loose as if he hadn't cared.

30

Malcolm had done things his own way, using his own set of contacts, with enough men on the ground in the know who understood the sort of language needed. The same sort of people who knew that he had plenty of money, that he would be able to raise the cash. He'd paid up on their terms, put the ransom in a bag and got his wife back alive. The bag had been left in a bin next to a betting shop. There'd been instructions there on how to find her, not so far away. He'd raced through the countryside skirting the wild wet areas, with the hills watching his back like some hooded keepers. Like a madman, he sped on uncaring of the small roads, watching for an iconic Irish landmark, a semi-derelict shack still standing next to a heap of turned turf drying in the sun. He found her close to the sea, where they'd said he would, so help them. Her eyes were closed and he'd fallen to his knees, overcome and frantic now he actually had her, sobbing relief as he lifted her into his arms, stroking her hair, like some injured roadkill animal that twitched, eyes glazed to die.

Minutes passed before he could take it all in and ring for an ambulance. He felt her wrist for a pulse as he leant over her, inspecting her face and gently feeling her for injury. He needed to think straight, to keep his cool and not panic. He ran back to his car to pick up a blanket and the thermos flask he'd brought, a bar of chocolate, and hip flask of whisky. She hadn't moved, not a flicker, and he couldn't take his eyes from her face, desperate for her to wake up, to respond to his voice. What was wrong with her? Was she unconscious? He didn't know, only he couldn't see any bleeding or wound or blow to her head that would make her so lifeless. There was no blood on her clothing, not even a bump or bruising other than on her cheeks and mouth, and on her wrists. The bastards had obviously tied and gagged her. Then it dawned on him she'd been drugged and was still under sedation. With a huge sense of relief Malcolm cradled her gently, caressing her skin, kissing her as she lay in his arms. He whispered in her ear, 'My darling Beth. I've found you. Sweet Jesus.' He sat with her, crying quietly, waiting for the sound of a vehicle. 'Hold on my sweetest, just a little longer, the ambulance is coming, it's on its way. You're safe now, my little one. I'm here.'

They'd been at her bedside, keeping vigil, waiting. Letting her sleep would be the best cure, until she was strong enough to tell them something, anything that might help him to catch her abductors. Bethan could remember very little, and although the medics had stabilised her, her condition remained poor. She was weak, and still badly disoriented and Clare could see her mother for only a minute. Malcolm saw her lips stretch slightly at the sound of her daughter's voice, her eyes still half-closed, glazed over. He had been shocked to find her so debilitated, that her abduction had caused such damage. But he was not as shocked as his mother, who was appalled at Bethan's transformation, that four days had reduced Bethan to such a deteriorated state, and Moira feared for her life.

It had been the best part of a week since he'd found her locked up in a shack and still they had little or no detail to go on, and now that the Garda were involved Moira had been made to feel that they, in some way were to blame for not alerting them earlier. Secretly she agreed with them that her son had been wrong not to call them straight away, even though his methods had found her alive. The police had quizzed her like a suspect because, thanks to Malcolm's recondite behaviour, she had had to be unforthcoming. Why had the O'Connor family waited so long? Waited until Mrs Malcolm O'Connor had ended up in hospital before the family contacted the authorities? It wasn't the natural thing to have done and it looked like a family very unconcerned of Bethan's whereabouts. Malcolm was less than forthcoming, and his lack of faith in them, or anyone in authority had kept him from contacting the police. In the event he'd been proved right and the only way to have got Bethan back in one piece had relied on swift secret action, and money.

She came back to them by degrees, a dried sponge opening to drops of water, a little at a time. She saw enough to recognise his face, to hear his voice as he bent down to kiss her. She could speak, her voice a whisper to his questions, gently probing about what had happened. She could remember snippets, half-caught flashes like shards of glass that she couldn't piece together to make any sense. To think exhausted her, and she was content to close her eyes and drift, float caught up in a neap tide that held her so she could not move, neither back to her past life of wife, mother, nor forward. Mother? Was she a mother or a mother's daughter? She couldn't recall but from somewhere within she understood that low primeval ache deep down that had un-netted her baby, slipping away from its own safe waters to a surface, drugged and gasping in her own poisoned juices, forcing it to let go of its link, breaking away from the capture of its premature birth.

He'd no idea that she'd been pregnant when the doctors told him she'd lost it. She'd been carrying for four months before the loss and she would need a blood transfusion, special care and a great deal of rest. She was in a delicate, perilous state, both physically and mentally, after all the trauma she'd endured. Already tottering, the realisation of having lost the baby could be enough to send her over the edge.

'How long had she been pregnant?' he asked again, still unbelieving.

'About sixteen, perhaps eighteen weeks. I'm sorry.'

Malcolm was at a loss, not as the doctor thought, about the miscarriage, but that he hadn't known. He was tempted to have the foetus retrieved, to check its DNA. He wondered if it were possible and if he could ask the question, and query it. The doctor smiled sympathetically, touching him on the shoulder as he prepared to leave the room.

'I don't see why, after your wife's had the time she'll need to get over this, you shouldn't have more children. It's almost certain that the trauma and the drugs that were used to sedate her were the cause of her miscarriage. Your wife has been through a terrible ordeal and when she gets home, she'll need to be very quiet.'

Why hadn't she told him she was expecting another child? He recalled their conversation of that night when they'd had fresh mackerel, and that she had some good news for him. Only he hadn't waited to hear; he'd been so angry with her that he'd stormed off. Had that been the time she would have told him she was pregnant and that's why she'd gone to Dublin? To find out he was going to be a father again? Only his petulance had kept him from the knowledge. Would it have made any difference? He asked himself this question over and over. Was it his, definitely? Would he, by knowing, have had any influence on any of the actions she had subsequently taken that would have prevented the kidnap? How could he answer any of it? How by knowing, would it have stopped anything? That by some reason she would not have been on that road on her own at that given time and he perhaps not away from her, in Cork, talking deals and horses. If not then, they would have seized another opportunity to snatch her.

He could not take care of her every second, or wrap her up in cotton wool. He could not detain her in her own home. Yet all this because she hadn't told him. He felt inexplicably angry with her for her secrecy. Underneath his show of care and concern, he was silently livid with her for her incompetence, her clumsy handling of the motherhood of his child, the son they told him he'd now lost.

31

The work wasn't quite what Tegwyn had anticipated it would be, and although his status had been significantly raised, he still gathered moss at the weekends with Dic and Frank, although he was now their boss. Dic and Frank continued to work at their own pace and didn't pay much attention to Tegwyn. It was Dr Arthur Trelawny who specified the sort of moss he preferred, leaving the rest to Tegwyn. He delivered bags of the partially dried stuff to the new business unit set-up with the help of the Welsh Development Agency in a prestigious business park south of Llanfeni. For all their teasing, Tegwyn Jones, for the first time in his forty-eight-year life, felt more gilt-edged. With the title of project manager came a better pay packet, far more than what he used to get for selling indirectly where the dealer had the best cut.

Tegwyn started each day with a clean shirt and jacket, looking more the part as Arthur showed him round the unit and the processes, a drying machine and automated conveyor belt that handled all the moss until sorted. When it was cleansed and sterile it was packed up and sent off to the elastoplast manufacturers to be implanted into the fabric that would lie directly on the wound. He showed him a box containing the finished product and Tegwyn was a bit disappointed not to see the strands of moss he'd collected across the lint.

'Of course it's indiscernible to the naked eye; the colour would put people off – you know what they are these days. But it's there all the same. Take a box, try them out on your colleagues. See if they work any quicker. They're not for re-sale,' he added. 'We're still at the trial stage. All the marketing and the brand name to come. Have a think – what would you call it?'

'My name on the box?'

'If you come up with something good enough I don't see why not, Tegwyn. After all, you are the project manager; you're the one gathering the raw material.'

His idea on a box that could become a household name. How impressive would that be? He played with names in his head: Jones the moss, moss plast, moss mend, etc, as he drove back towards the town, feeling things were very much on the up.

'I'll be moving away once the summer term's over.'

They had hardly spoken for weeks. Richard was aware of her presence, her car leaving each morning for work with Rhian sitting in the passenger side. She'd be back at four-thirty after he'd finished the milking; there'd be a quick curt exchange, but other than that they barely said a word. If he made an extra effort to catch them between car and house, he might get a gesture, a 'Hi, Dad', from his daughter before the inevitable shrug, the unspoken 'whatever' to anything he asked. He'd no idea of her prospects, of whether she would get any of her GCSEs. He wasn't a good parent like Penny, who took such an active interest in everything her girls were doing at school.

Coming into the room, he was taken off guard, not expecting anyone to be there at that time. His wife surprised him, standing there against the light and for a split second he thought it might have been someone else.

'Don't worry, I haven't come back, and what I've got to say won't take long.'

'Oh, it's you.' His voice made his disappointment plain. 'So what do you want?'

'I've accepted another post, so I'll be moving down to Swansea earlier than I thought.'

He shrugged, 'Oh.'

'Well, if that's all you want to say, fine. It's settled anyhow; I've given in my notice at Llanfeni and we'll be leaving in July.'

'Is that what Rhian wants?'

'We've been through this, Richard, you were there when we discussed it with her, remember? Of course it's what she wants. Ask her if you don't believe me.'

'I might just do that, without you adding your penny's worth.'

'She won't change her mind. You won't persuade her.' She paused, unable to resist adding, 'I mean what have you ever had to offer her here? Except cowshit and boredom. Nothing else. I want a divorce.'

'Don't let me stand in your way.'

'And I want it now.'

Now seemed so sudden, so final, even though he'd expected some sort of ultimatum for months. Divorce would be the end. It would mean money, a final settlement and it was her way of telling him what to expect, that he needed to get his act together and prepare for the sting in the tail. He'd have to pay her what she was entitled to, for the years of being his wife on the farm, and raising their daughter. Now that she was jumping ship.

'Now! You never were farmer's wife material and you only came back here because you failed to make it down in Cardiff. So, this is really it. What a surprise!'

'I didn't expect any thanks from you. All the years I've wasted in this dump. You ought to take a look at yourself. You're pathetic in your filthy overalls. I've had it up to here.' She raised her hand over her head before turning away to leave.

'As well as being a lousy wife, you're also a very second-rate pianist. It's the only reason you came back to Llanfeni, and I was stupid enough to have you. Because no one else would,' he added.

'You're just upping the ante. You've always been a fool Richard, and I've had enough of you. You'll be hearing from my solicitors.'

'Oh, I will, will I? No doubt for my money.'

'My share, actually.'

'Your share! What do you mean, your share? You never lifted a finger here other than to curdle the milk. I don't think you have ever helped once on the farm, have you? Not once, you bitch! I don't think you even have a pair of wellingtons, do you? No! All you ever did was fuck my brother and criticise me. Having mucked up your own life you're about to wreck Rhian's. Take my money and run!'

She pushed past him.

'Pity I ever asked you. I should have left you rot down in Cardiff.'

'Go to hell, Richard.'

'I bet you've already got a figure in mind, you conniving *hen hwch*.[19] '

It wasn't going well, and losing his temper served only to inflame his wife, goading her to go for the most she could squeeze out of him. He'd never hit her, never raised his fist, yet she felt his fury and it was only from the safety of the outside, in view of the cottage that she turned back to taunt him further.

'You can always ask your new business partner for a loan. I hear she's got a bit to spare.'

'Go jump.'

'You've always been as awkward and stubborn as a mule. I'm not going to waste any more of my time. You carry on, go on, rant on in this lousy yard of yours. Your crummy little farm. Talk to the cows – they'll be better at listening.' Spittle formed at the side of her mouth.

---

[19] old sow

'And more attractive!'

'There's a letter in the post with my terms.'

'Terms!'

She had a nerve. His anger welled up as he heard the engine start up and watched Nesta drive off through his yard. She deliberately left the gate open, forcing him to run to cut the cows off before they went up the lane and onto the main road. He stood panting, furious.

He clenched his hands at the departing vehicle, cursing her and, uncharacteristically, he smacked the nearest unfortunate cow on its rump in frustration. Never once in their marriage had he ever been violent, only now he wanted to kill her, to see her dead so that he could retrieve something.

His whole life had been put in peril by someone who had never been, or become family. He needed his mother's advice, as she had no doubt heard their row, her bed beside an open window. The row that would put the whole family in jeopardy. The generations of Davieses who had depended on this land that fringed the sea and mountain to eke out a living. Surviving until now, with that same family that had dug peat on the mountain, walked behind the horse, survived war, to draw a furrow for the next harvest, through rain and drought; human, bovine and plough. A persistence now likely to go under, to be made extinct by an ignorant modern law.

There was nothing Richard could do but worry and wait for the demand that would send him spiralling, a figure so sky high that he couldn't possibly contemplate finding it, not on his twenty thousand a year, not without selling up to release the capital, uprooting his family so that it no longer existed. He knew the demand would run into hundreds of thousands, silly money, the realms of fantasy that he couldn't think of a way round, even a deferment. It would eat him alive, the worry and anxiety, as he paced his farm, not knowing what to do or where to start. Who to contact, who to get advice from? He felt undone, without his land to support him, and alone with his distress, he sought out his mother. Without comment he unburdened himself of his woes as Elin sat impassively in her chair. He knew she understood what was happening and twice had tried to say something. Was it, 'Let her go?' He asked her again.

'It's not Nesta I care about, Mam, it's Tŷ Coch, our farm.'

Elin tried to speak, her words still quiet and slurred but Richard caught the drift about managing. They had before. He did not share his mother's optimism, but felt marginally better for sharing his problems with her.

He'd have to ring Bethan and Simon to tell them what had happened and how the farm would have to be sold. Perhaps they could add some pressure. This was far worse than any BSE crisis. Here there'd be no public inquiry, no culpability or blame apportioned to pave the way for any compensation claim, other than for a failed marriage. Whatever the outcome it would be to her advantage, a win-win situation. Sure, he would fight the amount, but as Britain was gaining a reputation for being one of the most lucrative places for wives to get a generous divorce settlement, he didn't hold much hope of any judge being sympathetic to him or his livelihood.

'Are you sure it's hopeless, Rich?'

'She's always hated this place. She loathes the farm, the smell of animals.'

'And you two? I know it's not been very good recently but is there nothing you can work on to try and patch things up?' Richard shook his head. He didn't touch the coffee his uncle had made him. 'What about Rhian? It'll affect her badly. Would you like me to have a word? Has she thought about the consequences?'

'It won't do any good. Of course I've raised the matter, Mervyn. Have you tried reasoning with her? She won't listen to me, and according to Nesta, Rhian wants to go as well.'

'Have you asked her on her own what she wants? If she stayed here it would make Nesta's case less strong. Walking out on her husband and daughter! Pah, she's bluffing. She'll come round. I can't see her forcing you to sell up. She was brought up round here, she knows what it means.'

'Oh, she knows all right. She's been to the solicitors and is determined to go through with it. She just doesn't give a damn.'

'I'm sorry, son.' The word caught him and he looked across at his stepfather, who'd done so much for him. He felt he'd already lost.

'Do you know I think I could kill her. I'm so—' He hit his hand upon his chest. 'I don't know where to go, Mervyn.'

'Don't despair. There must be a way. Do the others know? I'm sure Simon and Beth will help. Is it because of, you know your involvement with, you know that lady?'

'Penny? No, I don't think she cares about that. She's glad to have me out of the way. Our marriage had had it before that had ever started. And if she wants to throw any mud, it'll stick on her. I know that.'

'Could she help?'

'Who? Oh, you mean Penny. Even if she could, I don't want to involve her with any of this.'

'Then you'll have to ask your brother and sister. I'm sure jointly we can find a solution.'

'I doubt it.' He knew there was no quick fix, not sharing his uncle's optimism.

'They're not going to find the amount she's demanding. Win the lottery, rob a bank or hope she drops dead. Those are the options.'

'Now you're just talking silly, Rich. The family has always found a way.'

He wished rather than believed it, as he watched them leaving his house, getting into her car, to drive off to school. He hoped something awful would happen, imagining different scenarios that would conveniently dispose of his wife; that she'd fall or get pushed over the cliff edge in a high gust of wind, or vanish with no trace other than her clothes left on the beach, so that he'd be left in peace with Penny, to run his farm and sort Rhian out. Any poison, E. coli, or fatal disease, anything that would dispose of her. He'd never hated anyone so vehemently.

Nesta had put things in place so that she was ready to move when term ended. She could feel the firecracker she'd lit and enjoyed his agitation. Dull old Richard suddenly alight! She made sure she was out before he got the letter he'd been waiting for that confirmed her intent. Shaking with rage, he showed it to Mervyn, for him to see the impossible demands made on him, that other than winning the pools, the money demanded was unattainable. He had broken down in front of them. 'Look, Mam, look what the bitch is asking me for! Where the hell do we find that sort of money from? What do I do, Mervyn?'

Nothing, other than argue. He could and would fight it, drag his feet and contest each and every point to make the process as protracted and slow as possible but he could see no way out of the inevitable conclusion that he'd have to sell up in order to pay his wife off.

32

Richard cursed as he applied the brakes, seeing a line of vehicles slowing in front of him. He was already late for the afternoon milking, leaving Mervyn for the second time in the same week to do the cows. The meeting with the bank had not helped his mood and the last thing he needed was to be stuck in a traffic jam. There were no options, no short cut through to Llanfeni. No doubt some lunatic biker or holidaymaker had misread the dips and curves in the road that looked straighter than it was. Any hot weather and the inevitable procession of caravans seemed to bring out the worst in otherwise normal people, who lost their sense of reason and tried to overtake a caravan, stock trailer, tractor and silage wagon as if their life depended on it. There were always accidents at the height of the summer months on this part of the coastal road. Richard tapped the steering wheel of his car impatiently, unable yet to see what was the cause of the hold-up. He switched the radio on in case there was something on the Welsh news that would explain the blockage. Looking in his mirror, he saw the queue snaking back, and several of the occupants getting edgy in their frustration, looking out of their windows or getting out of their cars and standing in the middle of the road. For half an hour complete strangers stuck together, waited; for want of anything better they started up conversations about their destination, traffic, the weather, distracted only by kids beginning to misbehave, irritated and trapped inside the stationary cars.

The noise of sirens sent them scattering back to their vehicles, and an ambulance flashing blue lights sped by. Twenty minutes on, the traffic coming the other way started to trickle by. 'There's been an accident,' a middle-aged man, with his children gawking in the back, explained unnecessarily, unwinding his window to impart the news to drivers in the line of unmoving vehicles, many leaning out, eager to hear of someone else's catastrophe. Thankfully it hadn't been a personal tragedy. They ignited their engines, ready to resume their journey. Then it was his turn to move through the backlog, unable not to look, to rubber-neck onto the scene of the two vehicles, the small Fiesta concertinaed up onto the side of the hedge, a front indicator light still flicking in its broken frame, the four by four with caravan intact still on the road, hardly damaged, and a fair-haired lady talking animatedly to the police, a man by her side, hands in pockets. As Richard edged nearer, he saw the wide chalk lines drawn on the road where the impact had occurred, and a woman standing next to the vehicle who was visibly upset, shaking and dabbing her face with a tissue, looking at the wreck of the other car. There had to have been casualties – Richard was glad that the ambulance had already been and he did not have to witness any fatality: no bleeding body through a windscreen or child crushed inside the wreck. As he was waved through by a policeman he saw something that made him jolt, an object among the bits of battered door panel, plastic moldings and glass that seemed horribly familiar. Lying with the contents spewed out in the ditch, he saw a green army canvas bag, and as he braked to look more closely he could clearly read the black graffiti of 'New Model Army' on its flap. He remained halted, frozen, as a policeman came up to see why he'd stopped.

'I think my daughter might have been in the car. It's her school bag on the road there. I'm sure of it. I recognise the name. I'm her father! Richard Davies. Is she all right?' The policeman waved him over to one side so that the rest of the traffic could continue. 'Now, Sir, who did you say you were? If I can just take down your details.'

He watched as the officer wrote them down, speaking into his radio.

'I can't tell you too much at this moment, but there were five occupants travelling in the vehicle at the time of the crash. The injured have been taken by ambulance to A & E at the hospital. I can't tell you more than that. I'm sorry, Sir.'

He drove straight to the hospital, where he waited in A & E to find out if Rhian was one of the kids in theatre. She should have been with her mother in Swansea, not up here on this stretch of road and not with those bloody yobs. A curtain was drawn back and he saw her coming out of a cubicle, her right arm in a sling, her face cut and bruised on her cheek, and a nasty stitched gash

224

over her left eye. Nesta was with her, supporting her on her good arm.

'She's all right, Richard,' she said. 'They rang me at school and I came straight here. I didn't know where you were, but I left a message with Mervyn. He said not to worry about anything, he'd do the cows.'

'Rhian! Thank goodness you're OK. When I saw your stuff, I thought—' He attempted to hug her, but the plaster on her arm, her swollen face and general soreness made it virtually impossible. 'I passed the accident on the side of the road and I saw your school bag lying in the wreckage. I thought you'd been killed, Rhi.'

'I'm OK, Dad. One of the walking wounded.' She tried to smile, fighting back tears, sniffing, looking away so he couldn't see.

'I'm going to take her home.'

Home. Where was her home now? What did his wife mean, that they were returning to the farm?

'Did they say it was all right? It seems very early to discharge her?'

'Yes, Dad. The doctor's given me a thorough check-up, made sure I haven't been hit on the head. He said I was really lucky and that my injuries are superficial. Not like poor Jazz.' He was about to ask who Jazz was, if he'd been the moron driving, he wanted more than a word with him, but Nesta's look warned him to say nothing. He drove home sedately in front of them, trying to use the landrover as a buffer against any careless driver. Mervyn came out to meet them, relieved to see Rhian walking from the car and quietly hopeful as he saw father and mother go into Tŷ Coch on either side of her. But soon he heard Richard's walk across the yard, making his usual night-time checks, and then his footsteps coming to their back door, the sound of the kettle being heated and a tired sigh.

33

Each morning after the milking was done and the cows were back out in the fields, Richard dreaded the sound of the post van, expecting another letter rejecting his request, compelling him to meet her demands.

He moved the electric fence a few yards forward, allowing his cows a little fresh pasture in rotation. There were always a hundred jobs needing doing, as well as the twice daily milking. Only a few weeks ago he'd considered himself lucky, with things going his way, and as well as being happy for the first time in years he'd had some good weather to get his first crop of silage in. Added to the usual farm season, he had the extra pressure of making cheese, hoping to make double his normal amount in preparation for the four day Royal Welsh Show. Now just as one area of his life was beginning to flourish, his wife was about to jeopardize everything. He felt impotent, unable to do anything to prevent her, especially as her timing coincided with improving cheese sales and a shop window at the show for his Caws Tŷ Coch brand.

On the fourth and final day of a successful show, he came back to Tŷ Coch tired to find Nesta's car parked by the door packed full. The back was crammed full of oddments: bedding a bedside lamp, cushions and cardboard boxes stuffed with china and breakables, as well as two suitcases on the back seat. The boot was closed but he imagined it also to be full. The material stuff she could have, but he hated to see his daughter sitting in the passenger seat, waiting to go. Nesta's face wrinkled in displeasure at having been caught and having to speak to him. Reluctantly she wound down the window.

'Hi, hi, Rhian.' He peered into the car, looking at the items that had been part and parcel of her life. He wanted to register a hurt to make her realise what she was about to do. Not his bloody wife who he was only too glad to get rid of, but his daughter, who was about to leave him, her grandparents and her home. To leave when he wasn't about, only he'd come home early and caught them.

'You leaving? You were going to go without a word?' He looked accusingly at his wife. 'Like a sneak.'

'You weren't around, so I left a message with your parents. I thought it would be easier for us all if I went without creating a scene.'

'I wasn't talking to you.' He pointedly turned his head, looking directly at his daughter, who was too embarrassed to meet his gaze.

'What about you, Rhian?'

'Not now Richard.'

'Yes, now. She is my daughter.' He leant across into the car. 'This is what you want? Are you really sure?' Rhian didn't want to look at him, to see the anger and hurt in his face. To show him she also felt guilty for deserting a sinking ship. She looked down as she nodded.

'Is that it, Rhi? A nod is all I get? No other explanation?'

'I need a break, Dad, a change of scene. The accident, school, everything.' Seeing her sitting miserably among the junk, he couldn't bring himself to tell her she was making a huge mistake and that running away solved nothing, but he said nothing, standing there, everybody awkward.

'It's not as if we're going abroad, Dad.'

'He's just trying to make you feel bad, love, we're not even leaving Wales!'

'You know where you can go. It's Rhian I'm talking to.'

'If it doesn't work out, Dad, I'll only be a couple of hours away and I can come back to you anytime, can't I?'

'You know you don't have to ask. Your home is here. That's of course while I still have the farm and a roof over my head.'

He saw her looked surprised. 'Hasn't your mother told you?'

He looked enquiring at Nesta. 'Oh, she hasn't? Your mother's omitted to mention that little detail has she? Where do you think she's getting the funding for her brand new lifestyle? She's forcing me to sell up.'

'Is that true, Mam?'

'Tell her, Nesta. Your bloody mother's breaking up the farm. Your Nain and Taid, everything. We'll all be without a home by the time she's finished with us.'

He could see her shock at his revelation, questioning her mother with her eyes.

'You bastard, Richard! Only a shit would use emotional blackmail on his own daughter. None of it's true, Rhi, don't you believe him, whatever he tells you.'

'Emotional blackmail. That's rich!'

She started the car up as Richard made a lunge through the window for the steering wheel.

'Hang on, I haven't finished,' he said, but Rhian's expression was enough to make him release his grip on the steering wheel and pull his arm away.

'Sorry, Dad.'

Goronwy Roberts of Roberts, Pugh & Wright sat across the desk from him in a serious suit, white shirt and conservatively patterned tie, as befitted his position as elder partner of the firm. With his hands resting across his generous paunch, he sat impassively as he listened to his client. On the desk the letter lay between them like a black spot. The headed, embossed note paper indicated an expensive bill from the other legal practice.

Mr Roberts let Richard rattle on about his wife's unfair and ludicrous demands, quietly thinking of two things: that divorces, although messy affairs, especially where land was involved, paid very nicely, and on seeing his old colleague's name on the letter in front of him, he was reminded that he owed

John Jenkins dinner and quietly thought of what he might order. Where better to discuss the details of the Tŷ Coch estate as well as the Glamorgan cricket season, than over a good dinner at The Felin Hotel? He allowed himself a small smile as he thought of the very comfortable drawing room, warm log fire and glass or two of claret with views over the mill pond and stream. With these images in mind he nodded benignly at the agitated farmer, whose hands waved about as he aired his woes. When he finally came to a halt, Mr Roberts tried to press upon him that the two parties ultimately would have to come to an agreement unless he wanted an expensive court case.

'I'm not going to roll over for her, Mr Roberts.'

'No one is suggesting that, Mr Davies, but we will have to try and find a way for both parties to agree.'

In his present frame of mind Richard wasn't going to agree to any of her preposterous terms, and he was damned if he was going to give her everything he had spent a lifetime's work building. There had to be another way.

'I hope I haven't caught you in rehearsals have I, Si?'

'No, it's fine, Uncle Merv. Is everything all right at home? Mam OK?'

'Yes. She's getting better slowly. It's nothing like that. It's about Richard. Has he been in touch with you?'

'Richard? No, why has something happened to him?'

'Not physically. It's not an accident or anything. Did you know he and Nesta have split up?'

'No. Oh, I'm sorry to hear that. I knew things hadn't been too good between them, but I assumed as I hadn't heard anything, they were getting through it. Are you sure they've really split for good?'

'I'm afraid so. She's left Tŷ Coch.'

'Left? Where? When did she move?'

'Near Swansea. She and Rhian, after the accident.'

'Accident! What accident?'

'Car accident. You were abroad, and Rhian was all right. We didn't want to bother you.'

'What happened?'

'Well I'm back now, so tell me what happened.'

'She was one of the passengers and the lad driving went off the road. He killed his front passenger.'

'Good God. Was it anyone I know?'

'From Pen-y-bryn estate. He's up in front of the courts, facing a manslaughter charge. It was lucky for Rhian she was in the back. Since she's come home from hospital, they've been fighting all the time. It was no good Simon, they couldn't stay as they were. Nesta has moved, taking Rhian with her.'

'And how's Richard taken it?'

'How do you expect? He's up and down.'

'Does Mam understand what's happening?'

'I'm sure she does. She knows Richard's been very unhappy with the ways things have been going, and I think deep down Richard's known there was no future for them, but it doesn't stop him blaming himself for what happened to Rhian.'

'It wasn't his fault she had a car accident.'

'She shouldn't have been with them. Those Vaughan boys are a rum lot. Up to all sorts. It brought it home to your brother just how distanced he and Rhian had become. So he's beating himself up for not stopping it earlier, before it got out of hand. Dropping out of school, hanging around by the railway with the druggies. Not good is it, for any girl? And this time he can't make up, she's not a kid any more, and now she's moved away from him and from us, her family.'

'So he's on his own.'

'He's got us and the work and I suppose this new cheese business helps distract him.'

'You said something about that some time ago, with the organic milk. Will it make him money?'

'*Duw*, I don't know, Simon. But it shows he's not giving up.'

'He's had a lot on his plate this last year.'

'At least he's had a grant to help start up with his new business partner.'

'But it still leaves him with all this money to find which is why I thought he'd have contacted you, and Beth.'

'I've heard nothing, but then we've been away. Did you get my postcard?'

'Yes, we did. And one from Beth from Dublin not long ago. I know your Mam appreciates them, and they're a lot easier to hold than a letter.'

'Does Richard want help?

'With Nesta? A brotherly phone call, but don't tell him I told you. I don't want him to think I've been behind his back. I'm surprised he hasn't rung you.'

'He may have, only I missed the call.'

'She's been to the solicitors and started divorce proceedings. Big firm from Chester. She wants her full share of the money.'

'She would of course, I suppose it's only fair. How much? Do you know?'

'More than we can find, that's for sure. Even if he sells the house and here, I still don't think—'

'Wait a minute, Mervyn. She can't do that. Aren't you and Mam still in partnership with him?'

'Yes.'

'Then it's not freehold. There's the bank to consider. They must have quite a big share in the farm still? Where are the deeds, do you know?'

'With the bank, I think. Or with your brother.'

'Well, they may increase the mortgage, so that it can release some money to pay her out. But the bank is quite likely to say no, if they see it as risky. She is only entitled to half of his real assets and as he doesn't own the farm she can't have it, can she?'

'I knew you'd understand and be able to help him. It's too complicated for me.'

'And there's Rhian to consider. He will still have to provide for her, so that should help his case. Don't tell him that you've spoken to me Uncle Merv, not until I can get some figures. It might help if I pop over to see Beth. She's always so level-headed and a good influence on Rich.'

'Can you afford the time?'

'He'd help me, wouldn't he? If I was in his position, and it'll be easier if I ask, it's not quite so personal and Malcolm's not short of a bob or two. I'm sure they can help with a loan. So there'll be no need to think of selling up, OK?'

'I knew you'd be able to help, Simon. I told Richard to speak to you.'

There was no point in telling his uncle that Richard had already let him know some time back that the marriage was on the rocks and he needed money, and having heard nothing he'd put it on a back burner, hoping the problem would sort itself out. Simon didn't want his mother and uncle to know what had caused the rift, wishing to remain their golden boy.

'Don't tell him for now. I don't want to raise his expectations at this stage, but I'll ring Beth today and try and get a ferry over the weekend.' Simon preferring a rough crossing than the short flight into Dublin. 'Has Mam been able to give you her opinion?'

'She sits there, and you don't know how much of what she hears she understands. A lot more than she can let on. She tries to tell me with a gesture and odd word, and her eyes speak to me. She's known Richard has been struggling, and she'll only want what's the best for him. They've always been very close.'

'I know. Give her my love.'

We're all very proud of you, Simon.'

34

Simon decided he would make it a proper break, taking off the Friday and Monday, which would give him four days. Luckily the sea was calm on the morning of his outward journey, which allowed him to travel on the Stena Lynx rather than the larger ferry, cutting the journey time so that he arrived at Rosslare promptly. He tried ringing Beth on her mobile but each time he dialled the line was dead. Simon assumed he'd used the wrong code, reasoning to himself that it would make it more of a surprise if he just turned up. He'd also be less tied to a timetable and free to enjoy the drive down. Looking at the map, he'd make a loop, driving through Kilkenny to Tipperary towards Limerick and then down to Kerry, coming back along the southern side through Cork. Although he couldn't possibly see all of Ireland during his short stay, he would at least get a flavour.

After sorting out a hire car, he started off at a leisurely pace through the Irish countryside, stopping at Waterford where, like most tourists, he bought some crystal, slightly disappointed by the town, before he set off again going north-east along the main route.

As they ran a racing stud he knew either his sister or her husband would be home whatever time he called. On a whim, because he like the sound of the name, he took a detour to Carrick-on-Suir. The broad main street with trees either side made it seem bigger as he walked to stretch his legs. The town seemed full of young people. Not heavily tattooed or in hoodies with a mix breed bull terrier, these kids posed no threat, no hidden knives, their faces open, a friendly curious smile to the stranger. In the shop one of them told him where to go for a meal, if he didn't want the fish and chips, pointing him back down the street. He thanked them and wondered back the way he'd come, to the only hotel of any size. He was hungry, and the sea motion that had prevented him from eating on board had passed. Travelling with Welsh National Opera, he'd grown accustomed to good food and Simon was not disappointed in his choice of a freshly caught river trout, cooked gently in herbs and fennel. He had new potatoes, a side salad garnish with a sprinkling of the French dressing he'd asked for, as well as a beautiful beetroot relish to complement the fish that was attractively arranged on white bone china. With a flourish he turned the pepper mill in the otherwise empty restaurant. His first bite reminded him of trout he'd caught as a boy, the music of Schubert's 'Trout', so apt in the tinkling pleasure of fish in water. Not fussy about bones, he ate to the middle of the fish, washing his last mouthful down with a crisp glassful of Muscadet. All around the empty room there were reproduction prints of horses and hunting. Behind glass, a large salmon had been mounted on the wall, obviously a local record catch. On the waitress's recommendation he opted for the summer pudding with fresh cream, followed by cheese and coffee. In an act of largesse, partly because he'd been so well fed but also because he saw the place so bereft of any other paying visitors, he tipped generously, and listening to an organ piece by Bach on his tape, he continued on his sojourn across the green isle. It had much more to do with his genial frame of mind than any fact that he felt that the people he met were especially warm and friendly toward him. Perhaps they recognised him and it paid to be genial, smile and be liked. One thing that struck him was the pedestrian traffic on the rural roads. There was more of a foot tread rather than just men and machines, and there were horses everywhere. Far fewer sheep to see, as one would expect on the superior pasture, but there were still plenty of milking herds and beef cattle. Overwhelming in comparison with home was the abundance of the equine breed. In Ireland they seemed more ubiquitous than cars. All forms of breeds: racehorses, hunters, warm bloods, draught, cob, tinkers' black and white, skewbald and roan, the old colours of ancient breeding, tough, enduring. And with the horse, the man who led him. Simon would later describe him as 'a real character', leading a horse along, bow-legged, walking as if he'd lived most of his life in the saddle, waving a hand to any fitful passing traffic. Away from the trunk road, tarmac maintenance deteriorated and there was no warning, no white lines, and many road signs were faded or broken, rendering them unintelligible for the visitor, so without local knowledge it wasn't easy to follow a route, but as Simon was in no hurry, it added to the charm, and as long as he kept heading west he knew he would eventually stumble upon the main road.

He was happily singing to himself when too late he saw a large pothole in the middle of the road. He failed to react quickly enough to steer around it, and felt the heavy crunch as the car's front wheel hit the cavity, sinking into the large hole. Cursing, he managed to drive the car to the side of the road, where he got out to inspect the damage. Not only was the tyre punctured but the wheel's rim seemed bent. He lifted the boot to find the spare tyre and jack. Although he was a big man Simon was neither practical nor remotely mechanical, and apart from getting his hands covered in grease he was unable to loosen the last nut on the wheel. Even after several attempts at putting his considerable weight on the jack, he couldn't get it to budge. He looked at his phone but with the no network displaying, he knew he would have to sit by the side of the road and wait, and as he did so, the empty road that a moment earlier had been quaint, became an irritation that darkened with the passing of each quarter of an hour. There wasn't even a horse or cart to hail.

Eventually he heard an engine, not from the road but coming from behind him, and he got up to alert the attention of a man driving a tractor in the nearby field. With only a roll bar for a cab, the man had seen him waving his arms standing by the side of the road next to his car and had realised long before Simon had seen him that the traveller was stranded. In his own time the man was making his way towards him.

When he arrived, he made no attempt to conceal his smile as he saw the car's damage, knowing Simon had hit the hole and seeing the car couldn't be towed.

'I can't get the wheel off,' said Simon, feeling a bit of a clot. 'I didn't see the hole and went straight into it and it's buckled the rim. It's probably bent the nut.'

The farmer pushed his cap to one side, and jumped down from his tractor.

'Do you think you have something on the tractor that would help shift it? I don't know how far the nearest garage is. I don't have a signal to ring out,' he added, waving his mobile phone dismissively. The farmer tried the nut, which refused to shift, even when he used part of the jack as leverage. He kicked it ineffectively with his boot, grinning as he did so.

'She's on tight enough,' he said, smiling at Simon, standing back from the job, waiting for a solution to appear. Without saying any more, he walked back to his tractor and for a moment Simon thought he was going to give up and leave him stuck in the middle of nowhere. He climbed onto the hub of the back wheel and rummaged around in the tractor's tool box, bringing out a large, wooden-handled hammer. He took a labourer's swing to the stubborn nut, hitting the hub several times with the hammer as Simon looked on. Not every shot hit the target and the rim got several more dents. Initially the nut remained locked, but after a determined volley of blows, the man tried the spanner again and managed a slight give. Once started, it came out without much difficulty, and they were able to put on the spare tyre.

'Tracking's out, but she'll take you to the garage. You watch she doesn't pull you to the ditch,' he said helpfully, as if talking about a horse 'to see how she goes'.

Simon was grateful and although he wanted to offer to pay him for his time and services, he didn't want to offend the man. Apart from cash, he had nothing else appropriate to hand, so offered a note, which the farmer took.

'And the garage is a few miles away?' What seemed a simple journey became more complicated as the farmer explained the route. It didn't help that he described each section of his directions with minute detail: names, profession and every building of his neighbours' fields and other objects obvious only to him. Simon had no idea as to distance or the name of the town where the garage was and he felt it would be rude to try and get clarity and ask yet again, especially as he had come across the same problem in reverse in his native country where so many names were unpronounceable to visitors. He tried a different tack.

'The name. Can you tell me how many miles is it, approximately?'

'Pat, Pat Fletcher will see you right. Mind you keep following this way,' he said, raising his arm and pointing down the road. 'That'll see you there for fifteen minutes.' And with that he turned, lifting an arm in farewell. He walked back to his field and started up the tractor.

Simon drove off cautiously down the way he had been directed, feeling the severe pull of the damaged wheel veering him to his left while he tried to recall the jumble of landmarks he'd been given. Once out of sight, he stopped to look at his road map, hoping to stumble upon a village with a garage. As it turned out, going at his forced slow pace, it was easy to spot the building that served as a garage sitting back from the road's junction. Sitting in a field, surrounded by old cars, machinery and scrap metal, were a couple of petrol pumps on a small concrete forecourt and shed. There was an assortment of agricultural and car tyres piled in one corner of the concrete and what served as the workshop was no more than a corrugated round roofed shed. There was no lavatory or convenience foods here; there was a couple of pumps, unprotected from the elements, and an old advert for derv pinned to a fence. The place smelt of rust, oil and petroleum and it reminded Simon of the old black and white photos of his uncle's family at Yr Efail in Llanfeni.

The wheel needed more than a new tube and tracking and the job would take the rest of the day to sort out, leaving Simon no option other than to stay at the only bed and breakfast available.

From their guest house's landline he made the belated call to his brother-in-law.

'It'll be grand to see you tomorrow. Beth will be so pleased to have you here,' said Malcolm. If he was surprised to hear from Simon, his voice didn't show it.

'I'm sorry not to let you know earlier but I had no mobile signal and I've only now managed to get to a landline.'

'We'll look forward to having you; come whenever you like tomorrow. It'll do her good, it'll help to take her out of herself.'

'Why? Is she not well?

'She's not been.'

'What's been wrong? I haven't heard anything. No one told me from home? What's been the matter?'

'I don't want to alarm you, or any of your family, but as you're coming over it's better you know now. To be honest with you, your sister's been very poorly.'

'In what way? Has she had an accident?'

'You could call it that. She is getting better. It is something I need to talk to you about, but not on the phone. I'll explain it all properly when I see you; it's complicated, you see.'

Before Simon could quiz him further, Malcolm put the phone down abruptly.

Even though Richard had enough on his plate with his own problems, Simon wondered if he should ring him and find out if he knew anything about Beth. Obviously Mervyn didn't or he would have said something to him when he talked about going to Ireland. Weighing it up, he came to the conclusion that his brother was probably also in the dark. The timing of his visit, cap in hand for a loan of a fifty to a hundred and fifty thousand with Beth mysteriously out of sorts, was going to make his stay awkward, and he was none the wiser what had happened to his sister. Strange too, he thought, that his brother-in-law was so secretive, reticent to speak about it on the phone, as if the problem or illness had not completely cleared and there was some residue.

35

He recognised the place from her photos: picturesque, quaint and unmistakably Irish. Malcolm came out to meet him, hugging him like a brother, welcoming him in. There was no sign of his sister to greet him.

'Where's Beth?'

'She's upstairs. She's resting.'

A word usally used for an invalid, Simon thought.

'I didn't tell her what time to expect you so as not to over-excite her. Here, let me get you a drink. Come into my study and I'll explain it all to you.'

Malcolm led him along the stone corridor to his study, closing the door behind them and pulling up a leather chair for Simon, before pouring a slug of whisky into cut-glass tumblers for them both.

'Soda, water, or on the rocks?' he asked, his manner unctuously solicitous towards his brother-in-law.

'Soda's fine. So, what's all this about? Why all the mystery Malcolm?'

'Beth's been through a really bad time. She had a very bad experience and at the time I didn't know myself, but she was expecting our second child. She never told me—'

He seemed more bothered about this than about Bethan which irritated Simon.

'What has happened? Has Bethan had a miscarriage? Why all the mystery. Women often miscarry.'

'Why, indeed? In many ways I blame myself for what happened.' He gave an apologetic smile. 'After you've heard it all you'll understand why we kept it hushed up. If I had known, I would have been more careful; I would never have let her go on the boat. She went swimming off it, right out in the ocean and caught a chill. That was the beginning of it and then it dragged her down. She had a miscarriage and in the end she lost our baby.'

'Oh, is that what happened,' said Simon, letting go of his breath, thinking Malcolm was being overly dramatic about it all. 'Poor Beth. She must feel awful but none of us knew anything about it, or that she was expecting another baby. When did it happen? Why didn't she, or you ring us?'

'Of course I should have but with all the complications—'

'Complications? She's all right now, isn't she? I want to see her. I can't believe we haven't been told about any of it. We are family.'

'She's had the best medical attention, I can assure you.

'Yes, I'm sure, but I meant moral support.'

'There's was more, more to it than losing the baby. She had internal problems, you know woman's problems as well, and the bleeding made her very weak. She had to have several blood transfusions. She became very anaemic and this made her,' – he searched for a word that wouldn't send off too many alarm bells – 'very low.'

Simon was shocked to hear his brother-in-law describing a

scenario that sounded more life-threatening with every sentence he uttered. He hated to think of what his sister had gone through with no one in her family there to support her, yet alone know about what had happened to her. How could the O'Connors not contact them? What were they thinking of! He badly needed to see his sister for himself and had had enough of Malcolm's prevarications. Following him up the stairs, he felt he was being lead by a gaoler to visit a prisoner. At least her door was not locked as they entered her bedroom, but he was shocked at what he saw. His sister's pale face. On seeing him, her blue eyes blinked in astonishment before she grasped it was really him in person and her horribly thinned face brightened as she smiled. He tried to hide his shock.

'Simon!' she said, Is it really you?'

'Of course it's me, sis.'

'I'd no idea! Malcolm's very clever at keeping secrets; he never let on you were coming.'

'To be fair to him, he didn't know. I thought I'd surprise you both.' He leant over to give her a kiss. 'Dear Beth, I had no idea you'd been ill, and I'm so sorry to hear what's happened. Sweet sis. Hmmm?' He looked at her, 'You should have told us. Someone should have let us know,' he said, watching her, trying to read the language between husband and wife. Malcolm came across to hold her hand, kissing her on her forehead like a child. But there was no deception, no guile, only a loving grateful look up at him.

'I'm getting better, slowly, thanks to my very good and gentle nurse. He's looked after me so well; he's given me everything I could want, haven't you darling?'

Hardly, Simon thought, looking at the fragile, wasted woman and washed-out face that was his sister.

'I just want you well again – we all do. Back to your old self, filling this house with your fun. Not up here like a little shrew.'

'I know it's been difficult. I'm sorry to be such a pain.'

Why? thought Simon, was she apologising to him?

'But I am feeling stronger every day, especially now I'm home again.'

Malcolm smiled, patting her hand, aware that he was being scrutinized.

'I wish you'd told me you were coming Si, so I could prepare things ready for you.'

'And that's precisely why I kept it from you. The last thing we need is you exhausting yourself running round like a rabbit. We've got the spare room ready and Mother, has been busy in the kitchen sorting out the food with Clare's help, so there's no need for you to worry your little head. Everything's been taken care of.'

'It was all a bit spur of the moment. So here I am out of the blue, surprising you all! But I'm so sorry, Beth, to find you like this.'

What the hell did she mean home again? How long had she been in hospital?

'You can spend all your time with your brother while I'm here, instead of running round trying to arrange any sightseeing trips. I have enough of those, so it'll be nice just to be with you!'

'Yes, yes but I must get up,' she said pulling the bedcovers down as Malcolm rushed to help her.

'Only if you promise not to overdo it. You know what the doctor said. This is going to take some time, so we'll wait upon you? Promise? We'll let you get dressed in peace. There's a warm fire in the drawing room.'

They retreated from the room and Malcolm showed Simon to his room along the far end of the landing with views overlooking the sea. As soon as they were out of earshot, Simon caught hold of his jacket sleeve, somewhat alarmed.

'She looks terrible, Malcolm. I mean, at death's door.

Whatever has happened? It can't be just a miscarriage. Was it very late on?'

'I know it's an awful shock for you, but she's nowhere near as bad as she's been.'

'Is that meant to reassure me? She couldn't look any worse could she?'

Malcolm looked down, 'We nearly lost her. She's only recently turned the corner.'

'How close to death has she been?'

'Dangerously so. But you coming over will do her the power of good; it'll help put some colour in her cheeks. And if you can encourage her to eat she can start to regain some of the weight she's lost.'

'So why didn't you get in touch earlier? I don't understand what the hell you thought you were playing at!'

'We were so close to losing her – any upset could have tipped the balance. I couldn't risk it.'

'Is that what the doctors advised? Presumably she's sees a doctor every day?'

'Yes, Dr Flynn's been very good and he's pleased with her progress. He said it'll all take some time and it's going to be a slow, gradual process.'

Malcolm seemed to stare oddly at Simon, as if in some way he was to be implicated in how his sister was to recover and he added his warning, 'She and I have been through hell and I don't want anything to upset her. No excitement or questions. She's not ready. All that's happened has seriously unnerved her. She's lost all confidence and she's very insecure and jumpy. She overreacts to the slightest thing. It's not just physical, it's her mental state. We have to go very quietly and not let anything agitate her that'll set her off. Do you understand what I'm saying? It's going to take her months to recover.'

'But how has she got like this? What has happened to

243

make her so bad? I mean women lose babies quite often, it's not uncommon to have a miscarriage. You should have rung, Malcolm, I can't believe you didn't. I mean, look at her! What would her mother think? How many months gone was she?'

'I think about three-and-a-half months, may have been four. But it's hit her bad: psychologically it's been almost worse for her than what she went through physically. She's had a sort of breakdown following it.'

Malcolm pressed his lips together in an effort to control his emotion. 'I've been at my wits' end, worrying about her condition. I thought I might have lost her on more than one occasion. What was I to do? Ring you and say your sister's had a total collapse? And if your mother was in a fit state herself don't you think she would have been the first person I'd have called – but as she is, how could she have helped her?'

'There's me, Richard and Mervyn. One of us would have come over.'

'At the time all I could think of was getting her over the worst. It was dire, and the doctors advised a total shutdown to give her body time. She needed special treatment, and thank God I had the money to pay for it. The best professionals to help her.'

'So you saved her life?'

Malcolm allowed himself a slight smile.

'We have her here, thanks to modern medicine. For the first few days afterwards, she didn't recognise me, or Clare, her own daughter. It was that bad. Christ, can you realise how that was for me? My lovely wife, not knowing me. She'd lost the use of her voice or how to communicate, and she couldn't tell me anything. Can you think what that was like? The doctors said it was the shock, the huge amount of blood loss she'd suffered. And after the transfusions, she was still very anaemic. And then she sort of slipped into a depression.'

'It still doesn't explain why you didn't ring one of us. You could have told us about the situation and we'd have understood, rather than this!' He raised his arms, circling them outwards.

'And you would have stayed away? No, you wouldn't have. Look, don't you think I wanted to pick up the phone a hundred times? It would have been much easier for me to have shared this burden but I couldn't. I had to keep her totally quiet. You must see that. Beth was more important than you. I've lived through hell, watching her, unable to do anything. I only had your sister's best interests at heart. I'm sorry.'

'Not as sorry as I am to see her like this.'

'If I could put the clock back, I would. She'd never have come to this state. I wouldn't have left her that day.'

'If only I'd known.'

'What could you have done, that I haven't been able to do? And do you think you're more important to her than me or Clare?'

'That's not a good enough reason not to contact us, Malcolm.'

'I did try. I rang a few times but no one answered and I didn't want to leave a message.' He was lying, Simon could tell. 'She's so glad to have you. You saw how pleased she was, let's not spoil it for her.'

Simon was staggered by his brother-in-law's attitude and he would make it his business to find out exactly what had happened when he talked to his sister alone. How now to ask for money, to disclose his real reason for calling unannounced? It was impossible to even broach the subject with her, since she was so enfeebled. He would have to ask Malcolm for a loan in private.

Flushed at being up, Beth was both exhilarated and exhausted by the time supper was over. They kept off the subject of her illness, and encouraged by Malcolm's prompting, they talked of home, of the farm and the family. Simon was careful to talk up their mother's improvement. He didn't mention the fact that Richard and Nesta had parted or that Rhian had been involved in a car accident, and divorce proceedings were already advanced and proving acrimonious; disillusion, disappointment added to deceit. Oh, and the little matter of money.

Instead he made a fuss of his niece, painting a rosy picture to them of home, nostalgically cosy. He remained alert to any snippet that would shed light on the huge chunks of what had not been said. He would have to engineer some time alone with Bethan, not now, as she looked so washed out and she was about to go back to bed, but in the morning when her husband wasn't there.

As if to thwart his plan, Malcolm was most obsequious in his attention to his wife, hanging around her like a faithful dog, and if his sister thought he was just being conscientious, Simon was not convinced. There was something in his manner that Simon didn't like, and he wasn't looking forward to asking him for a favour. When the phone rang Simon quickly asked Beth if she wanted to stretch her legs, but before she could answer her husband put his hand over the mouthpiece, shaking his head.

'Surely we can go and sit in the garden?' Simon was not going to be put off.

'How the hell did that happen?' demanded Malcolm into the phone. 'Who was riding him? I don't care about a bit of plastic. He's a jockey, isn't he. That's what I'm paying him for.' He continued to listen to Liam, his face angry with the further news, the voice down the phone explaining the extent of the damage.

'I don't think it's broken. He's damaged his stifle, but we've got him back in the yard. He must have the vet.'

'Can't you handle it?' A pause before he cut the line. He'd already decided to get rid of his head lad and now needed no excuse.

'The bloody fools, you pay them to do a job! The horse is entered for next week, fit and with a good chance. I'll have to go down and sort it out. I won't be a few minutes. You're not to go out of the house, Beth. Remember what Dr Flynn said.' He pushed a tab on his mobile, 'Johnny, it's me. They've had an accident with the chestnut colt. I don't know. Can you get over here now?' You could see he hated to leave them, slipping his mobile into his pocket before he stormed off down the passage.

Simon knew he had no time for small talk and yet he did not want to alarm his sister, or to make any false accusations about things he didn't know. All he knew was what he saw; that she was changed, she had become damaged and he needed to know if she was all right and what had really happened.

'It is so good to see you Si, you must tell me all about home .'

'I promise I will, but first let's talk about you. Are you really getting better, Beth? '

She nodded, 'Yes, I am now.'

'Only, I can't lie to you. Seeing you as you are – well, I'm really shocked to see you looking so poorly, Bethan. And Malcolm, he's obviously been very upset as well?'

'Oh Simon, if you knew how much he's done to help me. And it's not as if he hasn't been through his own misery. It shows how much he loves me. All he thinks about is getting me well.'

'I'm sure losing the baby was difficult for him too, but it's not quite the same for a man.'

'He was very upset to hear I'd lost the baby. I wish he wouldn't blame himself. You see he thinks f he'd been here they wouldn't have got me.' It took a second to register.

'What do you mean? Got you? Who? What happened to you, Beth?'

'He had to go through so much to find me. You've no idea.'

'To find you?' Was she talking literally? 'What do you mean, Beth? Were you lost?'

'After they took me.'

'Who took you? Bethan you're not making any sense.'

'Malcolm told you, I was abducted.' Malcolm hadn't told him.

'Abducted? What do you mean, abducted?'

'It happened just before I lost the baby. I was out having a walk, I can't have been more than a few fields from home, on the road to the next bay, and these men came.'

He wondered if his sister had lost her senses, if she were making it up, talking a load of nonsense, but looking at her face so intent and earnest he knew it had to have happened, and it started to explain why she was as she was. At least now he began to understand the extent of her injury, and that her mind had been unbalanced by what she'd been through.

'Go, on, sis.' He said quietly, as she faltered.

'They grabbed me and bundled me off in a car. They tied me up and left me to die in a boot. I don't know how long. Days perhaps. Then they left me in a shed.' She started to shake, then to cry.

'Oh Si, I don't want to think about it,' she said, sobbing into her brother's arms. 'If Malcolm hadn't found me.'

'But why, Beth? Who would want to do that to you? It doesn't make any sense.'

'It was for money. Malcolm had to pay them off before they told him where they'd dumped me.' She was trembling, the telling of it all too much for her. Simon realised he'd overstepped the mark, and tried to soothe her before her husband returned.

'Oh Beth, I'm so sorry. You poor, poor thing. What you must have been through. But it's over, it's all right now. Sh, my little sis.'

He held her, not knowing whether to believe her story. Malcolm had conducted his business in double quick time but when he burst in on them he realised that he was too late and that Beth had been spilling the beans. His face was furious as he motioned to Simon to shut up as he came to take his wife from him.

'I'm here, Beth. There, let me hold you, there there. Come on.

Nothing and no one's going to hurt you, I promise.' He flicked his hand at Simon to tell him to leave them alone and, already feeling embarrassed and awkward at having reduced his sister to her present state, he was glad to get out of the house, to wander outside towards the yard and sea so that he could clear his mind to think.

He had many more unanswered questions which he saw it would be useless to put to Bethan, but he had every intention of quizzing Malcolm. He was still reeling from the news as he strolled past the bungalow and on along the road towards the bridge and village beyond. Nothing made any sense. Did anybody else know – the man's mother for instance, and the paid employees? The locals? If it had happened in Wales the bush telegraph would have spread the news. So where were the press and police? He had a lot of questions for Malcolm.

The stable lads were wary, as if they'd been primed beforehand. They gave polite but monosyllabic answers to his questions. The two girls were tentative, in and out of stables, using the horses as a barrier. Simon was nervous, as he didn't like horses, so he kept out of the box. He gave up and left them to their grooming, and as he started to walk back he spotted a man schooling a young horse over a few low poles in the jumping paddock. He watched politely, standing back from the rails until the man brought the horse back into a walk and, clipping a lead rope onto its head collar, walked towards him.

'Are you wanting something or looking for the Boss?' Liam asked him.

'No, no, I'm not. I'm staying with them. I'm Beth's brother.'

'Richard?'

'No, the other one, Simon.'

'Ah the great singer! I've heard a lot about you.' He proffered his hand, a firm, warm grip and grin that revealed several missing teeth. 'Liam. I'm his head lad.' The horse snorted, fidgeting on its toes. 'Here let me put him away,' he said, and led the horse up the other side of the paddock towards the exit. With the rails between them Simon was able to relax.

'I arrived yesterday, as a surprise.'

'Sure you did that, and she'd be right glad to see you.'

'She was, but I was shocked to see her not well. We didn't know. Do you know what happened to her? No one seems to wants to talk about it up at the house.'

'It pays not to ask too many questions.' Liam nodded, looking towards the house.

'You worked for them long?' Simon asked, feeling his way. 'So what's he like?' He lifted his head to look directly at the man. 'You know, as a boss?'

'He's got a good eye for a horse, but he's not an easy man to work for. He'd be a bad enemy, if you know what I'm saying. He doesn't like to be crossed.'

'I can see that.'

'As long as he's in the driving seat, and the horses are running well, it's all right. His family carries a bit of clout round these parts.'

'You worked for him long?'

'Long enough, and my father before.'

'So you know the family well?'

'As I said, they're a funny lot. His father was used to his own way. You ask Da, he'll tell you some stories about the O'Connors, that's for sure!'

'Do you think it would be possible to have a word with your father?'

'I can't see why not, if you can catch him in. How is Beth, Mrs O'Connor? When you have a minute, alone with her, will you let her know I'm asking about her?'

'Yes, of course I will.'

'Say I'm sorry for what's happened.'

Simon waited for Liam to explain but Liam just clicked the horse forward, 'About the baby and everything,' was all he said.

'Wait a minute,' Simon called, jogging to catch up as Liam continued to lead the horse back towards the boxes. 'Look, I just want what's best for my sister. I know something else has happened and I need to know how and why. I need to find out what's been going on here, and if Malcolm won't tell me perhaps your father could shed some light on it. Please, where can I find him?'

'You could try him on his fishing boat, just over there, down on the estuary – 'Little Maire' – ask for Peter, and if it's not there.' He pointed to the sea. 'I'm afraid he's already out to his pots.'

'Do you know what happened to my sister?'

Liam stopped the horse by the gate and waited for Simon to come beside him; he could see he was nervous of the horse. 'He's all right, he won't bite. I was very shocked and sorry to hear about it. The boss came running down into the yard like a madman, shouting at us to see if we knew where she was, if she'd taken a horse out. But afterwards he clammed up. Didn't tell us anything, so we had no idea what was going on. Not until she was found.' He looked up at the broad man. 'I can see the family resemblance,' he said to Simon. 'She's a lovely person, your sister. Sh, whoa boy,' he said to the horse, who had started to fidget. It would be safer if he said no more. 'I don't know what really happened – we didn't know anything until the Boss came down. He said she'd disappeared and one of us must have seen or heard something. He was furious, and he was threatening all sorts, rolling up his sleeves and shouting at us, he was so mad. But he calmed down when he realised none of us knew anything of her whereabouts. He started to think, you know, ringing round, and he sent us all out to look for her in case she'd had an accident. We only heard later about the motorbike and car. I bet he had to pay a pretty shilling to get her back safe.'

251

'So you think she was taken for ransom?'

'You can be sure of that. Everybody knows the O'Connors are worth a bit,' he said, rubbing his thumb over his fingers. 'There's plenty of those he's laying his hands on, and there are many who might bear a grudge. You know what I'm saying.'

'Fisticuffs?'

'And more.'

'You mean his business dealings.'

Liam deliberately didn't deny the question, adding, 'And don't let him know you've been talking to me, or it'll cost me. And you'd better not be asking any more questions, not around here at any rate.'

'Thanks, Liam.'

As they'd come back into view of the yard, Simon had pulled away from the head lad so that it did not look as if they had been in conversation. He knew Malcolm would be told even if he hadn't seen them together. Simon felt his movements were being watched. He had wanted to ask Liam if he thought they were a happy couple, and more to the point was Malcolm a good husband, even if he was a hard boss, but he had already gauged the answer in what had been said. There was an uncomfortable feel to the place, for all its attractive setting. As he strolled back in the direction of the house, he watched the slim lad lead the horse towards the stables, and he reckoned he was telling the truth, but he had also guessed that he was soft on his sister and may have overstepped the mark.

Instead of turning up into the drive he decided to wander down to the water and see if he could catch up with Liam's father. His time was short and he only had another day, before he had to set off back to Cardiff. He could change his ferry for a flight if he had to, which would free up some time and he could possibly be a day late for the start of rehearsals if need be.

As he walked down to the river, following it into the estuary and sea, he saw why Bethan had been attracted to the place. Once down on the shingle Simon looked back at the row of brightly painted cottages sitting back above the tide line. The only road out of the village curved back on itself, heading inland towards the higher ground. There were only a few boats on their mooring and none that fitted Liam's description of his father's. Apart from a couple walking with rucksacks on their backs, and a woman and dog, there was no one else on the beach. He called in at the local shop cum post office, just for a nose, where he bought the local paper and a few postcards to send home to make up for Beth's absent ones. Something quaint, a *clochan*, or *curragh*, or an old man with a donkey. The old peasant way of life still clung to the fringes of land and sea that the young had abandoned, escaping to enjoy life in the revitalised cities of the booming economy. The old woman barely acknowledged him. She muttered back at him in Gaelic, no doubt cursing him as she took his proffered note. It summed up the village, not so different from his own back home, tightened up like a clam against incomers.

By the time he got back, the table had been laid ready for lunch and he found Moira and Bethan in the kitchen.

'So you've been doing the rounds, Mr Davies,' Mrs O'Connor said. 'Tis a beautiful place and you've got the weather for it.'

'Simon, please. Yes, it is, Mrs O'Connor.'

'Moira.'

'Moira. And how are you, darling sis? Feeling better?'

'Much better every day now. It's lovely to have you here and the sun out; it's so often wet.'

'Like Llanfeni.'

'Yes, like home.' There was another pause as Bethan concentrated on folding a napkin.

'Beth, I thought after lunch and only if you feel up to it we could go for a little stroll. Not far, just to the beach and back.'

'It would be nice. I haven't been out since,' she sounded hesitant.

'Or along the lane if you'd prefer,' he added.

'No, I don't want to walk there.'

'Why don't you wait and see what Malcolm thinks, he'll be back any time now. Would you like a drink, Mr—?'

'Simon, please.'

'Whisky, gin?'

'A glass of beer would be nice. Or actually a cup of tea.'

After they'd eaten, the three of them took Clare for a gentle walk down to the beach and along the shore. Taking her socks and shoes off, Clare ran off towards the pools to look for shrimps to put in her bucket. In the old days he would have expected Beth to do the same, but she was quiet and reserved, not at all like her old self as she stayed close to her husband's side. She visibly brightened when Malcolm suggested they turn for home. Once inside she seemed to regain some of her composure and, reassured that they would not venture out again, Malcolm left brother and sister to have tea together. She behaved like a frail woman. He'd only known her full of beans, the first to dare, to race to take up any challenge, and he struggled to see or accept her as she was. This was not the real Beth, and he blamed Malcolm for her change.

'Are you really all right, Bethan? You seem so different. I know you've had a terrible experience and everything, but I find the whole thing very odd, Beth? Odd that we didn't know, were not told and that your family here wanted to keep it from us. It was very strange behaviour on your husband's part, you must see that Beth? Is there something you're not telling me?'

How could she tell him of her anguish, looking across at his face full of brotherly concern for her, wanting him to believe what she'd said? How to tell him of the darkness that had filled and remained in her thoughts? Her fear, her paranoia of being taken, snatched, in every corner of her mind, obsessing her? How to tell him, to even start to explain her feeling of being paralyzed? The long weeks, the rehabilitation that reduced her to a numbed inertia that prevented her from doing the simplest of tasks. Getting dressed, walking freely about the house, answering the phone had all been beyond her. She could only think wild, irrational thoughts in her weak, traumatised state and her brother's presence highlighted the extent of her feeling of exclusion from anything familiar. Although her mind raced with electric agitation, her body remained disconnected from it, making each movement deliberate and laboured. She took a deep breath, having been taught to breathe slowly and count to control the ever-present threat in her head. She concentrated on the armrest of her chair, as the doctor had shown her, until the moment passed, and then she tried to answer him.

'Because it is very "odd",' she eventually answered him. 'To have something like that happen to me, Si. I know it's affected me, of course it has, and is going to continue to and I know there is a difference in how I am. It couldn't be anything else. But I am getting better.'

'Dear Beth, I'm sorry, I'm not being very understanding, am I? I just find the whole thing so, oh I don't know, bizarre. It's out of this world what's happened to you. I can hardly believe it. And not knowing anything until yesterday, well, it's hit me like a bolt from the blue. All this secrecy, Beth? Huh? I suppose that's what has made it worse.'

Had he realised just how painful and potentially harmful his interrogation was, would he have desisted? But having no understanding of the mental battles she'd endured to come this far, he'd clumsily reminded her of what she had tried to obliterate.

'You know I can't be alone. I'm not fit to be left in my own mind and Malcolm worries.' She said it as a fact not to be discussed. 'He is worried for my safety and if it got out, became public knowledge, it would make everything, including my recovery more difficult. Without him I wouldn't be here.'

Without him she'd never have been in the position in the first place, Simon thought.

'I know he's no saint, Simon,' she said, reading his thoughts. 'People are envious of his success.'

'I'm sure you're right, Beth.' He needed to reassure her not add to her doubts.

'Malcolm's always been very protective of me and Clare. Home is horses and training and I should have been totally safe here.'

'You are now, Beth.'

'Yes, I am now, and there is always someone with me, so come on, no more quizzing, and promise me you won't go home and worry them all about something that's over and done with?'

'You can't expect me to tell them nothing? I can't do that, Beth. We're your family, *annwyl Dduw*! They have a right to know, don't you think? Look I'll do anything to help—'

'I suppose you can let them know about the miscarriage. But not the other thing. Promise me you won't?'

He sighed, frustrated.

'OK, I can see it's not fair to tell Mam, the way she is, but honestly, don't you think you ought to let Richard know? You always used to tell him everything, Beth.'

She shook her head.

He left it at that, and when he drove away the following day, being seen off by them arm in arm as they waved from the front door, he felt a bad taste in his mouth. His whole Irish trip had been irremediably soured, even though he was prepared to accept that he may have got things wrong and that he'd misread the situation. What did he know about other people's marriages, how could he pass any sort of judgement? He had to take it at face value and accept that if he'd been forewarned, he might have seen it in a more measured light.

Only a few months ago Bethan wouldn't have dreamt of having Moira back to live with them.

It wasn't the fact they'd found her near to death's door or that she'd spent days drifting in and out of consciousness, hospitalised, but when she'd come home Moira had seen her diminished and utterly lost, needing a mother. So she filled in when Malcolm had to be out, sitting by her bed, to begin with just making sure she didn't wake up disorientated and frightened or try and get out of bed. And when she cried, calling out for help in her frequent nightmares it was Moira who put reassuring arms about her sobbing shoulders, holding her and letting her grieve for her loss and the loss of her baby. In those bleak private times Moira mumbled Hail Marys and Our Fathers out of habit, her fingers trailing imaginary beads in repetition of the fruitless bedside vigil of a beloved son. Now her daughter-in-law needed her care, sharing in their female bond the anguish of the loss of a child.

It took time to bring her back, and as Bethan improved Moira would bring Clare in to talk to her mother, the three of them on her bed in a cosy infantile place of feather and cotton. For all her outward improvement, as her body strengthened the fragility of her mind persisted and she depended on the older woman for support. What Simon didn't know was how close Bethan had come to being confined for her own safety. That in her blackness, there had been a time when she gave up, no longer wanting to struggle for life and Malcolm had needed round-the-clock care for her and was filled with remorse and guilt that he had not been home when the abduction had happened.

Unaware of such catastrophes, Simon was glad to get away from the sombre atmosphere of the stud, and headed straight for the port.

36

'Did you ask her about the money?'

God, his brother could be blunt sometimes – no finesse, just straight out with it.

'No, I couldn't, not after seeing her. She wasn't up to hearing it.'

'But the whole point of you going there was to ask for a loan. Do you think she'll prefer to hear we've had to sell up, because you were too timid to ask for financial help? She could have said no, only you haven't even given her that choice. You could have asked Malcolm, couldn't you, Simon?'

'If you saw her Richard. Saw how she was—'

'Yeah, and I would have asked what the hell was going on. I would have found out. What the hell do we do now? The solicitors are already splaying their talons.'

In the middle of their conversation the noise of a vehicle pulling up distracted Richard, who looked out of the kitchen window and saw a four by four Mitsubishi drive into the yard. A plump middle-aged man got out, followed by a younger male. 'Look I can't talk now, the vets are here. Ring again tonight.'

He put the phone down, cross, not really thinking about what Simon had said of Beth's problem. Occupied with his financial difficulties, he grabbed his cap and went out to the vets.

Gareth Pritchard had been their vet for many years and his son Aled had newly qualified and come home to join the family-run business. The testing was routine and with his dairy herd well used to handling, Richard was not expecting the tests to take long. Not like beef herds where the cattle were less used to handling and were naturally wary of cattle crushes and men in white coats with needles. Mervyn came over from the cottage to lend a hand, driving the cow forward into the crush, each one lining up, placidly waiting in turn. He pushed a lever, and solid bars came around the cow's neck, preventing her from pulling backwards. Another bar was levered down at her rear end to stop the cow from trying to pull back and damage herself. Once she was secure, Richard read out the herd number, adding the specific tag number attached to each cow's ear, which Aled wrote down. Meanwhile his father clipped two coin-sized patches of hair away from the cow's neck as Richard watched over the proceedings, on hand in case something was needed from the vet's vehicle and to make sure all the numbers and paperwork were double-checked. Any discrepancy, however inadvertent, would cause a mass of extra bureaucratic paperwork and phone calls to the agriculture department and result in even more testing, papers and muddle. With a pair of calipers, the vet measured the skin on both sites, reading out the thickness in millimeters to Aled. The two sites were injected with two different TB viruses, one an avian virus which is used as a control measure in case the cow has a natural reaction to all TB viruses. The other site Gareth injected with bovine TB, before calling the all-clear, as Richard lifted the front latch of the crush, and with a pat on her rump, she rejoined the tested cows.

In three days' time the vets would be back to recheck the sights, but at least this was a much quicker procedure which took half the time. Although the cows were well behaved and there were no incidents, the initial test still took the best part of three hours, and Mervyn and Richard hardly had time to get some food in them, before they were back out and getting the cows in again for the afternoon milking.

In the evening Penny came over for supper, thankfully taking charge of the food. Having eaten, they sat down on the sofa with the rest of the wine and the reason for their excuse to celebrate, which was her nomination for a food award, with the ceremony to be hosted in Cardiff.

'We can make it a break of it, spend a couple of days to do

some Christmas shopping, catch a show, book a nice hotel. What do think? You can get someone in, to do the milking. Come on Rich, it would do you good to get away for a few days.'

He didn't want to dampen the pleasant evening, knowing he shouldn't be spending money on frivolities. Yet when he thought of his ex-wife seeking her share, he was tempted to blow it on a fabulous weekend away with his lovely Penny. He'd had nothing but bitching all week from Nesta and nothing had been resolved: all the while legal letters, each one costing an arm and a leg, were passed across like chess pieces, and to top it all, Simon's efforts in Ireland had produced zero. To hell that he couldn't afford to squander another few hundred for a couple of nights in Cardiff.

'It's a lovely idea, but—'

'Good, before you go all negative and think of the three hundreds reasons why you can't, it's settled. Remember we are business partners, this isn't just about me – it's our Mountain Range, just in case you've forgotten' She leaned across to kiss him, 'Oh, Rich you do worry so. Life's for living!'

As usual she was right, and after they'd made love he confided in her.

'You haven't got yourself a very good catch. In case you want to pull out.'

'What's brought this on, Rich? I thought you were happy with me?'

'I am. Very. I didn't mean us. I meant me, financially. Perhaps it wouldn't be such a clever thing for you do to, tying yourself up with me.'

'Tough, because I've just told the girls about you and next time they're down I want you to meet them.'

'I'm not sure they'll like that. A penniless bald-headed farmer!'

'It's not your money I'm interested in.'

'I could be going bust, Penny.' She felt the edge in his voice.

'Don't be silly.'

'Honestly, now.'

'Are you serious, Richard? Why? Is the farm in trouble? I thought you were going great guns, with the organic cheese and everything.' He could feel her tensing up, now fully awake. Neither of them spoke. The bedroom curtain fluttered in the open window as the loose pane knocked in the breeze. Richard heard the leaves rustling outside on the trees near the house, that slightly drier sound that heralded change, like the coats of his cows beginning to thicken, to lose their gloss. Late summer was turning to autumn. Penny idly stroked his arm across her tummy.

'It's not the farm. That's ticking along all right. It's my awful ex-wife. She wants a huge amount. It's in the hands of the lawyers, and I haven't a hope of raising the sort of money they're talking about. And to make matters worse, my brother had some bad news.'

'Oh?'

'I had hoped that Simon was going to secure a loan from my millionaire brother-in-law in Ireland, but when he was out there, he didn't even ask them. I was counting on Beth being able to help. At least to keep Nesta off my back, while I think of a way to release some capital that wouldn't jeopardize the whole farm. And there's Mam and Mervyn to consider.'

'Perhaps he's not liquid rich and like you, it's all tied up in capital.'

'I've never been out there. But he's very flash.'

'So why didn't your brother bring it up?'

'Quite! Apparently Bethan's been ill. She had a miscarriage and she hasn't had time to recover fully.'

'Your poor sister. It's a horrible experience. I had one once, I was only a few weeks gone, but losing it really upset me. It took me a long time to get over it and try for another baby. And even when I conceived again it wasn't quite the replacement everybody thinks it is.'

She tried to tickle him out of his sombre mood, 'It was a long time ago Richard, when we were first married and I was briefly happy.'

'I'm so wound up about saving my farm, I suppose I'm not being fair to Beth.'

'You come across as a real meanie!'

'Do I?'

'As if! I'm teasing you, silly. You've been very kind to me.'

'I wish I'd met you years ago, and then I wouldn't be in this mess. I could kill her for what she's done.'

'We have that in common, then. Ralph with his little tart hasn't exactly brought out the best in me, but revenge is always best served cold.'

'Do you know, I've wanted to push her over a cliff?'

'Understandable but not very clever, and you'd end up in the clink and lose the farm. No, you've got to play it clever, get yourself a smart solicitor, one who specialises in this sort of thing, land, tenancies and the like and fight your corner, Rich. It's what I've done to Ralph: I got myself one of the top business lawyers to squeeze every last ounce out of him. I told him to put Ralph through a mangle if he had to. At least I have the satisfaction of knowing he's really had to pay for his sex!'

'He's got a lot more money. I'm absolutely strapped for available cash as it is, without paying huge legal fees.'

'Yeah, but it will be worth it. You've got more to lose and it's not as if my husband had a long established family name to protect. Not like you, trying to save something that's been in your family for generations. No, Getting rid of me was easy for him.'

'I didn't mean to burden you with my problems.' He sat up, making her look at him. 'I've never been so happy as I am with you. Never have I felt like I do when you're with me, not in my entire life!'

She rolled over, covering his mouth with hers. 'Good. So let me help you. It's not as if I can't afford to. Think of it as Ralph's pay-off if it helps. And you needn't feel bad. He was and still is a very wealthy man. Have it as a loan and when the dust has settled, you can pay me back.'

'It's so kind of you, but absolutely not. I can't and won't take a bob from you. But thank you, my dearest Penny,' he said, kissing her.

'Don't look a gift horse in the mouth – take the offer.'

'I can't. It's against my principles. I know that sounds stupid,' he added.

'But rather noble and old-fashioned. So where else are you going to find the finances?'

He shrugged. 'I don't know. I've got a meeting with the bank.'

There never was serious money to make in his sort of marginal farming, even in a bumper year. Not like the financial markets.

'Call it a long loan from me.'

He shook his head.

'It's there if you change your mind.'

After Penny had gone, and feeling he'd not been entirely kind to Beth, Richard rang the Conna stud. Moira picked up the phone and kept him waiting several minutes before he heard Beth's voice.

'Beth, it's me, Rich.'

'Hello Rich. Is everything all right? Mam?

'Yes, we're all fine, Beth. I only rang because I wanted to know how you are and to say I'm very sorry to hear about your baby.'

'Yes it was sad, but I'm getting better.'

'You should have rung. I could have come over, or you could

come home to convalesce. Only we had no idea what you'd been through, not until Simon told me.'

'I asked Malcolm not to say anything. You've enough on your plate.'

'How did you know?'

'Because I know about stroke victims. I'm a nurse, remember?'

'Yes, of course.' He'd nearly blurted it out, assuming wrongly that she'd somehow heard of their plight.

'So how's everything at home, Rich?'

'You know we plough on. Everything much the same,' he said. 'But I didn't ring to talk about the farm. Simon said there were complications?'

'Did he?'

'That you'd lost a lot of blood.'

'Oh, yes I did, so I've been a bit slower to recover. I'm sorry I haven't been able to send Mam any postcards for a bit.'

'Don't you worry about that. And as soon as you're up to it you'll come over and see us? Or I can come over to you,' he offered hesitatingly.

'I'd like to come home.'

Before the allocated three days were up, he'd already noticed a swelling on three of his cows when he brought them in for their milking and when the vets duly arrived to check the injection sites, his worst fears were confirmed by Gareth. Meticulously he cross-checked the cows against their ear tags, and after measuring the amount of swelling, he read it off against his chart, making absolutely sure that the cows were definite reactors and not just inconclusive as some cases can be.

'At least you'll get some compensation, Richard.'

'How have I got it?'

'Don't know, just one of those things. Have you bought any stock recently?'

'No'

'And you use AI[20] and breed your replacements, so you've just been unlucky.'

'These aren't just any commercial cows; they don't pay anywhere near their worth. You know how long it's taken. Years of careful breeding to bring them up to this level. I'll be going back at least twenty years to get to this quality. What do they know, those men in grey suits? They've no idea.'

'Until there's a change in government policy, there's nothing we can do.'

'It's all right for you. They're not your cows and the testing pays well.'

He'd heard there were family problems and most farmers were prickly when there was a risk of an epidemic breaking out in their stock, so Gareth ignored Richard's comment.

'EU regulations, Richard. I don't like to see good cattle have to be destroyed anymore than you do, but my hands are tied.'

The vet understood the real loss to the farmer; he'd seen an increasing number of TB cases in recent years and whether dairy or beef, the loss to the farmer was infinitely greater. It had often taken a lifetime's work to build up a successful herd, more than any government payment could cover for the immediate slaughter. They both also knew that far from lessening the problem by instant cull and disposal, a full post mortem would result in a restrictive movement on all his, and his neighbouring livestock. TB in cattle was still on an alarmingly upward curve and no one knew why.

'At least the others are clear. If you can put them in, somewhere away from the rest of the herd, in isolation, I'll try and get them picked up as promptly as possible. You know the restrictions: no movement, no selling. And I'll need to look at the movement records. Can you remember if you've sold any stock off recently? If so, they'll have to be contacted and checked.'

---

[20] Artificial insemination

How could it have happened? Richard took such pride in his strict bio security measures. His yard was swept and hosed down twice daily. All the farm's fences were secure, the cattle's health and feet were frequently checked, and now as he was organic he'd done no buying in of any livestock or substances that could be harmful for his cows. Everything was checked: there were no harmful pesticides or GM on Tŷ Coch land.

He'd done everything he could to make his farm healthy, spending time planting hedges between the double fencing he'd erected, to allow for nesting birds and other wildlife, as the Soil Association had encouraged him. He'd even fenced off three small pieces of perfectly good grazing land to nurture natural scrub for wild mammals, birds, bees and other insects. The irony of it all, having made suitable habitats for wildlife, making his farm less reliant on artificial fertilisers, he'd been burdened with a disease he was unable to trace or do anything about.

Another equally worrying thought crossed his mind: what if he'd given Penny infected stock? He hoped to God the young heifers he'd sold her in the spring were not infected, or carrying the virus. He gave the vet Penny's details.

As soon as they could fit her in, the vets were down on her smallholding. Richard scrubbed his overalls and wellingtons with disinfectant and went over to help her get the cattle in. He looked at them, her Welsh Black cows first and then the younger Friesians to see if he could note a change, a look in any of them to indicate they were carrying a virus. But like his own cows they seemed healthy, with no outward signs of any illness.

Fair play to Penny, who must have been worried and cross about what had happened, as he would have been in her shoes, she remained unflappable and kept telling him it wasn't his fault, it could happen to anyone, and he had just been unlucky. But now the time had come and the vets had arrived, Richard could see she was anxious, and he felt as if he had brought a plague to her that could destroy her growing business. The older cows were sensible enough, not as quiet as his milkers which was only to be expected, but once in the crush, they had no option but to stand and have their skin pricked with the viruses.

The young Friesians were more skittish, cow kicking as they cantered around, and had to be channelled first into the shed and then, using a gate, Richard squeezed them, two at a time into the crush.

It was a nervewracking wait for any reaction that might occur and Richard called in the intervening days to see how they looked and to try and reassure Penny. On the third day, the re-examining took little time and it was obvious to the naked eye that there was no swelling on any of the patches of the cattle's necks. It was nevertheless good to hear Gareth and Aled confirm what they saw, that Penny's cattle were clear of the dreaded TB virus. His was an isolated case and with the restrictions in force, and with a bit of luck, his herd would not have a reoccurrence of the disease. Because he had not bought in any new stock to contaminate any of his herd, he remained convinced that badgers were spreading the disease from farm to farm.

37

It was raining, heavy and persistent, the sort of rain that would soak through. It prevented him from going out. Simon looked out at the sheets of rain that lashed the window of his hotel bedroom. He was tired from the demanding performances that allowed little time for rest. Too tired to do the sightseeing he'd planned. Instead he opted for a lazy morning rather than risk getting wet and catching a cold, sore throat, or any minor ailment that could effect his vocal chords and his singing.

After a prolonged shower he got dressed and wandered down to the lounge where he ordered an espresso with deliciously moreish Italian almond biscuits, and having made himself at home he flicked through the English papers before he picked up one of the glossies that was lying on the ornately decorated table. Sitting back down on the comfy leather sofa, he glanced through the features, turning over pages of illustrations of smart Italian houses and their interiors. He was about to put it down and think of doing something else, when he accidentally caught his coffee cup with his knee, spilling the dregs onto the magazine. As he clumsily tried to dab up the liquid something caught his eye and he peeled the damp page back. It hadn't helped that he'd covered it with strong coffee and he wished his Italian was better as he struggled to understand the article with its intriguing black and white photograph. He needed someone who was fluent in Italian to translate the piece as he studied the picture. One thing he could understand were the noughts at the end of the lira and if it turned out to be what he thought it was, then it could be exciting. 'However', he reasoned to himself. 'It would be highly unlikely that what he saw was in any way connected to what he recalled at home. All the same he clutched the magazine and he went off to see if the receptionist could help him.

'According to this, it's very old, Roman and rare, especially to find one still in one piece.'

'Is it worth a lot of money?'

'According to this article. Yes.'

'Thank you for your help.'

'You're welcome.'

Simon knew Wales had a lot of recorded evidence of the Romans, believing that all the names beginning with *Caer* had derived from the Roman word for fort. Caerllion, as far north as Caernarfon, Caerdydd, Caerfyrddin, Caersws. Although Llanfeni was not built on an ancient Roman settlement some old codger could have found it, one of his ancestors ploughing on a hillside and brought it back to use on the farm. One did hear of incredible finds. Like that bit of stone washed up on a beach in Gwynedd that turned out to be some priceless rare Roman relic. If it was, it would be a godsend to Richard, and he'd be the bearer of good tidings. A white knight!

In the privacy of his own room he looked at the magazine again, examining the photo and trying to remember the exact shape and markings of the stone at home, and when he'd last seen it. Was it still in the yard? He couldn't place it. He hoped his old fool of a brother hadn't smashed it up or got rid of it. To think the old Tŷ Coch pig trough could be the saving of the family farm.

38

'Malcolm, I can't find my mobile. Have you seen it lying around?'

'Use the landline.'

'I will, but it's cold in the hall. There's something I want to ask you.'

His lips compressed marginally. 'Now I'm so much better, what would you think of us going over to see them? Seeing Simon again has made me realise how much I've been missing them and I haven't been since Mam came out of hospital.' She seemed oddly distracted, lifting cushions and bits of paper in case her mobile lay underneath. 'I'm going scatty. I can't think where I put it!'

He smiled indulgently at her. 'I've taken it,' he said, and before she could ask why he added, 'I felt it wasn't safe. You could be traced by it and I didn't want, you know, any undesirables being able to locate you to where you were by your phone.' He saw her flinch at the thought. 'So darling, I had it cancelled, just to be on the safe side.'

'Can they do things like that?'

He nodded.

'Do you think they are still watching or following me?'

'Not if they've any sense. I didn't want to alarm you so that's why I got rid of it. To be totally secure.'

Her whole demeanour shrivelled, and he came over, putting his arms around her in a protective embrace. 'There's no need to worry, my pet, they won't ever be able to get you again. I give you my word, you're safe with me.'

She didn't answer him, turning away from his direct gaze. 'Here, use mine anytime,' he said. 'I'll leave it with you and whenever you need to, just use it.'

Such delicate progress, like a network of cobwebs glistening in a field of sunny dew easily destroyed; innocent or just clumsy, perhaps deliberate. The result was the same, a dislodging of her building blocks of improvement, leaving her precarious again. His remark was enough to stop her from wanting to pick up the phone, and all her enthusiasm and desire to speak to her family dried up. She couldn't ring, let alone contemplate a journey to visit them. It was still too early, she told herself, her hands fidgeting with her sleeves, suddenly feeling cold, sensing a breath at her back again, an old foe behind her neck, ghost riders with lidless yellow eyes watching her from behind. She did not trust herself. Her husband's innocuous remark unwittingly exposed her, bringing on her invisible tormentors, sending her spiralling.

Those had been her black days, standing at the edge of a storm unfixed, fluttering like a leaf. Starting light grey in a wisp of cloud, chased on to be consumed by the heavy sheet of black. That leaden menace that made her fractious, unpredictable, in the shifting shades of her despair. Sudden flurries of wind, whispering spitefully, until an oppressive stillness was released by weighty first drops and rumbles of thunder and she would break down and cry, like she had as a child when her father had drowned.

Memories flooded back from another time, when she had gone missing as a child. She'd been reported lost then, and searched for; she remembered a booming voice over a tannoy describing her, even down to the bobbles and hairband holding her pigtails, the attention to detail testament of her parents' love for her; her sweet mother frantic in panic, having lost her in the crowd. That cruel show day where it had started, the first domino to fall; over and over the scene which tormented her, and like her recent abduction, the subsequent events that followed leaving an indelible desolateness in her.

Private things that normally happen within families behind the scenes had been publicly exposed that heinous day when her family had been exhibited to a large, curious crowd. It may have seemed all part of the show to the amused audience, something they might comment about on their way home, but to the young Bethan it had been an appalling spectacle, one that she had caused that had left her with a permanent guilt.

It had been her actions, her selfishly going down to the fairground and getting lost in the first place, watched silently by Mervyn, that had brought it about. No longer the proud winner with his magnificent Welsh Cob stallion, her father Ianto was suddenly a callous, red-faced, livid man. Through the subsequent years, she could still recall his voice, menacing and thick from beer and whisky, threatening Uncle Mervyn in the main show ring. He'd slurred as he'd spat out his abuse with his fists up, and she'd remembered her Dad's eyes, accusing slits of cold hatred, and the ice cream, a 99 Mervyn had bought for her, dripping down her hand. She'd watched as he shouted at his wife, Elin standing mute, her mouth like a sick clown. Only there was no mask, no silly clothes or other props of make-up to

271

cover her pain at being made a public spectacle. Bethan felt the shame of seeing the person she loved most in the world unable to control his arms or legs, or mouth as he swayed drunk in the circle that had collected around him, baiting Mervyn on like a bear, all because of her.

It was bad enough that his glorious day had been hopelessly sullied, but back at Tŷ Coch it had got worse as she had lain in bed, listening to her parents downstairs. They had argued in the kitchen, their heated words dense in the airless, hot July night. She'd hidden under the sheets, hardly daring to breathe as her father's words rose in a crescendo, and then her mother shouted back, their voices reverberating under her floorboards. She'd gasped as she heard the smashing of crockery, and then the table being overturned and everything on it flying off onto the floor. Elin's alarmed cry, a thud and then silence, until there came the scraping of boots and the bang of the back door. The creak of someone going down the stairs, Richard's voice quietly anxious. She heard and remembered his entreaties, and the anguish in her mother's voice. Beth didn't dare go down the stairs; pretended to be asleep, but she had not come out of it unscathed. Perhaps this was how it had always been, their marriage unhappy, only covered up like parents do. Careful that is, until the day of the show when she had innocently blown their cover, and in her mind it had gone on from there, her father's untimely death in an accident followed by allegations. The fall-out, like a runaway wagon, with bits of her family life peeling away as it careered out of control.

No one would guess, seeing her later as a chilled-out, laid-back teenager that underneath the facade she still felt responsible for what had happened to her family. Those incidents that had irrevocably changed their lives were only alluded to, hushed up quickly so that Simon had been protected from his siblings' nightmare. Everything had been churned up like a rough sea, and somehow there had been worse to come in the days and months that followed. It was no wonder she'd become a withdrawn clingy child, frightened of the dark, of being left alone, always needing Richard's hand to take her. Wetting her bed, having bad dreams, always needing a light on and someone to be there.

School had been a relief, away from the hell of home. Miss Prydderch had warned the class to be extra kind to Bethan and for a few days afterwards they had remembered, but thankfully soon forgot and were the only ones to treat her as normal. They had bustled around her, noisy, banging about in the playground, letting her forget what had happened, at least until the school gates at teatime when her mother would come to pick her up. Only she'd preferred it when her mother didn't come, and she'd been able to prolong the illusion of normality, travelling on the school bus with the other children. She'd secretly wished she could go home with one of them and not have to face the chaos and mess of Tŷ Coch, which until her father's death had been her happy home.

It was different for Simon, who had been lucky never to have witnessed the scenes of hatred. He'd never known his father or been present to see the loathing that had crept into the walls of her home. It was an inherited loathing that infected Richard. And Mervyn had come, then uncle Merv. The man who came to live with their mother who everybody knew was Simon's father. The same man who'd lost an arm saving Richard's life, who'd rescued the farm, bringing them all back from the brink. This big blacksmith and horse farrier who had watched her getting lost in the fairground and who followed behind, to help her claim her prize of a goldfish and take her back to the showground, in front of her drunk father, publicly rubbing his nose in it. The fear of being lost had always stayed close, ready to surface, persisting through childhood. She was always worried in case she would be picked up and stolen by men she thought she could trust.

Once again for her own safety, Moira had moved back to live with them, so that Bethan was never left on her own. So vulnerable, they had become friends as slowly the older woman helped her daughter-in-law remount the blocks, the stepping stones across her divide towards a more stable sense of the world. The comings and goings of her daughter Clare helping her recover her balance so that the months slipped by and she found laughter again in brief snatches. With company, Bethan started to venture out, never straying, but at least taking the initiative to leave the four walls of the house. She remained anxious, telling Clare not to run ahead and never to go out of sight. She only went when Malcolm was home to ensure her security. She missed the sea, but for all her longing she had not been able to pluck up the courage to walk the short distance to it.

Today, however, was to be special and Moira led the way down the path to the beach, taking her daughter-in-law's hand as she hesitated, looking behind her.

'Come on, there's no one here, Beth. We'll go for a few minutes. Before the weather turns. We might see Pete on his boat. He's been asking after you, you know.'

'Why did Liam leave?'

The question surprised her.

'Oh, I think he felt it was time to move on, and he had a better job offer with Paul Shaunessy up in Meath.'

'He never called to say goodbye.'

'You were probably resting.'

She didn't say he'd been sent packing, kicked out without notice. He should never have gone boating with them, skinny-dipping with the boss's wife. It had been asking for trouble with a man like her son.

Beth bent down to touch the sand, sifting it through her fingers. A gull cried as it flew over the open water, making her start, looking up for reassurance to Moira who stood close by. Moira smiled as one would to a small child. Bethan felt a burst of pure joy for the first time in many months, glad to be alive again, gripping Moira's arm as her tears flowed. Clare came running back to them a piece of seaweed held at her side which she swished like a horse's tail.

'Why have you stopped? Are you sad? Has the sea made you unhappy, Mum?'

'No. Your mother's happy.'

'Don't cry. Look, there's the boat. Can we go and see if Uncle Pete is on it?'

'You run and see.'

'Only where we can see you,' Bethan cautioned.

'Giddy up.' She made to kick her pretend mount and trotted off along the beach towards the river where the boats were moored, her mother and grandmother in tow. They saw Pete's boat leaving the estuary and from the bank they waved across to him as he passed out into deeper water.

Seeing the trio standing at the water's edge he wished they'd come earlier so that he could have seen her up close and been able to speak with her to see for himself that she was better. It had been months since he'd last seen her and he'd been troubled by what he'd heard. What had happened to her? He wanted to hear from Bethan herself, not the gossips. From the day she arrived as Malcolm's bride, he'd often seen her on the beach, walking or riding, and had got to know her over the four years. She'd had the time for him and he enjoyed her company and liked having someone to take out on his boat. Until it had come to an abrupt halt. It came as a big relief to see her walking on the beach and raising her hand, and from the boat she seemed normal. Maybe he'd worried unnecessarily, imagining the worst when there had been no need to. Perhaps she would be able to come out for a fishing trip, just a little one in the bay, before the equinox that would herald autumn and inclement seas and he'd have to pull his boat in and up onto dry land for the winter.

39

'Gwyn? It's me, Simon, Simon Davies.' There was a pause at the other end, as the person tried to connect the voice and name that sounded familiar.

'I know it's been some time but your silence isn't very complimentary to an old friend! Gwyn! Come, on it's me!' He started to sing a little down the phone, ending in a laugh.

'Ah, you old devil Simon, of course I knew who it was! How are you? *Duw*, it must be a couple of years or more, old stranger.'

'No, not that long, I'm sure.'

'Ha! Ever since you said you'd get me those tickets you promised me, how long ago? Near enough two years. And you gave me a hell of a hangover. Do you remember, in Clwb Ifor?'

'Sounds like we had a good night.'

'And a skinful!'

'Time really flies by.'

'It's because you've become famous.'

'Nah. I'm older and wiser, and I can't party so hard!'

'There speaks a man feeling his age!'

'You and me both. OK, seeing as I promised and I genuinely forgot about it, how about the Ireland game in Cardiff? I'm sure I can get you a couple of tickets.'

'This time I'll believe it when I see them in my hands. Will you post them or—'

'I've got a better idea than that. Why don't we meet up for a pint and I'll bring them with me.'

'Brilliant, but I won't hold my breath!'

'No, seriously. I won't forget, anyhow there's something I want you to run your eye over for me.'

'Always a snag. Go on, tell me the worst. What do yo want me to do? You're not involved in any scandal or anything juicy, are you?'

'Not that sort of thing.'

'A beautiful damsel?'

'You'd be so lucky. Nothing to do with any of that, but more to do with your field of expertise.'

'Mine? Now, you do surprise me. So that rules out an all-expenses paid trip to some exotic place? Like the old days – you getting the pretty girl leaving me with the flat beer and dregs and pushed out to sleep on the sofa.'

Simon laughed down the phone.

'Ha, bloody ha,' added Gwyn. 'So long as you don't want me traipsing up some godforsaken Welsh mountain in the pissing rain where there's only a few bedraggled Welsh mountain sheep—'

'Something like that!' he replied easily, the image of Gwyn struggling with the Cader Idris climb in their college days making him smile. 'Just a photo I've got. I want an expert's opinion, that's all, in case I'm about to be ripped off.'

'Well, I hope you haven't bought it already, and mind you remember to bring the tickets.'

'Cheers, Gwyn.'

'O'Neills, seven thirty, Thursday, and mine's a pint of their best draught!'

Both men put down their receivers, pleased with the phone call. Flattering his old uni friend had got Simon what he wanted, and he knew he could trust Gwyn to keep it quiet. His advice would be invaluable and he'd be happy to give up a couple of international tickets, one of the useful perks of being a minor celeb. Gwyn Williams had studied archaeology. He'd gone on to do a PhD, specialising in Welsh human antiquities and was now a curator at St Fagans in Cardiff. If anyone could help him, Gwyn could, and at least he'd know something about it, or if not he'd have a good idea as to what to do and where to start. Gwyn for his part was chuffed that the rising star still counted him as a chum.

Penny had arranged that the girls would spend their half term with her and she'd been looking forward to having them back, thinking that the more time they spent in Wales, the more it would consolidate the idea of it being home. Away at school they grew up so quickly that each reunion exaggerated how quickly they were growing and becoming more indepedent in the time spent apart. She arrived early, pacing the platform and watching down the line. The signal dropped before she saw the train reducing its speed as it came into view. Only ten minutes late, it was easy to single them out from the other passengers alighting from the three carriages, their clothes and rucksacks the uniform of the young. They had earplugs dangling from their jeans pockets, and the taller of the two was busy texting on a mobile.

Penny raised her arm. Her loud 'cooee' across the platform was so un-Welsh that it made several people look at her. She was not in her anorak, tracksuit and trainers on an awayday trip to the coastal towns of Barmouth, Pwllheli or Aberystwyth.

Penny smiled happily at her two daughters. Slightly embarrassed, as kids are by any demonstrative parental show in public, the youngest, Sophie, waved back, nudging her elder sister, Charlotte. 'Come on, there's Mum.'

It was so uncool to run up the stairs and hug their mother. Penny's loud and plummy 'darlings' was too loud. At least, thought Charlotte thankfully, there would be no one from her school to witness the spectacle. Their mother would have gone unnoticed at Paddington or Euston but in Llanfeni she stood out, neither local or visitor, lodged like a pip between teeth to irritate her daughters. Trying to be ultra nonchalant, Lottie sauntered after her sister and held off as her mother flung her arms around her, gushing.

'You look fabulous! Oh it's so good to see you. I've been so excited. Do you know, I think you've grown since the summer.'

Exaggeratedly, she stood appraising her daughters, as if she was measuring a horse in hands. 'You've shot up, Soph, and you've got so slim! Did you have a good trip?' She took the overnight case from Sophie, noticing her elder daughter's lack of enthusiasm as she pulled up her rucksack, hunching her shoulders at what she saw. A backwater where sheep outnumbered people. A place where gas lamps on the station platform wouldn't have seemed odd. As they drove through the town it was virtually devoid of people, let alone anyone she would term cool.

'It's so lovely to have you home. I can't wait to show you what I've done and all the new animals.'

'How are the ponies?' asked Sophie.

'Fat and needing work. A week of riding will do them good.'

'We're not staying a week.'

She'd so looked forward to having them for the whole week and was not going to let Ralph have them back earlier than they'd agreed.

'Yes you are, you don't go back until the twenty-eighth. I've written it on the calendar.

'Yeah, back to school, but Dad's got us tickets for the U2 concert.'

'He's got what? Your father? I don't think so, Lottie.' Not that their phone calls or e-mails were other than clipped, to the point. 'Anyhow you're too young to go on your own.'

'We're not going on our own. Dad and Lily are going as well.'

'Your father going to a pop concert? You must be joking!'

She didn't want to start their holiday with a fight, but the thought of him at such an event was farcical. For years she had asked him to take her to see a show or musical and he had categorically and obstinately refused, and now she couldn't hide how galled she was. 'Ralph's always loathed pop music,' she said. Penny thought of her estranged husband, squashed against sweating bodies, in an arena full of loud noise, pretending to enjoy himself. 'No fool like an old fool,' she thought, picturing him in his trendy new black collarless shirt, which made him look even more scraggy-necked, trying to look in, wearing black jeans too tight for his middle-aged paunch, just to impress his new and considerably younger woman, 'God rot him, the bastard!' – and now here he was buying off her daughters with treats she couldn't compete with.

They were easily influenced and it was not fair to them, but it was difficult for Penny to appear impartial. When they got back to the house, she could hear herself trying too hard to say the right thing that would please them, overcompensating for the lack of the wow factor. Lottie slouched round looking at the farm with bored eyes, and whatever her mother suggested she resisted, finding a reason to say no. No to riding, walking or surfing. When her mother attempted to treat her as an adult and engage her with talk of her business plans she switched off, yawning. She showed absolutely no interest in the cows, bullocks or heifers and by the second day Penny gave up, leaving her to watch Sky TV.

She blamed Ralph and struggled to bite her tongue and hold back from exposing him for the boorish pig he was. It was tempting but morally wrong to slag their father off. It was so different from three years ago when they first saw the farm, where Lottie more than Sophie longed to have a pony and the space to ride around. She had insisted they buy surf boards and wet suits, which hung virtually unused with the pony tack in the garage. Fifteen going on twenty, wanting only the bright lights of London.

The night Richard was coming for supper, Penny had sudden doubts, knowing their first evening together with her two daughters could be a recipe for disaster. Did she want them to think of Richard as her boyfriend? Not yet, nor was she sure she wanted them to report everything back to Ralph.

On cue he turned up every inch the middle-aged farmer; driving up in his Land Rover, wearing a checked shirt and jacket that did not match his trousers, worn just a fraction too short on his brown shoes. He'd brought a bottle of wine and what he thought the kids would like – a box of milk chocolates.

'I only like dark,' Charlotte remarked as he handed her the box.

'Thank you Rich, and take no notice of her. My eldest daughter Charlotte is suffering from city surfeit.' At least Sophie's response was more normal.

'Can I have one?'

'Sure. Now you've opened them, I can have one. My favourite.' Richard took out a soft caramel, winking at the twelve year old. 'I've always had a sweet tooth.' Unwrapping it he popped it into his mouth, not minding the sweetness with his glass of beer. He could see he'd walked in at a moment when mother and elder daughter were at odds. She sat apart from them, not wanting to join in with her mother's little soiree. To begin with Richard tried to coax her but he was no match for her. She remained offhand, hardly bothering to answer him. His inane questions attempting to draw her out were clumsy and easy to deride. Regardless of her mother's grimaces and silent pleas, her teenage daughter was obstinately difficult, managing to make the meal as unpleasant as she could, becoming ruder as the evening wore on. When she cut across him with an exceptionally rude retort, her mother's exasperation burst and she lost her temper.

'Charlotte! Enough! Don't you dare be so rude. Richard was only asking you a question. The least you can do is be civil to him. He's our guest.'

'Since when? He's not my guest! Did you ask him, Sophie?'

'Don't you bring her into this, you little minx. He is my guest and this is my house. Now apologise.' Her serious misgivings had been well founded.

'It really doesn't matter.' Richard had had enough experience with Rhian to know a public showdown was something a parent didn't win.

'I never wanted to come down here in the first place. I want to go back to Dad and Lily. At least they treat me like a grown-up.'

'Pity you can't behave like one, then.'

Through her heavily weighted, off-centre fringe of straw-coloured hair, she looked daggers at her mother, trying to think of a bitchy comment in retaliation. Sophie, who had sat quietly, was looking down at her plate on the table focusing on her fork so that she wouldn't cry. She wished her sister would shut up so they could enjoy what she'd been secretly looking forward to. Home to Mum, where she could be herself instead of with her father and his girlfriend Lily. She wanted things to be how they used to be; their home cosy and lived in, with their dog, homemade food, and the smell of ponies. Only her selfish sister Lottie, was intent on spoiling everything, creating a scene centred on herself.

'Well you're not going back to your father—'

'I am. I've got my ticket and I can get a taxi to the station. You can't stop me. Coming here, I can see why Dad left.'

'You can be a spoilt little prig.'

'Lily doesn't think so! It's lucky I no longer have to live with you!'

'Sit down and behave, Charlotte.'

'And she's much slimmer than you and wears really cool clothes. She's years younger,' she said, getting up from the table.

'Nearer your age then!' That pulled her up, and instantly Penny regretted saying it.

'You remind me of my daughter Rhian. You are very alike.' Richard tried to butt in.

'You must be joking!' Charlotte looked disdainfully at the bald-headed, old-fashioned farmer.

'I'm going to ring Dad now. See if we can't go tomorrow instead of Thursday.'

'He's not at home, Lottie,' said Sophie unhelpfully.

'Lily is.'

'Lily is,' Penny mimicked. 'What sort of name is that!'

'Better than dickhead any day!' Charlotte moved from the table, upsetting her chair as she pushed her half-eaten plate and with her bottle of lager in her hand, stomped off, slamming the door behind her.

They looked across at each other.

'I'm sorry, perhaps I'd better go?' He raised his eyebrows in apology.

'No, you stay. I want you to. Is she always like this?' Penny asked Sophie who was still near tears. She shook her head.

'Sometimes,' she muttered.

'Does she fight with your Dad or is it just for me?'

'She has rows when she wants something.'

'And Dad gives in?' Sophie nodded.

'Did you really not want to come?'

'No, I did. Honestly Mum. I'm been looking forward all term. I much prefer it here to school or the flat. It's boring there and there's nothing for me to do. It's just Lottie prefers it.'

'It wasn't me who walked out on you. Your father chose to leave me Sophie, whatever he tells you now.'

'It's not that; she knows it wasn't you.'

'What is it then? Something else I don't know? You can tell me Soph, I wont spill any beans.'

'She's got a boyfriend that's all, and they've arranged to meet up in London this week.'

'Does your father know?' Sophie didn't answer 'I thought not. Do you know who he is or where she met him?'

'She'll kill me if I tell you.'

'I won't tell her Sophie; I give you my word.'

'I don't know anything about him, only that he's called Matt.'

Somehow she would have to contact Ralph without breaking her promise. 'Anyhow, Charlotte's not going to spoil your half term and tomorrow we'll get Sooty in and go for a lovely ride and if the weather's nice we could take the trailer down to the beach and ride through the dunes.'

'Can we, can we, Mum?' Sophie suddenly happy at the prospect.

'I don't see why not and if Charlotte doesn't want to come, I can ride Topper.'

Sophie got up from the table and hugged her.

'Brill! Thanks, Mum.'

Richard helped clear up, and stayed for coffee after Sophie had gone off to bed. The evening had not been a success and he felt for Penny, having to deal with the point scoring and hurt. He'd wanted to intervene, but instead he'd sat there, said nothing and been useless. He knew he was part of the problem and without him Penny would have sorted her daughter out. It reminded him of how ineffectual he was with his own daughter.

'Could have been worse, at least she's not taking drugs or—'

'You say that, Rich, but how would I know if she was! I'm obviously the last person she'd confide in. Oh, she was so rude, not like the old Lottie.'

'She's unsure and hurt and so she turns on the person she knows she can trust. She's just kicking out. Rhian's the same. Trying to put all the blame onto me. They need an excuse and where else but the safety of a parent. Unconditional love. It's little consolation, but your Charlotte isn't anything like as bad as Rhian's been.'

'That's not very reassuring,' Penny shrugged. 'Kids. Who'd have them!'

'Yeah. As if you mean that. We weren't much better, were we?'

'I would never have got away with being so rude.'

'The world's moved on and it's not so groovy!' The word made her laugh suddenly, reminding her of flower power.

'If ever a word dated you Richard, that was it!'

'At least it made you laugh! I remember making my Mam's life pretty difficult at sixteen.'

'It was a different sort of rebellion then, wasn't it?'

'The same. They're growing up and testing the boundaries and today there are so many things we didn't have to send them the wrong way. Everything's instantaneous. When I was young if I wanted to leave home after a row, I'd have to walk miles and by the time I got anywhere my anger had passed. Today everything's there in an instant for them. There's no waiting time to reconsider. Just push a button and it's gone.'

'Next time I have the bright idea that everyone should meet up, stop me.'

'Phew! So I'm off the hook with Rhian?' He laughed gently at her.

'Oh no, you don't. I've had my plateful of humiliation, it's only fair you reciprocate!'

'Thanks a bundle!'

Much later, after Richard had gone and Sophie was sound asleep, Penny knocked tentatively on the door of her eldest daughter's bedroom. She expected the silence, but still opened the door, knowing Charlotte wouldn't be asleep. Sitting up against the headrest of the bed and staring out at the dark sky, she made no acknowledgement of her mother's presence, her earphones stuck in her ears as Penny caught a regular heavy beat of drum. She knew it was going to be difficult, where to start to contain, if not heal the cut that, if she were honest, had formed before any split. Penny needed to build a bridge so her daughter could return to her when she needed. It was all so impossible now that they no longer lived together, and Charlotte was growing up so fast. 'I want to hold your hand,' rather than 'Up the Junction' or 'Fire Starter,' but it still all led the route away, a rebellion against parental control, a stretch of fledging feather ready for flight. The Beatles, Doors or Dylan, replaced by New Model Army, Faithless or Prodigy, but still the same prelude to departure.

She chided herself for not having faith in her daughter and letting her go and making her own mistakes in life. She sat down on the bed in the dark and put an arm around her, 'I'm sorry for being overprotective. Of course you can go to the pop concert, only promise me you'll be careful, that's all.'

Charlotte nodded. 'Thanks, Mum.'

'And try to treat here like home and come back whenever you want or need to?'

She nodded. It was better than being told to piss off.

'Goodnight, love,' her mother said, kissing her lightly on her shoulder. The feel of her under her pyjama top, was tense, vulnerable and so young.

40

At last Richard had some good news as the follow up TB test proved negative and the animal restrictions of the last months could be lifted. Only now did he feel able to concentrate on running his farm organically and increasing his cheese enterprise without the fear of another animal going down with the virus. The recent events made him more sceptical of the whole ESA[21] scheme. The whole area of Llanfeni was included in order to protect the natural habitats of the rare choughs and barn owls and he'd liked to pull out of the so-called green scheme but was contracted in. A group of mature oak near the road had caused two of his cows to become

---

[21] Environmentally Sensitive Area

seriously ill from eating too many acorns on the ground and on top of this, in a storm a large branch had ripped off, landing very close to the road. He could not afford the risk of leaving them standing in case they caused an accident and he'd be sued.

The odd small tree he could fell himself, but the old oaks would need a specialist and he made a mental note to have a word with Tegwyn. Sooner rather than later, if local gossip was to be believed. Tegwyn really was making a success of his new role and was giving up his forestry work completely.

Tegwyn was indeed enjoying being a businessman working several days a week in one of the units on the newly-built business park. Although half the units still remained empty, under the direction of Dr Arthur their project was expanding. With the scientist's expertise and connections in the medical services, demand had increased so that he'd invested in new equipment for the different stages that turned the gathered upland moss into the finished article. The sterilised, ready-to-use bandages were proving to be highly effective in medical trials. For all the glorified title that gave him a status among the small community, Tegwyn was still the hands-on part of the process. But for the first time in his life he had a salaried position rather than a price per hour or piecemeal work, even though he was still essentially the moss gatherer. Dr Arthur had left Tegwyn in charge of recruitment as the business grew, needing a larger workforce, a few local lads ready for hours of labour overseen by Tegwyn. He taught them how to collect the raw material most effectively, careful to pick the varieties the doctor had identified. He still drove to pick up Dic and Frank working alongside them, but now as their boss he was able to give them a pay rise.

In keeping with his new moss business, Tegwyn upgraded his contractual forestry work to 'tree surgery'. In the days he wasn't with the moss, he continued to take on forestry work, realising the smaller the job the more he could charge for it.

Tegwyn agreed to fell Richard's oaks, spreading his time over several weekends to fell what was needed, working early and late when the public sector was closed. Working for Trelawny had given him a new confidence, dictating his own terms as a tree surgeon rather than forestry labourer and working for himself was proving more lucrative, as both private landowners and county councils paid much better for felling and loping. Timber was an added bonus as the owners often didn't want the wood, leaving him to remove it. Once home he'd saw up the best for sale to the building trade. The rest he sold in large fertiliser bags as firewood to the increasing number of people whose homes had converted to woodburning as a primary source of fuel.

Driving up to Tan-y-bryn Richard noted the changes, reflecting how Tegwyn had gone up in the world as Richard himself slipped backwards, thanks to Nesta. Older and rougher than Richard, Tego used to call him a nancy boy and Richard had thought Ianto had shown a preference for his neighbour's son.

Tegwyn had also always had an unnatural interest in his sister, flirting with Beth, just to wind him up, and after she'd gone to college Richard had had little to do with him. He heard the farm labourer went through a bad patch, and was often in the boozer having to be dragged out by Dic and Frank. He ran the gauntlet with the cops, driving while under the influence, taunting them to catch him, but always quick enough to leave his crock of a car in some ditch and leg it over the fields. After one frozen Christmas period where he'd had a repeated skinful, he'd driven himself off the road, landing upside-down in some hedge. He'd landed up in hospital with broken bones in both arms and a pelvic fracture that kept him on his back for weeks. It sobered him up and he seemed to pull himself together making a go of things after the few tough years that followed his brief marriage. The gypo boy almost respectable.

There were no longer broken bits of machinery littering the

yard, but a county tractor, winches and trailer, all tidily stored under roof. A large circular saw took up what used to serve as the cowshed. Bundles of untreated fencing stakes, split logs and sawdust were all bagged up. He seemed to have made a handy little niche for himself, Richard thought grudgingly, as Tegwyn came out of a shed with his usual grin.

'What can I do you for, Richard?' he said.

'Place has changed.'

'Yeah, well you can't run a business today, not with all the health and safety regulations, without the tackle being up to scratch. I have to keep everything well maintained. It's got to be safe or I'd be out of business quick as that.' He clicked his fingers. 'So what brings you over? Fencing stakes? Firewood?'

'No, not that. Do you still do felling?'

'Yeah, I can. Depends how much, where and when. I'm pretty busy with the moss, but I dare say I could fit you in. Have you got something needing to come down?'

'A couple of oaks, you know, on the top near the road.'

'I think I know where you mean, the far side.'

'Yes, those. One of the branches came down last autumn and I think it's made the tree less stable. Could you take a look? I don't know how much you charge?'

'Depends. Oak isn't it?

'Yes, they are all oak there.'

When do you want it down?'

'Before the winter.'

Tegwyn looked at his watch. 'I've got an hour spare now if you like.'

'Good. I'll drive you up.'

When they reached the site Tegwyn examined the trees, leaving Richard to look on.

'Have you applied for a felling licence?'

'No, I didn't know I needed one.' He should have known he'd

come up against opposition from some nosey vociferous little group of busybodies.

'Can't fell a tree this size without a licence.'

'Isn't there a way round it?'

'Always a way, depends how dodgy you want to be.' Tegwyn walked round the trees again, looking at their trunks and roots. Did he want to help his neighbour? Not unduly, only he happened to be Bethan's brother. 'I suppose you could say they were dangerous.'

'Does that help?'

'If the trees are likely to fall or cause an accident then you wouldn't need a licence to cut them.'

'Brilliant. Are they dangerous?'

'Well, you've lost a branch. But look here. At the roots. You've got plenty of badger holes, and over here quite a few fresh ones. All helps to make them less secure.'

'Do you think you could wangle it for me?'

'Depends.'

'How much do you want for the job?'

'This tree? A couple of hundred.'

The amount surprised Richard.

'And for the lot?'

'You want them all down?' That's quite a bit of timber.'

'You can have the timber as part of the job.'

'Yeah, but I'll have to think. We might need traffic lights on the road, there's the cost. I suppose seeing as we're neighbours I could do it for five hundred.

'Is that with the timber?'

'OK. Say four fifty and the timber, and I'm doing you a favour.'

Richard extended his hand, confirming the deal with a handshake.

With the business done Tegwyn asked him, 'And how's the lovely Beth?'

'She's fine.' Then added, 'No, she's not been well,' knowing it would provoke a response from Tegwyn.

'What's been the matter? I haven't seen her home for a long time.'

'She had a miscarriage and there were some complications. But she's getting better. Simon went out to see her last month.' The news would serve as a reminder to Tegwyn that she was spoken for, and well out of his reach.

'Tell her I was asking after her, won't you?'

'Sure,' he lied.

When he told Penny of his revised plans for the farm, he had prepared himself for her adverse reaction and was surprised when they weren't forthcoming. Far from being against the felling, she was all for increasing his herd numbers and wanted him to introduce goats into his dairy equation. They'd decimate any saplings or shrubs and she was keen to introduce goat's cheese to complement their existing cheese list. A warm goat's cheese starter was the new prawn cocktail. She kept quiet about her ideas on ice cream, the usual flavours, and extra ones like elder flower, blackberry and Welsh heather honey. Cheese and ice cream would be a better way of making use of his milk rather than selling it too cheaply to the supermarkets.

41

Leaves turning their colour heralded the onset of cubbing and another national hunt season, and this year would prove pivotal for the O'Connor stud. After all the summer build-up, Malcolm's horses were to be tested, ready to face the obstacles they'd been bred for, and the new head lad was keen and able, all for pushing the horses early in the season. He wanted them racing before the winter set in, when heavy rainfall would make the ground bottomless and only stayers would win.

Malcolm had waited long enough, showing a generous amount of patience, hanging around at home offering Beth support. Now she was on the mend he could afford to leave home, knowing her to be safe with his mother about. Clare had started school properly and now he was freed up he could concentrate on training and racing his horses. He wanted to see them over fences jumping to win and win again to pay the bills and keep his name on the tip of the national hunt tongue. To be one of the best, better than his father.

For the last two months since Simon's visit, Bethan's progress had been steady and she had had no relapses. She talked again of visiting her family in Wales, only she'd have to wait until next spring and the end of the jumping season. Perhaps then, he placated her with a half-promise.

Once racing and away from the yard, Malcolm slipped back to his old ways, leaving Bethan in the dark as to where he was or when he'd be home. He stopped bringing any syndicate home, knowing how crowds and noise, and people, especially an unexpected nudge or even a handshake was capable of unnerving her. By keeping them away, he controlled who called at the house. His protectiveness towards her left Beth on her own and alone in the house now that Moira had moved back to her bungalow, leaving her with too much time on her hands, not knowing what to do but still lacking any confidence. She was unable to act impulsively without first taking precautions. If her mother-in-law wasn't accompanying her, she made sure she rang her before leaving the house to venture the short distance down to the stables. Only in the last few weeks had she dared to go further. First she went to the village and back along the tidemark, always with her home in her sights.

She had to learn how to drive again, lurching the car forward with jerky actions. Always anxious, she looked almost constantly in her mirror just in case she was being followed, driving permanently in third gear with her foot semi-poised, ready. She kept the windows shut, radio off and had made sure all the doors were locked. No wonder that she felt claustrophobic, sweaty and anxious and found driving one of the worst hurdles to overcome. To her credit she persisted, fighting her panic. She always parked and locked her car where it could be seen, preferably on the main street in full view of people. She didn't like too many people but worse was to be down a side road on her own where she could be taken unnoticed. An unexpected movement from a passer-by would make her jump involuntarily. She would often start in fright, letting out strangled gasps, provoking odd looks as someone pulled out a car key, or some other harmless movement. She would shout her alarm and run, jelly-legged in fear, away from people. It wasn't so much the banging but that soft subtle firm click of a car boot, a suction seal, rubber-lined, sound-proofed. Like those expensive, top-of-the-range silent, dark cars capable of slinking, stalking. She searched for bustle, preferring to be involved without the necessity of involving herself. She could only manage the small grocery shop or stand still by the school gates waiting for Clare, not too close to other mothers.

She had to fight the persistent urge 'not to bother', to stay at home, aware that she was in danger of becoming reclusive, enclosed in a prison of her own making, hating what it had done to her but powerless to change. Always prevaricating, she allowed the negative, the black to win, to keep her numb, holding her fast and out of life.

What her husband did not understand was that Beth might want to do anything on spec, for no reason other than she wished to. She'd lost her spontaneity, the buzz that made life interesting, and she loathed herself for her caution those men had imposed on her. She'd become a coward and her battle was to fight for the fun, the *hwyl*[22] of living. There were days when she was able to control her fear, venturing further from home as she gained confidence. Like a new swimmer moving close to the edge of a pool, Beth made herself go out of her depth, where she wasn't in control, to keep moving slowly, fighting the urge to run that would cause her to panic. She hung onto her determination not to let the loss of her baby affect the rest of her life, her resolve.

Perhaps it had something to do with growing up on an isolated farm with no option other than managing to get by that taught self-reliance and sufficiency of mind. Perhaps being tough through necessity was helping her pull through now. With her health improving Bethan thought more of why she had been the target. She knew Malcolm had money, but was it solely this or some sort of revenge for something he might have done in the past? She couldn't say: her thoughts were like pebbles in surf, churning over in her mind, knowing that some of her husband's connections felt less than safe.

When the time came to take her place by her husband's side at the race meeting, Bethan couldn't face going. She hadn't been on a racecourse since the last jump season and fretted beforehand, even though he'd deliberately chosen a quiet meeting in November with a small syndicate. She knew she'd be under scrutiny, that they'd look at her, like they did at their horses, rugs off. Perhaps pass on their condolences on the loss of her baby, or say nothing.

Man and wife had agreed to keep the darker truth secret – 'least spoken, soonest mended,' he'd said. She couldn't endure the handshakes, hugging, or kissing near her. The whoops of joy as an outsider came first past the post or the flatness of disappointment, of money bet and lost. Dirty notes in fingered pockets flitted away to the rows of smiling bookies. When the next race meeting came Moira went in her place.

---

[22] joy

42

At first Moira assumed she'd bitten something hard that caused her jaw to jar, and she carefully avoided further aggravation by eating on the other side. She tried to reason it away in the hope it would dissipate to nothing, but for the third night in succession the throb woke her. It was always in the middle of the night when the pain was less manageable. She'd tried sensitive toothpaste, a mouthwash, graduating from boiled, warm salted water onto stronger remedies: a tincture of cloves, soluble aspirin and neat alcohol. Eventually Moira resorted to attacking the tightened gum with a toothpick which at least gave her the satisfaction of a sharper pain. The throbbing intensified, running along her bottom jaw into her middle ear and throat, to the extent that she was no longer sure which tooth was causing her such trouble.

She had stupidly tried to endure another day, anything rather than go to the dentist, but the pain was such that she spent the night pacing up and down her bungalow, as pills and whisky were no longer effective. She sat, then walked with a hanky wrapped around her jaw, unable to do anything other than think of ridding herself of the toothache. By lunchtime on the fourth day she could stand no more and rang Beth. She didn't pick up the phone but that didn't mean she wasn't there, so Moira walked over, her coat collar turned up to protect the side of her mouth. Pain prevented her from calling out to reassure her daughter-in-law, as she knocked on the back door. Not expecting anyone, the knocking startled Bethan, who immediately hid, hoping the caller would leave. Quietly she crept to an upstairs window to look down at the back door. When she saw it was Moira she tapped gently to let her know she was there.

'I'm at my wit's end. You'll have to take me. I can't stand another minute of this agony.'

'Take you where, Moira? Is your tooth still troubling you? Didn't you see Mr Docherty?'

'He's off until next Monday. I can't wait 'til then. You'll have to drive me.'

'Drive you?'

'The pain's driving me to distraction!'

Bethan knew Malcolm and the lads were away at a meeting, but the thought of driving to an unfamiliar destination scared her.

'There's no one else to ask, Beth. I'll be with you; it's not like going alone.'

'What about Clare? I can't leave her on her own.'

'We can pick her up from school as we go past. Do hurry up, Beth.'

She was allowed no time for her ritual of preparing herself to go out, the checking and rechecking that had become an obsession. Moira groaned at her to get a move on.

Moira had found someone through her racing connections to see her at short notice, and as fast as she could get her daughter-in-law to drive, they journeyed south and inland to Killarney, where Mr Cleary a retired dentist and keen follower of hounds waited in his front room, ready to pull out her bad tooth.

'Why's Granny got a hanky round her mouth?'

'Because she has raging toothache darling, and we've got to take her to the dentist. She can't talk to you. It hurts too much.'

'Poor Gran.' So they drove in silence, Bethan concentrating on the unfamiliar roads as Moira sat silent, no longer caring what it took as long as the tooth would be removed and she knew by going to Cleary she would not be fobbed off with an X-ray or course of antibiotics.

It was after five when Bethan got to the town, where she parked the car in the first available space. They got out and proceeded up the street, mother and daughter behind Moira, who seemed to know where she was going. On the corner she turned left, so that she was briefly out of Bethan's sight.

Bethan caught sight of Malcolm suddenly but unmistakably. He stood with his back to her in the hotel car park that backed onto the street. Her view was partially blocked by parked cars, but she recognised his shape, his walk. He was with someone, bent forward in conversation. She had half-raised her hand, about to call out to him, when she heard the engine, that distinct 'tink' sound she instantly recognised as it started up. She froze, her eyes watching in disbelief as the man on the motorbike, helmet down, threaded his way up through the car park away from her, to the only exit under the hotel's archway, and out of sight as the hollow noise of the bike roared off onto the main road. Had she seen him hand the biker an envelope? It happened so quickly she couldn't be sure but she did see her husband pat the biker on the back before he strolled back to his own car and followed him out through the arch. All she could think of was the bike's sound that had echoed through her nightmares. There was something else about the bike that made it unique, something about its shape that she couldn't identify, but nonetheless knew it had to be the same one. The incident was over in a matter of minutes but it brought everything back; distended, warped, but horribly real. She couldn't speak, or make her legs walk. She was glued to the pavement, and Clare, only a few paces up the street, turned to see her mother rooted to the spot. Something was amiss, Bethan was staring across the road, her face in anguish. Sensibly Clare didn't wait for any instruction, but ran on to her Granny, calling out to her.

'For God's sake, what's happened, Bethan?' Moira said, coming back to her, angry but anxious, her tooth still jarring with the sudden movement. 'Did you see anything?' she asked turning to her grandchild. Clare shook her head. 'Well, we can't just stand here, Beth. You have to move. Talk to me, Beth. Tell me what happened?' Now was not a time for a panic attack, and Moira couldn't afford to leave her stranded in the middle of the street. 'Look, there's a hotel over there. Let's get you there. Then we'll—'

'No!' Bethan shook her head vehemently. 'Not over there. Please don't leave me.'

'I've no intention of leaving you, Bethan. I only went ahead of you to find the dentist's door. If I'd known it would do this to you. Look. I'm here now. We'll all go together.'

Bethan seemed reluctant to move. 'Clare you take your mother's other hand. Right, now you're safe between us. Come on Beth, we can't stand here in the middle of the street for eternity.'

Joining hands on each side of her, they walked with her like an invalid supported between them to the top of the street, round the corner and along the pavement until they came to Mr Cleary's villa. There was no front garden, only a bare patch of gravel. Once they were inside the front porch Moira pushed the bell, looking through the frosted glass pane of the front door, trying to check she had the right house, looking for the telltale signs of a dentist's chair, the sound of a drill and the smell of antiseptic. They heard a shuffling of soft-shoed feet on an uncarpeted floor and the door was opened by a man older than Moira had expected, his smile not the best advert for his profession.

'Mrs O'Connor, I presume. So you had no trouble finding the place? Good, good,' he said standing back to let them enter. 'And I see you've made a trip of it and brought the family. Come in through to the lounge where the lighting's better.' When he noticed Beth's uncertainty he added, 'No, no come on through. You never know, I may need you to help if the tooth's troublesome!' He showed Moira to the dentist's chair near the bow-fronted window. 'There, now we've got Mrs O'Connor comfy, if you two take a seat over there, to be at hand.' He winked again irritatingly. 'Now, if you could just open your mouth for me and point to the tooth.' Moira opened her mouth, 'Ah, ah, ah,' she muttered, her finger preventing any coherent speech. He adjusted the spotlight to get a better look, and with a pick proceeded to feel along her jaw. 'Ah, it's often the way with a sore tooth, the pain moves. I don't want to be extracting the wrong one.' It felt as if he was tapping her teeth with an iron crowbar and when he touched the offending molar the intensity was such that she let out a yelp in pain. 'I thought so. Good. Now we're sure, I'll numb you up.' He filled the syringe, flicking his finger against the glass. 'Now, just a little prick,' he smiled encouragingly, deftly squeezing a portion of the liquid into three different areas around the offending tooth. 'We'll just wait a while for it to take effect. You'll be no doubt looking forward to the new season?' he said conversationally to his near prostrate patient. 'You had that lovely grey a few years ago – what was he called – Fergus something?'

'Fergus Blue,' she said, her precise diction numbed by the effect of the anesthetic, and a bit of saliva escaped down her chin. The easing of her pain made her chatty, and she wanted to keep the conversation light, aware that Bethan was still looking withdrawn. Moira didn't know what Bethan might do and felt that the sooner he could pull the tooth and she get her home the better. She did not want some hysterical scene at the dentist.

'Yes, he was exceptional.'

'The late Mr O'Connor had a good eye for a horse. I don't mind telling you I won a few bob on him.'

'I wouldn't have had you down as a betting man, Mr Cleary.'

'A flutter. Something to keep the interest.'

'Get this tooth out and I'll give you one of my son's "ones to watch" for this season.'

It came away in bits, denoting the state of the rotten roots and with the fragments of enamel a most unpleasant odour of puss and decay. Yet for all its rot it was stubbornly rooted and the dentist had to use considerable force, going onto his tiptoes and pushing down to dig out the last stubborn ends. It took the best part of half an hour, and once he was satisfied he pumped the chair back into a sitting position, dabbing Moira's mouth with compact rolls of cotton wool to suck up the bloody seepage.

'Now, this young lady will drive you home carefully and if it starts to bleed, bite gently on the cotton wool. When you get home, but not for a couple of hours you can make up a cup of warm, previously boiled water and add some salt and very gently let it sit in your mouth. No wild swilling or the like mind, or you'll start a bleed.'

'Whisky?'

'Not for a few hours. Any severe pain, go to your doctor. The throb should lessen by the morning. No nuts or toffee for a bit!'

The air outside felt raw and she was in a hurry to get home before the numbness wore off.

'Are you all right to drive?' she asked Bethan although she did not feel up to driving herself. She turned to Clare. 'And you've been such a good girl, haven't you my pet.' Not a word of complaint for your Mammy. Granny will get you something special.' She looked across at Bethan, who nodded. 'We'll see how we go. You can always pull over and we can change round if you find it too much.'

Before Bethan started the engine she looked in her mirror half-expecting to see Malcolm and the bike rider. 'You won't tell Daddy. Mam's better now, see.' She smiled at Clare, catching Moira's eye.

'Not even about Granny's tooth?'

'You can tell him about my tooth. But we don't want him worrying about Mummy being frightened, do we?'

'Mummy, you're not going to be ill again are you?'

'No, no, I'm not Clare. I had a fright, for no reason, and

Granny's right, we don't want to upset Daddy, not with all the work he's got. As you've been so good we'll buy you something.'

'What?'

'A surprise!'

She didn't like buying her daughter's silence with a bribe, but until she could fathom out a simple explanation for what she had seen, her instincts told her to keep it from them and her husband. The drive made her concentrate on the road, but her mind kept pulling back to Malcolm, and the image of him handing a bulky envelope over to the biker. She was sure that they'd shaken hands. Was it possible he was still paying for her safety? Equally worrying but more sinister, did he know the man, as his actions suggested? She was convinced it was the rider who'd sped past that fateful day and helped her assailants bundle her into the boot. Could she be sure it was even the same man on the bike? She couldn't see Malcolm ever befriending a blackmailer, even though that's what it had looked like. She remembered now that he'd said something about a bumper at Listowel, running 'Ballylad' for a new syndicate. She tried hard to recall what he'd said that morning before he'd taken off. She needed to remember, to recall his exact words, so that she could make sense of what had happened in the car park and then broach the subject with him. Until then she couldn't afford to bring it up. How could she ask her husband what he was up to without revealing that she had witnessed their rendezvous? She had felt like a voyeur violating some secret tryst. How could she find out if it was just Malcolm doing what he had always done, brokering a deal? She'd learned not to eavesdrop. 'See a man about a horse' was a euphemism for everything else, she knew that. Who to trust? Who could she turn to for help in finding the answers? Hardly his own mother, who was sitting across from her, watching her behaviour, one eye on the road in case she panicked and put them all in a ditch. Who'd believe her? They'd think she'd gone doolally.

'Are you sure you'll be all right? Malcolm should be home before long.'

'No, we'll be fine. I don't know what came over me, but it's passed.'

Moira needed a good night's sleep before she made up her mind whether she'd tell Malcolm about Bethan's panic attack.

'So where have you been to, my little rose?' He picked her up, his mood happy as he swung her up. She looked at her mother before answering her dad.

'Granny had to have her tooth out.'

'Did she?'

'Yes. And she had to lie down and it was bleeding and broken. She showed it to me. It smelt ugh!' She wrinkled up her nose and laughing he squeezed it gently between his thumb and finger.

'And that's why you must brush your teeth every night.'

'I do don't I, Mum?'

'Yes, you've been a very good girl.'

She could tell he was in a good mood. There was a bottle of champagne on ice on the table and a packet of smoked salmon ready to be opened.

'Are we celebrating?' she asked him, after putting Clare to bed.

'I had a good win today. Ballylad beat the favourite.'

'Oh. Where was that?'

'I told the boys to spread it, do an each way. I thought with a good draw he'd be there or thereabouts but I didn't think he'd win. Bit lucky coming off the bend, but he stayed on well, came in a neck in front. The lads were pleased. Their first winner. There'll be a few sore heads in the morning, that's for sure.'

'You always have luck at Killarney.'

'Killarney? It's not until the end of the month. No, I was down at Listowel.'

'You mean you had a bit of luck there.' Perhaps he hadn't

even been to Killarney that day and she had mistaken him for someone else.

'So, now's your chance to ask for something. A bit of bling or new dress while I'm feeling flash!'

Or a slap on the back with an envelope full of wads, she thought, picturing them in the car park.

'So who did they have in?' She looked puzzled by his question. 'I thought Docherty was away on holiday? If my mother was in that much pain she should have gone to Johnny, he'd have pulled it for her no trouble. So where did you go?'

She was nervous of his persistence. Had he seen her standing on the pavement, snooping?

'Someone your mother knew. We went along the coast somewhere. I don't think he was still in regular practice. He was an elderly man.'

He smiled, noticing how tired and drawn she looked.

'You look tired out, my little one. Come and sit down. I'll light a fire and get you a glass of the bubbles and we can have a quiet, cosy evening.'

Sitting in his arms on the sofa her legs up across his lap, she relaxed with the champagne, salmon and warmth of an open fire, and she realised she had been wrong, that her judgement had been impaired and it couldn't have been the same bike or biker or even him.

She wanted to ask him, to hear him reassure her, his mouth close to her ear, nibbling her lobe. But since she'd started by not telling him the truth of their whereabouts he'd find it very odd if she came clean now. Especially as she was punctilious to the extreme in being where she said she would be at all times. She left her question unasked, pushing her doubts to one side as she let him take her upstairs to bed.

43

Two days later and it all seemed so normal that Beth almost believed she'd imagined everything, that she'd had a blip. He'd been up early for the first of the exercising and then over breakfast he pored over the newspapers and the racing channel, checking the runners, then gave her a quick kiss before going down to the yard with Clare at his side, who was holding her new jewellery-making kit tightly in her small hands. Watching them go she was apprehensive that her daughter would mention the incident without thinking, especially if Malcolm asked her about the trip to the dentist.

Relieved of her toothache, Moira had gone off for a couple of days to her daughter Rosaleen, leaving Bethan on her own for the first time since her miscarriage. There was nothing to prevent her from going out, down to the stables, to the beach or from driving to town, but she'd regressed. The incident in the car park had unnerved her, leaving her panicky and feeling unsafe.

She tried all she'd been taught to control her feelings, but her misgivings resurfaced in waves. A gentle, soft roll in the back of her mind built up forcefully, leaving her unanchored in her wreckers' sea. Could she or was she in a fit state to deal with the truth if it turned out her husband was in some way involved with what had happened to her? How could she possibly point the finger on the basis of such a loose premise, and how if she dared voice her troubled thoughts would she be able to live with the consequences? Either way it would destroy any chance of their living together as a family and she couldn't possibly accuse him on her flimsy evidence. Had she been made delusional by his loving words and actions? No, of course not, he was devoted to her and Clare. How could she think otherwise? The sound of his friendly slap on the leather-clad shoulder replayed over and over in her mind. Her brain, which had run unhinged in her months of trawling unfathomed depths, had gained nothing but loose debris. She had to be mad to suspect her husband of complicity. Yet for all her reasoning she remained convinced there was something there to mistrust, an animal instinct warning her to watch, to sniff the air, to catch a whiff of deceit. Her dilemma was when and how to unearth what she'd witnessed without showing signs of any of the digging.

She did not want to ask him anything that would put him on his guard, and set off alarm bells. So she waited. She was nowhere near as good as him at concealing things, but she forced herself to contain her rising fear, her paranoia, to sit still like a trapped mouse under a cat's paw, until she had some proof.

She watched him drive off to another race track, waiting long enough to know he wouldn't turn back, before she felt it safe enough to pick up the phone. What she heard herself saying sounded ridiculous, and with each question she could hear the incredulity in the person's voice. It soon turned to sarcasm as she tried to explain. Although he assured her that they'd look into it, she knew he hadn't believed a word and in the ensuing silence after she'd replaced the receiver, she felt even more exposed.

Sergeant O'Shea went through with the pretence making a few superficial enquiries, knowing full well that he had been dealing with a nutter. No one had reported a missing person from their small community. If such a thing had occurred he and half the county would have heard about it. He'd wait another week and then he'd ring back to explain there had been no such incident reported. It was common knowledge that the young Mrs O'Connor had had a miscarriage and that it had affected her adversely.

For days she waited near to the phone, nervous that he'd pick it up before her. She checked early each morning to see if she had any post.

'Are you expecting a lottery win?' Malcolm asked her, seeing her eagerly search through his already sorted post.

'No, I was hoping to have a letter from home, that's all.'

'So go and ring them. Look, I'll dial out for you. Get a chair and talk for as long as you like.'

She didn't want to talk in front of him, not trusting herself to keep the hysteria from her voice, and early morning wasn't a good time for Richard, who'd be busy milking.

'No, he'll be out. I won't ring them now. Perhaps I'll get a letter tomorrow.'

'OK my darling, whatever you want. It'll do you good to talk to them. Let them know how you are that you're getting along just fine.'

They both knew he was lying and she would not use the phone with him listening, imagining his breathing as she talked. She felt permanently tense, strangulated by his presence, yet she was fearful of being alone. Like a long lost friend she was excitedly pleased when he told her that her mother-in-law was due back.

The next day Moira walked to meet Clare from school, leaving Beth in the house to get the tea ready. Bethan's deterioration was immediately obvious. Just as they were coming in through the back door Clare tripped, spilling all her beads across the floor. Bethan came to her aid, getting down on her hands and knees to help pick them up. From the passage she heard the telephone ring and Moira voice as she picked up the receiver.

'Ah, Mrs O'Connor, I was just about to put the phone down, thinking there was no one at home.'

'Yes?'

'It's Sergeant O'Shea. I've looked into the matter you raised,' There was a pause. 'You remember you rang a week or so back. We couldn't find any incident of a reported abduction or kidnap. Furthermore I have made enquiries about the motorbike in the car park that so upset you. Let me see – yes, I have it here in my notes; "the 24th of last month, at quarter to six in the afternoon in the car park of The Brandon Hotel where you say you saw your abductor taking a packet, which you think could have been money from your husband." There has been no report, other than what you told me to substantiate this. I think the best thing I can suggest is if I come over and have a word with you and your husband? Is he there?'

'I think you may have the wrong person.'

'Mrs O'Connor?'

'Yes. I'm Mrs Patrick O'Connor. I think you want my daughter-in-law, Mrs Malcolm O'Connor. Has she contacted you?' she asked, lowering her voice so that Bethan wouldn't hear.

'Well, I'm not supposed to, but seeing as you're family, she did ring up. She was very nervous and agitated, especially when she got to the bit about this supposed motorbike she'd seen. I tried to reason with her. I was very worried about her state of mind. I didn't want to put the phone down on her in that state, not knowing if there was someone with her.'

'I see. I understand. Unfortunately my daughter-in-law has not been very well lately.'

'I understand, but because of the seriousness of the complaint I couldn't ignore it and had to look into it.'

'Of course. You were only doing your job. I'm afraid what she needs is medical help – a doctor, not a policeman. But thank-you. I'll look after her now and see that my son knows, but I'd be grateful if it went no further because of her delicate situation.'

'Who was on the phone?' Bethan asked anxiously when Moira came back.

'Someone wanting Malcolm.'

'Oh?'

'Nothing important. He was wanting to bring a mare over in the New Year to be covered. Why, where you expecting a call?'

It had to have been the afternoon she'd driven her to the

dentist. Something had happened to her walking up the street and her sudden strange behaviour was explained by what the policeman had told her. It was unlikely that a wife would make a mistake of her husband's identity and there was no reason to suggest Beth had. But the nonsense about the man and the motorbike? Her abductor with her son? Absurd.

She would have to talk to Malcolm about it to clear up the misunderstanding and hopefully put Beth's mind at ease. Yet the more she mulled it over the more it bothered her, not because she didn't believe what the police had told her, but by going to her son she was in some way going behind Bethan's back, betraying her, and it might be enough to send her over the edge. She had obviously made a point of ringing the Garda without telling her husband, and however deluded she was, Moira did not want to be the person to expose her. She already saw her regression and didn't want to do anything that would push Bethan further.

The two women had become much closer: Clare's birth and then Bethan's need of her mother-in-law had cemented the female bond, so that Bethan knew she could rely on Moira's support. Moira had become her friend and safety net. Moira owed it to Bethan not go to her son first, not until she had had the time to talk it over with her daughter-in-law.

Unexpectedly it was Bethan who came to seek her out. She peered through the bungalow window to see Moira doing her daily crossword, the racing on in the background. Moira beckoned her to come they were in and once in the lounge, Bethan came straight to the point.

'You know the phone call yesterday? Was it for me? Because I've been expecting someone to contact me.' Bethan was agitated, not able to be still, trembling as she looked around the room.

'Beth, why don't you sit down and have cup of tea?' Bethan shook her head. 'I was going to come over and tell you.' Moira saw Bethan jump at the prospect of some news. 'Whilst you were picking up Clare's beads, that phone call was for you.'

'The man with the mare?'

'Yes. Anyhow, the person,' – she was careful not to say man – 'wasn't ringing about a horse. It was the Garda, the sergeant you'd rung. He informed me of his investigations into your enquiry.' She put her hand across to touch her. 'Dear Beth, why didn't you tell me what you saw that day at the dentist's? All this time, keeping it to yourself and there I've been, worrying about you, racking my brains to try to understand what had so upset you there. You've been coming on so well and then, all of a sudden there was this. You should have told me, Beth. I could have helped you.'

'What did he say? Did you see them?'

'No. See who, Beth?'

'Malcolm. With that man.'

'Malcolm? In Killarney?' She thought back, 'That wouldn't be so strange, would it? In a day's racing with two courses within throwing distance. If it was him, why should it have given you such a terrible fright? If only you'd said, we could have gone over to speak to him and sorted it all out there and then.'

'I know it was him.'

'Yes, OK. So it was him, but why ring up the police?'

'I'd know that sound anywhere.'

'You're not making sense, Beth.'

'The motorbike. The man on the motorbike was the same man and he was talking to Malcolm. Don't you see, Moria, they knew each other? He handed him a package. I had to tell the police in case they were planning something else. What if they were threatening to steal Clare and were blackmailing him!'

'Now you're just being crazy. Could you ever imagine Malcolm allowing himself to be blackmailed?' She tried to sound reassuring. 'As if he'd contemplate talking to someone whose intention was to hurt his daughter? He wouldn't let a fly hurt a hair on her head. You know that, Bethan.'

What Moira was saying was correct – Malcolm adored his daughter – but just as she knew this, she was equally sure of the identity of the biker. Having failed to convince Moira, Bethan was on her own. Malcolm must have had something to do with her abduction. No wonder they would think she was mad, and as if Moira had sensed her thoughts or just stumbled on the idea, she lowered her voice as she asked as gently as she could, 'Beth, why on earth would your husband have anything to do with such a heinous plan? To hurt you and lose his own baby?'

She sat perched on her chair, trembling with emotion, fighting to keep control of her shaking, compelling Moira to put her arms out, and pull her into her to comfort her. 'There, there, Beth.' It was like soothing a child after a nightmare.

'He didn't know I was pregnant then,' she said in a small voice. 'I hadn't told him. It's why I went up to Dublin to see the gynaecologist. I had a scan. That's how I knew I was carrying a boy. I had the photos to show Malcolm: sixteen weeks old. Only I never got the chance. This happened before I could.'

'He still wouldn't—'

'Because he saw his wife having a good time without him and he didn't like it. It's why he got rid of Liam, because of a boat ride.'

She pulled away from Moira, standing up ready to remonstrate, excited she'd finally understood why. 'Don't you see? I wasn't under his thumb anymore, and he didn't like it.'

'So he planned your kidnap?'

'Yes.'

'I've never heard anything so preposterous in all my life. If you could only hear yourself, Bethan!'

'He's been very clever. He's been counting on it that no one will believe me, his crazy wife. I had no option but ring the police. And they don't believe me either.'

'It's not that I don't believe that you think it is true, Beth. I'm not for one minute blaming you. I just want to find a way of helping you over this.'

'There is no way.'

'But if we go together and talk to Malcolm. That, surely, will be a start?'

That would be playing into his hands; he was like a fox waiting until the silly little hen passes too close.

'No, no, please, I beg you. You mustn't say anything to Malcolm. He'll have me locked up.'

Bethan broke down, sobbing.

'I give you my word Bethan, he will not do anything to hurt you. I won't let him. We have to get to the bottom of this so that you can move on and put this ghastly episode behind you.'

'He'll kill me.'

'Bethan! Bethan. He won't. I'll be with you and I won't let anything happen. No one is going to take you away, or hurt you or Clare.'

Her mother-in-law's kind words struck a fatal blow for her freedom, exposing her madness, as she'd be obliged to relate their conversation to her son. She knew the look he'd give his mother as she told him. Incredulous, he'd enjoy the drama, show his astonishment. He'd already cornered her, ready for the kill. Bethan knew she had to act, to do something before it was too late. She and her daughter had to leave, to escape him before Moira had a chance to tell him. Somehow she had to go off, innocently as if on a walk, without raising any alarm. She had to shift and make her move, slip through a small hole before he had the net pulled up tight with her inside.

44

The recent warm weather had dried only the surface earth, leaving the soil underneath wet and heavy. Sloe, blackthorn and elder filled the lanes. Occasional trees of Welsh wild plum with fruits of ripening purple stuck out from the straggly hedges, offering an abundance of food before winter made it scarce. Blackbird and thrush waited for bunches of mountain ash and hawthorn. The air smelled distinctively autumnal.

At the edge of the wood, the unmistakable scent of fox lingered in the early morning hoar, failing to conceal its brown scent and trail, covered over by the spent fronds of bracken, breaking out onto moss. His frequently-used route ran through the wood and up along the wire fence; it was easy to spot from a distance, until near the top his path changed direction, crossing out under the wired fence and onto the open hill. Here Tegwyn lost the fox's trail, which petered out among the prints of grazing sheep.

He was happy to be out, under bough in wood, earthy in his surroundings, his *cynefin*,[23] where nature went its way. It reminded him of growing up, his lost youth spent out of doors with stick, net and ferret, flogging rabbits for pocket money. Poaching trout and salmon as they swam up the small streams and popping off pigeon, pheasant and any duck that came his way. Once he'd shot a swan, passing it off as a goose.

Things change; life moves on, and he wasn't grumbling. His lot hadn't turned out so bad, working for Dr Trelawny. But he hadn't lost his roots as a country boy – he was still a bit of a lad, a cowboy at heart hankering for days out of any office, on his own, working in some remote spot.

He stopped to look over the job he'd been doing, wiping his

---

[23] Habitat

nose on his sleeve, satisfied with the progress he'd made. Oak trunks lay felled, their stumps a smooth yellow circle in the gap left by the fallen tree. He'd been pleased to get the timber thrown in on top of the cost of doing the job. Most of the wood was only fit for firewood, but what Richard hadn't realised was the value of the bark. Tegwyn did, which was one of the reasons he had agreed to take on the job. Always keen for a bargain, knowing oak bark was selling at around seven hundred pounds a ton, he'd played hard to get, only saying yes so he'd get to talk about Bethan. Although Richard had let on she'd been unwell, Tegwyn took it as being unhappy rather than physically ill, and using a spoon-like tool he attacked the bark, thinking of Malcolm as he pushed up under the moist growth, stripping the tree bare of its skin. Once off, he stacked the strips, bark side down in bundles to dry. Later he'd store it in one of his sheds in the yard before he sold it on to the tannery. Where the bark wouldn't lift, normally on the smaller twisted gnarled branches, he put his chainsaw through them, ready to make up into bundles of firewood. Initially the stripped trunks glistened but within a matter of hours they dried and darkened in colour. Never idle, Tego worked vigorously through the morning, stopping only for a coffee and a couple of roll-ups; he ate convenience foods – a packet of crisps, pork pie and cake. He had a quick pee and then he went back to his work. It was only when he downed tools that he felt the afternoon chill. He left the bulk of the wood lying, loading up his trailer with some of the sawn logs and his valuable bundles of bark. Having stopped he felt the damp cling in the fading light, and rubbing his hands he decided he'd done enough for the day. He collected up his tools, his can of fuel and chainsaw, putting them inside his pick-up. He reckoned he deserved a pint.

From the road, the white shadow to the side of his headlights caught his eye, and Richard pulled in to see just what it was. It wasn't too elongated to be an animal and too still to be an owl in flight. He switched off the lights, leaving only the side ones on, and peered out at the dark shape. As his eyes grew accustomed to the lack of light, he realised Tegwyn had wasted no time felling the trees. He hadn't expected them to be stripped of bark, and it had been their whiteness that had caught the landrover's headlights. He got out to inspect the work, running his hands over the pale lengths. The place was strangely empty without the oaks and he knew his mother would have regretted their felling. Shrugging it off, Richard decided that rather than returning home to an empty house, he would call in to the pub for an evening pint.

There was a small but effective open fire, throwing out a welcoming heat. He acknowledged the smattering of locals with a nod and smile as he leant on the bar, automatically rubbing his hands towards the warmth the fire. At his back there was a loud tap-tap on the table nearest the fire, 'Knocking again! *Wyt ti wedi stitchio'r gêm i fyny eto, Teg?*[24]'

He turned to see the three of them playing dominoes, older but the same as ever – Dic, Frank and Tegwyn noisy over their beer. Frank chuckled as he lay down his domino, finishing the game. 'Mild with a spot,' he said, handing his empty pint glass to Teg as he got up to get the next round in.

'*Duw, Duw*, we don't often see you in here, Richard! As I'm getting them in, want a drink?'

He hesitated, 'Go on then, half a lager.' When his drink came he thanked him. '*Hir Oes*[25]' – 'I see you've already started on the oaks.'

'Tidy job, too. I hope you pay as quick.'

'I need an invoice first. Did they come down all right?'

'It wasn't easy by the road there, but with the right tackle and a lot of know-how,' he said, tapping his nose with a stubby finger. 'Professional job.'

---

[24] You've fixed the game again, Teg!
[25] Long Life

'Yeah, I'm grateful. Thanks, Teg.'

'Better safe than sorry,' Tegwyn added trying to make it sound significant.

'I couldn't afford a tree falling across the road. Tell me, why did you take the bark off?'

'Dries better. And it's more effective if you want to treat the wood.'

'New one on me.' Richard said. 'Will you use it for fencing posts?'

'Lots of it is poor quality. Twisted, so most of the stuff's not fit for anything but firewood.' He didn't want Richard knowing he'd sawn some of the trunks into planks for the building trade. There was quite a demand for oak beams in barn conversions.

'Have you got any firewood for sale? Not the green stuff you've just felled for me. I was looking for some seasoned hardwood. You know, in lengths, for a wood-burning stove.'

'For you?'

He could mind his own business, always wanting to know other people's business, sniffing about with his piggy snout to see what Richard was up to, knowing he didn't need to buy wood for himself.

'No, not for me. For someone else.'

'Oh, like that, is it? You'd be surprised just how many people are converting to them. I'm selling a lot to the greenies. Probably be able to fix you up, for the right price. Delivered?'

They both knew Richard was buying for Penny, who wanted some for her wood-burner, but he didn't want Tegwyn delivering them to her.

'No. I'll collect it with my trailer. I don't mind ash or alder, any hardwood as long as it's properly seasoned. About a foot to eighteen-inch lengths?'

'I'm sure I've got some in the shed. Do you want me to saw it up to the right length for the lady?' Tegwyn added with a wink.

'No, I'll do that, but it's got to be dry. What do you charge for a trailer load, say?'

'As we're neighbours, I'll do you a special price, a hundred pounds for a load.' It seemed reasonable enough and should last her until spring if the winter wasn't too cold. He followed his farmer's instinct to haggle, to see if he could knock off another tenner.

'Tenner off, as I'm collecting?'

'Get on with you! I've already given you a discount. It's only because you're Bethan's brother or I'd charge you the full whack. You said she'd been poorly. Is she better?'

The question reminded Richard of the postcard he'd received that morning, and in his rush he'd stuffed it in a pocket and forgotten about it.

'That reminds me,' he said rummaging around in his pockets. 'I had a postcard from her this morning as it happens.' He fumbled as he pulled out a bit of baler twine, cow's ear tag, a nail and a shop receipt before he found it in the inside of his jacket pocket. 'Ah, here it is,' he said, pulling out a somewhat bent postcard. On the front was a large seagull perched on a quayside post. The seabird had been covered over with spots.

45

The old pig trough hadn't been moved once Richard had remembered where he'd stored it, and although it would have been much easier to have used a power hose, Simon had advised against it, telling him to handle it very gently, as if it were precious. It was a large slab of stone which Richard had spent several hours cleaning with a brush and water to remove some of the dried cow dung. Once it was a bit cleaner it still didn't look very promising, but what did he know about ancient Celtic stones? He had his doubts that it was worth anything, but would wait until his younger brother and an expert showed up.

'I can't tell you immediately. I'll need to take some photographs and to do some tests. There's no need for you to hang around. I'm sure you've got plenty of other much more urgent things to do than watch me.' Gwyn preferred to work alone without them hovering over him. 'I'll come to the house when I'm through.'

So the two brothers went off to the farmhouse, and Richard was glad of the opportunity to have a moment's privacy with Simon. He needed to speak, to quiz him face to face.

'Before you go over to see Mam, have you heard from Bethan? I can't understand why she's become so uncommunicative. It's not like her. Even if she's been ill.'

'Not for a bit, no.'

'You were the last to see her, and you didn't say much when you came back.'

'You knew I wasn't happy. I told you, Rich I didn't like leaving her there. I said there was something amiss then, even though she insisted she was on the mend. There was something odd about the whole set-up.'

'Yes, but what do you mean by odd? Tell me what you mean.'

'I can't. It just felt strange. Wrong, out of synch.'

'Were Malcolm and she all right together? He seemed just the type to have, you know, someone on the side.'

It wasn't a subject they normally discussed.

'No, I don't think it was that sort of problem. If anything, he was too concerned, almost smothering her with his need to protect her.'

'Probably guilt.'

'That's what I thought and what Bethan tried to impress upon me. But, and it's been niggling at me because I can't put a

317

finger on it, there's something not right. I've been really worried about her, Rich.'

'You won't like this either then,' he said, and going to the sideboard pulling out the postcard he'd shown Tegwyn earlier from under some letters. It's probably nothing, but I got this in the post yesterday. I can't make head nor tail of it. Unless it's Clare's work. I mean has our sister gone off her rocker? I can't make any sense of it, can you?'

As Simon studied the card, Richard went on, 'It seems bloody ridiculous. Here we are, almost in the twenty first-century and I can't get hold of my sister, by letter or phone. She doesn't seem capable of answering any calls. She could be on the moon for all I know!'

'So speaks the caveman,' Simon thought, knowing how useless Richard was with mobiles or computers.

'And then all of a sudden, I get this weird card from her.'

'She's got a phobia about the phone. She wont pick it up, and she's given up her mobile. She's convinced that's how she got caught and so she lets the phone ring if her mum-in-law or husband isn't there to answer.'

'What do you mean, caught?'

'She's convinced it was because of her mobile that it all happened.'

'What happened? Have I missed something, because I don't understand what you're saying. How can a mobile phone cause a miscarriage? Mind you, I've told Rhian they'll mush her brains.'

Simon had given his word not to reveal what had really happened to their sister, but he wanted to tell Richard. The card confirmed his fears that Bethan was losing the plot. He was about to explain when the phone rang and as Richard went to pick it up he said to his younger brother, 'I'm going to ring tonight and I'm going to insist on speaking to her. We've got to find out what's going on there.'

Simon looked back out of the window and across the yard, wondering what to say as his brother spoke into the phone. 'This afternoon. As long as you bring it before the milking, otherwise I've got my hands full. Sure. Ta ta.' He turned back to Simon, 'So are you going to tell me what really happened or will I have to force it out of Malcolm?'

'You'll find he's very plausible and persuasive. He'll assure you everything's fine, like he did with me. It was only when I got the opportunity of speaking to Beth alone that she opened up a little. But then he came in and she clammed up.'

'Why? Is she frightened of him? Has he hurt her?'

'No, I can't say that, quite. She seemed incapable of having or at least expressing her own thoughts, as if his being there stops her from behaving normally. She wasn't rational. And she agreed with everything he said. Only thing is, I didn't believe her and I still don't. It was phoney, but what could I do when she kept saying it was all fine and she was better and Malcolm was looking after her 'like a saint'? Those were the words she used to describe him! Now you can understand why I never raised the question of a loan.'

'I wouldn't have asked if I'd known how serious things are.'

The noise of footsteps followed by a knock stopped them speaking further as the door opened and Gwyn let himself into the kitchen his face beaming.

'Good news?' asked Simon

'The kettle's on. Would you like a cup of tea or coffee? Should be some biscuits somewhere,' said Richard, trying not to look too anxiously keen for anything that meant he might not have to sell.

'Coffee. Milk and two sugars. *Diolch*.' Gwyn took the mug, blowing on the surface and making a show of warming his hands, as if it was winter and not autumn outside.

'It's cold once the sun goes.'

He'd no idea, Richard thought, sitting in a warm office, as he smiled pleasantly, offering a packet of chocolate digestives.

'Put it like this, I'm hopeful. All the tests I've been able to do in the yard so far haven't discounted it. But it's early days. We'll need to do a lot more testing. Probably have to move it from here. When I get back to Cardiff I'll make a start. I'll need to bring in other professionals before anything can be properly validated. All I can say is from what I've seen today, the signs are promising.'

To think of Richard, Ianto, his grandfather and how many generations of Davieses, throwing slops into a trough that was worth a fortune! As the pair left, Richard pulled Simon on his sleeve, letting Dr Gwyn walk on to the car. 'Thanks Simon, for bringing him over, and you know, for helping.'

'Fingers crossed,' Simon said, smiling, aware that it was the first occasion in a long time his brother had thanked him for anything. 'We need to sort things out with Beth, but I'm in Germany next week. You've got my mobile number and I'll leave you the hotel details once I know them. I'll be in touch before I go.' He added, 'Don't tell them,' nodding his head towards the cottage. 'They don't need any more to worry about.'

'I wasn't going to. Let's hope we can give them some good news soon, eh?'

The morning she got the idea, and before she lost the impulse, Bethan left home, walking briskly down to the village. Her time was running out and, feeling unnerved since the scene in the car park, she knew her husband was watching her ever more closely. He was solicitous, almost obsequious in his condescension, as if he revelled in her reduced condition, treating her as if she were sadly deranged. Clare had started playing up, reacting with tantrums if she didn't get her own way and unlike other kids, she had neurotic over-protective parents. She was never allowed out on her own to play, nowhere without someone nannying her and

Bethan had instilled her own abnormal fear and paranoia in her daughter. 'If only she'd had a baby brother,' she thought bitterly to herself, watching Clare pout, bored and spoilt at having had a no changed to a yes too often.

So on that fateful morning her only choice had been the local shop, which was within quick walking distance. The selection of postcards wasn't great; Bethan searched along the display rack, through the pictures that had become faded by time and light, the demand for them being slight. Choice was limited to crosses, ruined remains and a few coastal pictures, as well as the proverbial donkey, but nothing she was looking for. A lone seagull would have to do. It stood on a post that was part of a sea break, perched above the water at high tide. Luckily there were two of them, and she bought them both. Considered a seaside pest, a scavenger of the promenade, who'd steal chips and cornets from holidaymakers, there was something about gulls that Beth had always liked. Eager to be out of the shop so she could write them without being caught and post them quickly.

On the quayside she tried to compose herself, thinking of what to write on the blank square, some message that her family would understand. Instead of filling the back, she turned the postcard over and proceeded to cover the gull's body with spots, defacing the picture with her biro. She did the same on the other postcard before addressing each one. Stupidly, in her haste and agitation she'd forgotten to buy any stamps and needed to return to the shop. Holding her cards tightly she got off from the damp sea wall and hurried back towards the shop.

Pete climbed the wall ladder, hauling his pots up onto the quayside, ready for winter storage. He never liked autumn the dying off of summer to be replaced with empty long evenings where he had too much time and little company. At least mending his pots and tackle would help pass the interminable time until spring.

He looked up and saw her walking his way and normally he'd have waited for her to come to him, but because of everything that had happened, he felt she might walk past without speaking. He started towards her and although she greeted him with a smile, she seemed distracted and was keen to move on, all the while looking edgy and unsettled.

'It's good to see you out and about, Beth.'

She smiled nervously, and seeing something wrong, he moved closer to her. 'How are you doing, missy?' he asked gently. 'I'm so sorry about everything that's happened to you.' He shrugged, opening his hands upwards. Her lips trembled before she managed to reply.

'I'm well, thank you,' she said stiffly, her manner in stark contrast to their former easy friendship.

'They wouldn't let me help. They kept me and Liam away. I called, but he wouldn't have me in the house, saying you were too ill for company. My company anyhow.' He had expected to see her pale, but not this withdrawal from him. Only her eyes showed how frantic she was, blue fear, trapped like an animal, shifting, unable or unwilling to look at him. He looked across at his pots piled against the quayside wall.

'I was just bringing my pots in before the winter. There'll be no more pots for a bit. Never mind, it'll soon be spring and with a bit of luck, you'll be back out. I'll need a hand now Liam's away in the north.' She didn't reply, fidgeting with something in her hands. A card close to her breast. It was awkward for both of them and he was about to move on when he noticed her husband walking purposefully from the opposite direction towards them. 'Seems like your husband's come looking for you,' he nodded indicating his direction. She turned, rictus-mouthed, to see Malcolm approaching.

'Quick. Please, you must post them,' she said hurriedly handing him the two postcards. In her agitation and rush, she dropped one, and before she could pick it up, an arm like a heron's beak stabbed it up. An involuntary gasp escaped her lips as she put her hand to her mouth, too late to cover her fright.

'Sorry, darling. I didn't mean to startle you. There,' he said holding up the card. 'You seem to have dropped something. A postcard, how nice.' He turned it over in his hands. 'But look, it'll need a stamp before we can post it.' There was no mention of its blankness; he continued talking to her in front of Pete as if she was an imbecile. Taking her arm in his, with a show of solicitousness, he steered her away. 'You'll catch your death of cold standing here. The wind's really raw.' He felt her hesitate. 'I'll make sure your card gets posted, don't you fret your little head. We don't want to bother old Pete with things like that,' he said, smiling patronizingly to show he understood and appreciated the fisherman's concern, but that she was in capable hands. 'Now, come. We can go back to the house together.'

He led her away from the quay and moored boat, away from the water's edge and the old man, and without a backward glance she allowed herself to be taken back to the stud.

In the privacy of his cottage Pete studied the one postcard she'd given him. The gull had been crudely speckled over, but the address was seemingly written by a controlled hand. There was no other writing, no message or name. His was the dilemma, knowing she needed him to help her but not knowing how to. No clue, no signature or even name other than Davies, Tŷ Coch, Llanfeni, Wales. He assumed O'Connor had caught her before she could write anything and perhaps he should fill in for her? But what to write? That she was unhappy for sure, but did that give him any right to write something that could be misconstrued, or turn out to be completely wrong? It was none of his business, and who was he to tell her family she had, or was, losing her mind, that he didn't trust her husband and there was something untoward going on? He had no proof other than her sad dejected form in a mind locked away. Perhaps they already knew, were kept informed on a day-to-day basis. Only she had come to him, obviously in a desperate bid, and he had to help her.

'There, it's not been improved from being squashed in my pocket all day.' He had tried to flatten out the crinkled lines of the photo. 'Odd,' he said flicking it over. 'Either she's used a very faint pencil that I can't read or the silly *malwoden*[26] has forgotten to say anything!'

'And look, someone's scribbled ink spots all over the gull.'

'Spoiled it,' Tegwyn had said when he had looked at it in the pub, and as he handed it back had commented on it being a strange thing for Bethan to send.

With a rush of clarity, Richard thought of her daughter. 'I've got it,' he thought to himself. 'It was probably Clare,' and he wished now that he hadn't brought it out to share it with Tegwyn.

Walking the cows back down to the fields after he'd finished the milking, Richard dismissed Beth's postcard, occupied with the information Simon had relayed to him. He didn't dare hope too much, but couldn't help hoping all the same, feeling that perhaps at last his luck was changing

Walking to pick up Dic the next day, Tegwyn was still thinking of Bethan's postcard. Odd that Richard had showed it to him and stranger still that it said nothing. The sudden noise startled him as Tego felt the starlings, before seeing the upsurge of a dark mass and whoosh of wings fly over him. As if in some orchestra of music, coming together in a mass of movement, a huge flock of starlings swarmed above him. Up and down to some fantastic composition, they swerved on iridescent wing, crescendo-close, to spread and surge again in shoals, in breath-taking display until something unseen signalled the end and they

---

[26] Snail

flew off as one to land and settle in a nearby field. Compelled, Tegwyn followed them to where they had landed where without baton they started up their chatty song once more, filling the air with their playground noise. He banged the door loudly, calling out, 'Come on, Dic.' A call from inside was followed by a low grumbling voice. Then Dic came out of the back door, slamming it to, his picnic box with pickled egg, pork pie and thermos flask of strong sweet tea inside his worn canvas bag, which he carried over his shoulder. A creature of habit, he would not be hurried by Tegwyn stamping impatiently by his door. He scraped his hobnail boots on a stone, relieving them of their dried muck from the previous day's droving in the market.

'*Duw*, you're early.'

'Time's money, Dic. I can't wait all day for you to get up. There's moss to be gathered, Frank'll be waiting and I've got some lads starting. You'll have to set a good example.'

'Take the shirt off my back, they will. What about looking after the old workhorse? You're going to work me 'til I drop.'

'Come on Dic, you know you want to show the young ones how to do it.'

As if bored of what they heard, the flock of starlings took to flight once more, swooping up and away in waves to land in a group of birch trees. 'Fantastic, aren't they? Must be hundreds of them.'

'It's a common enough sight. It's the single starling you want to watch out for.'

'What?' The old codger was onto something else.

'Clever birds starlings, part of the mynah family. They're good mimics.'

'What are you on about, old man?'

'Can't think of the Latin name for them.'

'Yeah, well you're not on University Challenge, and if you don't get your skates on—'

'You ever seen a starling on its own? No, I thought not. A solitary starling is a warning. Foreboding. It's a sign of something bad.' He spat on the ground, disgruntled.

Tegwyn laughed at the old man. 'I don't know where you get them from Dic; you've got a saying for everything – there's nothing that isn't a sign for something, according to you!'

'You may mock, but who was right about the moss? Hm? You mark my words, if you see one of those on its own, it's a sure sign of trouble,' he said pointing to the trees,

Crossing the yard on his last check before bed to see a cow due to calve, he heard the phone ringing from the kitchen. In case it was Penny he went towards the house. He was still half-expecting the voice to be Penny's when he picked up.

'Sorry, I didn't quite catch that. Let me close the door.' He put the phone down, closing the back door firmly so that outside noises didn't impede the already bad line. 'Can you start again. Who did you say you were?' A man he didn't know, ringing quite late, with an accent that needed careful listening to in order to comprehend fully what he was saying.

Richard didn't interrupt the caller, but his breathing quickened as he listened, moving his cap up and down on his forehead, not quite sure whether to believe what he was hearing. 'Are you sure? You mean my brother Simon Davies. You met him personally? He didn't mention any of this.'

'It's the gospel truth.'

'I'm sure he would have told me.'

'Perhaps he didn't know. They hid it from him.'

The excuse sounded hollow but as Richard continued to listen to the explanation, he recalled his brother's anxiety. He'd been convinced everything was not all right with their sister. Then the caller told him about Bethan and the postcard incident he'd witnessed.

'But why?' Richard couldn't help interrupting. 'Even if what

326

you say happened is true, what possible motive would he have to do such a thing?'

Only it had been this man Peter and not Simon who'd met her on the quayside, who'd witnessed at first hand her distressed state when she saw her husband coming towards her. Then she'd panicked, thrusting the postcards into his hand, pleading with him to post them.

'She'd dropped one and her husband picked it up and pocketed it, but luckily he hadn't seen there had been two and I managed to slip the other one in my pocket without him noticing. I remember them being exactly the same,' he said. 'Each one with a seagull she'd covered in spots. She said you'd know, you and your brother would understand.'

'That all?'

'Yes.'

'And the other card, was it meant for Simon?'

'Yes.'

'He never got it, or he'd have told me.'

'Because O' Connor never posted it, you can be sure of that.'

Richard continued to listen, trying to remember exactly what Simon had said. At the time he'd been taken up with the business of the pig trough. All he could remember with complete clarity was the question he'd asked and disappointment he'd felt at Simon's answer, that he'd been unable to ask for a loan. Now he needed to speak to his brother urgently to see if anything of what this man, this so-called friend, was someone he could rely on and if what he was saying had a modicum of truth to it. He took down his name, address and phone number, and at the man's persistence gave his word he wouldn't ring the stud about the matter. He said that he'd ring again and Richard needed to be ready at short notice.

46

'Come on Mum, the party will have started,' she'd said, stamping her foot, the carefully wrapped present in danger of being squashed in her impatient hands. Beth regretted having ever agreed to take her, wishing now that the time had come that either Malcolm or Moira were there to drive Clare. But they were not and she could not disappoint yet again. She would have to drive her there herself. She had no intention of staying with the other mothers amid the noise and jelly and party games. Yet when the time came Mary had been very persuasive, insisting she stay, at least to have a cup of tea, and a piece of cake. In the end she had sat, smiling tensely, trying to listen, to absorb what was being said over and above the racket of children. She needed to escape; she felt that she was in danger of suffering a panic attack. She tried taking deep breaths, not wanting to draw attention to herself. There would be less of a scene if she could endure other people's boisterous children in the crowded house, and where would she wait? Not in some lay-by, or empty road locked in her car.

Almost the first to leave, her nerves already shattered, Bethan steeled herself for the drive home in the dark. It wasn't a long journey; it was a matter of miles. Clare sat in the passenger seat excitedly chattering to her as her balloon bounced irritatingly against the car's gear stick. Behind the wheel, Bethan tried to calm herself, fighting the sensation that she was being stalked. Somehow she had been followed and was being watched as they drove home. If she'd known the place had a long lane and farm gate at the end she would have never agreed to come, as she was now forced to get out of the car and open and close the gate in the dark.

There was a moment of apprehension, that quickening of step when walking alone through an unsafe place; a woman's instinct to be wary. Whether down an alley, subway or underpass that opened out onto the sluggish ooze and dull light of a city river it didn't matter, it was the same: a dimly lit space with limited exits. Any footpath sparsely peopled, in shadow. Women would walk, the clack of shoes hurried in eyeless time, on sharp gravel, soft towpath, or concrete, their laden bags like their gender, a burden ripe for the violating.

For Beth it was that short space after opening a gate where she'd have to walk back into the headlights of her own car, sightless so she could not see if someone was hiding in wait to strike. Frozen by her fear of being jumped and tied up and bundled off, she made Clare get out and open the gate while she sat, ashamed later of being a coward, knuckles taut on the steering wheel ready to shriek, to hit the horn, as she watched. The little girl complained but obliged running out into the car's full lights and pulling the gate open for the vehicle to pass. Once through Bethan slammed on the reverse lights so that she could see Clare, watching her as she pushed the gate clip into its lock, always with the feel of something at her back. With horror she caught the flickering of lights through trees, moving in their direction. She panicked, wanting her daughter to hurry up so they could make their escape before the car following them up the lane caught up with them. A dead leaf fluttered like a bat onto the windscreen, making her jump. She banged on the windscreen to beckon Clare to hurry. Once in, she set off looking anxiously in the rear mirror as the light behind dipped, the closed gate between them.

She had felt something had altered, an imperceptible tightening in the room when she came in that night, frayed and exhausted from the party and journey home in the dark. Malcolm swung his daughter up in his arms, tickling her as she giggled, letting go of her balloon which floated up, the ribbon dangling down from the ceiling. He put her down onto the sofa, still tickling her, her party dress riding up over her wriggling body. As always he didn't know when to stop, going too far, making her protest that she was going to be sick. Couldn't he hear the change? The inflection in her protests that were no longer a joke, begging her daddy to desist. He ceased only when they turned to screams, her mother rushing to her to pull him off, 'to spoil their fun,' he said. Only she saw his look, a look she knew, of rapaciousness, waiting for the plea. The power he liked, that in a split second between pleasure and pain, he sought before he relented, showing his mercy. His wife knew then that he had her, that Moira must have told him. She'd have to make a run for it, like a coursed hare with no gaps in the fence, only lurchers and cruel men. No longer flat-eared and still, now she was cornered she would bare her teeth, raise her arms and put up a fight.

The killer whale had his injured seal where he wanted it, in deep water so that he could have his sport with her uninterrupted.

She rang the police the next morning, asking specifically for Sergeant O'Shea.

'No, Mrs O'Connor. We've had nothing, nothing at all. It's exactly as I told your husband—'

'My husband? You spoke to him? When? When was that?' she hurried her question, the hairs on her skin rising as she quickly looked behind her.

'He rang yesterday.'

'Oh?' She tried to sound casual.

'Mrs O'Connor? Hello, are you still there?'

'Yes, I'm still here. Sorry, what did he say? He confirmed my story of what happened, of course.'

She could feel the policeman's awkwardness, struggling to choose the right words before he answered her questions. He had softened his tone, as one would to a child.

'Yes, he told me what happened. How you'd been under a

330

great deal of strain and you hadn't been yourself since losing your baby. We do understand Mrs O'Connor, and I'm very sorry.'

'That's very kind of you. I appreciate your help. I'm sorry to have bothered you. Goodbye.'

After he'd replaced the phone he felt a short burst of pity for the lonely, sad woman, shaking his head as he went back to his mundane paperwork.

So, she was already too late, and his lying to the police had given her the evidence needed to substantiate his involvement in her abduction. The softly spoken sympathetic policeman had been forewarned of her delicate position by her caring husband. No wonder he'd been sympathetic; he'd been expecting a call from her. Malcolm, ahead of the game as always, the inductor of plot and his own subterfuge. Already discredited, she'd been stitched up and he'd seen to it no one would believe her. She had no allies to turn to.

She was tempted to go to him and taunt him. To tell him he'd been right and it hadn't been his, but Liam's baby he'd had murdered. How ridiculous, but perhaps it was this that had launched him on such a wrecker's mission. It was proof he had lost control over her. Only he hadn't known then that she was pregnant. She tried to recall their conversation, the exact timing in that sulky evening when she had been about to give him her good news, but he'd thwarted her. The news of her skinnydipping with the lads enough to provoke a jealous sulk, and he'd stomped off. So why had he done what he did? Because he hated her, that was the only possible answer.

With no further choice other than wait to be chewed up, she welcomed the fight, her weapon of vengeance that would take him to the edge. She'd marked time ready with her words carefully selected for maximum damage. She wanted to nudge him closer, designed to incense, to push him over, like he'd sent her. To watch him and witness his ride; the rollercoaster race, out of his control that would initially make him lose his temper. Then it would all come out. In her mind she'd prepared it all, planning to start by asking him why he'd ever wanted to marry her in the first place. Only then, she hoped, the mechanism of his foul mind would spew forth. And she could easily picture him, taking things up a notch, perhaps to threaten her as he'd warm to his task, relating all his nasty little plans, the details of how he had planned to deal with her.

But when you take such a treacherous road, who can be sure of the end result? Who can predict anybody's reaction to severe provocation? Bethan believed her controlling husband was capable of being very nasty if it meant he would get what he wanted. He'd have no scruples, and would easily resort to using Clare as a pawn if need be.

No, she could not afford to fight him openly, not until she'd got Clare and herself clear of him and his influence. She had to get out and quickly, but how and who to go to? Where to trust? She could not get caught, not at any cost and so she was forced to play the waiting game. For weeks she had pretended that everything was as it had been and he had his wife exactly where he'd put her; a little touched, insecure and isolated.

With her nerves steel tight she tried to hide her thoughts from his sly look as he monitored her behaviour, sliding towards her, a luxurious indolence in his sibylline eyes. Like a snake, his pink tongue flicked, sensing her as he moistened his lips, touching the turned-down corners of his mouth in anticipation. She felt the thick of him, his mouth on her bare lips, pulling her close, feigning nonchalance as he coiled himself around her, and with each revelation, he'd make her gasp, allowing a further tightening. Unrelenting, daring her to make her move so that he could squeeze the life out of her.

His mother was her only hope, and he could not prevent

her from going to see her, not in broad daylight. Anyhow it amused him to watch her play the scene, the pretence of some spontaneous decision, a short walk to the shops and then back to the stables and call on Moira for tea.

Ashen, yes, nervous and distressed – all of that – but Moira, who'd been with her at her worst, noticed an added urgency in Bethan. Before uttering a word Bethan put her fingers to her lips and she pulled a crumbled bit of paper and pencil from her pocket and wrote. In silence Moira read it. She took her glasses off and looked across to her daughter-in-law.

'Beth, I can honestly, hand on heart promise you there is no way this house, my house is bugged. It's an absurd suggestion and there's absolutely no need for you to start writing everything down. Look, there's no one here to hear us and no one has been to wire up my home. You can trust me, you know that. What the hell has happened to make you so fearful?'

'I don't know how to say it, but Malcolm is involved. He was from the start. He set up my kidnap!'

'Beth, we've been through this, I don't know how many times—'

'I've got the evidence now. He lied to the police. Malcolm's been lying all along.'

'I don't think—'

She cut Moira off. 'It's true. Don't you see, by telling them I was never kidnapped and it was all in my imagination, he's hiding the truth. Why would he do that if he wasn't involved?'

'To protect you?'

'You don't believe that. No more than I do.' Seeing Moira's doubt she carried on, 'You know, all that stuff about losing the baby. He managed to unhinge me, oh yes, he was very clever, making me delusional; it was all a smokescreen for what was really going on. Can't you see that, Moira? You were there. You know it happened. It wasn't in my mind. You witnessed it.'

Moira couldn't deny her daughter-in-law her manic kind of logic and she struggled to think of something that would show her that she'd got things wrong, all muddled-up and upside-down. Looking at the younger woman's animated, wildly excited face, there was nothing she could think of that would help explain things. No words that could offer comfort. What could she say that wouldn't expose her as being crazy? She sat there silently pleading with Bethan to stop her wild accusations. Accusations that if Malcolm heard them, would only serve to push her nearer a mental institution.

'You don't believe me either, do you? I've no hope if you don't.'

'Bethan I do believe that what you think is in your mind is what you truly believe happened. I don't doubt you for a second. But I don't think it happened in reality.' But Moira could think of nothing that exonerated her son during the events of her daughter-in-law's disappearance.

'If he's innocent he wouldn't have lied, not to the police. He lied to stop them looking into it, Moira. Why can't I make you see this!'

'OK, Bethan, try and calm down. Now, for argument's sake let's say he is involved. Why would he lie to them?'

'In case they dug up something that would incriminate him. His name coming up through his associations, the people he used to do it.'

Moira couldn't deny Bethan her reasoning. It had all happened and she had been there when her daughter-in-law had been snatched, but could her son have been the instigator? No, she would not believe that. Nothing would have induced her son to come so close to destroying Bethan. It had lost them their unborn son, her grandson.

Bethan watched Moira struggling with what she had said. She could understand and sympathize with a mother's dilemma, of not wanting to believe the worst about an offspring. She softened her voice, pleading with her.

'But you were here Moira, when it happened. You were the only person who saw him when it was being done to me. You know how he reacted, and you know him better than anyone. How genuine was he really when he heard the news?'

'He was very upset, and deeply concerned for you. All he wanted to do was to ensure you were got back safely,' Moira said without total conviction.

'But he refused to ring the police; he was insistent on keeping it within the family group, wasn't he? That's what you told me. Didn't you think it a bit odd at the time?'

'I can see it might seem strange to you Beth, but he felt it safer if the news was contained.'

'Safer for whom? Not me, that's for sure!'

'That's were you're wrong. It was safer for you that way, Beth. You know how things are today, in the world we live in. Once the media gets hold of anything, it's impossible to contain it – Malcolm was frightened it would pressurize the kidnappers into doing something that could have fatal consequences.'

She should have known she would protect him. A mother's first instinct is to protect her children. In her place, Bethan would do exactly the same; she'd protect her children above all else. Thieves, murderers, hit-and-run drivers. She'd been naïve to think Moira could or would react differently, especially as she didn't even believe her. Only she had nowhere else to turn. Nowhere to go.

'Oh, it turned out pretty toxic for me, wouldn't you say?' she said. 'No, you're not right and deep down you know it, Moira. You doubt him, don't you? The only thing Malcolm was frightened of was having the press dig around and find out the whole thing was a charade. A story that would set the newspapers alight!'

'That's not true, Beth.'

'This happened to me; it's not some fanciful story. It happened in the here and now, Moira. Your son didn't want any outside involvement because he's guilty. Don't you see it's why he kept the whole thing cosy within his 'family', using you for credibility. Only it was me – I was the object of his nasty little game. He's hoodwinked you and paid off the rest of them. I know what I saw in Killarney and I'm not going off my rocker; I'm not the one who's delusional. I'm not insane. It's your son who's sick. He's the one who needs locking up!'

Moira waited, letting Bethan finish her rant before she said, 'There's one thing you haven't explained.'

'What?'

'Tell me Bethan. Why? What on God's earth would make him, my son your husband, Clare's father wish to do such an appalling thing to his own family. His own flesh and blood! Where is the gain? What could he hope to achieve from it? Tell me that if you're so sure of his culpability.'

'Do you think I haven't asked myself that question? I've racked my brains as to why! More than anything else, why would he do such a thing? Ever since I twigged his involvement, I've been asking myself over and over, trying to make some sort of sense, an explanation. But I can't. The man I thought I loved, living with him these past six years. I don't understand him at all.'

'Because you've got it wrong.'

'No. Why would my husband, my Malcolm, want me so damaged? I mean, look at me. What do you see? Not the same person, am I? Hardly a happy-go-lucky Welsh girl now!'

'Then tell me what you must have done to make him hate you so much?'

'Me? Do! You're asking me what I did! Nothing. You tell me Moira, you're his mother. It's him who's sick, not me. He's a dangerous man, and I need to get out and to take Clare with me before he kills me.'

336

The words seemed to unbuckle her, to make her bend as she leant onto the table. 'And do you know, when I first came here, at the time I used to think it was all your fault he was as he is. Yes, I'm sorry I was so wrong. Wrong to blame you for his inadequacies.'

'Me?'

'Because you had hurt him, as a little boy. He said it was why he grew up warped, and why he ended up hating you as much as he did his father. He even had me feeling sorry for him.'

The old woman broke, tears seeping from the corners of her eyes, running down her lined face. She'd never seen Moira cry and put her hand across to hers. 'I see now I was a fool ever to have come here. When he vanished I should have counted my blessings, realized I was lucky to have escaped. But I was what he accused me of, I was desperate to get married and have children. You know that stupid old-fashioned stigma of being an old maid, as if any of it matters. Pathetic really. I should have stuck to nursing and stayed in Wales. I can see why you despised me.'

'I don't—' Moira started but Bethan raised her hand to stop her. 'I'm glad you did.'

'Look how it's turned out. Your son's a good liar, I'll give him that. All that "little boy lost", about him being misused and unloved, fooled me – he's a nefarious bastard. He even had me believing that you and Patrick had wished him dead, rather than Kieran. Like a sucker, I fell for it all.'

'I did.'

She said it very quietly but unmistakably. 'I wished then and I would again now. If I could have I'd replaced his living body for Kieran's lifeless one. I would have sold my soul to change them over on that cold slab in the hospital. What he heard was true. So you see, he did have a reason for hating us. He'd always been jealous of Kieran.'

'Oh God.'

'Another generation on, and still we learn nothing. I'm no better than my own mother.'

Bethan looked at her questioningly wondering what else was going to be revealed. 'She gave me away. She kept my sister but didn't want me. But you have to believe me Bethan when I tell you I really tried afterwards. I tried so hard to put Keiran's death behind me and to forgive Malcolm. Only I couldn't and he knew it. He was behind the wheel when the car left the road and I blame him for Keiran's death and wish it had been him instead.'

Both women slumped, defeated by the enormity of deceit. Now Bethan saw, like scales being torn from unseeing eyes, why he'd married her. It was a payback to his mother and father.

'He'd deliberately chose me to get back at you! Because I'm not Irish, not Catholic and come from a poor background. Is that what you're saying?'

'As usual he got it wrong. I don't care about religion or give a fig about being Irish, or if you're poor. It's about love, or the lack of it. What he never understood about his father was he might have been a wild, rough man, but he saved me from lovelessness. When I met Patrick, for the first time in my life someone showed me love. Malcolm tried to emulate him, and he failed to match up. Simple as that. So he became jealous and deliberately turned back everything I've striven against, worked my life to become distanced from, almost to where I started: lost and loveless. As a species love is our only redeeming feature and I wasn't going to let him ruin it in my family. Then Kieran died.'

'And he married me for spite.'

'Perhaps.'

'He thought the baby was Liam's.'

'Ah.' She seemed uninterested, resigned.

'It was some silly remark Clare made, that was all. Lucky Johnny was there at the time.'

'Flew up like a fireball.'

'Yes, If you could have seen the look on his face then.'

'I know it, I'm his mother.'

'If I'd realised any of this would happen, do you think I'd have gone near the boat? ' She raised her hand, 'let alone a silly fishing trip! And no, you don't need to ask. It was Malcolm's baby, only I wish it had been Liam's. At least then, to his way of thinking at least, there would have been a point to all this. Do you remember the time I went up to Dublin, when you were cross with me for leaving Clare with you? It was to have it all confirmed. I even had the photos of my scan, but he'd already made up his mind. There was no stopping him. He was on a crash course, deaf-eared, already ballistic.'

'What will you do?'

'Get out. I've got to escape, and get away from him. There's no other option.'

'No. And you'll take Clare with you?' She already knew the answer. Of course a mother would want her only child with her.

'If I stay, he'll kill me. You know that.'

She'd known it, known he wouldn't be able to let go, incapable of accepting defeat.

'You don't expect me to help? To betray him?'

'No, I wouldn't ask you to do that, Moira. Don't help him though; let me get away first. Please.'

'So that I'll never see my granddaughter again?'

'If need be, yes.'

'He won't let you go. He'll stop you. And even if you get away from here, do you think he's even capable of letting it rest? He'll search until he finds you.'

'That's something I'll have to sort when the time comes. I can't look that far into the future. For now I've just got to get away, put some distance between us. Which is why I have to pretend everything's normal, so he doesn't suspect, not even

339

until the minute we go. Then we'll just vanish. I'll need someone I can trust.'

Both women understood. Bethan placed her hands on Moira's. 'I shall never forget what you've done for me. I wouldn't have survived without you.' She leaned down to kiss her mother-in-law's thin-skinned cheek, before straightening up. She saw herself out of the bungalow.

47

Now for their final coupling, a gross game; each groping for purchase on the greasy board; a snakes and ladders, fox and goose. She heard him move, forcing her into the open to make a desperate dash to avoid his sharp salivating jaws.

Hers was the living nightmare of always being watched, surveyed covertly. That was until now when at last, he had come out of hiding, keeping her in his sights. As she was already caught, he seemed in no hurry to pounce, leaving it to her to make a bolt for it. She had to decide what was the safest option for her and Clare. Either to risk trying to sneak away in secret, or to do it loudly and boldly, making sure everyone saw her leave, daring him to detain her publicly. Living under threat, Bethan oscillated between the two possibilities; to go undercover, through the unlit underpasses where they waited with intent, hooded or balacalvered, loitering for an easy prey, or to take her daughter and run openly, dodging his traffic across dual carriageways, hoping she'd be able to swerve to avoid a head-on smash. Blatantly, standing in bus stations, and from there, another bus, train or taxi east. At last she knew she had to, and knowing gave her courage.

For a week she kept up the same routine, walking Clare to school and then carrying along the coast line to the village where at the bridge she turned to come home again. She knew, he'd be spying on her or kept informed, as he was always at the end of a phone, using his binoculars to watch more than a horse's gait. She'd have to be transparent, play it safe. She knocked at Pete's cottage door and disappeared for fifteen minutes before coming out and continuing her walk homeward, a couple of dabs in her bag. She grilled them for their supper, with lemon, tomato ketchup and chips.

'I called on Pete on my walk and he gave me them. Said they'd do me good. Thought I still looked pasty.' She spoke light-heartedly, only she wasn't fooling anyone. He toyed with the white clean flesh, eyeing her to see if she gave anything away. Her nerves were a jumbled wreck.

'Do you like them, Clare?' he asked, playing with the hooked line that lay in his wife's mouth. 'This fish lies flat in the sand just near the water's edge.'

'With their eyes sticking out?'

'Yes. Their eyes watch for danger. And see the colour of their skin?' he interrupted her eating, turning the flat fish over, 'See it's all grey and speckly: that's its camouflage so when it lies in the sand you can't see it. You could tread on it and you wouldn't know it's there.'

'Don't be silly Daddy. It's all slippy and wriggly.'

'But if it didn't move – look at its eyes, they're all on one side so it can watch you without moving to see what you're doing.'

'Eat it up before it gets cold darling, then we can watch *The Jungle Book*.' Bethan tried to change the subject. 'All of it.'

'Did Uncle Pete catch it in his boat?'

'What?'

'The fish.'

'No, from the shore.' She wished Clare didn't call him Uncle.

'Silly little fish, all aflounder! Now Clare, a clever fisherman will know of its hiding place, and then they're easy to catch. If you were a fish like this one, and I was after you, you'd need to watch out or I'd come and get you!'

'Dad!' she said, unsure if he was teasing her or not. 'You're not a fisherman!'

'But I might be.'

'Don't put silly things into her head Malcolm, you'll frighten her.'

'I'm not frightening you, am I darling? Can't your Mam take a tease?'

For all the insinuation and veiled threats directed at her, she had no option other than continue to share the space of married life, those intimate moments between a couple. The act of undressing, of pulling a jumper over one's head, the undoing of shirt buttons, rolling down nylons, pulling off a sock, unhooking a bra, stepping out of boxer shorts, all states of vulnerability, the baring of unprotected flesh that had once been erogenous, reduced to an act of embarrassment. She wanted to cover up in flannelette, to conceal herself. With such animosity why continue to share, to change and sleep in the same bedroom? Because he was happy to wait, to watch her prepare to break from cover and until she did she'd have to go along with the charade. In her remaining time she would have to let him watch her undress, as she fumbled with pants and bra, her back to him on the bed as she slid her nightdress over her head, half expecting to feel him, a hand or shaved cheek against her skin, in mock deference. She knew he enjoyed seeing her in her state of fright; any tremor, start or shudder that showed her fear amplifying his position of dominance over her. Bethan steeled herself, tossing back her fair curls, smiling back at him to show him she wasn't intimidated, not looking at his eyes as she pulled the bedcovers up, and if he forced himself she would acquiesce, in the knowledge it would be for nearly the last time and then he could go to hell.

'I posted your postcard, my little dove. Your family should have it by now.'

She lay holding her breath waiting for him to finish. Had he guessed what she was thinking? 'They'll think it a bit strange of you to send a card with nothing on it! And spoiling the picture with all those spots. I wonder what were you thinking of Bethan? Hm? What was going on in that little brain of yours?'

She smiled in the dark, letting her breath go. So he didn't know and he lied, he never sent it.

'That I've gone mad, doolally.'

'Well that's a shame, as I'd hate to think what it'll do to Clare, knowing she's got a loony for a mother. We mustn't let it get out of control, I wouldn't want to have to put you away. Then no one would see your pretty face except the psychiatrist.' There was no concealing his threat there as he leant across and bit her on her earlobe. 'You need to pull yourself together. Goodnight, sweetheart.' She resisted his goad, keeping shtum, trying to control her racing heartbeat. In the darkness she lay awake, squeezing her lips tight in grim determination not to get up. To put on the light and have it out with him, all the things he'd done that showed him to be the one with insurmountable problems. It was her turn to damage, to want to hurt him, only restrained by the need to safeguard her child.

He moved away, rolling onto his side as she remained unmoving in cold disgust, waiting for him to fall asleep. Knowing that Pete had sent her postcard and it had reached Richard she could afford to think of home, of getting back to Llanfeni. A bright star in her soft-moss, black sky to guide her into safe arms. She only had to let him taunt her for a few more days, letting him think he had her where he wanted her, relaxing him into a false sense of security, believing she was incapable of doing anything, maimed and wingless so that nothing she could do would upset his plans for her.

He went away, off racing while Bethan kept as low a profile as he'd allow, all mousy and quiet, nibbling through the line that held her hooked.

It would be the meeting at Tralee that threatened postponement on her planned day. Three days of rain came in off the Atlantic, and for a few anxious hours Bethan had to hold her nerve, to pretend she didn't care whether his race fixture was on or off, suggesting all was not lost and he could get to another. Stupid cow, what did she understand about training horses for specific races? It was like suggesting Usain Bolt win a swimming race. 'If you can't say anything sensible, best to say nothing,' he said adding 'dear' with his mouth turned down in an ugly slant. She wanted to rattle him, watch him twitch, clenching his fist resisting the urge to hit her, impotent against the uncontrollable weather.

She secretly rejoiced in her short-lived, tiny victory that could wreck her plans as well.

She was to be lucky on two counts. First, the wind picked up, helping to dry out the sodden ground, and with the whole of Ireland rained off and itching to race, a soggy course wasn't going to deter the diehards. The second, that in the event of the wet roads, he'd left earlier than she had expected, leaving her on her own.

Once clear of him she had to act fast. She would leave the collecting of Clare from school to the last minute, the very last thing she'd do before she left Conna. Although she'd planned it all, now the time had come she felt flustered, panicking when she needed to be calm and decisive, wondering what she would say when she called in at the school. The headmistress would give her a looking-over, judging her, and Malcolm had of course been very thorough, warning anyone who she was in contact with of her difficulties. She had to make sure she seemed as normal as possible so that they would let Clare come with her. She could not afford a scene.

But first she had to make sure she had everything they would need. She looked round their bedroom, at her clothes in the wardrobe untouched, shoes tidy in pairs underneath her dresses. She'd leave her large waterproof coat and wellingtons, she thought her trainers would be the most practical. She could run in them.

No make-up or personal items, nothing other than what she stood up in. She left the bed unmade and only cleared the breakfast things as far as the kitchen sink. From her daughter's room she collected a warm fleece with a hood and from the assortment of toys, she picked her favourite; a rag doll from her grandmother which had comforted her through teething and infant ailments; it had been her *cwtsh*, its arms testament to her sticky love, stretched and dulled by years of thumb sucking. She knew Clare would miss her Gran but nowhere near as much as Moira would miss her, and Bethan felt a rush of guilt at the wrench of their parting, knowing their flight would cause inconsolable grief. Moira had become her friend and ally as well as a loving grandmother to Clare, making herself an unspoken go-between for husband and wife. Perhaps when it was all over, she'd be able to come over to stay with them, if she wasn't in hiding from Malcolm. She wondered if he'd let it go, and behave as a rational reasonable human being, or, as she feared, if he would be driven by revenge, determined not to let her win. She was going ahead of herself; she hadn't even got out yet.

She looked around the kitchen for the last time, hoping she'd left it as if she'd just popped out for one of her short walks just in case he came back early or unexpectedly, so he'd think she was about and just being her absent-minded, strange self. He wouldn't wait long, a quarter of an hour at most, but hopefully enough time for her to get clear. What she needed most was him tied up racing, having a busy day and for the races to keep him occupied for another couple of hours. Carefully, she hid the doll in the bottom of her canvas bag, covering it with her daughter's fleece and then an old woollen coat of hers. One he would not recognise, as she had barely worn it in Ireland, and had kept it folded away in the bottom of a spare chest of drawers on the landing.

A noise made her stop. Had she really heard something? There was a crunch on gravel that made her heart lurch as she stopped, holding her breath, waiting. Standing, straining her ears to catch a nuance of him. There was no other sound, only that of the empty house, but her ears were ringing, high-pitched like a bat, making her unsure of the noises outside her head. She could not afford to wait, so she steeled herself to tiptoe to the window, standing back from the glass so she remained in shadow. She looked down the lane towards the stables. Nothing, no car or person in sight, no horse or lorry, only horses head down, grazing in paddocks. She moved closer to the glass looking directly down at the door, half-expecting to see him look up, mouth open, gloating. Perhaps he'd slinked round to the back of the house and let himself in. Perhaps he was silently waiting for her to come downstairs. She froze on the top step, pressed against the wall for support, waiting to hear him give himself away, the house warning her with a creak as he mounted the stairs.

She had to stop herself from screaming in terror forcing her hand into her mouth, listening, expecting to see him waiting for her to come down the stairs into his net. She needed to move quickly and get herself outside, out into the open, into space where she had a chance to run. Trembling, she ran down the stairs and without looking back she slipped out of the kitchen door. Still her heart pounded under her rib cage forcing a dry hard intake of breath, in, out.

She told herself to concentrate and walk as she would usually, holding herself close, tight about herself, her movements sharp yet without purpose. Only when she passed the bungalow did she falter, looking across at the window to see Moira watching for her from behind the glass. She pulled the strap of the raffia bag further onto her shoulder, shrugging it upward as she raised a finger to her lips, a gesture of silence and goodbye. A brief expression that said thank you to the woman whose unseen tears fell as she stood, her palm open against the enclosed pane. Anyone observing would hardly have noticed her pause other than to hitch up her bag as she continued to walk down the road towards the village.

48

He waited for them as arranged, keeping Bethan and Clare tucked away in the hold for as short a time as possible, knowing how Bethan found small confined spaces almost unbearable, each minute a test of her endurance. The Stena Line ferry had already docked at Rosslare, and he'd given Richard and Simon instructions as to drive down and find Kilmore Quay.

From his boat he watched the comings and goings on the quiet quay. Standing out from the local fishermen, there were two men loitering. From where he was, they seemed nondescript, middle-aged. He watched them, needing to be absolutely sure before he beckoned. He pretended to check his boat's ropes which he'd moored, tied to the quayside wall with warps, while all the time scrutinizing the men for several minutes before he was sure it had to be them. The Welshmen. Quietly he slipped down the few steps to ask Beth to come up and look, just to double-check, telling her to keep low in the boat so as not to attract any unwanted attention.

'Yes that's Richard,' she said to him. 'But I don't know who that is with him.' She looked more closely, watching Richard's companion before she recognised the shape, the turn of the head to see the profile that she knew. 'It's Tegwyn. I'm almost sure it is, but what's he doing with Richard?'

'Why? Is he a danger?'

'No, no nothing like that. He's a friend, a family friend and our neighbour. It's just I never thought Richard would ask him, that's all, and why?'

'No doubt to help get you home. Is he any good in a boat?' suggested Pete.

She'd never known Tegwyn go near water and thought it highly unlikely he'd suddenly acquired nautical skills. But she was quietly pleased to have him there. 'You'd better get back below, and stay down there while I go and pick them up. I don't want anyone noticing you on the deck. It won't be for much longer and once we're out at sea you can come out.'

He climbed the vertical ladder concreted into the wall and once up he walked along the quayside towards the two men who were obviously waiting for someone. With the briefest of acknowledgments, the three of them walked quickly back, wasting no time with any obvious greeting. Following the fisherman gingerly down the ladder, they climbed aboard the 'Little Marie'. Unlike Pete, the two men were both a bit clumsy aboard the gently moving wooden vessel, putting out a hand to steady themselves and get their balance. Neither had any sea legs as the boat bobbed gently on her ropes in the ebbing tide and Richard realised the task he was about to embark on, an immense stretch of water to cross in a small boat, but it was too late for any self-doubt or change of plan.

Pete had checked some pilot books and, more crucially, got first-hand knowledge from one of the local fishermen as to the exit manoeuvre and, without giving much away, had the best route across confirmed. It would be the easiest if not the most direct route across, setting a course two miles south of The Smalls, and once there, he'd head for Milford Haven. The local boatman had warned him to give the notorious area between The Smalls and Grassholm a wide berth, so Pete's chosen route would take them to the edge of the Celtic deep. By going this way, he would also avoid the Rosslare to Pembroke Dock route of the Irish ferries, in case Malcolm had people aboard scouting for them.

He was in unfamiliar water so decided to wait, to leave on the flood tide, so that if he mismanaged the tricky exit and ended up grounded outside the narrow channel, he could rely on the rising tide to re-float them.

In the cramped cockpit which wasn't designed to hold five, Richard hugged his sister who looked small and frightened but so glad to see them. He couldn't hide his shock at seeing her so depleted, her appearance so altered. She'd obviously lost a lot of weight and there were heavy darkened bags under her eyes, showing some of the strain she'd been under. She also seemed very nervous, jumpy at any movement or gesture. The jeans and jumper she was wearing swamped her.

'Duw, Beth fach beth sydd wedi digwydd i it? Fo 'nath hyn i ti?'[27]

She looked down, shaking her head, coming into his outstretched arms.

'Diolch byth, Rich, fod ti wedi dod. Ac annwyl Tegs.'[28]

'We've come to take you home, *cariad*, to where you belong.'

Hiding behind her mother's legs, Clare's face peered out as Bethan indicated her presence and that they needed to be careful, not to ask too many questions in front of her. Not yet.

'And who's this?' asked Richard, having never met his niece.

Suddenly shy, she hid behind her mother, pulling on her hand.

'Say hello to your Uncle Rich and to Tegwyn, Clare.'

---

[27] Heavens, Beth, what happened to you? Did he do this to you?
[28] Thank goodness you've come, Rich, and dear Tegs

It had started as revenge, a payback to the Connor family for his sacking after years of service, but after he befriended Bethan, Pete had grown to love her as the daughter he'd never had. He was a lonely old man who when he saw how they'd misused her was prepared to put his neck on the line to help. He'd come so far from home, first down and then along the South Irish coastline, clinging crab-close to rock and travelling quietly, and, he hoped, inconspicuously in his boat which he'd paid to moor for a few days in Kilmore while he took the several busses home. He warned her to pack virtually nothing, just enough for the boat journey, and in an act of sheer lunacy he'd taken them in his car, having to drive out of their village with Beth hidden in the boot and Clare on the back seat, wearing a hoodie over her head, pretending it was all a game, hide and seek in fancy dress.

He allowed a few hours' distance before he dared to stop in some small out-of-the-way lane surrounded by trees and fields. He understood her torment as she'd come out shaking uncontrollably, the brave, lovely woman, who hugged him gratefully for releasing her, the white of her eyes wild with terror. He'd be back from his day's racing by now, but Pete hoped their pursuers were still searching for him offshore, looking for him and his boat among a couple of his lobster pots, which he'd put back out as bait.

Until Beth was missed, they would not have noticed the absence of his boat, that it had been gone for over a week and he in it. Only now would Malcolm begin to panic, to pull the threads together and to hear that the old employee had been away for ten days. That precious time he counted on, no more than a few hours but enough, he hoped, to make their escape from the Conna stud.

'I think she said she was going to the beach, Malcolm. I know she didn't go down to the village.'

He stared at her, hostile and hating her. Ugly, thin-sticked mother.

'How can you be so sure?' He didn't trust her and he came closer, threatening her by grabbing her frail wrist. She did not cower but stood pulling herself straight, returning his stare with her cool steel eyes embedded in aged skin, her elderliness her only vulnerability. He'd liked to have smashed her face in, to see her grovelling on the floor begging him, but he needed answers. He shook her off, feeling her thin bones under his hands, knowing it would take little to snap her in two like a chocolate bar. He almost smiled to himself, and his sneer was not lost on his mother.

'She took a towel, and their swimming things.' It was far too cold to go swimming, he thought, knowing his wife wouldn't dream of going into the water unless she was planning on drowning herself, in which case she wouldn't have taken Clare. So he let his mother continue uninterrupted, watching her all the while with disturbing eyes, an obsequious smile on his lips. She couldn't resist adding, 'I'm pretty sure she said they were going to meet up with Pete, to go in his boat to get the lobster pots up.' Another lie, he thought, as he remembered the fisherman on the quayside with his wife only two weeks ago; his lobster pots had already been hauled up for winter storage. 'Carry on, Mother,' he said. 'Dig your own grave.'

She ignored his remark. 'She promised to bring me a spider crab home for supper. She was very happy, carefree. Remember Malcolm? Beth as she used to be, before you did what you did to her. You always were a bully; you used to boss Kieran around, jealous that he was better than you at everything. You destroyed him and now her. Don't think I don't know what you've done.'

'There's nothing you can do about it, you old bitch.' They held each other's stare, then he let her go, brushing his hand as if it had been in dog muck, turning away in disgust. 'You'll be sorry if you're wrong.'

As if she cared any more. She'd already lost them.

Like soldier ants, rows of spies with black antennae raised, his men had spread out, searching for any trace of Bethan and her daughter. Questions were asked and answered before moving on, trying to catch a scent of her. She had not been seen on the beach that day and Pete's boat hadn't been on its mooring for days. 'The fecking woman, his mother lying to him, to help her.'

Pete drove as he'd never driven, through places he'd never been in, choosing the smaller backwater routes eastwards to the opposite coast. He knew they'd be on to him, scouts watching for them; each car he saw in his rear mirror was a potential hit man, tracker or informer. Bloodhounds up for the blood. He stopped only when he had to, for petrol and snacks. In the night she did the driving, with her hair pulled back and a flat cap that helped disguise her. He sat next to her, watching for her and advising her not to dip the headlights when they met any traffic to prevent recognition. They needed to remain unidentified, but not to break any traffic laws. Malcolm wouldn't have gone to the Garda to raise any alarm or alert their attention; he did things a different way. Only she must not stop, not think who was where, only keep driving to get away. Keep the car door locked from the inside, fighting her paranoia of being confined. The knowledge that it was him, and him alone who had done this to her kept her from losing control and Pete from falling asleep.

At last, near to the water's edge in the daylight he parked up, leaving mother and daughter holed up a few miles away from the water in a nearby patch of scrub wood, while he went to check that his boat was still there and ready. He tried to look like an ordinary old man, without cares, an old sea dog fiddling with his boat. He had come back to them in the afternoon, and led them to the quay and onto his boat sitting on the silky water, waiting for them, for brother and tide.

49

With the boat still tied up to the quay, Pete had started the engine, letting it tick over in neutral, and Richard went across to him, raising his voice to be heard over the engine, 'I can't thank you enough for all you're doing for us.'

Pete nodded, putting a finger to his lips. He leaned closer to Richard so only he would hear him, not wanting to further alarm his nervous passengers. 'We're not clear yet, and he'll be onto us.'

'Can't we leave now?' Richard asked, looking around the quay for any sign of a man or men searching for them.

Satisfied with the sound he knew so well, the fisherman turned the engine off, shaking his head.

'No. We can't go just yet, but the engine's primed and once I get clearance.'

'Who from?'

He smiled at the farmer's misunderstanding.

'Nobody. Look down. See. I've got to wait for the tide.' Richard was still not sure what he meant. 'Look,' he said, pointing below the boat's hull. 'It's that shallow most of the way out, so it's very easy to get it just wrong and end up stuck on a sand bank. And I don't want to be a sitting duck for them. Give it another half an hour. Tell your sister we should be on our way soon. Not much longer to hold on for, and once we're in open sea they can come up onto deck.'

In late afternoon on the incoming tide, the 'Little Marie' pulled away from the fishing harbour of Kilmore Quay, leaving behind the smattering of cottages that fringed it. In the evening sky, the imposing church on the hill watched in outline shadow as their fishing boat departed the harbour.

The old fisherman kept a careful eye in this shallow water, steering his boat through the narrow channel with sand banks on either side. To stay in channel he kept the two transit marker posts astern in line, holding the boat steady in the strong cross tide, concentrating through the deep, but narrow passage of water, where there was little margin for error.

On the mainland side of little Saltee was another narrow channel to negotiate, to the east at what the locals had called 'St Patrick's Bridge,' marked by a pair of buoys, red and green, like a small airstrip through the passage, and then he headed southeast out to sea, leaving the windswept islands of the Saltees behind them.

No, he would not let them get caught now, not with open water in his sight, and having achieved the tricky exit without mishap, Pete felt suddenly exhausted. His age, catching up with him, made his bones ache and his rheumy eyes struggled with the light. He was and felt an old man, but at least he was in his element, on his boat that he trusted like a sure-footed horse, as she began her race, rising over the waves. At about six knots, and barring any major problems he'd calculated that the trip would take around twelve hours, and fixing her on a southeast course, for the first time in nearly two days, he allowed himself to doze off to the boat's lullaby as they made steady progress, chugging their way over the Irish Sea hour upon hour, with nothing but a rise and fall in the swell, with a few odd gulls floating above the stern, hoping for some slops.

It was not an easy place to talk, not seriously, confined and against the noise and movement, too open and painful in front of Pete and Tegwyn, and there was Clare. She mustn't hear of what Bethan had been through, of what her father was really like. Not now, but perhaps when she was older. So Bethan's story, of what had happened would have to wait and be told when they got back to Llanfeni, to the farm where brother and sister would have the time. She thought of the quiet and peace of their shared childhood home, a land she knew and loved, a place to which she was hefted, where she'd be able to feel safe again in the fold of family.

Nor was it the right moment for Tegwyn to voice his undying love for her. It was enough to be with her, staying silent, his look enough to understand. He was there to help her home, whatever it took. Inadvertently it had been Dic's argument that had shown him the light; her seagull poorly adapted into a starling that had alerted him. Later he'd sort out the shit who'd done this to her.

Suddenly, from some distance off, Richard caught sight of something travelling at speed towards the boat. He alerted Pete and the others who watched as in a spectacular torpedo of speed, a lone grey shaped mammal, a shark or whale, honed in on the boat, coming hard at them, its fin clearly visible, swimming close to the surface as if to hit them midship. Awe turned to fear and Clare screamed as she watched the dark shape aiming directly at their broadside with no let-up of speed. Her mother held her tight, also a little afraid that it meant them harm before it dived effortlessly only to reappear. It was a dolphin and it seemed only to wish to inspect them, to check them out first and then to want to race the boat in play, in exuberance, a joy of life. It sent up fantastic sprays of water, as if seeking their attention and the little girl's fear quickly subsided as she realised it was not going to hurt her. Soon she was laughing as she watched the speeding dolphin, clapping her hands in glee as another came to join in, jumping up out of the water, high in front of the boat, to dive and vanish.

'Was it a seal? Like the one we saw at home?'

'No, it was a dolphin, Clare. A bit like a seal. It just came over to say hello and see what we were doing.'

'We're travelling over its home,' said Richard. 'And do you know, Clare, there're lots of them where I live? We have several pods in Cardigan Bay and you can often see them from the cliffs, just by my farm. I'll take you if you, like.' She nodded her head looking at her mum for approval. 'Of course you can go with Uncle Rich.'

'Now,' he said, leaning over her and pointing to the water. 'If we're very lucky and we watch carefully we might see some more.'

Richard was right and within minutes, seemingly having reported back, the whole pod of dolphins now came to inspect the boat, swooping alongside, one or two in tandem arching effortlessly out of the water, their hourglass markings on their flanks plain to see, making them look as if they were smiling, their mouths grinning up at their onlookers as they raced alongside them. Then, in demonstration of superior speed and skill, they swam ahead, to play in the boat's bow wave, a mother and toddler jumping in unison, easy and relaxed. It came as a real pleasure to see them, keeping them company in *hebrwng*[29] that made them feel that they were being looked after in the sea. Just as unexpectedly as they had come, they abruptly vanished as a single group, and the sea suddenly seemed all the more empty and lonely without them. Perhaps they had got bored by the slow moving, thud-thudding noise of the boat, or they'd become distracted by a shoal of fish, or who knew what these clever sociable animals were thinking, only the crew had felt it a privilege to watch them for the short while they had shown themselves, bringing a little light relief to the anxious travellers.

---

[29] Old Welsh custom of escorting guest halfway home on foot.

50

Penny was quietly pleased with the way she'd handled the afternoon milking, and at Mervyn's suggestion they left the cows in for the night. With a predicted forecast promising heavy rain and high winds there was no point in leaving them out to stand against the hedge for shelter getting wet and cold. It was not good for them or their milk production to be huddled together in poached ground, miserable. Far better for them to be kept warm and dry and ready for the early morning milking.

Mervyn had kindly offered but she'd declined his invitation to stay for supper at Y Bwthyn, preferring to be on her own in Richard's kitchen, closer to him among his clobber, overalls, coats and wellingtons. She wanted to be on hand, in case he rang. Richard, 'my boyfriend', she liked to think of him, to say the words out loud rolling them around her mouth like a boiled sweet; telling his cows, and sharing it with his dog as he walked by her side, back across the yard. Her voice carrying on the wind over his fields and his land, willing him back safe. He had plenty on his plate already, and his trip to Ireland was not without danger, without having to fret about his Friesians and farm. Penny had been proud he'd had the faith in her to ask her to step into the breech and look after his precious cattle. She was fine in the early evening, working with Mervyn and later doing the jobs he'd listed, keeping herself busy until it had become fully dark outside. She had become used to living on her own and wasn't nervous. Nevertheless she was unfamiliar with the house and its sounds; the wind gusts that rattled a loose door. Being alone in his home she felt anxious for him, knowing his plans, and the increasing strength of the wind outside did nothing to allay her worries. It was not a night to be at sea.

She'd tried to suggest delaying his journey if the forecast turned out to be accurate, at least until the seas abated. All she could do was hope he'd managed an earlier crossing and was nearing Fishguard, ahead of the worst of the weather. Waiting for the telephone to ring she half-regretted taking the option of staying instead of going home, sitting in the farmhouse, its proximity to the sea emphasizing the high wind and rough weather. Mervyn could have managed the few jobs on his own, and she'd have come over for the five a.m. milking, only at the time, in the quiet daylight of a few hours ago, it had seemed easier for her to stay. Farms were notorious places for getting hurt and what could she do in the event of an animal falling ill? Would she even risk going out in such weather where a slate could be blown off a roof, and where any yard debris could cause injury, buffeting her in the wind. She hoped she had closed all the barn doors securely, as she had no intention of venturing out again. She'd wait until morning, she thought, consoling herself that Richard was happier knowing she was there about the place even if she could do little until the brewing storm abated.

Penny spent the remainder of the evening watching the telly, the picture often flicking as the wind shook the aerial on the roof, and several times she got up to answer the ringing telephone to have no voice at the other end of the open line, only a crackle and then the dialling tone as it rang on and off intermittently. Twigs hit the wire as they swayed between the poles and she hoped the line wouldn't go dead during the night. She could not settle with a book, waiting for Richard's call. She longed to hear he was on dry land and safe. When the phone eventually rang properly, she was preparing for bed and had to race down the stairs to catch it before it rang off, answering it breathlessly, hoping for a voice and not another fault on the line.

'Hello, Richard? Is that you?'

'Sorry I must have dialled the wrong number,' a man's voice said at the other end. 'I wanted Tŷ Coch.'

'This is Tŷ Coch,' she answered, the farm's name not sounding very Welsh.

'Oh? The Davies farm, Llanfeni?'

'Did you want to speak to Richard?'

'Yes, is he there?'

'No. I'm afraid he's away until tomorrow. I'm expecting him to ring any minute. I thought it was him now. I can give him a message when he gets back.'

'Sorry, I didn't catch your name. I'm Simon, his brother, by the way.'

'Oh, Simon.' She felt huge relief and she let out her breath, 'Hello. I'm a friend of your brother's, I'm Penny Jordan. I popped over to help Mervyn with the milking whilst Richard's away.'

'Hello Penny.' The line crackled, threatening to break up. 'Can you tell him I rang and if he could ring me back as soon as he gets back. I've got some important news for him.'

'Do you know where he is, Simon?'

'No. Should I? Why, are you worried?'

'Yes. I know where he's gone but I've been expecting him to ring for some time.'

'He probably got held up. He's never been a good time-keeper. You know what farmers are like, they go by the weather and not the clock!'

'I suppose you're right. And this wind doesn't help.'

'Ty Coch can feel very windswept. But Mam and Uncle Mervyn are there aren't they?'

'Yes. No, I'm fine. Just being silly.'

'Don't you worry. Richard's very good at looking after himself. He doesn't take risks. When he does come home tell him to ring me.'

'I will.' She didn't want him to put the phone down. She felt reassured by a rich deep voice at the other end, an intonation similar to Richard's. 'So you're the famous Simon. I've heard an awful lot about you from Richard and Mervyn. The brilliant, tall, good-looking opera singer!'

'My ears are burning!'

'In case you're wondering, I'm his new business partner.'

'He had mentioned a new business venture and partner but he never told me it was a woman. Trust Richard to have kept that bit out! Of course I knew about him going organic and his cheese-making, but I don't think he told me your name.' Nor, he thought, that if she looked as she sounded, she would be very nice.

'I'm meant to be looking after the farm, helping your uncle out because Richard's gone dashing off to Ireland to help Bethan. It was all a bit last minute and a rush.'

'Not in this weather?'

'No, he left yesterday but I hope to God he hasn't got caught in this storm.'

'I'm sure he'll be all right. The ferries wont sail if the weather's too rough. Has something happened?'

'Yes. I don't know the details but he got a letter – no it wasn't a letter, a postcard from Bethan that really bothered him.'

'What did it say?'

'I don't know, but it was the catalyst for his racing over. I'm worried about the weather. It's got pretty rough here and I think he said he'd be crossing about now.'

'Yes, but the ferries won't go if it's over a certain wind force. They'll wait in harbour.'

'He's not on a ferry. Look, I know this sounds very silly and we've never spoken before, and you must be thinking quietly to yourself who the heavens has Richard got himself involved with, this neurotic woman who can't stop talking.'

'Not at all. You sound very sane and it's reassuring to hear from someone who obviously cares about my brother. He's been through a rough patch of late.'

'I'm glad you haven't taken it the wrong way. I'm not normally this het up, but he said it was a fishing boat.'

'A fishing boat? Why and whose?' Perhaps she had misunderstood him and meant a trawler.

'Look, I don't want to say something I shouldn't, or give you the wrong information. Richard was very sketchy about his exact plans, but I am very concerned for his safety.'

'Would it be easier if I ring Mervyn?'

'No, they don't know anything. He told me that much. All I can tell you is that this postcard set things off. Then he had a phone call from the fisherman in Ireland. Someone who knew Beth.'

'Called Pete?'

'I think that was his name. Someone rang to say Beth wasn't safe, her life was in danger and he was going to try to get her out and away from the stud and needed Richard to help. So he's gone off with Tegwyn.'

'Tegwyn, Tegwyn Jones Tan-y-bryn?'

'The bloke who lives nearby. A neighbour who does work with trees, oh, and the moss medical supplies.'

'Yeah, that's Tego. Why the hell didn't he ring me first?'

'I think he did. He told me he'd tried several times but couldn't raise you and there was no time to wait. They had to get the next ferry across.'

It wasn't the right moment to query whether his brother had rung him or not, as whatever had happened, it sounded as if Beth was in trouble and his suspicions of a cover-up were well founded. He knew his sister was unhappy – he'd told Richard as much – but he hadn't let on just how much her condition had troubled him. He should never have left her there. There had been something he really disliked about her husband, not just his phoney concern, but his obvious enjoyment at being the unctuous slippy shit, dominating his sister like a raptor, lizard-tongued, out to kill her. All Simon had done was to accept the lame duck excuses, leaving her to fend for herself.

'I know it's a bit late, but if there's anything at all I can do.'

'I'll pass your message on as soon as he rings.'

'Oh, I nearly forgot the reason I rang. Please tell him I've got good news about the trough.'

'The what?'

'The pig trough, He'll understand. Let me give you my mobile number and please do ring, it doesn't matter what time of day or night, when you hear from him?'

'I will.'

After all the excitement of seeing the dolphins which had been so much more thrilling than fishing for mackerel, Clare had fallen asleep in the cabin tucked up under a blanket. It was getting cooler and darker as the day slipped away in the dusk. With the child asleep, Richard moved across to the back of the boat to talk with Pete.

'I can't thank you enough for what you've done for them and for what you're doing now for us, Pete. From what little Beth's been able to tell me without Clare hearing, I know you've risked your life for them both. And by doing so, you've scuppered your options. You know you can't go back after this, not there?'

'Pah! His father was a hard man, but not a bad one like his son.'

'What will you do?'

'Me? They can't do much to an old man that'll make any difference. Liam's left, and I can look after myself.'

'I don't know what to say or how I can ever repay you for what you've done, and all this,' he said. 'For my family.'

'I don't want anything. I wasn't prepared to stand by and let the fecker do what he was doing and get away with it. Ah! What he put your sister through—'

He looked away out to the dark-blue, moving swell of the sea. 'She's a real good'n, been like a daughter to me.'

'I sound pretty lame don't I – it's not good enough to say that I didn't know what was going on, but I would have done something if I'd realised. It was only when I got her postcard that I began to realise something was terribly wrong. That really frightened me.' He omitted to say that it had been Tegwyn's reaction that had sounded the alarm bells. 'Then you rang.'

'The gull? The one she covered with spots! I wondered if you got it?

Richard nodded.

'The bugger caught us on the quayside. Luckily she managed to pass one to me while he was busy picking up the one she'd dropped, and I was able to post it, away from the village. You see she'd got two identical cards, one for you and one for Simon and he picked up the one she dropped. Never saw yours, thank Jesus. She said you'd understand, that the penny would drop.'

The word penny immediately conjured up his Penny, and he smiled at the thought of her back at Tŷ Coch, in a warm rush of her. He longed to get home and put his arms around her. Smiling, he admitted to the fisherman, 'It wasn't until after I'd been to the pub where I met up with Tegwyn. When I showed him Beth's postcard, he understood what she was trying to say. That's why he's here. He's always loved her.'

It might have been the flock of starlings that had danced for Tegwyn and his conversation with Dic that triggered a childhood memory, a story told by the schoolmistress of an ancient Wales, but he didn't share it with the fisherman – a myth tenuous and intangible and so intrinsically Welsh. 'That and you ringing me. Simon never told me she was as bad as she is.'

'Malcolm's a sly one. I live there and I've had trouble enough finding anything out about what had happened. They wouldn't let me visit her, even though I called at the house several times. They're a family who keeps things tight, so your brother wouldn't have got much out of anybody.'

'I suppose so, and living so far away, you lose regular contact. But it's no excuse. I should have read the signs.'

'He hid it. Cunning as he is. I don't even think his mother knew and she was living under his roof.'

'I knew things weren't right when she came home to see Mam. She wasn't the same Beth, you know, but I was too busy with the farm and my own problems to see, or to ask her what was wrong. It was none of my business, was it? What goes on in other people's marriages.'

Pete sucked on his pipe. 'You'll have her home now, soon!'

'I'll be forever in your debt. We'd never have been able to do this without you and she'd never have left without her daughter.'

'He can't get us, not in international waters, and he's always hated the sea. We're safe from him out here. Your sister will need looking after. A gentle time after what she's been through. Someone with a lot of kindness and patience.'

'And she'll get it. It'll be good to have her home where she belongs.'

Pete grinned at Richard as the boat suddenly rocked on a bigger than average wave, and Richard grabbed the side to prevent himself from losing his balance. Holding onto the boat's side Richard looked across at Beth sitting with Tego and Clare. He stood upright and put his hand on the older man's shoulder, before crossing the slippery floor of the boat to join the others.

Progress was slow but the diesel engine made steady, reliable knots over the rolling sea. It was the old man who sensed something was wrong, knowing his wooden craft so well. He didn't want to show any alarm about the subtle but certain shift in the wind direction; from a westerly, south-westerly, backing towards the east. It didn't take the rest of them long to pick up on the change as the waves were now coming at them onto the boat's bow, accentuating the rocking motion. It came just at the point where they touched the channel of deep water, that marked the edge of the Celtic Sea.

The old sailor did not like the wind's change of direction nor its increase. He left it for as long as he could afford, allowing the little boat to battle head-on in the aggravatingly short, sharp, choppy waves, cresting at the top as she lifted and fell to each one. He called to them, motioning to them with his free arm to get down below, down the few steps and into the safety of the cabin as the spray increased, sometimes breaking across the bow. There had been no weather forecast of an easterly wind, or any sudden change of direction or ferocity, and having to sail head-on would not help their progress. Pete knew his passengers would be frightened, not knowing the ways of the sea or movement of his boat, and what they must be feeling, their unease as beneath them the ocean's movement deepened, the strength and potential menace of an easterly gale whipping up white spray.

Down below, Clare had woken up and become very frightened at the unfamiliar noise, amplified in their enclosed, cramped quarters. The boat crashed and groaned under the strain of each wave, and to its inexperienced occupants it sounded as if the very wood was going to split and shatter. Oh, brave little boat that had not been built to face such seas, fighting to hold her course, all steady. Still out sitting by the tiller, Pete kept her straight, letting her ride each crest and trough as the wave force increased.

Stronger than the gaining wind, he heard the call, unmistakable in its resonance. Not out here any comforting boom of a foghorn, or friendly ship light but a low groan, no, he thought not a groan, more of a deep moaning sound, defying the depths. It was eerily beautiful as it floated up and outwards over the water, strangely earthy in its strength. Something more solid yet fluid in the watery mass. It was calling one of its own in an ancient music. Somewhere deep below, away from the surface turbulence, this whale sang her own song, her singing call uplifting the abandoned sailor. He strained to catch her again, but she did not repeat her call and now, with everything dark around him, Pete scanned the water, hoping he would see her surface not too close to his boat.

He was too old and out of practice for these sorts of water. He hadn't ventured onto real open seas for years, but at least he knew his boat and could find his way blindfold on her deck. He knew her rudimentary instruments by touch and the course he'd set was etched in his mind. At least there were patches of clear sky where he could find the stars if he needed further guidance. They were in the lap of the gods now and it was too dangerous for him to risk having anyone else on deck; inexperience would only be a liability. He decided to do what was needed himself, as their lack of knowledge and ignorance of how the boat would react would make it all the more dangerous.

Richard watched him from the comparative shelter of the companion-way hatch as Pete fastened the tiller with a rope to prevent the boat from turning as he tried to erect the mizzen, which would help stabilize her in the heavy seas. As he was pulling up the sail, the knot he'd made, done quickly in near darkness with cold, tired hands, had not been tied off properly. In a matter of minutes it allowed the tiller to work free and once unfettered, the boat was swung sideways onto the swell. Before Pete could get back to the tiller a rogue wave hit them, causing him to lose his footing and from the hatch Richard watched, as in horrified slow motion he saw Pete swilled in the rush of water and carried along, unable to help himself as he was washed overboard. Wild to wind and water, the mizzen then snapped. Blinking hard and staring into the blackness Richard yelled out, 'Pete, Pete.' There was nothing, no answer, no one on deck and no sign of the sailor. God, what to do? He indicated to Tegwyn and Beth that he was going above and went out to look for him. How to search as he peered helplessly into the ever-moving, swirling, thick, green-black mass of water. How could he hope to spot a head in all this?

Abruptly he thought he saw not Pete but a more familiar face in the turbulent, swirling, mossy sea. What sudden turn after two score years, would have brought up in a glimpse of moonlight his father's face, with still a ghost of a smile as it seemingly lurched upwards in water, beseeching him to lean over and pull him from the waves. Like some ungainly puppy he was inept; hardly able to stand let alone manipulate the boat; or to reach over and out like some fantastic magician to haul his father in, as the boat pitched and lunged. Clouds covered the moon like a final curtain and the image was lost. Another wave broke over the deck, sweeping him off his feet. Defenceless in the rushing water, he was sucked to the side, where luckily the weight of water pinned him down, wedging him under the rim of the boat, preventing him from following the hapless sailor overboard. Drenched, he held on grimly to the guard-rail. There was no hope of any rescue now: even if he did see the body again, how could he possibly get him back into a boat he could not even stand up in? He had never sailed and didn't know how to steer her properly, or which way she should face the waves to keep her upright as her broken sail flapped loose and ominous above the stern.

51

In the mountainous swell, Tegwyn left Bethan with Clare below, and came out on deck to look for Richard. He found him face down as the boat bobbed hopelessly in the roar of the sea whipped up in the gale. The wind greedily snatched any voice before it could be heard so that, anchored only by his rope, it was he alone who could make any decision. He'd no idea of time, of how long they had been marooned, tossed like a bubble that he felt would break with each crash of wave. Somehow he managed to drag Richard's unconscious body back into the cabin. Utterly remote and wild, through the din of furious water, he could see no sight of land or rock, only each wall of ever rising wave above him in a tsunami of saltwater. The stick of broken mast looked pathetic in the vastness of it all.

Petrified in the cabin, Beth had tried to keep calm, hoping not to transfer her fear to her daughter, who lay huddled and shivering. At least she'd stopped being sick and was quiet in the frightening noise. She'd endured hours of the timbers crying out as the sea battered her from all sides, below, above and sideways on. The groaning noise had become constant and she was beginning to get used to it, as the little boat although still groaning and creaking as if fit to burst, had so far held firm. It had dawned on her that the dirty water under their feet was not caused by a leak as she had first feared, expecting them all to drown, but it was the drag water created by large waves swamping the boat, the residue of which had dripped through the window openings as each wave crashed over.

In the cabin's dim light and small space, she'd done what she could for her brother, wrapping the top half of his body in a bit of partially dry blanket and resting his head on a fender to stop it being banged as the boat fought through the storm. She couldn't stand up in the limited headroom, so she had to crouch or sit, bracing herself against the pounding of the water. From the outside she could catch the violently rocking motion of red and green lights fixed to the boat's bow as the vessel was pummelled, wave on wave, near horizontal, seemingly about to go under, before righting herself, bobbing like a cork. What lunacy had she brought upon them, putting them through such an act of madness that would ultimately consume them? And where now was Tegwyn? Where now was his horse to ride down and lift her from such treacherous seas and save them? Out in the face of the storm, flailing on deck, beyond hope in such atrocious conditions. She wasn't even sure he was still there, unable to see through the flood of water. She longed to open the hatch, to let it all wash away together, hoping to get to him, or at least to see him before she slid under the waves, but she'd given him her word. On no account was she to open the door, under any circumstances, even if the boat turned upside-down, and so she was forced to crouch in the damp eerie little den, not knowing if he lived, when they would keel over, with no knight to cling to.

She could hear nothing but the lashing of the sea crashing onto the small windows battered by the near gale-force wind that had curried up the Celtic Sea to its wild frenzy. To try and help stop her shivering, she pulled on her old green coat from her bag, one of the very few things she'd taken as they'd fled from the stud. Damp in places, it was at least another layer and would help stop her teeth from chattering and in the event, the weight of it, like stones, would help her drown quickly. She put her hands inside the pockets and felt the bits of debris that always collect there, pulling out remnants of a dried-up sprig of heather still wrapped in moss. It nearly broke her, finding that silly charm he'd given her from the Welsh moorland of her home. A few years, a lifetime ago, that she could have brought them to this! In the wilderness of the sea, if ever she needed to believe in a God it was now, and for the first time in years she prayed, begging him for their lives, for their survival. *Ein tad, yr hwn wyt yn y nefoedd. Sancteiddier dy enw*[30]. Save us! Holding the brittle twig, knowing she had always loved Tegwyn, she begged they would not drown, peering out to the blackness, at a brief sickening glimpse of the boat's swinging lights, in between the huge sprays of water.

The red sea seeped iodine salt from mossy fronds of seaweed as dead men's fingers poked through the crevices of rock on the ocean's floor. Nicotine stained, beseeching from their watery grave, a silver cross in lighting flash, a shoal of herring danced. Another desperate love in the same history, William Morgan and his beloved Martha.

Hold hard, Bethan, do not falter whilst you have life, your daughter beside you and the man you love, fighting for your survival.

She had only ever taken such a rash course of action because her husband had driven her to it, making her mad and desperate. What error of judgement had made her resort to her perilous action, putting the lives of those she loved in peril? Was he so overwhelmingly powerful or dangerous, this small-time, tin-pot dictator? Better to have stayed and been killed than have all her family go down lost to another sea, in different time. Black, Celtic.

52

Briefly a break in the racing, heavy clouds revealed what he thought to be a small beacon of light. A candle of God against glass. He dared to stay, striding his horse in the race, the saddle his deck to ride the next crest, clutching onto the tiller like a flying mane as she rode relentless waves, a brave little charger,

---

[30] Our father who art in heaven, holy is thy name.

upwards once more. Tego strained his eyes, searching ahead for a snatch at salvation. What was it he saw? Some giant on stilts standing firm against the sea's torrent like some monstrous spider crab with a single ray, an eye of hope shimmering light from its head. Was it a colossal fiddler crab claw or an arm in the blurred distance that beckoned them out of this white-tipped, whipped blackness? A doubting Thomas, or was it Griffith, no, it was another. A raging Thomas Howell who kept The Smalls lighthouse lit, drawing them home past the lethal rows of jutting teeth of treacherous rock set in a grin, surfacing and resurrecting through each wave.

Worse, more macabre and off his rocker, he was seeking revenge for his abandonment, using each surge to draw their pathetic vessel closer to the rocks of disaster. In each trough Tegwyn felt another ever powerful suction weighing them down. Grasping with green-grey limbs those nails flailed greedily; there was a livid, white scraping around the boat to pull them to ocean's depths where in the sea of it all, he saw an eruption: a red leeching light of water, a hell's furnace of jet streams, hissing up to boil them alive. Oh, what poisonous deceit in that realm between The Smalls and Grassholm where, pouring from the huge cauldron came a spew of re-made bodies in disturbed eyes, no pearls but all dead men renewed, glorious blood crimson, intent on drowning his small cargo of people.

At the helm a King wore a golden crown. Was it Neptune who'd taken such affront? What had he done to deserve such wroth? And as he turned to look closer, like a child enchanted by the splendour, the image surged up from the depths, coming up to meet Tegwyn like some gross animal come alive under the glass of a microscope. There was no mistaking his old enemy, grotesque in magnification but the same renegade. Malcolm, camouflaged as Matholwch, his eyes still mocking as he ordered his feckless army to attack, galloping astride wild horses of the sea, swords drawn to take once again what was his, his wife and daughter.

What wicked madness had brought Tegwyn to this! How could he hold out? Endure against such odds? He would die rather than surrender twice, and, finding a last morsel of strength, he waited for a gap, that lapse caught between tides where water seems strangely mute, to attempt to haul himself, crawling like a hermit crab, vulnerable and unhoused, on hands and knees across the soaking slippery deck, all the while holding on for grim death to his rope, as he pulled himself back along towards the tiller. Somehow he had to steer her away from the rocks, her engine still steady in the noise and rage of the demented storm all around them. Other lights, perhaps all imaginary, flashed off and on, black and white in his head. Skokholm, South Bishop or St Annes? He didn't know, other than he was nearing the Welsh shore, and now, what were those breaks ahead that sent such white froth high and smashing?

In that early greyness he thought he saw another darker grey. Something stationary amid the movement? A hueless lump due south, like a humpbacked whale singing its last lament? Or like them, a stranded dying elephant that had given up? No? He wasn't imagining it, it was solid, a block of rock, basalt sticking out above the waves, with a white headed dome to it. Almost euphoric at the sight of land, he whooped with joy, that there would be a homecoming, some divine intervention that had saved them, and as if to share this sudden salvation, the thousands of gannets soared above. Only as they neared the perilous sheer rock, did he see the futility of such senseless joy as Grassholm loomed more treacherously solid than any volume of unfettered sea. Although the smallest and remotest of the islands off Pembrokeshire, it was still surrounded by dangerous currents that had been cajoled by a devious wind whose terrific clapping sounded like an invisible audience, that would witness their wrecking. Now it seemed they were to be shattered into fragments against its rock. Oh, to be so close and so helpless, pitted in the currents' whims, all the while longing for a shore, petrified of impact. What to do to change her course so she could avoid such impending disaster? He'd no idea the Hats and Barrels lay like crocodiles, ready to snap their lumbering prey. Tegwyn could no longer differentiate fact from fantasy, land from sea, rock from water; his only anchor was that she was there with him, hour on hour, crouched in fear beside his own and they would go together to a watery grave, to be brought home or so nearly, on the Welsh shore.

He wasn't even sure if Richard was still alive, lying mute on the cabin's floor. At the time he'd been proud of his endeavours managing to get Richard back down from the deck, under a roof where saltwater sloshed around his feet. Beth had managed to raise his head above any water, resting it on her rucksack. The few hours that had passed felt more than a lifetime away.

Gripped in her mother's arms, Clare slept finally, as if she'd succumbed to the storm's torture, ceding defeat to the necessity for sleep. It no longer mattered how much the boat rose and fell, creaked and groaned under the weight of the sea; the child slept, unaware of rock and catastrophe.

He'd tried in vain to aim his lame boat toward the safe deep harbour of Milford Haven, but in a strong running tide the sea would have it differently, pulling and rocking them north, and he now aimed for land he thought he recognised, that distinct contour of Ramsey with the city of St Davids standing stark in their grey dawn. In the continuous clamour of ferocious water he felt certain they would all drown, and he tried to hold in his memory the coastline of his home as dawn broke in yellow-tinged, limestone burning across the skyline, illuminating the land against the sky.

The boat was being sucked hopelessly north in a tidal drift, even though Tegwyn tried valiantly to steer her towards St Bride's Bay. Only the tide-run was having none of it; the boat's engine was still fighting but pathetic against the strength of the race that pulled them ever nearer to the Bishops and Clerks, whose names had nothing to do with faith, being those of nautical men who'd perished on the rocks that bore their names. If only he could steer her for the small safe harbour of Porthglais where, empty and disused, he saw the stone pairs of limestone kilns like giant honeycombs that lined the harbour wall. Behind, fertile fields and traces of original whitewash on old cottage walls nestled in rock, standing the test of time.

The malevolent current continued to tear them along; Carreg Rhoson and Llech Uchaf, stubborn stacks leaning to them from their deep water, rooted in perpetual race, in a one-sided game of fox and geese with rock and current, hiding nasty overfalls of tide against water where they had no hope.

Not here the season for puffins, manx shearwater, kittiwakes or guillemots as Tegwyn recognised the island of Ramsey. Sitting in the little boat on a curling mass of liquid that tunnelled them now, like some colossal unplugged bath water, with dangerous eddies and swirling whirlpools towards more reefs.

Thinking the vessel was very likely to break up on the nearby rocks, Tegwyn pulled out the inflatable from one of the lockers. He called for Beth and together they took it in turns to pump it up. Once it was inflated, they hauled Richard's lifeless body into it, propping him up as best they could against the side. Then he double-checked their lifejackets, making sure they were securely fastened, before he ordered Beth and Clare into the dinghy. He made them sit at the back of it, holding onto the rope so that if their boat hit any submerged rocks she would have a chance at least to stay afloat, the inflatable needing very little water clearance to shoot off. As long as it wasn't punctured, it should bounce along on the top of the water like a bit of balsa to come through the gaps safely. They must not let go and at least now they were in daylight and the wind had dropped significantly at last, so they could hear each other, although the sea remained churned and roughed up.

He so wanted to hold her in his arms and tell her how much he had always loved her, in case anything should happen to him, but he did not want her to see his fear that they would not make it to the shore. He remained mute, his arm on hers, his eyes saying it all as he looked at them for the last time, their small white faces, already given to grief, pinched with fear, knowing he would not be with them on their craft when it hit the water.

North of the sound he saw a curve of beach, a stretch of Whitesand, the bay of Porth Mawr, which he thought he could steer the boat into. Looking like a swimmer in trouble, with an arm raised in forewarning, he managed to avoid the thin pillar of rock which came up briefly black before submerging again with every wave, another man drowning to his tired eyes, in ever-rolling breakers on the beach's southern side. He could feel the pull, the will of water and with each wave they were carried on another stronger surge of water mass that spurred them temptingly closer to their land. Only as he neared the shore, trapped in their power, did he realise their size, huge rollers pouring down onto the beach. The volume of each rising crest, feet high as he heard them break in front of their boat, pounding down, leaving behind only white tips that curled away, the creamy soapy froth flying back at them as each wave thundered up the beach.

He knew then it would be like going over a precipice, as in the big unbroken surf their boat streamed on wave, salmon-like along the crest in search for the river-mouth of its home, but unlike those graceful kings of fish, this skipper could only flounder in the wooden craft on the top, his instinct to survive as keen, homing in for a safe channel.

He was powerless to prevent the wave that would break on

them, picking them up in a show of strength and pitching them forward with such force that the boat's stern skewed around, horizontal on the wave before she capsized under the tip of white water as it crashed down. Before relinquishing his grip, in one last final effort he thrust out at the dinghy to push it off the boat before the 'Little Marie' rolled over in the surf.

He thought he heard her shriek, and caught a flash of black, bouncing off, carried forward by the wave, before he was out and under in the open water, tumbling over and over, as helpless as a bit of clothing in a washing machine. Was it sand he felt as his body was rolled under the water in the bottom of the wave? It didn't matter he couldn't swim, as the power and weight above him gave no option, dragging him to her motion, unable to breathe, even to know which way was up to air, eventually succumbing to take in a lungful of water. Drowning and not realising he could stand up in this, the sand solid under him in a neck-deep wave that washed over him, pushing him further up the beach towards her frantic form, waiting at the surf's edge.

She left her daughter by the battered dinghy to watch over her uncle's still form knowing that soon there'd be another person at hand: an early morning dog walker, surfer or park warden.

She had to go back into the sea, calling for him unheard in the roar of surf, as she searched for a sign, an upturned keel, splintered wood or other flotsam in the running waves. Wading out she thought she saw something black, lolling semi-submerged in a wave. Pushing herself waist-deep through the water, she kept her eyes on the solid form that rolled like a soaked log in the surf. With outstretched arms she grabbed him, turning his face upward and using the waves to help her, she found the strength to haul his sodden body to the shore. Her desolate embrace caused an involuntary spasm that gave her the power to pull him out of the sea and up onto the beach.